William Pitt Lennox

Drafts on My Memory

Being men I have known, things I have seen , places I have visited. Vol. 2

William Pitt Lennox

Drafts on My Memory
Being men I have known, things I have seen , places I have visited. Vol. 2

ISBN/EAN: 9783337218591

Printed in Europe, USA, Canada, Australia, Japan

Cover: Foto ©Andreas Hilbeck / pixelio.de

More available books at **www.hansebooks.com**

DRAFTS ON MY MEMORY:

BEING

MEN I HAVE KNOWN, THINGS I HAVE SEEN,

PLACES I HAVE VISITED.

BY

LORD WILLIAM PITT LENNOX.

IN TWO VOLUMES.
VOL. II.

LONDON:
CHAPMAN AND HALL, 193, PICCADILLY.
1866.

CONTENTS.

CHAPTER XII.

CHAPTER XIII.

CHAPTER XIV.

CHAPTER XV.

CHAPTER XVI.

CHAPTER XVII.

CHAPTER XVIII.

CHAPTER XIX.

CHAPTER XX.

CHAPTER XXI.

CHAPTER IX.

CHAPTER IX.

My last chapter ended with two instances of misplaced hospitality—that which gives you too little, and that which gives you too much. It is difficult to say which is the more reprehensible. The first is most felt at the time, but the effects of the latter endure afterwards. True hospitality consists in supplying the wants of a guest—in not stinting him on the one hand, or pressing him on the other. A pleasant, though amusing, case in point was furnished by the late Sir Charles Shakerley, who died in 1857, and who, though eccentric, was one of the kindest-hearted men imaginable.

The popular owner of Somerford Park, Cheshire, was devoted to theatricals, and during the run of the Christmas pantomimes he might be seen every night in the private boxes of the respective theatres. The Royal Adelphi was his favourite place of entertainment, and it was within those walls that the following circumstance occurred. To reach his private box Sir Charles had to cross the stage, and as his good nature and liberality were proverbial, he was an especial favourite with all behind the scenes. Passing one evening to his box during the pantomime, just at the moment when the clown had knocked over a tame duck out of a poultry yard, he heard one of the stage carpenters say with a sigh, "I wish that was a real one; how I should like to have it for my missus and myself for supper!" The man picked up the wooden bird, looked at its plumpness, and gave another sigh. "Are you fond of ducks?" inquired the baronet. "Very, Sir Charles," responded the other, "and my missus is longing for one." "Tell her I will send you a brace to the stage-door to-morrow morning. What name?" The name was soon given, entered into Shakerley's pocket-book, and before eleven o'clock the following day two fine specimens of these aquaceous birds were left at their destination. That very evening the baronet was again at his post; and as he trod the boards while the preparations for the harlequinade were being made, he heard around him sundry exclamations, all bearing the same purport, viz., a love of ducks for supper. As the stage manager happened to be present, Sir Charles passed through the phalanx of sage-and-onion fanciers without quite understanding the point of the conversation. After remaining in his box until after the transformation scene, the worthy baronet proceeded to Drury Lane, where a scene from the ballet of the "Revolt of the Harem" was being represented. Crossing the stage, his ears again caught the sound, "What a beautiful bird! I quite long for a real one for supper." Some young ladies of the ballet met the patron of the drama, especially the Terpsichorean part of it, with smiles, referring to his kindness to the "guardian naiads of the Strand," at the Adelphi, in furnishing them with ducks and game. "Let me have the pleasure of forwarding you some," responded Shakerley. The Turkish beauties acknowledged their thanks, little dreaming that their wishes would so soon be realised. Three days afterwards, about ten o'clock, a cart from the London and North-Western railway drove up to the stage-door of the Theatre Royal, Drury Lane, just before a rehearsal. "Some game for the guv'nor, I presume," exclaimed a "super," as a brace of hares was handed out to the Cerberus. "There's nothing to pay," said the railway man; "but where can you stow them all away?" "All!" said the doorkeeper, looking at the furred animals with some surprise. "Oh, I've lots more," responded the man; "here's the parcel bill;" and from this he read the names of at least twenty ballet girls, some bearing the unassuming titles of Sims, Jones, and Roberts, while others aspired to English names Frenchified or Italianised into Le Brun and Chikeno. "Here's a hamper for Alfred Bunn, Esq., and the rest are all in twos, directed to the respective parties."

No sooner had the game been deposited in the small hall in which the porter sits in all the glory of power, than the lessee drove up to the stage-door, and nearly came in contact with the game-cart, as it might truly be called. "Why, what's all this?" inquired King Alfred.

"There's a hamper for you, sir," said the man, "carriage paid, and the other game is for the ladies of the ballet."

"Out with it," thundered the poet, as he was facetiously called by *Punch*—though, judging from the words of some of his songs, he was really entitled to the name—"out with it! Why, you had better at once turn the hall into a poulterer's shop, with 'Licensed to sell game' painted over it. Turn it out in the street!"

At this sudden mandate, a cry of female voices was heard:—"I won't attend rehearsal if I don't have my hares!" "I'll not go on the stage this evening unless I have my game!" "Hand me

that hamper." "This is not for me, it's for
Miss Collins." Shouting and scrambling were the
order of the morning, and affairs began to look
serious, when the lessee, in a stentorian voice, exclaimed, "Well, young ladies, the game may remain
here until after the rehearsal; but, in future, I hope
it will be sent to your private residences."

Peace was now restored, and the threatened
"revolt of the *harem*," as Bunn called it, was at
once quelled.

Another anecdote of the baronet may not be out
of place. Somerford Park was within an easy
distance of the large and populous manufacturing
town of Congleton, and whenever Sir Charles's
stag-hounds met near it, the field was more numerous than select. On one occasion a stag was to be
turned out upon the race-course on Easter Monday,
and a very large assemblage was expected. Long
before the appointed hour thousands flocked to the
place, and when the hounds arrived, the sportsmen
who had come out with a view of enjoying a good
run were disheartened to see the deer-cart so closely
surrounded with spectators that there was little or
no chance of the antlered monarch making his
escape. A place had been railed off for carriages
to draw up in, and the hunters, huntsmen, whippers-
in, and hounds were all assembled in the enclosed

front before the stand. When all were on the tip-
toe of expectation Sir Charles appeared, admirably
mounted, and neatly equipped in a costume of
Lincoln green. "What is to be done?" asked a
hundred voices. "It will be next to impossible,"
said one, "to uncart the deer, and if he is uncarted
he will be mobbed, or hunted to death by every
species of animal, from a thorough-bred bull-dog
down to a costermonger's cur." "Wait a minute,
my good fellow," said Sir Charles, "and all will be
right." The hour had now arrived for turning out
the deer, when a band of music struck up some
popular air, and marched down the course to a
wooden building which had hitherto attracted no
notice. They ascended the steps, when, as if by
magic, an enormous scroll appeared, with the words
"Grand National Circus" emblazoned in gold on a
gaudy-coloured ground. In the meantime the
music, the bills that were gratuitously given away,
and some fluttering banners and flags that had been
displayed, told of the performance that was to come
off, and nearly all the pedestrians flocked to the
arena. In the excitement of the moment the deer
was quite forgotten, except by those who came
together for the chase, and, as the door of the cart
was opened, the animal bounded from his wooden
prison on the turf, and flew off "upon the pinions

of the wind." At that moment the clown of the circus rushed on the platform, turned his knees and feet in, opened wide his mouth, winked his eyes, and with his arms in his huge pockets, large enough to hold a string of sausages or a young baby, exclaimed, " Ain't I a pretty *dear!*" This jocosity was followed by all sorts of antics and contortions of body, ending in a somersault. The object of the hunters was gained, the hounds were laid on after twelve minutes' law, and a splendid run was the result.

Sir Charles was one of the first to adopt that useful style of carriage called a brougham, and now so common. His was made in the shape of a *vis-à-vis*, with a hammer-cloth and a coachman in full-dress livery, curled wig, shoes and buckles.

One day, when I was calling upon the baronet at Mivart's Hotel, I heard the following dialogue between him and his valet :—" Is the brougham at the door, Lowther?" " Yes, Sir Chorles." Here I would pause to ask why baronets are favoured with their titles so much more than dukes or any other Corinthian " pillars of the state." I will be bound to say that for one " your grace" or " my lord" you will hear ten " Sir Johns," or " Sir Francises." It would appear that this extra mark of respect paid to those who bear the badge of the " Red or Bloody

Hand of Ulster"—that honourable badge commemorative of the bold adventurer who, vowing to be the first to touch the shore of Ireland, and finding his boat left behind, cut off his hand and flung it before him—is to console them for the decree issued by James I. in 1612, fixing the precedence of younger sons of barons before the baronets.

" Is the coachman's wig properly curled ?"

" Yes, Sir Chorles."

" Has the horse the rosettes Miss —— (a popular *danseuse*) admires so much ?"

" Yes, Sir Chorles."

" Are there many persons assembled to look at the carriage ?"

" About eight or nine, Sir Chorles."

" Let me know when there are a dozen, and I will get into it."

" Yes, Sir Chorles."

And Sir Chorles did get into it, among the jeers of a few idle young men and boys, who, in a most irreverent manner, compared his coachman to "one of them Old Bailey lawyer chaps," called his brougham a " pill-box," at the jocose suggestion of an apothecary's lad, and hinted that the " old buffer" was got up "like a lover in a Christmas pantomime."

Among other eccentricities, Sir Charles gave a dinner at Crockford's, at which a supposed luxury

from the Celestial Empire was to be introduced,
namely, bird's-nest soup.   Francatelli was at the
time *chef de cuisine*, and a better one never existed.
All his talent was to be devoted to this epicurean
repast.   About sixteen members of the club sat
down to dinner, when, to their great surprise, apologies were made for two individuals in Chinese costume, who were to have appeared.   It was said that
the host, having failed to procure the attendance of
two Chinese boys, who were, through the kindness
of the Queen, being educated at some establishment
near London, had sent to Drury Lane Theatre to
borrow two "supers" from Mr. Bunn to take their
parts, but the "supers" also were unfortunately engaged.   The result was, that we had the soup without native attendance.   Every one was anxious to
"go birds' nesting;" but a taste soon showed that
it was not suitable for English palates.   We felt
like the Austrian general, to whom some Milanese
nobleman sent a present of a parrot.   The gallant
officer, not being much acquainted with natural
history, fancied the bird was meant for the spit,
and accordingly gave orders to his cook to have it
roasted.   The day after the gallant officer had
indulged in *perroquet rôti*, he met the donor, who
asked, "*Come vi piacque l'uccello?*"   "*Così, così,
un poco duro,*" responded the general.

Fortunately, at our dinner a remedy was soon

provided.   Francatelli, with great forethought, introduced some turtle-soup, which was greedily
devoured.   The evening passed off delightfully.
Shakerley drank the healths of all present, and one
absent, namely Francatelli.   These toasts, with a
return thanks for his own health, entailed no less
than eighteen speeches on the worthy baronet.
Every one has heard the old Joe Miller, of a party
of Welshmen, who, meeting at dinner, began by
toasting themselves, and ending by toasting the
cheese; and, as far as number of toasts went upon
the above occasion, we were fully equal to the
Welshmen.   In such a company, it was difficult to
introduce appropriate allusions to each member, so,
as Shakerley was supported on the right by Lord
Chesterfield, and upon the left by myself, we, and
others, promised to prompt him whenever he required our aid.   Lord Chesterfield's health was
first proposed.   This was an easy task, as a more
kind-hearted or popular nobleman never existed.
Next followed others, which call for no comment,
till Sir Willoughby Cotton's name occurred.

"Where has he served?" asked Shakerley, the
quantity of wine we had all drunk having produced
a slight effect upon his memory.

"We will name the battles," responded those
near him, including myself, simultaneously; and, as

the host proceeded in his eulogiums, just ones, indeed, towards this brave warrior, we alternately gave the speaker the word, "whose services at" "Seringapatam," said one, "at Assaye," whispered another, "at Mooltan," "Peshawar," "Benares," "Egypt," cried others, *sotto voce*, until the speaker began to suspect a hoax was being practised, and sat down.

Under Ude, as under Francatelli, Crockford's Club was famous for its dinners. During those palmy days in St. James's Street, when the culinary department was under the direction of the immortal Louis Eustache Ude, that truly popular nobleman the fifth Marquis of Queensberry dined in the coffee room early in August; and, among other delicacies, a young grouse was served. To a canny Scot, and a sportsman, such an open defiance of the game laws was intolerable; the bird was sent away, and the *cordon bleu* was compelled to make his appearance at the police court in Bow Street the next morning, to answer the charge of Lord Queensberry for having thus forestalled the 12th. A suitable admonition from the magistrate, and a small fine for this, the first (proved) offence, was the result. In the course of the day the noble lord again dined at the club, and, on thoroughly scrutinising the bill of fare, found that the illegal luxury had been crased from it. As he was about to sit down to dinner, the late Lord George Bentinck came in, and proposed joining tables. This was agreed to; and orders were given to the waiters to serve the two dinners together. The soup and fish were removed, and two *entrées* were placed on the board.

"I have ordered a *suprème de volaille*," said the Marquis.

"And I," responded George Bentinck, "am about to try a dish I never heard of before; but Ude recommended it strongly. I forget its name. Waiter, bring me the bill of fare."

A very careful observer might have perceived that something untoward had occurred, from the anxiety of the attendant, himself a Frenchman, and his master, Le Grand Louis. While they kept nervously in the background, an English waiter took the covers off, and the olfactory senses of the Northern laird soon told him the nature of the dish.

"Why it's a *salmi* of grouse," he shouted, with an exclamation which, had he been in Bow Street, would have added five shillings to the cost of his dinner. "It is not down in the bill of fare. Let me see it."

The fatal paper was handed to him by the terrified Ude, who now approached the table.

"Why, what is this?" asked the Marquis. "*Salmi de fruit défendu.*"

The culinary artist was silent, looked unutterable things, and merely shrugged up his shoulders.

Either the ingenuity of the *chef*, who had suggested this new gastronomic appellation, or the remembrance of his past services, produced a favourable effect upon the complainant, for a good-humoured smile played upon his countenance, as he remarked—

"Well, Ude, I presume this is a part of the bird of yesterday; but recollect, in future, no forbidden fruit must be plucked before the lawful day."

Few men among my friends and acquaintances gave more agreeable dinner parties and concerts than Samuel Cartwright, or *Toothems*, as Cannon irreverently called him. The worthy dentist's *tusk*ulum—I again quote from the Dean of Patcham —was the rendezvous for many of the notorieties of the day; and our host being a member of the Catch Club, and a most liberal patron of the musical profession, could always command the services of the best native talent. The usual number at his festive board was eight, when they dined at a table that formerly belonged to the extinct Octagon Club. Sometimes, however, the number was doubled. His dinners were plain but excellent, his wines faultless. Among the guests that I have met there may be mentioned the sixth Duke of Argyll, Saltoun, one of the heroes of Hougomont, Napoleon III., then Prince Louis, the Duke of Leinster, Count D'Orsay, the late Earl Fitzhardinge, Hon. Henry and Augustus Berkeley, Charles Dickens, Thackeray, Charles Kemble, Harley, W. Knyvett, Henry Phillips, Hon. Fitzroy Stanhope, &c., &c. Cartwright never allowed his dinner to be spoilt, as dinners are often spoilt, by not sitting down punctually at the hour named, and he waited for nobody, duke or commoner. After a time every one got into his ways, and a late guest was unknown. Indeed, what with the good things that were to be eaten, and the wine that was to be drunk, it would have been impossible to have got through the selection of music unless regularity had been the order of the day.

Cartwright's hospitality was not confined to London; for at Delabere, near Twyford, and Nizells, near Tunbridge, he kept open house, with the addition of excellent fishing and shooting at the former, and shooting only at the latter. I recollect upon one occasion Charles Kemble forming one of the snug eight. He was then so deaf that he could not hear without a trumpet; and some one remarked, *sotto voce,* " I would give anything to hear

Kemble's opinion of Edmund Kean." As nobody seemed disposed to put the question, I screwed up my courage to do it; and, premising that I was spokesman for the company, asked his real opinion of Edmund Kean in his palmy days. Charles smiled in his most gracious manner at the compliment with which I began my question, and proceeded to give a criticism upon Kean, which was as lucid as it was just. Admitting Kean's great genius, he gave passages from "Othello," "Hamlet," "Richard III.," as Kean gave them, and then as he thought they ought to be given. One remark struck us all forcibly; it was in that scene in "Othello," where the Moor exclaims,—

> "It is the cause, it is the cause, my soul—
> Let me not name it to you, you chaste stars!
> It is the cause."

"Kean," said his critic, "gave the lines quick and abruptly, without that tenderness of expression which the author evidently intended should be adopted."

He then proceeded to go through the whole of the scene, with a pathos unequalled, until he came to the line,—

> "Had all his hairs been lives, my great revenge
> Had stomach for them all;"

which he gave with a power second only to the great Edmund.

"Mark what a contrast there would be," said he, "if the burst of indignant revenge had been reserved until his jealousy was roused beyond control at Desdemona's expression on behalf of Cassio,—

"My fear interprets then,—what, is he dead?"

After a time Kemble proceeded—"I pass over 'that speaking thick, which nature made his blemish,' but which I regret has become the natural accent of some of his followers, and frankly admit that there are some splendid bursts of passion in Edmund Kean's performances. *Sir Giles Overreach* is a masterpiece of acting; so is *Richard III.*, and *Iago*, and portions of *Othello* are magnificent; but I humbly object to his dividing words, such as, 'I am your pris—prisoner;' suppose the word happened to be 'assassin,' how would it sound?"

Considering the different schools in which the Kembles and Kean had studied, and allowing for a certain amount of prejudice, Charles Kemble's criticism was just and forcible, and it was a great privilege to hear it. The death of this great actor was an equal loss to the stage and to society; he possessed a fund of anecdote which, added to his refined and gentlemanlike manner, rendered him a welcome guest among all who could appreciate talent, honourable conduct, and noble bearing.

At one of Cartwright's dinners the conversation turned upon certain dishes which were not admissible at fashionable persons' houses. Among them the awful name of "tripe" occurred. "In Paris," remarked one of the guests, "the *plát* goes under the title of *Gras-double à l'ail*, and is highly esteemed; in former times there was a restaurant famous for it." "Do give us a tripe dinner," said another to our Amphitryon. "Willingly," he responded, "with this condition—that there shall be no other dish on the table. It shall be boiled with milk and Portugal onions; it shall be fried and curried." Every one agreed, including two ladies who were of the party, though with a reservation from one of them that "we are not bound to partake of this very extraordinary dish if we do not like it." "Certainly," responded the host; "you can of course lay by for the sweets, for there will be tarts and puddings, but neither soup nor fish." The party was arranged, and in due course of time the dinner came off. When we entered the dining-room two large tureens were uncovered and sent out an unmistakable smell of onions. One of the ladies, determined to judge for herself, tasted the unfashionable condiment, and declared it was very good. The other, remembering Theodore Hook's comparison of tripe to a pair of leather inexpressibles cut up and boiled with onions, said she would wait for the curry. The curry was brought, but the prejudice could not be conquered, and the young lady made up her mind to go without her dinner—no small sacrifice in days when the five o'clock tea was unknown. At that time people were satisfied with a breakfast at nine or ten o'clock, a sandwich or a biscuit for lunch, instead of the hot joints, game, fowl, pastry, and wine, which now compose the mid-day meal, a dinner at six or half-past, and a cup of tea or coffee after it. Now, tea, coffee, cake, bread and butter are served at five o'clock, within three hours of a most substantial lunch, and within an hour and a half or two hours of dinner. Byron writes that "great things were to be achieved at table," but he could not have said so, had he lived to see ladies take a few spoonfuls of soup, decline fish, flesh, and fowl, and perhaps play with an oyster *pâté* or an *entrée;* while the lords of the creation, who have contented themselves with a biscuit for lunch, and have declined tea, are left alone in their glory.

But to return to the old Burlington Street dinner. Cartwright finding that the young lady preferred starving to eating tripe, told his butler to bring in another dish, which, being uncovered, displayed a fine brace of pheasants. It was more than five

weeks from the day upon which shooting terminated, and, according to the gastronomic rule, the
birds had hung by their tails until they dropped—
a sure test of tenderness. Unfortunately the
weather had changed from a severe frost to a mild
temperature, and it was soon apparent to all, that
not even the high odour of the onions could get
rid of the scent of the game. "I am afraid,"
said Cartwright, "that they have been kept a little
too long." "High and dry," remarked another in
an under-tone, for the culinary artist had "devilled"
them, in the hopes of making them a little more
palatable. "Will any one try a wing?" asked the
host; but there was no reply, and the pheasants
were taken out of the room. During this pause it
occurred to me that if properly disguised the tripe
might pass muster; so I wrote a few pencil-lines to
Cartwright, suggesting that if the whitest part of
the tripe could be placed in a dish of spinach,
which the hostess told me was coming in the second
course, it might pass for breast of veal *a l'épinards*.
The hint was taken, and in a few minutes the dish
was placed before me. "What a gallantry," said
I. "Let me send you a little, Miss ——. It
seems quite hot and tender." Placing a layer of
spinach on the plate, and half covering the tripe
with the same vegetable, I sent it to the fasting

lady, who ate it with evident relish, and, moreover, sent for a second helping. The cook had assisted the disguise by adding a few mushrooms, and few would have detected the real nature of the dish. Our host insisted on tasting the "breast of veal," and loudly extolled it, premising, however, that it was not to be compared to the tripe. "I know not what that very anti-aristocratic dish may be," said the young lady, "but this in Paris would ensure a *cordon bleu*." Cartwright smiled and made a sign which I at once understood and obeyed. Some months after, I met the victim of our hoax at dinner, and ascertained that the secret had not been disclosed; and to the present day (for I am happy to say the lady is still living) she is under the same delusion. Cartwright's musical reunions were most delightful. In addition to professional talent, he occasionally introduced amateurs of the highest order. Miss Constance Roden, who is now an established singer, often enchanted us. Fitzroy Stanhope was ever ready to troll one of his cheery ballads; and Henry Berkeley would vie with Thalberg on the piano-forte. Poor Samuel Cartwright! no one felt his loss more deeply than I did. To a sound judgment and pure classical taste he added charity, and those social qualities which endeared him to all.

If there is one sin against the laws of hospitality which ought to be more severely visited than another, it is that of giving your guests bad wine. I knew a man, and a rich man too, whose many virtues were obscured by that one fault in an aggravated degree. Before the reduction of the duty on foreign wines, which has conferred due immortality on the name of Gladstone, though it has very improperly conferred the name of Gladstone on inferior claret, my friend asked me one day what I thought of his claret. My reply was, "If you really wish me to give you an honest opinion, I should say, it was not claret." "Not claret!" he responded, "I bought it as such." Of course, after this remark I was silent, and the conversation took another turn. One morning when I happened to call, I found a stranger in my friend's room. "You are the very person I wish to see," said he to me; "let me introduce you to Mr. —— my wine merchant." The introduction took place, and before I had time to utter a word, my friend proceeded, "Lord William Lennox says, your claret is not claret." The importer of foreign wines and spirits looked aghast, and I was what the sailors term, "taken aback:" but not wishing to retract what I had said, I quietly remarked that the wine I referred to did not come up to my notion of claret.

"Your Lordship is right," said the wine merchant,
whose reputation in the city stood second to no one.
"The wine I sold is what is termed in France, *vin
ordinaire*, price thirty shillings a dozen, a light
dinner wine. I understood that you, Sir," addressing the owner of the house, "had a large stock of
Crockford's choice *Chateau Margaux*." "I have
some," he responded. "In future, Sir," continued
the wine merchant, "let me entreat you not to give
my *vin ordinaire* as after-dinner claret. It might
prove highly prejudicial to me. I have claret of
the finest growth at ninety-six shillings a dozen."
Here the conference broke up; but before I conclude, I must add that my friend had purchased
two dozen of Crockford's best claret, the appearance
of which was, to adopt the hackneyed saying, "like
angels' visits, few and far between:" still it gave
my host the opportunity of saying, and truly saying, "he had some first-rate *Chateau Margaux*."
My reader will readily understand what claret at
thirty shillings a dozen was before the duty was
taken off; it probably cost ten sous a bottle, perhaps
only five at Bordeaux.

As a companion to this anecdote let me tell of
what happened to a man who prided himself upon
his wine, and who had some of the best claret of
the celebrated '34 vintage. "Be careful," said the

host; "you will find it in bin 5." The wine was brought, and as the old butler, who took a real pride in his master's cellar, poured out "the purple regal stream," N—— remarked, "Yes, this is the '34." " 34 ?" responded a country visitor. "Remarkably cheap, I've got some that cost 48 (this was long before the Gladstone cheap wine movement), and it is not half as good." There was no further demand upon bin 5 that evening.

In these days, instead of first growth Moet's sparkling champagne, dry champagne, Lafitte, and *Chateau Margaux* clarets, old bees'-wing port and hock, exquisite sherry, we meet with—there are many honourable exceptions — home-made gooseberry, a perfect stranger to France, at thirty-two shillings a dozen, fizzing moselle at the same price, the Chancellor's St. Emilion at two shillings a bottle, Cape, or South African port, or "young and fruity" Portuguese port, varying from eighteen to twenty-three shillings a dozen. Hochheim, Nierstein, and Hattenheim, at a less price than the port, and Gladstone's sherry (the senator, not the wine merchant), at a pound per dozen, while some of "exquisite quality, very old and scarce, not usually met with, their prices putting these beyond the reach of ordinary consumers," may be had at sixty-six shillings a dozen. It is now unfortunately the fashion for almost every Amphitryon to give champagne and claret, both excellent wines when good; but why not call things by their right names? The former reminds me of a saying of Wright's at the Adelphi theatre, "Since champagne suppers have been introduced, there's not a single gooseberry to be found on the bushes," and the latter, though a nice summer dinner beverage, and even then better as "Badmington," is no more fit to be placed on an Englishman's table after dinner, than a fricasseed frog would be to take place of a sirloin of beef.

Neither French wines nor French cookery are to be despised in their proper places. The glories— alas that I must say, the departed glories!—of the *Rocher de Cancale*, and the *Café de Paris* are too fresh in my memory to let me be ungrateful.

In a very amusing book entitled, "*Paris à Table*," most graphically written by Eugène Briffault, and cleverly illustrated by Bertall, the dinners at the *Rocher de Cancale* are thus described :—

"On commença par six petites huîtres de Marennes, et autant de cuillerées de potage qui neutralisent la froide sensation des huîtres ; on essaya plusieurs potages, le verre de madère suivit. Le premier service fut digne du début. L'admiration du nar-

rateur s'exprime ainsi : 'Ce n'est pas que le nombre
des plats fût grand ; mais ils étaient si bien gradués,
et la façon, la mine, la fraîcheur, la force et la saveur
étaient si excellentes, que tout le monde dût les
admirer' . . . . L'historien se plaint ici que, pour
le coup du milieu, on ait employé le punch à la
romaine au lieu du sorbet au rhum. Il ajoute, ' on
nous servit dans une argenterie d'un goût parfait et
chaude, de plaque anglais, et à la lueur de bougies
brillantes.' Il cite ensuite quelques mets exquis,
puis il s'écrie : 'Le reste du petit et magnifique
dîner fut parfait. Si vous voulez, dit il, en avoir
une idée, figurez vous M. de Talleyrand ou Laurent
de Médicis donnant à dîner à neuf gourmands de
ses amis.'

"Les chroniques du vieux Rocher de Cancale
regorgent de prouesses de ce genre. Ce dîner, qui
était donné par Lord W . . . . . et auquel prirent
part neuf convives, couta 100 francs par tête."

Whether the writer had the author of these pages
in his "mind's eye" I know not, but I must plead
guilty to having ordered a dinner which, through
the mistaken liberality of the Amphitryon, amounted
to a hundred francs per head. The circumstance
was as follows: In the year 1832 my friends
Harold and Edward Littledale, the late George
Russell, my brother Arthur and myself, passed

Easter week in Paris. Harold Littledale, in the generosity of his nature, proposed giving all the party the very best dinner that could be served in the city of frivolity. I, who had passed some time in France, was consulted, and I suggested that the best way would be to invite a French nobleman, a friend of mine, to join us, empowering him to give the necessary order. This arrangement was agreed to, and the Count gladly accepted the proposal. Upon the morning of the dinner, our host and myself drove to the *Rocher de Cancale*, and asked to see the landlord, but, as he was absent, we were ushered into the presence of the landlady.

" Everything will be ready, my Lords, punctually at six o'clock; my husband has gone about the fish, which we expect every instant from Dieppe."

" How much per head ? " inquired Littledale.

" Fifty francs," replied the landlady.

" Fifty ! " ejaculated my companion. " Double, double ! "

" Certainly, if you wish it."

" Oh yes ! " and with that we took our leave, I remonstrating a little at my friend's profuse liberality. At the appointed hour we met, and certainly a better dinner was never placed upon the table, but I question much whether it would not have been equally good had we confined it to the original price, and that, I believe, was the opinion of the Count, who, no doubt, laughed in his sleeve at the extravagant notions of Milords Anglais. Even the waiter looked astonished when presenting *l'addition*, which, with wine of the finest growth, added not a little to the sum agreed upon.

Talking of expensive dinners reminds me of two, one of which took place in Paris, the other in London. Three gamblers who, after winning a large sum, had reduced it to a thousand francs, determined to spend that amount upon one dinner, and spoke to Borel upon the subject. The honest *restaurateur* observed that they reminded him of the grenadier who, upon receiving some prize money, asked for coffee at six francs the cup. The others, however, insisted upon having what they had ordered, notwithstanding the urgent request of Borel to add to the number of the guests, if they were determined not to reduce the price. All remonstrances were in vain, the dinner was to be one thousand francs for three, or it was not to take place. The prices of expensive dishes were then discussed, but none appeared extravagant, when all of a sudden an idea flashed across the mind of one of the party, which was to have a dish of frogs. As the time of year at which the dinner was held was the month of December, the intensity of the frost had closed every pond, and, in order to get the frogs, it was necessary to employ at least fifty workmen to break up the ice. The result was that a hundred frogs cost five hundred francs, and a soup was made of them which none of the party tasted.

The other instance occurred in London. A party at White's were discussing how much a dinner could be made to cost, when it was agreed that each should order a dish, and whoever selected the most expensive one should dine for nothing. Alvanley came off victorious, having desired the cook to introduce a fricassee of that part of the fowl called the oyster, which, to make a dish, required at least a hundred fowls, at a cost of four shillings each.

"*Louis XVIII.*" (says M. Briffault) "*a laissé une réputation de mangeur qui, du reste, parait être héréditaire chez les Bourbons de la branche ainée. La Princesse Palatine dit dans ses mémoires : 'J'ai vu souvent le roi manger quatre assiettées de soupes diverses, un faisan entier, une perdrix, une grande assiettée de salade, du mouton au jus et à l'ail, deux bonnes tranches de jambon, une assiettée de pâtisserie, et puis encore des fruits et des confitures.'*" The author tells an excellent anecdote of Louis *des huitres*, as he was called, which we shall take the liberty of translating. "For a long time

Louis XVIII. had the doors thrown wide open when at dinner with the royal family, but near the close of his reign they were always closed. The reason assigned for the change was as follows:—M. Portal, the King's first physician, had forbidden his patient to eat spinach, to which he was greatly attached. At dinner, the monarch asked for his plate of spinach; when the Duc D'Aumont, first lord of the bedchamber, informed his Majesty that none of this choice vegetable was to be procured. Upon this the King insisted upon some being produced, and said, that if there was none in the Palace, they must send to the different *restaurateurs* to obtain it. The Duke attempted to appease his master, who, roused to·a pitch of frenzy, and swearing most royally, exclaimed, "*Comment, je suis roi de France, et je ne pourrai pas manger des épinards.*" At these words, his Majesty heard a shout of laughter from the adjoining room, which was occupied by the *gardes du corps*. Upon this, the doors of the royal dining room were ordered to be closed, and from that time they were never opened during Louis's repast, although history does not record whether his Majesty continued to indulge in spinach." Before taking leave of Monsieur Briffault I must quote two more anecdotes from his amusing work. "The first Napoleon's uncle, Cardinal Fesch,

whose cream-coloured horses may be remembered
by many visitors to Rome some years ago, received
a present of two magnificent turbots of equal beauty
and size during his residence at Paris. There was
a question what was to be done with them. To
give one away was to court rivalry, to eat both was
impossible, and to sacrifice either was quite out of
the question. While the whole establishment was
in perplexity, the major-domo exclaimed that he
had thought of an expedient by which he could
turn both fish to account. The Cardinal and his
guests sat down to dinner, and after the soups were
removed, the door was thrown wide open, and with
great pomp a magnificent turbot made its appearance. The sight called forth a burst of admiration
mingled with astonishment. During the height of
the excitement, to the great horror of the company,
the servant who carried the dish stumbled, and
rolled with its contents upon the floor. At this
untoward event, an exclamation of horror was heard
on all sides. Nothing daunted, the major-domo
calmly said that he would immediately repair the
damage; at a given signal another door was thrown
open, and a fac-simile of the first fish was ushered
in, much to the amazement of his Eminence and his
guests, who, on tasting the Apician luxury, expressed their surprise that the sea should have

yielded two such specimens of equal size, and no doubt of equal delicacy of flavour.

"In England, during the French revolution, the Duke of Bedford invited the emigrant Duc de Grammont to a splendid dinner, one of those magnificent entertainments which English noblemen pride themselves on giving to crowned heads, and their good feeling prompts them to offer to exiles. During dessert, a bottle of Constantia was produced, which for age and flavour was supposed to be matchless. It was liquid gold in a crystal flagon, a ray of the sun descending into a goblet, it was nectar which was worthy of Jove, and in which Bacchus would have revelled. The noble head of the house of Russell himself helped his guest to a glass of this choice wine, and De Grammont on tasting it declared it to be excellent. The Duke of Bedford, anxious to judge of its quality, poured out a glass, which no sooner approached his lips than with a horrible contortion he exclaimed, 'Why what on earth is this?' The butler approached, took the bottle, applied it to his nostrils, and to the dismay of his master pronounced it to be castor oil! The Duc de Grammont had swallowed this horrid draught without wincing. This sublime trait reflected the greatest honour on the aristocracy of France; one must ever entertain the most exalted opinion of a country where politeness is carried to such a degree of heroism."

Worthy M. Briffault! I have endeavoured to preserve his solemn, but rather inflated style, in the anecdotes I have translated. Heaven defend me from such heroism!

Perhaps the exiled Duke thought castor oil was the wine of England, as a courier said that mud was the gold of Norway. Stories of similar mistakes are so frequent and so familiar, that no Englishman is surprised at any Frenchman, and no Frenchman is surprised at any Englishman, getting into the absurdest scrapes. Most of these stories, however, are made up, and fastened on those who are quite innocent of them.

For years, all imaginable French and native *Malaprop-isms* were given to a lady whose husband had a short reign and a merry one in the world of fashion; and personally acquainted as I was with her, I must in justice say that her reported sayings were "mere inventions of the enemy." Some of them, indeed, ill-natured as they were, were highly amusing, which is a sufficient excuse for their appearing in these pages. It was said that the lady in question had found fault with her fishmonger for not having sent her gutta-percha *soles;* that she returned a pair of globes, terrestrial and celestial, because they were

odd ones; that she declared, when she went to
Paris, she would ask for the celebrated makers,
"*Droit et Gauche*," as their names appeared conspicuous in almost all the shoes she had seen; that
she went to Falke's for her *virtue* (vertu) and to
Hunt and Roskell's for her *bigotry* (*bijouterie*); that
she proposed importing her Charlotte Russes from
the land of the Czar; and that she never could
understand why a hotel should be called the roasted
friend, *Hotel D'Ami roti* (*Hotel D'Amirauté*).

Having alluded to sayings which I believe were
got up, I will refer to others which actually have
been made use of by eminent persons. I remember
full well a gallant colonel, who was on Wellington's
staff with me at Paris, in 1815, entering the breakfast room, and asking me whether I would accompany him to the theatre that evening. "I thought
you never went," I responded. "You are right,"
he replied; "but I have just come in from my
morning walk, and I see placarded in Rivoli Street
the playbills of the day. They act the same piece
at every theatre. It must be a wonderful one. See
here; it's in '*Galignani.*'" I referred to that universally popular paper, and read out, under the
head of the respective places of public amusement,
the following announcement:—"*Relâche au Théâtre.*"
"*Relâche!*—that's the name," my brother officer

exclaimed. "I wonder what it means?" Not a word more was said, as the party assembled at breakfast were in great hopes that the good-humoured and kind-hearted Scot would proceed to the Ambiguous, as he called the *Ambigu,* or to the Port of St. Martin's (Porte St. Martin), and there discover his mistake. The joke, however, was marred by the worthy *maitre d'hotel* informing the colonel that *reláche* meant "no performance."

CHAPTER X.

CHAPTER X.

In talking of dinners, we must not forget that there is something as important as the quality of the food and wine, and that without this something the most lavish host cannot pretend to real hospitality. This further requirement may be summed up in the word "courtesy." If I was asked to point out any one person who was a model in this respect, I should name the late Marquis of Anglesey. The grace, affability, and playfulness with which he did the honours, whether under the lofty shades of Beaudesert or in Old Burlington Street, were unsurpassable.

The first time I ever met him was at my father's house at Brussels. He was then the Earl of Uxbridge. Before dinner I was presented to him; and there was a charm in his manner which contrasted most favourably with the stiff, erect, martinet school of other general officers, who, as a rule, treated young ensigns and cornets with pride and contempt. As a large party had assembled round my father's hospitable board, I, with another youth of my own age, my brother aide-de-camp Lord Hay, sat at the sideboard, and we enjoyed ourselves quite as much as if we had been at the grand table. After a dead silence of a minute, the voice of Lord Uxbridge was heard. "I shall be happy," said he, "to take wine with the sideboard." Of course we hastily filled our glasses, rose, and acknowledged the compliment, which was truly gratifying to us. It was by gracious acts like these that the dashing hussar won all hearts. Although Lord Anglesey was not satirical, he could expose any little faults of his friends and acquaintances in a manner that, without offending, produced a beneficial effect. Upon one occasion, a guest at Uxbridge House took out of his pocket a handkerchief redolent with some strong perfume, which completely impregnated the room. "Nothing disagreeable, I hope," said the host, with a slight curl of the lip. "I fancy the smell of the paint is entirely gone." This gentle rebuke produced a good result, as the musky handkerchief never again appeared during the evening. What a contrast was this to a similar reproach attributed to the late

Lady Holland, who, at her dinner-table, desired a servant to fetch one of her pocket-handkerchiefs, and give it to Mr. M—— instead of his, for she could not bear the smell of lavender so near her. Lord Anglesey was punctual in his movements, and set an example of early rising and regularity that might well have been followed by many younger men. I remember dining with him one day, and after waiting some little time for an absent guest, the dinner was announced. Just as the soup was being removed the gentleman arrived, and commenced an apology. "I beg your pardon, my Lord, but I was detained so long in Rotten Row that I had scarcely time to half dress myself." "Under those circumstances," responded Lord Anglesey, "it's almost a pity that you did not stay to finish the other half; but better late than never. What say you to a glass of sherry?" The proposal completely took the sting out of the first remark, and set the *late* Colonel —— at his ease.

There was one colonel to whom the Marquis was not inclined to be equally merciful, and whom he would not let off as cheaply. He was wont to tell an excellent story of this man, as a proof that the keenest observer may be deceived by appearances. The event to which the story referred took place at the battle of Waterloo. Early in the day of the

ever memorable 18th of June, the attention of the
Marquis was attracted to a very smart cavalry regiment, happily, as it turned out, not one belonging
to the British service; and hearing that it was a
newly-formed corps, he gave orders that it should
retire till it was wanted, and form out of reach of
the enemy's guns, then keeping up a heavy fire.
The colonel, a fine, dashing looking fellow, obeyed
the order, and the men took up their new position
in a perfectly soldierlike manner. Later in the day,
when cavalry was likely to be required, Lord
Anglesey (then Earl of Uxbridge) told his aide-de-
camp, the late Sir Horace Seymour, to order the
above regiment to come to the front. The gallant
officer galloped off, gave the order, and returned as
speedily as possible to his general. A few moments
afterwards Lord Anglesey looked round, and saw
the regiment advancing.

"That's a fine fellow," remarked his lordship to
one of his staff; "see how beautifully they advance
—quite in review order. Mark the colonel; no
bustle, no confusion. They are bringing their right
shoulders forward; they are retiring. Depend
upon it something has occurred that we cannot
make out. The colonel is about to make a wonderful move, probably to cut off a regiment. How
quietly he goes to work; no one can suspect his

movements; perfect strategy. I knew I could depend upon him. He looks every inch a cavalry soldier. Why, what on earth is he about? The regiment is trotting away to the rear; they are actually running away. Horace Seymour, lose no time in bringing the colonel to his senses."

Away galloped the trusty aide-de-camp again, and soon caught up the retiring corps.

"Lord Uxbridge orders you to the front."

The reply is not recorded; all we know is that the mandate was not obeyed. After trying for some time the *suaviter in modo*, Horace Seymour, who was a fine athletic young fellow, proceeded to the *fortiter in re*, and catching hold of the commanding officer's *aiguillette*, tried to drag him back. He was, however, unsuccessful; so, with imprecations loud and deep, he left hold of the recreant knight, and rejoined his general, to whom he reported what had occurred.

"The cowardly rascal," said the noble Paget; "and yet I never saw a fellow in whom I should have placed more confidence."

The battle went on. In the course of the day Wellington told Lord Uxbridge that he had sent an order to bring up all the cavalry that had been held in reserve, more especially the regiment above referred to.

"All I hope," said Lord Uxbridge, "is, that you have sent a more powerful fellow than Horace Seymour, for he tried with all his might and main to bring the dastardly colonel to the front."

By the time Wellington's aide-de-camp had reached the spot where the *brave* corps had temporarily halted, the dashing men who had attracted Lord Uxbridge's attention, and drawn down alternately his praise and anger, were half home on their way to Brussels.

Cyrus Redding, in his "Fifty Years' Recollections, Literary and Personal," gives so faithful a description of the late Lord Anglesey, that I must transfer it to my pages :—

"Death has since deprived his country of this distinguished nobleman, full of years and honours, one who, in a great nation, stands among the foremost for many of those high qualities which belonged to the best of the old school rather than the new, of the heroic era rather than that of traffic, better estimated in lofty historical records than in the staple of common panegyric; in other words, more calculated for the admiration of the discriminating few than the applause of those who judge by the vulgar standard of every-day opinion. The Marquis of Anglesey was singularly disinterested, highminded, candid, chivalrous, without a particle of guile, in honour sensitive, in kindness foremost, in dealing gentlemanly, plain, and somewhat abrupt of address, affable, never suffering his social superiority to be felt; he was the last with whom an ill-bred person could take a liberty or a well-bred one feel constraint; his manners were natural, and not the offspring of study or affectation; his carriage elegant, but perfectly simple; he was one of nature's gentlemen, and from always thinking in accordance with the character, it governed his personal bearing. A mean action on his part was an impossibility. With high spirit, his sterling courage tempting him in some instances to hazard his squadrons farther than was politic, leading them personally, with a daring impetuosity that looked more to the impulse of overflowing valour than to the rules of military conduct, as at Sahagun, where, with four hundred men, he defeated eight hundred, sword in hand, and at Mayorga, Benevente, Corunna, and Waterloo. To have shown more of the strategist, he would have exhibited less of his bold and generous character as a soldier; in all, exhibiting the more distinguished qualities with which he had been gifted by nature. All around him prevailed the spirit of order, his establishments exactly arranged, and everything in its place. No stranger saw him but was struck with the grace of his

manners and the manly elegance of his bearing.
He showed the old hardihood in his living. He
never indulged in luxurious appliances, for which
he might well have been excused, particularly after
the loss of his leg. He suffered at one time severe
attacks of the tic-douloureux, which he sustained
with extraordinary firmness. He was an early
riser.

"There was a singular contrast remarked in regard
to the two Lords Lieutenant, Anglesey and Wellesley,
who followed one another in filling that post in
Ireland. Lord Anglesey, unaffected, simple, manly,
with his tall, graceful figure, asking no extrinsic
aid from pomp and circumstance, and full of self-
reliance. Lord Wellesley, insignificant in figure,
scrupulous in the display of snow-white linen and
dangling jewellery, a singular mixture of talent and
frivolity, fond of show, and destitute of that manly
simplicity which was a distinguished trait in the
character of his brother, the Duke of Wellington."

There were, however, few men that prided themselves more on neatness than the late Marquis of
Anglesey, and he was ever conspicuous for being
neatly dressed, and having neat equipages, and the
neatest of yachts. The deck of the *Pearl* was as
clean and as bright as attention and scrubbing could
make it, and the noble owner always prided himself

upon it. One afternoon in July, Adolphus Fitz
Clarence and myself, who had just returned from
Brighton, were about to get on board the Ryde
and Cowes steamer at Portsmouth, to convey us to
Cowes, when we saw Lord Anglesey in his well-
manned gig pulling off for the yacht. He hailed
us, and asked if we wanted a passage; we replied
that we did. "Perhaps," he continued, "you
are disengaged; if so, come and dine with me
at the castle: with this breeze we shall soon be
there." Gladly availing ourselves of the gallant
"skipper's" invitation, we got into a waterman's
boat, and were soon alongside the "gem of the sea."
In a few seconds we slipped our moorings, and were
under weigh, a strong breeze blowing from the east.
For half an hour all went well, and Lord Anglesey
was expatiating upon the neatness that prevailed
throughout. "If there is one thing more than
another," said he, "that I take pride in, it is my
deck. Look, there's not a speck of dirt to be seen
on it." Adolphus and myself fully endorsed the
remark, and were praising the admirable manner in
which the duties were carried on under Captain
Martin, when a heavy shower of rain came on.
"Get some waterproof cloaks," said the owner;
"the storm will soon blow over." The cloaks were
brought, and in less than a quarter of an hour the

sun burst forth, and the rain ceased. We doffed
the waterproof garments, and Fitz Clarence went
forward to watch the sailing of a new yacht that had
recently been launched. "Why, what on earth is
that?" exclaimed the Marquis. "Some one must
have broken a bottle of ink in his pocket." And
upon looking I saw large black marks on the
glassy deck. In the meantime Adolphus had rejoined us; and as he approached it was quite evident
that he was the culprit; for it was as easy to trace
the track of his feet as it was for Robinson Crusoe
to trace that of Friday. "Get a swab," said Lord
Anglesey, "and follow Lord Adolphus wherever he
goes; but first send a man forward to wash the
deck." "I beg a thousand pardons," said the
good-humoured son of the sailor king; "it is the
French polish that has come off my boots. How
could I be so stupid as not to have remembered
that wet will make it run?" "Never mind," responded the Marquis; "accidents will happen; but
to avoid further mischief, suppose you keep your
feet on the mat until we reach Cowes. A piebald
deck is not a very pretty object." Fitz Clarence
was so upset by this gentle rebuke that he sat quite
motionless, when it occurred to him that a pair of
canvas shoes which he felt assured he could borrow
from the captain would be better than his French-

blacked boots; and this change being made, "Dolly," as he was familiarly called, was again soon at his case.

Lord Adolphus's fatal boots remind me of another adventure of his, in which his French polish was severely tasked. Upon one occasion he visited Bedlam in company with the late Sir George Wombwell, and among other patients in that excellent and admirably arranged asylum, was a female suffering from temporary derangement of intellect. When the two visitors entered her apartment, she asked Lord Adolphus what his name was, and without thinking he replied Mr. Brown Nothing more occurred, and the circumstance had completely departed from his memory, until he again visited the building, where almost the first person he met was the female in question. He addressed her politely, and inquired after her health. He saw plainly that something embarrassed her, and not wishing to prolong a conversation which seemed from some unknown cause to give her pain, he was about to walk on, when gazing at his good-humoured countenance, the poor deluded creature said, "May I speak a word to your lordship?" His answer was "Certainly." "I felt hurt," she proceeded, "at your deceiving me by giving a false name. I knew you well at the time from your

likeness to the King on the gold and silver coin."
Adolphus stammered out an apology. "Say no
more," continued the female. "But perhaps as you
did hurt my feelings, you would not object to
render me an act of kindness." "I shall be
delighted," rejoined the kind-hearted nobleman.
"Then," she added, in a most impressive tone,
"convey this message to your father. Tell him I
am mad, often very mad, although I have lucid
intervals; but mad as I am—and promise me to
repeat my words—I am not half as mad as his
Majesty was when he signed his name to the Reform
Bill."

Far be it from me to endorse this statement. If
I had no other reason for questioning the lucidity
of the interval in which the patient uttered such a
sweeping assertion, I must remember that I myself
have sat in a reformed Parliament. I never held
with the amusing, but none the less gloomy pre-
dictions of my friend Hook, that in a short time
the masters would be waiting on the servants, and
the very coach horses would be impregnated with
reformers' principles, so as to refuse to stir from
their stables. I was not as fastidious as the late
Mr. Croker, who vowed that he would never sit in a
reformed Parliament, thinking that the menace of
losing his company would prove so terrible as to

ensure the rejection of the Bill. Not only did I sit in the reformed Parliament, but I voted for reform, and was personally acquainted with some of the chief reformers, among whom I may specify O'Connell, Sheil, and Joseph Hume.

Many of those who came in contact with O'Connell would, if asked for their recollections of him, have nothing to say but that he abused them roundly. Like Marryatt's midshipman, whose only interview with his Admiral began and ended with a threat of a flogging, or the gentleman who boasted that the King spoke to him, and when asked what he said, replied, "He told me to get out of the way," O'Connell's antagonists might record passages of sarcasm or invective. My experience of him was pleasanter, and he always treated me with that courtesy which marked his intercourse with his friends, and contrasted so strongly with his treatment of his enemies. It may be interesting to quote the words in which Prince Pückler-Muskau describes the great liberator. "He is about fifty years old," wrote the Prince in 1828, "and in excellent preservation, though his youth was rather wild and riotous. His exterior is attractive, and the expression of intelligent good nature, united with determination and prudence, which marks his countenance is extremely winning.

He has, perhaps, more of persuasiveness than of genuine large and lofty eloquence, and one frequently perceives too much design and manner in his words. Nevertheless, it is impossible not to be interested in his arguments, pleased at the martial dignity of his carriage, excited with laughter at his wit. He looks more like a general of Napoleon's than a Dublin advocate. His understanding is sharp and quick, and his acquirements out of his profession considerable. His manners are winning and popular, though occasionally tinged by what the English call vulgarity."*

I once crossed from Bristol to Waterford with Sheil, in the most lovely weather, and I particularly remember the passage from the absence of all agitation. The only thing that at all disturbed us was the squeaking of some very noisy pigs, who might almost have been Sheil's constituents surprised at his calmness. We arrived at Waterford at about three in the morning, and while I was getting something to eat in the hotel, Sheil dashed off to the stables and secured the only fly that was to be had.

Sheil's oratory was far more fervid than that of O'Connell, and superior in brilliancy and finish. He was a small spare man, with quick piercing eyes

---

* "Tour in England, Ireland, and France," by Prince Pückler-Muskau.

and a face wonderfully mobile—a little Gascon
figure, as an eminent Frenchman called him. One
of his schoolfellows described his face as pale and
meagre, his limbs lank, his hair standing up from
his head like a brush, a sort of muscular action
pervading his whole frame, his dress foreign, his
talk broken English, and his voice a squeak. There
was something theatrical in his oratory; but the
expression of his face, while he hurled forth his
sarcasms, or rose into the highest flights of eloquence, was perfectly sublime.

Hume, who was one of the chief butts of Theodore Hook and the *John Bull*, as witness the lines
in " Michael's Dinner "—

> " Where was, on that famous night,
>   Hume the surgeon, Hume the surgeon,
> Who pretends to set us right
>   By constant purging, constant purging?
> No division yet expecting,
>   Fond of work, he—fond of work, he
> At that moment was dissecting
>   Michael's turkey, Michael's turkey "—

was in no sense an orator. But few men worked
harder in the cause of reform and retrenchment, and
few succeeded better in expressing their opinions
openly and fearlessly without giving offence to the
opposite party. I happened to be one who was
antagonistic to him in his attacks on the General
Post-Office, of which department my late brother

the Duke of Richmond was at that time head.
Wallace, the member for Greenock, and Hume,
were loud in their complaints against Sir Francis
Freeling and his general management, and they
occasionally brought forward charges which were
unfounded. Anxious to defend the Liberal Government, and my brother who held office under it, I
was in the habit of accompanying him to St. Martin's-le-Grand two or three times a-week, so as to
make myself thoroughly acquainted with the work-
ings of the office, and be prepared to combat any
fresh charge that might be brought against it. In
all our skirmishes, no one could behave with more
gentlemanly feeling than Joseph Hume. He confined his attacks to the system, not to individuals, and was ever ready to do justice to the
motives of those who opposed him. Upon one
occasion he had given notice of a question he was
about to ask which affected my brother, and I was
in my place to defend him. The night before I
had been at a party at Lady Blessington's, in Seymour Place, and, as it rained heavily, D'Orsay
offered me the use of his cab to take me home. No
sooner had I got into it, and the diminutive "tiger"
had clambered up behind, than I found one of the
reins was unbuckled; the horse, accustomed to go
at a fast pace, trotted on, and as I pulled he naturally

hugged the pavement. At last, finding the rein dangle on his back, he started off at a canter, ran against an iron paling in Curzon Street, and tipped me out. I was taken into a chemist's shop and had my wounds, which were not very severe, dressed; still, the plaster about my nose and forehead made me appear worse than I was, and likened me not a little to the print one sees of Baron Munchausen.

The next evening Hume was in his place, and as I entered the House he, perceiving the maimed state I was in, got up, and said "if it would be more agreeable for the noble Lord that he should postpone his question he would do so, however inconvenient it might be to him." This courtesy was duly appreciated by all, and by no one more than myself, and in declining it, I publicly expressed my thanks to him.

During the above time I often sat, on the Liberal Government side, next to one with whom I had a slight acquaintance on the turf; I refer to the late John Gully, Esq., Member for Pontefract. There were few men in the House at that period who attended more to their parliamentary duties than the gallant ex-pugilist, and his opinions (which diffidence prevented his giving utterance to in the House) were ever good and sound. I have often heard him, after listening attentively to the members of the

Opposition Benches, make remarks to those around him, among others to myself, which we all gladly embodied in our speeches. Upon one occasion, when we happened to dine together at the same table in the House of Commons, I referred casually to the late Earl Fitzhardinge, which drew from my companion a most graphic description of his lordship, then Colonel Berkeley, calling in his carriage for Gully before his great encounter with the Game Chicken. Gully at that period had been unfortunate, and was pounced upon by the myrmidons of the law, who, for the smallest of debts, took him into what was termed a sponging-house, as a preliminary measure. The late Sir John Shelley and Harry Mellish rescued Gully from the fangs of the law, and from that moment he never again became involved. I have been told that the name of the Game Chicken was derived from Pearce being called Hen Pearce, which degenerated into Hen Peck'd; "more of a game chicken than a hen," said a friend; and hence the name.

It may not be out of place here to give a brief description of Gully's prowess in the ring. His first encounter took place at Hailsham, Sussex, October 8th, 1805, when he fought Harry Pearce (the Game Chicken) staking £400 against 600 gs. After a gallant fight of one hour and ten minutes he was obliged to give in. But, though vanquished, his determined resolution and spirit raised him high in the estimation of the sporting world. On the 14th of October, 1807, Gully met the herculean Gregson at Six Mile Bottom, near Newmarket, and, after a severe contest, was declared the conqueror. Gregson's friends, not being satisfied with the result, challenged Gully to fight for £200 a side, which was readily accepted, and, on May 10th, 1808, they met in Sir John Sebright's park, Hertfordshire; after fighting fifty-eight minutes Gregson was knocked out of time by a hit under the ear. When we consider the disparity of the men, the Lancashire champion being six feet two inches in height, and weighing fifteen stone, and Gully being two inches less in height and a stone and a half less in weight, the success of the latter was wonderful, and was alone attributable to his science. This was Gully's last appearance in the pugilistic ring, and for some time after he was the popular host of the "Plough," Carey Street, Lincoln's Inn. As "Speed the Plough" seems to have been the motto of his house, he in due course of time retired from business, and during an honourable and long career on the turf he realised a handsome fortune.

To show the gentleman-like and liberal feeling that influenced Gully in all his transactions in

private life, I will name one in which I was an
interested party. It is now nearly forty years ago
that I rented a small house in London, which I
placed in the hands of an agent to let furnished
from May the 1st to November the 1st. I soon
received a notice that Mr. Gully was willing to
take it at the terms named, and the bargain was
concluded. A day or two before Goodwood Races,
I happened to pass the house, and saw it was shut
up, and being anxious to see whether some bars
that I had ordered to be placed on the back
windows, had been put up, I rapped at the door to
make the inquiry, and found my orders had been
executed. "Have Mr. Gully's family been long
out of town?" I asked. "They have never
arrived yet to take possession," responded the
woman. "There has been an illness in the family,
indeed I heard of a death, and so Mr. Gully engaged me to take care of the house, and keep it
thoroughly aired until the first of November." At
Goodwood I mentioned the circumstance to Gully,
telling him how sorry I was that he had not informed me of it, as I might possibly have let it to
another. "I felt, my Lord," he replied, "that it
was not fair to make such an appeal, a kindly feeling might under the circumstances have induced
you to release me from my bargain, but I could not

have told you of the cause until the first month, the month of May, was over; so I much preferred paying the whole amount, and that I shall insist upon doing. We may perhaps occupy it shortly." The latter was said merely to satisfy my scruples.

Although never devoted to the prize ring, I occasionally for fashion's sake attended a fight, and well do I remember going with Ball Hughes, and a party on the 11th of September, 1821, to see a second contest that attracted a great interest in the pugilistic world, between Jack Randall, called the Nonpareil, five feet six inches in height, and Jack Martin, named after his profession, the "Master of the Rolls," five feet nine inches in height. Randall's weight was ten stone ten pounds, while the baker nearly turned the scale at twelve stone. In the first fight, which lasted forty-nine minutes and ten seconds, the light weight had come off victorious. The match was for three hundred guineas a side, and the "office" was given to the Golden Ball by Jackson to be at Reigate at a certain hour. Here we were informed that the fight was to take place within an easy distance of that town, but owing to the interference of the magistrates, the men were obliged to proceed still farther south, and the stakes were pitched nearer Brighton than London, so much so that after the contest we proceeded to dine and sleep at that watering-place. Having travelled at least forty miles, some of the party were disgusted to find that the fight only lasted one round of eight minutes and a half, ending in a second defeat of the baker, who after much fine sparring fell violently against a stake, and was stunned by the shock. To me the result was most satisfactory, as the beaten man soon recovered, and I had an opportunity of witnessing as fine a sparring exhibition as could be imagined between two men in the finest possible condition, without all the horrors that attend a prolonged fight.

CHAPTER XI.

CHAPTER XI.

AMONG the "Stately Homes of England" few are more interesting than Berkeley Castle. Shakspeare refers to it—"There stands the castle by yon tuft of trees;" and the road-books tell us that it is pleasantly situated on an eminence in the delightful vale of Berkeley, about a mile east of the river Severn. This ancient pile appears to have been founded soon after the Conquest, but has at different times since received important additions. Its present form approaches to a circle, and the buildings are enclosed by an irregular court, surrounded by a moat. The entrance to the keep is through an elegant sculptured arched doorway, leading to a flight of steps, over which an apartment is shown as the place where Edward II. was barbarously murdered. The building is flanked by three semi-circular towers, and a square one of later construction. During the civil wars, this castle was for-

tified for the king, and sustained a severe siege in
the year 1645. About the same time the town and
neighbourhood frequently witnessed the disastrous
effects of skirmishes between the contending parties.
I must, however, refer the reader to Holinshed,
and other authorities, ancient and modern, for a
fuller account of the old castle, as I am not concerned with it in a topographical point of view.
It is more worthy of record that the castle was
always noted for the most genuine hospitality. As
the present Lord Fitzhardinge married my sister,
I was a constant guest at Berkeley Castle and
Cranford, and was always mounted with the hounds,
or offered a place out shooting.

The late earl was a thorough-bred sportsman,
and his hounds were second to none. The shooting
was also excellent. It was a favourite maxim of
his, that punctuality was as necessary in pleasure
as in business, and he always acted up to this principle. In the kennel and hunting-field nothing was
wanting; to adopt a household saying, "there was
a place for everything, and everything was in its
place." The same with regard to shooting; the
beaters were regularly told off, and each knew the
duty assigned to him. When the decoy pool, or
when wild-goose shooting on a cold frosty evening
was the pursuit, the utmost regularity prevailed,

and all was carried on in a business-like manner.
The same system was pursued on board his lordship's yacht, the *Imogine*. Nothing the earl dis-
liked more than to have any one staying with him
who had not a stud of his own. "It's all very
well," he would say, "you profess not to care for
hunting, but when the morning arrives, and all are
equipped for the chase, you would look as if you
wished to go, and I should be annoyed at not being
able to mount you. So, bring a horse or two, and
I'll do my best to mount you the days your stud
wants rest."

The living was perfect; every one did as he liked
as far as breakfast was concerned, and could have
it any hour. Luncheons were unknown, but a
glass of wine and a biscuit were ever at hand, while
punctuality prevailed at dinner, and it was served
to the moment. A rubber of whist for small stakes
was usually got up, and the smoking-room was
always ready at eleven o'clock. There was no
pressing to keep any one up at night, and a guest
might retire as early as he liked, or sit up to the
small hours. During the alternate winter months
Lord Fitzhardinge kept open house, when, in addition to his London friends, many of the neighbours
flocked round him.

The interior of the castle, despite its age, is as

warm and comfortable as any modern house. It contains many valuable pictures and historical relics. In the great hall, now used as a dining-room, is a splendid specimen of modern workmanship in silver, representing the fatal combat between the seventh Lord of Berkeley and his relative, Talbot, Viscount Lisle. The cause of the quarrel was as follows :—

"Upon the Countess of Shrewsbury's death, Thomas Talbot, Viscount Lisle, succeeded to her claim of right to Berkeley Castle; and, having failed in the several underhand methods and stratagems he made use of to get possession thereof, at last sent the Marquis* a challenge, requiring him—'of knighthood and manhood to appoint a day, and to meet him half-way, to try their quarrel and title, to eschew the shedding of Christian blood; or to bring the same day to the utmost of his power.' Unto which the Marquis returned an answer in writing :—'That he would meet him on the morrow at Nybly Green, by eight or nine o'clock, which

---

* "William Lord Berkeley being created Viscount Berkeley, 21 Edward IV., and two years afterwards made a privy councillor. He was in like favours with Richard III., who made him Earl of Nottingham; but he entering into the interests of the Lancastrians, and joining the Duke of Buckingham in endeavouring to dethrone King Richard, was forced to fly into Brittany, to Henry Earl of Richmond, by whom, after he had mounted the throne, he was constituted Earl Marshal of England, and in 1488 was created Marquis of Berkeley."—*Magna Britannia Antiqua et Nova.*

standeth (saith he) on the borders of the Liverode, that thou keepest untruly from me.'"

They met accordingly, and, the Viscount Lisle's visor being up, he was slain.

In the old billiard-room there are two interesting pictures, one of which represents the celebrated affray with poachers, which took place on the night of the 18th of January, 1816, and in which one of Lord Fitzhardinge's keepers, William Ingram, was killed. As the particulars of this affair may have been forgotten by many of my readers, I give an account of it, as taken from the Coroner's inquest and trial :—

" On February 1st were committed to Gloucester gaol John Penny, late of the parish of Hill, in Gloucestershire, charged with the wilful murder of one William Ingram, in the night of the 18th ultimo, and John Allen, William Penny, Thomas Collins, Daniel Long, John Reeves, John Burley, James Jenkins, Thomas Morgan, James Roach, and William Greenaway, severally charged with having feloniously been present at the said murder. Greenaway and Burley were afterwards admitted King's evidence. The trial commenced on Tuesday morning, April 9th, at the Booth Hall, Gloucester, before Mr. Justice Holroyd. Scarcely ever did any criminal trial excite more interest than the present.

Eleven young men, nine of whom were farmers'
sons, and respectably connected, the youngest nine-
teen, and the eldest not more than thirty years of
age, led on, in the clandestine pursuit of game, to
the destruction of human life, and, consequently,
making their lives dependent upon the decision of a
Court of Justice, could not but create an interest of
the highest degree in the feelings of the public.
The chief witnesses deposed to the following facts :—
Thomas Clark, park-keeper to Earl Fitzhardinge,
at that time Colonel Berkeley, stated, that on the
evening of the 18th of January last, he and his man
went to the Round House at the end of the Round
House wood, where they met seventeen other
keepers (seven of them belonging to his employer,
and ten to Lord Ducie) between eleven and twelve
o'clock at night. One of the keepers communicated something which induced them to leave the
Round House almost immediately. They were all
without arms. They had short sticks in their hands,
and went all together across the Bowling Green, to
the wicket gate leading to Catgrove. There they
separated into two parties, nine remaining with
him. His party went to Catgrove, where he
shortly heard a gun fired. They then pulled off
their great coats, when he went up the main ride,
opposite to the gate. After proceeding a little way,

he saw a number of men in a road to the left. Ingram was then close behind him, and the poachers about twenty yards from them. He saw them by peeping round a corner, and said to Ingram, in a low voice, 'Here's a lane full of them.' On his speaking, the poachers began to form in a line, and said 'Hist, hist!' as if they had heard him or his party approach. One man on the right was very active in forming the poachers into a line, who now advanced two or three deep. Witness did not say anything until a gun was fired; he then stepped into the middle of the ride, and exclaimed, 'Huzza, my boys, fight like men!' The poachers still kept moving towards him, and he retreated a little to the right, keeping about the same distance from the poachers, to leave room for his party to come up to him. The poachers were about fifteen yards from him when a second gun was fired, which took effect upon William Ingram. A third gun was fired within a very few seconds, a single shot from which struck witness on the inside of the right thigh. The body of poachers then made a rush towards witness, one of them striking him on the left shoulder, either with a stick or his fist, as he was turning his head to look for the rest of his party, who were then coming up the main ride. The poachers came close up, went over Ingram, passed witness, and turned the corner into the main ride. When the poachers passed him they were fronted by the keepers, a cluster of five or six guns were then fired together. After this the two parties were intermixed, but the keepers appeared to be running in all directions, the poachers keeping together. An outcry was made by some of the keepers, when he saw one man, Davis, lay down on the right of the ride, apparently dead. The poachers advanced down the ride, and as still they pushed on he heard a man cry 'Glory, glory!' When they were gone, he stood to see who were wounded, and only found Davis and Ingram.

"William Greenaway (who had turned King's evidence) said he was one of the persons who were with the poachers. Allen, whom he had known for seven years, came to him upon the Sunday before the 18th of January, and asked him if he would go out poaching, saying there was a party going out, and desired witness to get some party to go with him. They were to meet on Lord Fitzhardinge's or Miss Langley's liberty. Witness went to John Penny's house, and told him what Allen had said. Did not learn till the 18th at what time they were to go out; on the evening of that day Allen asked him if he would go out that night, and told him to come up a quarter before nine o'clock. The party

met at Allen's house, where ammunition was produced, and the guns distributed among the poachers.
They then had their faces blacked, and their hats
chalked. Something was then said about an oath
not to peach on each other,' and some person remarked that Brodribb should swear them. Brodribb, who was an attorney, then swore them
solemnly upon a book not to 'peach upon each
other.' The witness then corroborated Thomas
Clark's evidence, adding that John Penny fired the
second shot, which took effect upon the keeper;
and that upon witness picking up the butt of a gun,
which John Penny claimed as his, the latter said,
' Now Tom Till's debt is paid.' Till had been
killed by a spring gun on Lord Ducie's liberty a
little before.

"The learned judge then commenced summing up
the evidence, the recital of which occupied four
hours. The jury then retired, and, after a deliberation of about two hours, brought in their verdict,
by which John Penny was found guilty of the
murder, and all the other prisoners guilty of aiding
and abetting therein; but they recommended to
mercy all except John Penny and John Allen. The
sentence passed upon the two latter was carried into
effect on Saturday, April 13th. Brodribb, who
was tried at the same Assizes for administering, or

causing to be administered, a certain oath or engagement, purporting to bind William Greenaway and
others not to reveal and discover an unlawful combination and confederacy, was found guilty, and
sentenced to seven years', transportation. In his
defence he declared that Greenaway had confessed
to him that it was he who had shot the keeper."

The other painting represents the late Lord
Fitzhardinge, the Honourable Augustus Berkeley,
John Austin, Esq., and others, as the principal
characters in "Julius Cæsar." The scene is the one
in which the "great Cæsar" has fallen beneath the
daggers of the conspirators; the noble owner of
Berkeley Castle and his brother Augustus, as *Brutus*
and *Marc Antony*, are in the act of delivering
those splendid passages beginning :—

> "O mighty Cæsar! dost thou lie so low?
> Are all thy conquests, glories, triumphs, spoils,
> Shrunk to this little measure?"

and ending with the lines of Brutus :—

> "Prepare the body and then follow us."

Our readers need scarce be reminded that under
the auspices of the late Earl Fitzhardinge, amateur
theatricals were carried on at Cheltenham, Gloucester, Tewkesbury, Birmingham, Guildford, Worthing,
Richmond, and the Tottenham Court Road Theatre,
London, with very great success. Some of the best

of Shakespeare's plays were put upon the stage in a manner that could not be equalled upon the metropolitan boards. Witness the performance of "Othello," "King John," "Julius Cæsar," "Henry IV.;" while others were equally successful, namely, "A New Way to Pay Old Debts," "Pizarro," "Catherine and Petruchio," "Heir at Law," "Bold Stroke for a Wife," "The Wonder," "Follies of a Day," "Roland. for an Oliver," "Simpson and Co.," "Lady and the Devil," "Mayor of Garratt," &c.

One night in December, when a large party, including the late Sir George Wombwell, Colonel Jenner, John Dawkins, that prince of good fellows, Johnny Bushe, and other particular friends, were staying at Berkeley Castle, the noble host, then Colonel Berkeley, was to appear on the boards of the Gloucester Theatre, to take a part in one of the amateur performances that were carried on under his auspices. During the day, Wombwell had asked his host to give him a lift, jocosely adding that without it, it would be quite *un*possible to quit the well-piled wood-fire of the castle for the cold boxes of a country theatre. "It won't do, Master George," responded the Colonel; "I must be there punctually, and upon such occasions I take no one —not even my valet or a servant." "I shan't

occupy much room," replied the good-humoured
baronet, "and Bob Jenner's dying to go; as
Shakespeare says, 'I'll be the bare bodkin.'" "No,
no," persevered the owner of the castle; "I'll send
you all over to Gloucester, but I go alone." Carriages were ordered to take the party over, and at
five o'clock to a minute the Colonel's travelling
chariot, with four good posters from the Berkeley
Arms, was at the door. The night was dark, cold,
bleak, and stormy; a regular nor'wester blowing
strongly, and as punctuality was the Colonel's
motto, the moment the turret clock of the old
church struck five, he was snugly ensconced in his
comfortable vehicle, and the horses were bowling
away through the town at the rate of twelve miles
an hour. The orders given were brief but characteristic—"Make the best of your way to the stage-
door of the Gloucester Theatre. Seven shillings a-
piece, or nothing."

Upon reaching a small farmhouse about a mile
from the castle, the Colonel called out to the
boys to pull up for a minute, as he wished to get
out. The carriage stopped, and he descended,
leaving the door open; in a few seconds the "boy"
(a man of near fifty) who was riding the wheel-
horse, heard the carriage door bang, followed by a
stentorian voice, which, amidst the heavy gusts

of wind, was not distinguishable. It very naturally occurred to him that his employer had resumed his seat, so, clapping his spurs to his well-conditioned horses, he started off at an awful pace. The voice was heard again. " Seven shillings or nothing," seemed to sound upon his ear, so the pace was increased, and in a wonderfully short time the carriage reached the Gloucester Theatre. The attentive manager was anxiously waiting at the door, the ostler from the hotel was in attendance, the colonel's valet was at his post, and the postboy on the wheelers jumped off his panting steeds to receive his orders, when, to the surprise of all, the carriage was without an occupant. Consternation was strongly depicted upon every countenance. " What can have happened to the Colonel?" exclaimed one. " I shall be ruined," sighed forth the manager; " I must close the house." " Where can he be?" said the driver with fear and trembling. " Here, you double stupid fool!" shouted forth a well-known voice, and a well-known form appeared on horseback, covered from head to foot with mire.

The reader will at once unravel the mystery: the carriage-door was closed by a gust of wind, and the voice heard amidst the howling storm was that of the Colonel, left to his own meditations by the road-side.

Fortunately for him, his tenant was at home; but unfortunately the only horse that he could offer had been in the hands of the veterinary surgeon. "If anything happens to him I'll make it good," said the Colonel, as he mounted the animal, and giving him a strongish pressure with his legs, was soon in chase of his own carriage. "It's all well that ends well," said the amateur to the now delighted manager. "I am in plenty of time to dress, and, on future occasions," he continued, turning to the despairing postboy, who thought, like Othello, that "his occupation was gone," "keep your ears wide open, and attend to my voice, instead of listening to the howling of the wind." With this admonition, and the promised handsome gratuity, the drivers were dismissed, and his carriage and pair ordered after the play to take him to the hotel where he was to sleep. In less than an hour the postboys were both perched up in the gallery, shouting forth their delight, not only at the admirable performance of their "lost one," but at the generous manner in which he had overlooked an unconscious, yet flagrant error of judgment. The late Earl was liberal to the greatest extent, and many were the generous acts that he did towards those less favoured by fortune. He was also constant in his friendships, as was proved by the annual gathering of his old "chums" at his birth-day.

About three years ago, when a young lady, famed for amateur histrionic and musical talent, was staying at the castle, it was suggested that a play should be got up in the old baronial hall, and the piece was selected, cast, and rehearsed. I was appointed architect, machinist, scene-painter, and manager, with one stipulation made by the present noble owner, that no damage was to be done to the walls. To this I cheerfully consented, and arranged with the carpenter that only two large hooks should be inserted in the woodwork, the beams furnishing us ample means of hanging the scenery. For the proscenium I selected some paper representing knights in armour, and soon obtained enough materials from the paper maker for the interior of two drawing rooms and the wings. This, with the aid of a red curtain and drapery, was all I required, as the stage was to be made on the raised dais; the audience to be placed in the centre of the hall, with the gallery at the back for the servants. In addition to the duties above mentioned, I was called upon to take the part of a testy old gentleman,—one which the bother I was subjected to would have made perfectly natural,—and to write an occasional address, to be spoken by the star of the evening.

This young actress, with a niece of mine, were to be the leading ladies. All was going well, when, unluckily, we received a telegram, stating that the author of the piece we were to perform, who was to have acted with us, was unable to leave home. We could not find a substitute, and the play had to be abandoned, much to the annoyance of the *corps dramatique.* I give the address :—

ADDRESS WRITTEN FOR THE OPENING NIGHT OF THE BERKELEY CASTLE PRIVATE THEATRICALS, BY LORD WILLIAM LENNOX. SPOKEN BY MISS PUSEY.

Within these solemn walls, where once did ring,
Shrieks of an agonising murdered king,
Where Cromwell's soldiers—rude and lawless band—
Spread devastation o'er this fertile land;
Where battles raged, where still the ghost of Lisle*
Haunts the blue chamber with its ghastly smile;
I come to ask your favour for our play—
Kind Host and Hostess, prithee don't say nay.
All feuds have ceased. No more the din of arms
Or brazen trumpet sounds wild war's alarms.
No more the cannons roar, or lance is hurled,
No more the blood-stained banner is unfurled,
For verdure springs where carnage held its sway,
And waving corn-fields smile midst summer's ray;
Garden and terrace decked with flowers bright,
Fragrant in odour—beautiful to sight;
While hospitality with pleasure reigns,
And mirthful joy relieves our cares and pains.
Long live our host; may blessings him attend;
In him both rich and poor will ever find a friend."

Berkeley Castle has long been famous for hunting, shooting, and wild duck decoying; and there are few

---

* The ghost of Lord Lisle, who was slain by the seventh Lord of Berkeley, is still supposed to haunt the blue chamber.

places in England which afford more sports of those
kinds. Hunting, especially, the most English of all
pursuits, has found a series of devotees in the Berkeleys. But what shall I say of that noble art, or how
can I find words that are worthy of it? What new
thing can be said of a subject which has employed
all pens in all ages, from the frequent similes drawn
from the chase by Homer, to the hunting sketches
of one of the most popular of our novelists?

> " En age segnes
> Rumpe moras ; vocat ingenti clamore Cithæron,
> Taygetique canes, domitrixque Epidaurus equorum ;
> Et vox ascensu nemorum ingeminata remugit."

No one took a greater delight in hunting, or could
have quoted the above lines of Virgil with greater
truth, than the late Earl Fitzhardinge. So devoted
was he to the "noble science," that he spared
neither time nor expense in carrying it out to perfection. *Vulpecides* were unknown in his country,
and there was not a farmer in it that did not feel
a pride in preserving foxes, and rendering every
assistance in his power to promote this manly recreation. I believe that if the noble owner of
Berkeley Castle had expressed a wish for a new
gorse cover, there was not a squire, or a yeoman,
who would not have converted his best piece of
clover land to that purpose. "Gentleness of manners, with firmness of mind," says the refined Lord

Chesterfield, "is a short but full description of human perfection on this side of religious and moral duties;" and if occasionally the gentleness was eclipsed by the firmness, it was when the sport of the million was marred by the reckless conduct of a few in over-riding the pack. When the mild yet firm expostulation, "Hold hard, gentlemen!" was not attended to, anathemas, deep and loud, were heard, added to an occasional threat of taking home the hounds. Upon one especial occasion, the field had been very unruly, and his lordship had rated them considerably. The rating had produced due effect, and, for the next few weeks, they became quite orderly. One day, when the hounds met half-way between Berkeley and Gloucester, a large muster took place, and among the numbers were two young cornets recently arrived from India, who had taken up their head-quarters at Cheltenham. These youths had been boasting of their prowess in the East after jackals, and declared to a confidential friend that they were determined to "cut every one down." This boast reached the ears of the present Lord Fitzhardinge and his brother Augustus, who at once agreed to do their best to retain those honours they had richly earned in the hunting-field, of always being "first or thereabouts." Fortunately for them the noble master of the hounds was laid up with an attack of the gout, so that there was no one to keep order except the huntsman. "Give 'em time, gentlemen," exclaimed this valued servant, as a fine woodland fox broke cover. "Pray don't ride over them, sir," he continued, addressing a stranger, who, mounted on a tear-away animal, had lost all control over his steed. "I must ride at that fellow," said one of the cornets. "By all means," responded his brother officer, and away they went helter-skelter, racing pace, over the finest grass country. The runaway hero, although he could not check his hard-pulling hunter, managed to guide him in the direction the fox took, which happened to be towards Berkeley Castle. Away he went, like a second Mazeppa, "upon the pinions of the wind," followed by the two cavalry officers, unmindful of all consequences, and caring for nothing so long as they could keep in the first flight. But they had "reckoned without their host," for they were closely followed by Frederick and Augustus Berkeley, who, both belonging to the "never say die" school, resolved not to be beaten by two interlopers. "It's lucky my lord is not out," remarked the first whip, as the yelling of a hound showed that he had been most unceremoniously ridden over when getting through a fence. "Should not we get a wigging!" said the culprit; "I would not have the

peer out for fifty pounds." Scarcely had these words
been uttered, when another yell was heard, and the
shouts of the huntsman reached the ears of the
offenders. "You'll kill the whole pack if you go on
in that way. What will my lord say?" And what
my lord did say can hardly be laid before the reader.
"Why, who on earth is that?" asked one of these
wild huntsmen, as he pointed to a garden chair
tenanted by a gentleman encased in a warm great
coat. "It's Fitzhardinge himself, by all that's wonderful," exclaimed Frederick Berkeley. "We're in
for it," responded Augustus, as he charged a "bull-
fincher," and again a yell was heard. True it was,
that the earl, attracted by the melodious voices of
the pack—a pack

> "So well proportioned, that the nicer skill
> Of Phidias himself can't blame thy choice,"—

had ordered his groom to bring round the wheel-
chair, and had placed himself on the bridge, under
which a broad and sluggish river ran. "What's to
be done?" asked Frederick; "the hounds must
cross the bridge close to his lordship." "Follow
me," responded Augustus, as he dashed into the
water, swam under the archway some twenty yards
down, and landed on the opposite bank unnoticed.
His companion turned short to the right, took an
awful fence, and was soon out of sight. Unaware

of Lord Fitzhardinge's presence, the two cornets went a-head, and received the whole weight of his lordship's anger, both asserting that the real " Simon Pures," who had charged hounds, fences, and brooks, had made their escape.

One of the heroes of this adventure, Frederick Berkeley, the present Lord Fitzhardinge, was a first-rate amateur jockey and rider of trials. He rode upon one occasion a trial for the late Duke of Richmond, and was mounted on Swindon, to try the speed of some young ones. No one knew the trial horse better than Fred Berkeley, who had ridden him in his celebrated race against Lord George Bentinck on Mr. Poyntz's chesnut mare Olive, which was won by superior riding on the Captain's part. After the trial, which ended in the defeat of the young ones, was over, John Kent, the Duke's trainer, complained to his employer, " that the Captain cut the young ones down in the first half-mile." " Why, of course I did," responded the gallant sailor. " The object was to win by any means I could; do you suppose that during a race their opponents will not do their best to cut them down as soon as possible?" The answer was un-answerable, and completely satisfied the owner of Goodwood, however much it might have discon-certed his trainer. Not that we wish to censure

Kent's conduct, for it is human nature to give all young ones a chance, and Kent acted on the Latin adage — "Fere libenter homines id quod volunt credunt."

As a sailor Lord Fitzhardinge has seen much service, and distinguished himself greatly afloat and ashore. No one ever performed the duties of a Lord of the Admiralty with more credit. His prowess at sea has been chronicled by our great naval historian, James, who thus records his services:—

"On the 3rd of November, 1803, while the 18-pounder 36-gun frigate *Blanche*, Captain Zachary Mudge, was lying at an anchor off the entrance of Mancenille Bay, island of St. Domingo, the French cutter *Albion*, armed with two 4-pounders, six swivels, and twenty muskets, and manned with forty-three officers and men, was discovered lying close to the guns of Monte-Christi, waiting to carry her cargo, consisting of fifty-two bullocks, to the relief of the garrison of Cape François. As the cutter, notwithstanding her proximity to the fort, which mounted four long 24-pounders, and three field-pieces, appeared to be assailable, Captain Mudge, on the same day, despatched the launch, barge, and two cutters, with sixty-three officers and men, under the command of Lieutenant William Braithwaite, to attempt cutting her out. The boats

returned unsuccessful, not owing to any lack of zeal
in officers or men, but to their having proceeded to
the attack in open day, with the sea-breeze blowing
right into the bay. The battery, in consequence,
had begun early to fire at the boats, and soon convinced Lieutenant Braithwaite that, should he even
succeed in capturing the cutter, it would, in the
state of the wind, be impossible to get her from the
shore without a great sacrifice of lives. With more
judgment, a night attack was determined upon,
and Lieutenant Edward Nicolls, of the Marines,
volunteered, with one boat, to attempt cutting out
the vessel. His offer was accepted; and on the
evening of the 4th the red cutter, with thirteen
men, including himself, pushed off from the frigate.
A doubt respecting the sufficiency of the force, or
some other cause, induced Captain Mudge to order
the barge, with twenty-two men, under the orders
of Lieutenant the Honourable Warwick Lake, first
of the *Blanche*, to follow the red cutter and super-
sede Lieutenant Nicolls in the command. The
second boat joined the first, and, as soon as the two
arrived abreast of the French cutter, Lieutenant
Nicolls hailed Lieutenant Lake, and pointed her out
to him; but the latter professed to disbelieve that
the vessel in sight was the *Albion*; he considered
that she lay on the opposite or north-east side of

the bay, and with the barge proceeded in that direction; leaving the red cutter to watch the motions of the vessel, which Lieutenant Nicolls still maintained was the *Albion*, the object of their joint search. It was now half-past two, A.M., on the 5th, and the land wind was blowing fresh out. An hour or two more, and the day would begin to dawn, and the breeze to slacken, perhaps wholly to subside. The men in the boat were few, but their hearts were stout; in short the red cutter commenced pulling, cautiously and silently, towards the French vessel, the crew of which, expecting a second attack, had made preparations to meet it. As soon as the boat arrived within pistol-shot, the cutter hailed. Replying to the hail with three hearty cheers, the boat rapidly advanced, receiving in quick succession two volleys of musketry. The first passed over the heads of the British, but the second severely wounded the coxswain, the man at the bow-oar, and a marine. Before the French cutter could fire a third time, Lieutenant Nicolls, at the head of his little party, sprang on board of her. The French captain was at his post, and discharged his pistol at Lieutenant Nicolls, just as the latter was within a yard of him. The ball passing round the rim of the Lieutenant's body, lodged in the fleshy part of the right arm. Almost at the same moment a ball, either from the pistol of Lieutenant Nicolls, or from the musket of a marine standing near him, killed the French captain. After this the resistance was trifling; and the surviving officers and men of the French cutter were presently driven below and subdued, with the loss, besides their captain killed, of five men wounded, one of them mortally. As yet not a shot had been fired from the battery, although it was distant scarcely one hundred yards from the cutter. Judging that the best way to keep the battery quiet would be to maintain the appearance of the *Albion's* being still in French possession, and able to repulse her assailants, Lieutenant Nicolls ordered the marines of his party to continue firing their muskets; the seamen, meanwhile, busied themselves in getting the vessel under sail. A spring having been run out from the cutter's quarter to her cable, and the jib cleared, the cable was cut, and the jib hoisted to cast her. At this moment the barge came along-side, and Lieutenant Lake took command of the prize. Scarcely had he done so, and the musketry by his orders being discontinued, when the battery opened a fire of round and grape, which killed two of the *Blanche's* people. However, the breeze being fair, and blowing moderately strong, the captured cutter, with two boats towing her, soon ran out of

gun-shot, and without incurring any further loss,
joined the frigate in the offing.   Between the two
attacks upon the *Albion*, another boat-party from
the *Blanche* captured, in a very gallant manner, a
vessel of superior force.   On the 4th, in the morning, the launch, armed with a 12-pounder carronade,
and manned with twenty-eight men, under the
command of Mr. John Smith, master's mate, attacked, and after an obstinate conflict of ten
minutes, boarded and carried, as she was coming
out of the Caracol passage, a French schooner,
mounting one long 8-pounder on a pivot, and
manned with thirty men, of whom one was killed,
and five were wounded.   The launch had one man
killed, and two wounded.   The prize was a beautiful
ballahou-schooner, and had on board a considerable
quantity of dollars.   In his official letter, announcing the capture of this schooner, Captain Mudge
says, 'She is one of the finest vessels of her class
I ever saw, and is fit for his Majesty's service;'
adding in a postscript, 'I have omitted mentioning
the Honourable Frederick Berkeley, but the only
apology I can make is saying he behaved nobly,
and was much to be envied.'"

Besides gaining such laurels for himself, Lord
Fitzhardinge was ever ready to give full credit to
those who had served under him.   He used to tell

the following story of a man under his command during the late war with France.

A marine of the name of Clements, when attacking the boats of a French frigate, received a bullet in the calf of his leg, a part of which he was particularly proud. While he was smarting bodily under the pain, and suffering deeply in his mind at being thus maimed, the boat in which he was overtook that of the enemy. He raised his cutlass, and was about to strike the French coxswain, when a feeling came across him, that it would be un-English and cowardly to attack an unarmed man. Passing the cutlass from his right to his left hand, he doubled his right fist and gave the enemy such a blow, that he fell as if he had been struck by a sledge hammer. Whether, in the phraseology of the ring, the gallant Gaul had his "claret tapped," his "ivories" damaged, his "frontispiece" smashed, his "ogles" blinded, or his "smeller" flattened, is not stated; all I know is that the coxswain lay down in his boat, and never showed his head again.

Among the guests that I was in the habit of meeting at Berkeley Castle and Cranford was the late General Buller, who had formerly served in the Guards. He was a *bon vivant*, and a very good whist player; and, unquestionably, it was more agreeable to sit next to him at dinner than opposite to him at cards, for the slightest mistake would draw down " curses loud and deep." The general was a *gourmet* of the most refined order, and was famed for the excellence of his salads. He possessed a secret which he considered would have made the fortune of any one, and thrown Sydney Smith's recipe into the shade. But before I proceed to describe General Buller's salad, I must quote the recipe which it was to eclipse. Some worthy men no doubt can say it by heart, but there are others who do not know it so well, to their shame be it spoken :—

> " Two large potatoes, passed through kitchen sieve,
> Unwonted softness to the salad give.
> Of mordant mustard add a single spoon—
> Distrust the condiment which bites so soon ;
> But deem it not, O man of herbs, a fault
> To add a double quantity of salt ;
> Three times the spoon with oil of Lucca crown,
> And once with vinegar procured from town ;
> True flavour needs it, and your poet begs,
> The pounded yellow of two well-boiled eggs ;
> Let onion atoms lurk within the bowl,
> And, scarce suspected, animate the whole ;
> And, lastly, in the flavoured compound toss
> A magic teaspoon of anchovy sauce.
> Oh, green and glorious ! Oh, herbaceous treat !
> 'Twould tempt the dying anchorite to eat ;
> Back to the world he'd turn his fleeting soul,
> And plunge his fingers in the salad bowl.
> Then, though green turtle fail, though venison's tough,
> And ham and turkey are not boiled enough,
> Serenely full, the epicure may say,
> ' Fate cannot harm me—I have dined to-day.' "

Similar confidences, poetical or otherwise, were not to be extracted from the rival salad-maker. Every attempt to worm his secret out of him was futile. It was to live and die with him. Once at Cranford a strong pressure from without was exerted to induce him to disclose the ingredients, but it met with no success, and fair means having failed, foul ones were resorted to. Every day before dinner the general was wont to retire into the butler's pantry to prepare the salad, and every condiment was laid out, including mustard, pepper, red and black, salt, oil, vinegar, ketchup, cream, boiled eggs, Harvey's sauce, and others of a similar nature. The room was then closed, and Buller, "left alone in his glory," mixed the ingredients in as mysterious a manner as the witches in Macbeth, or the wild huntsman in Der Freischütz. One adventurous youth tried the door, but a gruff voice told him "that there was no admittance except on business." A party then assembled to try and outwit the salad-maker. "Let us try the window with the steps," said one; "we can easily command a view of the general's operations." A small pair of steps was procured, and an intelligent individual mounted them, pencil and paper in hand. The first thing that caught his eye was the gallant officer, with bowl before him, and spoon in readiness to mix the coveted recipe. The general looked cautiously round the room, and placed a napkin over the keyhole, little suspecting that there was a very formidable specimen of a Paul Pry looking through a small pane of glass at a considerable height from the floor, in which quarter the butler had told him he was perfectly safe from inspection. It would be an additional breach of good faith were I to say how many spoonfuls of the required ingredients were used; suffice it to remark, that every article was duly noted down, and the son of Eve who had adopted his first mother's love of curiosity, might have exclaimed, "*Eureka!* I have discovered the secret!"

Descending from the steps, my friend sent for a salad-bowl, and the usual quantity of "green forage," and, aided by myself and others in the housekeeper's room, made an identical salad. Nothing more was said until dinner was served, when we naturally brought on the subject of the best mode of salad-dressing. Our host, who had a most retentive memory, and who, by the way, had been informed of our proceedings, quoted Sydney Smith's poetical recipe, another mentioned the usual French way, when the principal conspirator said, "My Lord, I have tried a salad to-day, not equal, I fear, to the general's, but one upon which I wish your opinion." "I'll back mine to be the best," remarked Buller, with a grunt, and in a tone of defiance that seemed to say, "My throne must not be invaded." "What say you to a little bet?" "Well, as far as a new hat goes," responded the other, "I have no objection; the bet is, that his lordship does not pronounce yours to be the best." "Agreed," replied the general. "Bring me two cold plates," said Fitzhardinge; "and the salads; you know," continued he, addressing the butler, "in which bowl the general's is?" "Yes, my Lord," answered the man. After helping himself, and tasting both, he said, "I can find no difference; but the general shall decide himself." Buller took both, tasted both, drank a glass of fine old sherry to cleanse his mouth, and was speechless. "There's been some foul play," proceeded he, after a moment's pause; "I own I have fairly lost my wager, but whoever has discovered my secret, let me entreat him to keep it to himself, and not make it public." This was urged in so imploring a tone, that we all felt for the general. "Perhaps," said he, clinging like a drowning man to a straw, "my ingredients were enough for and used in both." "No, general," replied the butler, "yours was kept under lock and key from the time you gave it to my charge until I myself placed it on the sideboard." Buller's face elongated; then, recovering himself, he said, in a most desponding tone, " I do not ask who has solved my riddle, but I trust to him to keep it in his own breast." "We promise," exclaimed the whole party simultaneously. " You've not lost your wager, general," said our host, " it is a dead heat—a drawn bet."

Buller's principal study was, to use a phrase of Dr. Johnson's, " one of the arts that aggrandise life—cookery." His *precept* was " *In solo vivendi causa palato est;*" his *practice*, to devote his best energies to his masticatorial duties. How often would he quote the following panegyric on the delights of the table !—

"An excellent and well-arranged dinner is a most pleasing occurrence, and a great triumph of civilised life. It is not only the descending morsel, and the enveloping sauce, but the rank, wealth, wit, and beauty which surround the ' meats,' the learned management of light and heat, the silent and rapid services of the attendants, the smiling and sedulous host proffering gusts and relishes ; the exotic bottles, the embossed plate, the pleasant remarks; the handsome dresses, the cunning artifices in fruit and farina—the hour of dinner, in short, includes everything of sensual and intellectual gratification which a great nation glories in producing."

This oracle of culinary lore piqued himself upon being a *gourmet* of taste and sentiment, and he possessed *une érudition gastronomique tout-à-fait effrayante.* "Nothing like' good eating and drinking to bring out the humanities."

> "La table est mon seul amour.
> Manger, jouer à whist, et boire,
> Voilà mon ordre du jour,"

were his constant words, and he acted up to the maxim they implied.

His sarcasms, when put out of temper, were very severe, fully realising the sentiment of him who thus faithfully describes bitter irony :—

"A true sarcasm is like a sword-stick, it appears at first sight to be much more innocent than it really is, till, all of a sudden, there leaps something out of it sharp, and deadly, and incisive, which makes you tremble and recoil."

Anyhow, his care of the inner man was successful in preserving his life, for he died at the age of eighty-three, at his house in Bury Street, St. James's, November, 1855. He entered the army in 1790, served the campaigns of 1793 and 1794 in Flanders, as well as in the West Indies, and was present at the siege of St. Lucie and reduction of Grenada. In 1810 he was appointed aide-de-camp to George III., with the rank of colonel.

Men of his stamp generally consider that the cook is the doctor's greatest enemy, and that a good dinner is of more real service to the body than any quantity of medicine. The theory is confirmed by the general practice of doctors, who, as a rule, live well, and prefer the taste of their cook's prescriptions to that of their own. An amusing anecdote of the way mankind in general regard doctors was told me by Sir William de Bathe, who was aide-de-camp to the late Lord Strafford, the Sir John Byng of Wellington's army. Sir William was with Byng, when the latter commanded a district in Yorkshire, and, shortly after they settled down at some country house which the general rented, they drove through the adjoining village. There the first person they met was the Esculapius of the district, who with a smiling countenance, an eye beaming with satisfaction, and a most impressive manner, pulled up his horse, stopped the carriage in which Byng and De Bathe were driving, and said, "I'm happy to see you look so well, Sir John." "I don't believe you are," was the curt reply, much to the dismay of the doctor, who, clapping spurs to his steed, was shortly out of sight. Sir John, who was very warm-hearted, took an early opportunity of calling upon the medical man, and removing any unfavourable impression his truism had created.

CHAPTER XII.

CHAPTER XII.

SOME of the pleasantest hours of my life have been spent at Cowes, the great abode of yachts, the scene of so many trials and exploits. A stranger arriving there would think it a toy harbour. He would see diminutive craft of the most exquisite build and cut, moored a little way out, or lying close to the shore. Small forests of raking masts, hulls with the most graceful run, would attract his eyes in every direction. If he stepped on board he would find the same grace and neatness, but it would be equally difficult to realise that any use was made of these tiny craft—that men lived on board them, and rank and beauty delighted to cruise in them. The sight of their miniature cabins would confirm the impression. At first sight one would no more think of making a voyage in a yacht than of riding from York to London on a race-horse. And yet there have been instances of

H 2

long cruises in the smallest of these playthings; one hardy spirit accompanied the Baltic fleet in his cock-boat, and rode out the fiercest gales with the courage of a three-decker.

The primary object of a yacht, however, is speed rather than endurance. It is the racer of the ocean, and must keep up the pace of an express for a short distance, instead of braving storms and riding mountainous billows. To see it then you would no longer think it a mere toy. The spectacle of two yachts leading the squadron and straining every nerve to win another fathom, is as exciting as a well-contested Derby. They are so buried beneath the spread of canvas that their hulls have almost vanished. A small dark line breaks the connection between the swelling white above and the white crests below. Every possible device is tried to get their utmost out of the sails, its utmost out of the hull. Whip and spur, the last resource of jockeys, are useless here to disguise failure or cover excitement. Yet failure is as keenly felt, and the excitement is more protracted.

The yacht race of all others to which these remarks apply, was that in which the palm was carried off by the *America*. In former days the thought of such a defeat would have been a fearful blow to the pride of England. We have now come to be more tolerant. The cheers which greeted Gladiateur on his carrying off the "blue riband of the Turf" for a Frenchman, proved that John Bull has made considerable progress towards cosmopolitan feelings. All he demands now is "a fair field and no favour," and he takes all beatings with equanimity as lessons for future success. The crowds of people who visited the *America* were moved by admiration as much as curiosity, and the extreme courtesy with which they were received by the gentlemen on board her, Commodore Stevens, his brother, and Colonel Hamilton, was fully appreciated. The newspapers of the day have recorded the prowess of the *America* in the match round the island for the cup, open to yachts of all nations, and in her single contest with the *Titania* iron schooner, in both of which she proved victorious. It is not generally known that the late Earl Fitzhardinge was the first person to come forward to test the sailing qualities of the New York clipper, as he proposed to sail against her for two hundred guineas, provided Mr. Weld would lend him the *Alarm* cutter — Mr. Weld to have the entire control and management of his vessel. In the event of this match not coming off, the noble owner of Berkeley Castle offered to give a cup of the value of one hundred sovereigns, provided any two

yachts would enter against the *America*. The
veteran Weld, of Lulworth Castle, who was a most
liberal patron of yachting, felt the honour that had
been conferred upon his vessel, but declined making
the match as the *Alarm* was not in trim. Subsequently Mr. Scott Russell, the builder of the
Titania, came to Cowes, when he and Captain
Claxton, both practical men, and intimate friends of
Mr. Robert Stephenson, agreed to recall that yacht,
which was cruising off the coast of Yorkshire, and
try her speed with the American. Stephenson at
once assented to the proposition, and placed himself
in the hands of the Earl of Wilton, Commodore of
the Royal Yacht Squadron. The result was, as has
already been stated, in favour of the Stars and
Stripes. For myself, I had only one opportunity of
personally judging of the powers of the *America*,
and that was in company with the late Earl Fitzhardinge. His lordship in the *Imogine*, a powerful
vessel of about eighty tons, Claxton in the *Fire
Fly*, a small cutter of two-and-thirty tons, and
the Yankee skipper in his craft, formed the trio; as
the latter had come out to try his speed with us,
at the request of the late Lord Anglesey. It blew
a bit of a gale, and while we had all reefs down,
the far-famed clipper had two reefs down in the
mainsail, the bonnet off the jib, and the whole fore-

sail. Under this she stood up well, and beat us all
to shivers. I noticed she did not use the boom to
the jib; nor did she reef the mainsail to the boom.
This day's trial entirely confirmed the opinion I had
previously formed of the schooner's superiority over
all vessels of her tonnage. Before this I had paid
her a visit, having previously procured a letter of
introduction to Commodore Stevens.

Nothing could exceed the courtesy I met with
on board the *America;* and no vessel that ever
yet appeared in our waters could surpass her in
comfort and cleanliness. Upon her appearance and
sailing qualities I must dwell a little more at length.
The Earl of Winchilsea, in his spirited poem of
"Abd-el-Kader," seems to have had a prescient view
of the far-famed schooner, for he thus writes :—

> " O'er Benin's unhallowed waters
>   Lightly skims the demon barque;
> At her peak the *stripes* of freedom—
>   Steady in her wake, the shark—
> Nobly found! a fairy schooner!
>   Miracle of builder's art."

The lines, too, which follow are not inappropriate
to many a vessel that tried to compete with the
clipper :—

> " What is this comes drifting slowly
>   In the fairy schooner's wake,
> Struggling hard for vile existence ?"

To leave, however, the poetical strain, and descend

to humble prose, I must remark that few of the
accounts of the *America* which appeared in our
newspapers give so accurate a description of this
wonderful clipper as the one which came out in the
New York Herald on the day of her departure from
that city.   It will be read with interest.

"NEW YORK, *June 21st,* 1851.

"This superior piece of naval architecture takes
her departure from this port at seven o'clock, to test
her sailing qualities with the choice yachts of Great
Britain, and, we believe, with those of any other
European country who may think fit to place themselves by her side in a sailing-match. As the result
will be watched with much lively interest on both
sides of the Atlantic, it being a trial for the superiority in the sailing powers, beauty of model, and
symmetry of construction, between the vessels of
England and the United States, a description of the
America cannot be otherwise than interesting to our
readers, both here and in Europe.

"She is 95 feet on deck, from stem to stern;
80 feet keel; 23 feet amidships; and her measure-
ment 180 tons. She draws 11 feet of water in sailing
trim. Her spars are respectively 79$\frac{1}{2}$ and 81 feet
long, with 2$\frac{1}{8}$ inches rake to the foot. Her main
gaff is 36 feet long, and main boom 58 feet. She

carries a lugg foresail with fore-gaff 24 feet long. Length of bowsprit 32 feet. The frame is composed of five different species of wood—namely, white oak, locust wood, cedar, chestnut, and hackmatack; and is supported by diagonal iron braces, equidistant from each other 4 feet. From stem to midships the curve is scarcely perceptible, her gunwales being nearly straight lines, and forming with each other an angle of about 25 degrees. The cutwater is a prolongation of the vessel herself, there being no addition of false wood, as is usual in most of the sharpest-bowed crafts of similar description. Her after-cabin is a spacious and elegantly fitted-up apartment, 21 feet by 18 feet in the clear, on each side of which are six neat lockers and china-rooms. It contains six commodious berths. Joining this cabin are two large state-rooms 8 feet square, with ward-rooms, &c., attached. Between these and the fore-cabin there are two other state-rooms, joining which are a wash-room and pantry, each 8 feet square. The fore-cabin is ventilated by a circular skylight of about 12 feet circumference, and it contains fifteen berths. Directly under the cockpit, which is 30 feet in circumference, and which forms the entrance to the after-cabin, there is a tastefully fitted up bath-room on the starboard side, and opposite, on the larboard side, a large clothes-room.

Farther aft, under the cockpit, is the sail-room. She has a plain raking stern, adorned with a large gilt eagle resting upon two folded white banners, garnished with beautifully-carved flowers of green colour. Her sides are planked with white oak 3 inches thick, the deck with yellow pine $2\frac{1}{2}$ inches thick, three streaks of the clamps are of yellow pine 3 inches thick, the deck-beams are also of yellow pine; all the combings are of the finest description of mahogany. The rails, which are composed of white oak, are 14 inches high, 6 inches wide, and 3 inches thick. She is copper-fastened throughout, and copper-sheathed from the keel to 6 inches above the water-line, making $11\frac{1}{2}$ feet in all. Her sides are painted of a uniform lead colour, and her inside pure white. There is an open gangway extending through the whole length, from the extreme points of the after and fore cabins.

" It is impossible for the pen of the most graphic describer to convey anything like an accurate conception of the beauty and perfection of the *America*. She can only be seen to advantage when viewed at a distance, from different points, by the natural and living eye—under such circumstances only can her symmetrical and swan-like model be appreciated. She will proceed to Havre, France, where she will remain for a few days, for the purpose of getting her sides painted black, and every part of her fitted up in the most splendid style. Thence she will proceed to Cowes, where she is also to remain some days before exhibiting herself in the Thames. Mr. George Steer, the modeller and builder of the *America*, takes passage in her to London, for the main purpose of being able to judge, by practical observation, where rests the material difference between the model and construction of English and American-built yachts, and also to see which nation will win the palm of superiority in point of sailing qualities. Whether the *America* shall come off victorious is yet a problem; but be the result as it may, she cannot but be an object of deep interest and admiration on the other side of the water; and the elegant appearance which she will make in gliding up the Thames to meet her competitors must call forth applause on Mr. Steer, her builder and fashioner.

" She carries eight men before the mast, besides the captain, Mr. Richard Brown, first and second mate, and carpenter. Her cabin and state-rooms will be fitted up in a style that the people of Europe cannot but admire, and her accommodations are sufficiently ample to entertain a large company. The cost of the *America*, when all completed, will be 20,000 dollars."

The "whipping" we received from "Brother Jonathan" gave rise to many skits, and among others to the following from my humble pen. I may remark that I purposely attempted to vie with the poets laureate of Messrs. Rowland, Moses, Warren and Co., if not with the late lamented Catnach himself, and that, for fear of ranking far below these great luminaries if I came in open competition with them, I printed my poem for private circulation. Great was my surprise at finding it copied into a New York paper, with a very flattering allusion to the "good humour" of the writer. I will let my reviewer speak for himself. "The lines," he says, "contain so faithful an account of the proceedings at Cowes that we cannot refrain from giving those parts which more essentially bear upon the subject of the *America*. The air is 'Yankee Doodle.' They commence:—

> 'The '*Merica* to England came
>   And caused great consternation;
> She vow'd she'd sully British fame,
>   By flogging all the nation.
>
> 'To beard the lions in their den
>   At Cowes the gallant skipper
> First challenged all the squadron men
>   To sail his rakish clipper.'

The song then proceeds to describe the startling effect produced upon the noble and popular commodore, and his despair in thinking that perchance—

> '*Zarifa*, once the crack,
> Should have her fair fame blighted.'

It then delicately hints at the distress of the vice-commodore at being unable to take the *America* by the 'horn,' or rather 'Capricorn.' Allusion is subsequently made to the 'alarm' created among the Royal Yacht Squadron :—

> ' The *Arrow quivered*, *Dauntless* quailed,
> The *Stormfinch* feared foul weather,
> The *Champion's* wonted courage failed,
> The *Eagle* showed white feather.'

The challenge from that clever and spirited engineer, Stephenson, the owner of the *Titania* iron schooner, is thus graphically given :—

> ' *Titania* then, that playful elf,
> The queen of all the fairies,
> Cried, "Let us touch the Yankee pelf,
> And stop his. wild vagaries."

> ' So Stephenson to Stevens said,
> "I hear you've got a notion
> That '*Merica* can go a-head
> As mistress of the ocean.

> ' "Let's try my luck, and if I fail,
> 'Twill be my consolation
> To know at least you cannot *rail*
> 'Gainst all the British nation." '

The playful and *ironical rail*lery of the above stanza from the Colossus of roads—railroads—contrasts happily with the more serious peroration :—

> ' But should Columbia's stars so bright—
> So justly famed in story—
> Shine forth to dim our feeble light,
> We'll hail the New World's glory.

Chorus.

' Hey, Yankee doodle do,
   Hey, the Yankee skipper;
Hey, Yankee doodle do,
   Oh ! is she not a clipper ! ' "

While I am on the subject of yachting, I cannot refrain from mentioning a ludicrous circumstance which took place upon one occasion when the Royal Yacht Squadron were about to proceed to sea for a cruise, and afterwards to land upon the Hampshire coast for a pic-nic. The yachts, under the command of the gallant and noble commodore, the Earl of Yarborough, were to leave their moorings at a given signal, and by twelve o'clock every vessel was awaiting orders. The decks of each were crowded with fair ladies, and the weather being propitious, all were anxious to take advantage of it in the run to the Needles. I was on shore with Adolphus Fitz Clarence, who had promised to make one on board the commodore's yacht. He, however, having had a good deal of real sailing during his naval career, did not care for the amateur cruise, and proposed that we should have out his ponies, and drive to Ryde. To this I gladly assented, and suggested that we had better keep out of sight in the club-house until the squadron had got under weigh. In the meantime great preparation was going on, especially on board Lord Yarborough's

yacht, when its public-spirited owner ascertained
that one of his passengers, Adolphus Fitz Clarence,
was absent. Independently of the friendship that
existed between the two noble lords, the commodore was most anxious to have his old ally with
him, to show him how the work was carried on on
board the *Kestrel.* " Make a signal to the club-
house," exclaimed Lord Yarborough, " and ask if
Lord Adolphus is coming."

In a few seconds the signal was made. " What
is the reply?" Here a young fashionable landsman,
who had volunteered his services as signal midshipman, drawled out, " I'll make it out in a minute,"
took a Vienna opera-glass out of its case, and
pointed it to the shore. After a considerable delay
in adjusting the glass and turning over the leaves
of the signal-book, during which process some loose
memoranda of private signals were wafted over-
board, the " West End man" exclaimed, " I've got
it." " What is it?" asked the commodore and
others, who were beginning to get tired at the
delay. " Lord Adolphus Fitz Clarence says, ' No
go.'" This unexpected reply, repeated in a lisping
tone, raised a loud laugh, which was shortly sup-
pressed, and the mystery was explained. 3174 and
3259 had been made, the former meaning " no,"
" not," " nothing," and the latter " go," " going,"

"gone." Instead, then, of "No go," the reply meant "Not going."

When we take into consideration the difference between nautical language and what is termed Her Majesty's English, it is wonderful how a landsman ever gets on afloat. There are few things that surprise him more, among the terms used on board ship, than the animals, domestic and otherwise, which form part of the nautical nomenclature. I own I was surprised, when first I trod the deck of a man-of-war frigate, as a passenger bound for Quebec, to find that in stowing an anchor they must haul away the *cat* before they can hook the *fish*—that in bringing up a ship in bad weather they stopper with the *dog*, while it was quite a usual thing to talk of "handing in the *leech*," "clapping on a *lizard*," "raising on a *mouse*," "seizing with a *fox*." Articles of ladies' dress are also introduced, as the "*bonnet* off the jib," and "being in *stays*." But the course of my yachting experience enlightened me on all these mysteries. I have already mentioned that Captain Claxton, R.N., often sailed on board my yacht, and I learnt from him much about the navy without going through the painful process by which such knowledge is generally acquired.

Claxton, among other things, took much interest

in great circle sailing, and related an incident which
occurred to him when a lieutenant in the Royal
Navy. I give it in his own words :—

"One morning watch, the day of our making
Cape Race, a frigate under full sail was seen at
day-dawn on our weather beam, about four miles
off. Numbers were exchanged, she was the vessel
in which our new ambassador for the United States
was to embark and sail for New York the day after
we sailed; so it seemed odd that she should be so
far on to us, who thought no small beer of our own
ship's sailing. She passed within hail, under the stern,
after—'How are you ?' and 'How are *you?*' came
'How long are you out?' 'We sailed on 20th,'
(two days after us). 'What sort of weather have
you had ?' 'Fine all the way.' 'We've been, as you
may guess, in a deuce of a gale ; almost all up at
one time.' 'See you're all amiss—rather odd—so
could not have been far off;' and the captains shaking trumpets to each other, away she went, three or
four more points away than us, for Cape Race was
then close. 'How could this be ?' inquired some
one of me. 'Why, through the ignorance of the
master, and the captain's indifference.' I pointed
out the course he ought to have taken ; but with his
Mercator's chart before him, he could not be brought
to understand that, in high latitudes, if for any dis-

tance you follow the chart scale (which, for convenience, is laid on an apparent plane), you increase your distance unnecessarily, going easterly or westerly; the farther you keep north in north latitude, or south in south latitude, the less you find, if you look at a common globe, are your degrees of longitude. If you take a thread (showing it on a small globe) and hold one end in the fair way off the Lizard, and the other end in Halifax, or, better still, New York, you will find the south nook of Ireland, part of Newfoundland, Nova Scotia, and Long Island, all in your way; but as you must go clear of Cape Race, the point now in sight, put your finger there, and you will see the northermost part of the line several degrees north of Cape Clear, which you must also clear—I mean no pun. Now, we have never been farther north than that Cape; so by making something to get there, we have certainly unnecessarily increased our distance over a good day's run, while the other frigate, more 'wide awake,' has taken the proper course, and has escaped the hurricanes which made mincemeat of us, and which seldom reach the higher latitudes.

"Much, of late, has been said about great circle sailing," he continued, "as though it were a new discovery; why, I know men who have all their nautical lives practised it; and the first Atlantic

Steam Company, the Great Western, which was got up by Brunel, myself, and others, to my knowledge, prepared charts on this plan for their captains to sail by. Although a mighty fuss was made in the papers about poor Captain Hoskins going north of Ireland, almost every steamer in the contract now uses that passage from Liverpool. I think I may say always, if it does not blow strong from the northwestward."

"Then," I inquired, "why are not navy charts made differently?"

"The very question I lately put to a distinguished admiral; he replied, 'Why, for general purposes, Mercator's is correct enough; it saves trouble, and helps to make easy what otherwise is complicated; to make steady at a glance what varies almost every hour, every day, at any rate. Great circle sailing is only of much service well north or south of the tropics; and there are reasons why—as, for instance, between the Cape of Good Hope, Australia, Polynesia, and the Horn, the frozen regions interfere; and in other latitudes constant trades make passages shorter *in time*, though longer in distance.' Between England and the northern parts of North America, all north of Delaware, Canada, Nova Scotia, New Brunswick, and Newfoundland the case is different—the traffic great; the race between England

and America—now that the English laws (the igno-
rant laws, under the goad of Manchester quacks)
have given the latter all advantage, and have half
ruined the British shipping interests—being a fearful one, on which cutting off yards is of more
importance than cutting off degrees heretofore. The
continents of Europe and Asia, away to the one
hundred and fortieth degree of longitude, east of
Greenwich (nearly half the globe), travellers must
take their land tacks on board, and the map, and
the high road, and not the chart and salt sea; but
in the North Pacific and North Atlantic, ay, and
south of the Hope Cape, miles may be saved, and
distance shortened.   In conclusion, I am in no way
connected with Great Circle Reid, and the difference
between us is wide, although connected in a way—
his science being *his own*, and *sound about winds*,
mine borrowed, and only about courses."

Another of my nautical associates in my yachting
days, was the Honourable Augustus Berkeley, of
whose naval career I will give a slight sketch. He
was about fourteen years of age when he was
appointed midshipman on board his Majesty's ship
Donegal. The discipline of those days was very
different from what it is at the present time, and
the life of a reefer was anything but agreeable. On
one occasion he was ordered to the foretopmast-head

for the *serious* offence of skylarking with a favourite dog over the captain's cabin, and remained there for more than twelve hours. The secret of his having been mastheaded for that length of time was that the circumstance had entirely escaped the memory of the first lieutenant, and the middy would probably have fallen a victim to hunger and cold, had not his messmates stealthily handed up a warm jacket and a cold pumpkin pie. When we add the tricks of the mischievous urchins in the mess, the dogholes called berths, from which the sun and air of heaven were carefully excluded, the fragrance of the bilgewater, the brilliancy of the purser's "dips," the delicacies of the table—weevilly biscuits, not alone the staff of life, but life itself, salt butter, briny junk, and fiery rum, we can only wonder that so many fine young fellows were found to enter the service and prove an ornament to it. Another adventure of Captain Berkeley's may be worth recording. For some days the ship he belonged to, cruising off Ushant, had been on the look-out for a French *Chasse Marée*, and he was midshipman of the middle watch. Now, if there was one thing in the world he detested more than another, it was the middle watch. He cared not for any other duty; to board an enemy under a sharp fire of musketry, to go aloft when the wind was blowing great guns,

to lay out on the topsail yards to tie a reef point, or
pass a gasket in a gale of wind, were a pastime to
him compared to the horrors of being awoke at
midnight from a sound sweet slumber, such as youths
of fourteen, free from the cares of life, enjoy; with
perhaps the further torment of being cut down in
his hammock, and running the risk of fracturing his
skull in the fall.

Upon the night in question he had tried to induce
his messmates to sit up with him, knowing that if
once he turned in, nothing short of the strongest
means could eject him from his canvas cradle; but
they all pleaded fatigue, and dropped off one by one.
Left to himself, the middy was soon undressed, and
was shortly locked in the arms of Morpheus. His
thoughts wandered home; he dreamt of the scene
when, decked out for the first time in his naval
gear, dirk by his side, he was the admiration of his
sisters, the housekeeper, and the ladies' maids.

In the midst of one of these dreams, he was suddenly awakened by the well-known voice of the
captain, exclaiming, "Man the boats; where's the
midshipman of the watch?" Augustus Berkeley
started from his slumbers, and hearing the question
repeated, sprang from his hammock in search of his
clothes. Knowing the disgrace that would cling to
him through life if, even from uncontrollable cir-

cumstances, he appeared to shun this duty, he at
once made up his mind how to act, and without
further consideration rushed upon deck, and made
the best of his way head foremost through one of
the ports into the boat, in which he landed safely.
" Shove off," cried the lieutenant ; and in a few
seconds they were at every stroke leaving their
good ship in the distance.

After a long pull, and a strong pull, their boats
came in sight of the well-armed *Chasse Marée*, when
a bullet whizzed by our hero's head and entered
that of a brother reefer in the next boat. Poor
youth ! so sudden was the fatal shot, that even the
crew merely thought the victim had dropped his
head from sleep, death's counterfeit, not the grim
tyrant himself. Before Augustus had time to
mourn over the loss of his companion, the whole
party were actively engaged with the enemy.
They fought and conquered, and after an absence
of four-and-twenty hours the boats were within hail
of the *Donegal*. Berkeley had been put on board
one of the captured vessels, and triumphantly
steered her under the stern of the two-decker.

When he got on board to report himself, he was
ordered into the captain's cabin, for his " skipper,"
although a strict disciplinarian, did not wish to
lecture him on the quarter-deck, for the not very

venial offence of oversleeping himself, when he had made such exertions to attend to his duty in the boats. The reader will bear in mind the middy's costume, which consisted of a long night-dress tied round his waist with a rope, so as to look like a Roman tunic or a Highland kilt. Of nether garments he had none; and when, elated with success, he entered the presence of his captain, he for the first time remembered the state of nudity he was in. A burst of genuine laughter showed him that his offence would be pardoned. "Be more circumspect in future," said the worthy captain, afterwards a distinguished admiral; "attend a little more to the regulations and"—with an additional titter he added—"dress of the service."

The latter injunction was not a little needed one day when I landed with Augustus Berkeley at Southampton. We had been on a yachting cruise together, and, as we had been beating about all day with an adverse wind and a heavy sea, we preferred a bed and dinner at the "Dolphin" to a berth and "pot luck" on board our respective yachts. As we had got completely soaked to the skin in landing, we exchanged our wet gear for a dry suit more suitable to the deck of a cutter than the boxes of a theatre. It was a question if we could appear in the dress circle to witness Mr. and Mrs. Charles

Kean in "The Stranger" and "The Wonder," which were to be performed for their benefit.

"Our pea jackets and nautical hats will do admirably for the pit," said I; "and as in my days it was always considered the critic's seat, we will brave the opinion of any of our swell friends who may be in the boxes, and ensconce ourselves safely in it."

"Agreed," said my companion. "We had better dine early so as to be able to ensure a tolerably good seat."

Soon after the doors opened we found ourselves at the pit entrance, where a great crowd had already assembled.

"Perhaps," I exclaimed, "we might get one of the upper boxes over the stage doors; they are seldom or ever let."

As well might we have asked the box-keeper to have cashed a bill for ten thousand pounds. "Not a place to be had in the boxes, and the pit and orchestra will not hold another being."

What was to be done? "Let us try the gallery," said my companion; "we must get in somewhere, for there is nothing else left us to do, now we have dined."

Losing not a moment, we rushed to the gallery entrance, were told that there was scarcely standing

room at the back of it, but that we might take our
chance. Getting with some difficulty to the top of
the rather perpendicular steps that led to this upper
region, we found it to be what is usually termed
" chock full; " and in attempting to proceed, we
were assailed with anathemas that cannot be
repeated, interlarded with, " Where are you shoving
to, my hearties? " " It's no use a trying to get in,
there's not space enough to swing a cat in." " Mind
my feet." " I shall faint, and you'll kill the blessed
baby, if you don't mind what you are about." To
retreat was as difficult as to advance; so there we
remained jammed up, surrounded by half-suffocated
individuals, men, women, and children, who were
principally employed in shouting, singing, stamping,
crying for music, squalling, sucking oranges, and
drinking every liquor under the sun save good
liquor. After a few moments' deliberation as to
what we should do, I espied two boys, who looked
as if they had come out of the stoke-hole of a
steamer or the forecastle of a collier-brig, perched
up on the ledge of an open window quite at the back
of the densely-crowded gallery. They were yelling
and cat-calling in a manner that reminded one more
of a wild troop of Ojibeway Indians than civilised
beings.

" We'll get up to them, if possible, and buy their

seats," said I ; "anything is better than our present position."

At that moment the woman who purveyed eatables and drinkables to the "upper" classes happened to squeeze past us, and under the plea of diminishing her stock of provisions, we followed in her wake, until we found ourselves immediately under "the two little cherubs perched up aloft, looking out for the presence of Kean."

" I say, youngsters," I proceeded, "will you take a couple of shillings each and these nuts and pears between you, to give us up your seats ? You shall have your entrances paid another night."

"Won't we, that's all. Here goes ; let them gemmen pass; take care you don't tumble through; you'd come a header into the street. Thank ye, gemmen. All right."

During the above conversation the seats had been vacated and re-occupied, the money paid, and the urchins, who seemed delighted with the transaction, begun to attempt to make their way through the crowd.

" Why, there's Bill Cooper in the front row," exclaimed one.

" All right, Jem," replied his companion ; "let's make a dash to join him."

So ducking down their heads, they "gored" their

way through the mass of people, despite of kicks, pushes, and punches, until they wriggled themselves in between the above-mentioned Cooper and a friend in shirt sleeves, who was bellowing, " Silence—shame—turn 'em out—bravo—music ! "

The curtain drew up, and so great was our delight at the whole performance, that we sat out both plays, and did not vacate our " reserved " seats until Mrs. Charles Kean and her talented husband had made their curtsey and bow amidst a shower of bouquets. We say " reserved " seats advisedly, for when, between the two pieces, we left them for a few moments to refresh ourselves by standing up, no one attempted to take possession of them.

Let me conclude this chapter by a song which celebrates the chief beauties of the Thames Yacht Club, and which is therefore an appropriate pendant to the scenes I have been describing. It was written for a meeting of the club, and was sung after dinner.

" The goblet now fill while I give you a toast,
  The bulwarks of Britain, our pride and our boast,
  And the meteor flag which, for freedom unfurled,
  Has spread fear and dismay o'er her foes through the world;
  To the *Thames Royal Yacht Club*, our comrades, and crew,
  With heart native oak, like our colours, *true blue*,
  So fill up a bumper—I ask you no more—
  To the Queen, and our Squadron, and brave Commodore.

" We can boast of a squadron, the pride of our isle ;
    We have hearts without envy, and lips free from guile,
    We leave the world's turmoil, we quit life's dull care,
    All we ask is a breeze, be it adverse or fair ;
    And man's stormy passions will cease to prevail
    When our barques swiftly bound with the soul-stirring gale.

" We've a ' Stormfinch,' a ' Kestrel,' trim, gallant, and gay,
    May she long o'er our waves her broad pennant display.
    If you ask us for treasures, we've jewels most rare ;
    We've a ' Turquoise,' a ' Topaz,' and ' Amethyst ' fair,
    And a gem, which both landsmen and sailors agree,
    Is the ' Pearl ' of the ocean, the gem of the sea.

" We have Eve's loveliest daughters, ' Andromeda ' fair,
    ' Thetis,' ' Maid of Bermuda,' ' Zadora,' ' Gulnare,'
    ' Anne,' ' Ada,' ' Elizabeth,' ' Kate,' ' Jane,' ' Victorine,'
    ' Mary,' ' Julia,' ' Sophia,' ' Caroline,' ' Imogine ; '
    But midst all these beauties, 'tis sad to advert
    To a sly ' Little Vixen,' a ' Termagant,' ' Flirt.'

" We've ' Mab,' ' Sylph,' and ' Psyche,' ' Fleta,' ' Fairy,' and ' Fay,'
    ' Zephyr,' ' Sea Nymph,' and ' Mermaid,' ' Triton,' ' Nereid,' and
      ' Spray,'
    A ' Gnome ' and a ' Phantom,' how like shadows they fly,
    An ' Enigma ' who, sphynx-like, all will puzzle who try,
    And a ' Mystery ' great, how she flies to the breeze,
    Like the famed phantom Dutchman, the sprite of the seas !

" We've a grand Northern beauty, ' Czarina ' the fair,
    How she skims o'er the deep like a bird through the air !
    She scorns the dull Thames, seeks the wild Baltic wave,
    Where her ruby cross banner floats proudly and brave ;
    Long, long may she flourish, undaunted and free,
    Our English ' Czarina,' our queen of the sea."

When the *Kestrel*, the *Pearl*, and the *Mystery*
were mentioned, the whole party cheered in compliment of their popular owners, Lords Yarborough,
Anglesey, and Alfred Paget.

CHAPTER XIII.

CHAPTER XIII.

AMONG the light and graceful schooners or cutters that float about Cowes your gaze is sometimes attracted by the heavy hull, short masts, and powerful yards of an American man-of-war. Any eye accustomed to shipping at once detects the difference of naval nationality, and I remember my friend, Captain Claxton, showing his skill in this particular while we were crossing from Southampton to Cowes during the yachting season of 1850.

When off the west buoy of the Bramble, we were delighted at the appearance of a noble ship, under all plain sail, to the westward, which Captain Claxton immediately set down as a double banked frigate, and which soon proved to be the United States' ship *St. Lawrence*, a vessel well known in these waters. Upon nearing her, we saw her shorten sail to topsails, courses, and jib, with the evident intention of anchoring in the Roads. Her manœuvres were strictly and critically scrutinised, not alone by Captain Claxton, as a professional authority, but by myself and other amateur sailors. The voice of the first lieutenant was distinguished from the quarter-deck giving his orders in that quick and decisive manner which at all times ensures ready obedience. "Haul taut!" "Shorten sail!" "Stand by the small bower anchor!" were all respectively heard; and in a few minutes there was a splash, and the transatlantic ship swung majestically into her berth. The men were then seen swarming up the rigging, and in an inconceivably short space of time the flowing white canvas was rolled on the yards, and reduced to the minimum space allotted to it. After this the men descended from their lofty position; yards were squared, ropes hauled taut, and the warlike ship floated tranquilly upon the deep, a model of symmetry and silence. The appearance of this leviathan frigate, with her lofty spars, frowning battery, and high bulwarks, contrasted beautifully with the graceful models of the yachts anchored around her.

Upon the following morning three well-manned boats, with the "stripes and stars," came on shore; and having ascertained from one of the officers that the *St. Lawrence* was to sail for the North Seas at

noon, I lost no time in applying to the American
consul for a letter of introduction to the first
lieutenant. This was cheerfully granted, and
Claxton, another naval officer, the late James
Maxse, and myself were shortly on board the
ship.

The *St. Lawrence* had been built in 1817, but
had only been in commission a few years. When
she was taken out of ordinary not a plank was
defective, and her timbers were found to be as
sound as they were on the day she was first
launched. She mounts fifty-two guns, and is
pierced for sixty-two. She carries on her main-
deck twenty-six 32-pounders of nine feet, and four
68-pounders; quarter-deck, fourteen 32-pounders
medium, and two 68-pounders; forecastle, six 32-
pounders medium. She has four spare ports on
each gangway; two spare ports on the quarter-
deck, and two on the forecastle. Her tonnage
is under 2,000, and her complement, on the peace
establishment, 480 men. She is a fine roomy
ship, clean and clear for action; her fittings are
plain and substantial, all for service, nothing for
show. Her guns are rather closer together than
in the British *rasée* 50-gun frigates or ships of the
Pique and *Inconstant* class. She is very high out
of the water, carrying her main-deck guns remark-

ably well. The captain's cabin is spacious and airy,
furnished with great simplicity. The gun-room is
equally commodious—the more so from having no
after-bulkhead. The officers' cabins are all that
can be desired. The steerage is enclosed as a mess
place for the subordinate officers—a great deside-
ratum, and one well worthy the attention of our
Admiralty. Half the ship's crew are berthed in
the main-deck—there are no mess tables or stools
in the lower deck.

The gunners' store-room and arms are in good
order. A new carbine loading from the breech
attracted our attention, it being admirably adapted
for boat service, as the man charging it need not
expose himself to an enemy's fire by standing up.
A sword, resembling in shape those used by the
ancient Roman legionaries, is a formidable weapon,
being short, double-edged, sharp-pointed, basket-
hilted, and loaded by a tube conveying quicksilver
down the centre, increasing its deadly effect by the
weight of the thrust. The men are a fine, strong,
active looking body, neat in their appearance, and
attentive in their manner. The dress of the marines
is plain and serviceable. The galley fire consumes
nothing but wood, and the absence of coal dust is
an advantage which the smoke-dried Londoner can
easily appreciate. A good look-out was kept on

deck, for every yacht, however small, that dipped her burgee to the frigate, had the compliment returned.

Nothing could exceed the courtesy with which we were received by the captain and the first lieutenant; and it was gratifying to us to learn that every preparation had been made to render due honours to her Majesty, on her passage from Osborne to Gosport. The ship was decorated with flags and colours, and a look-out was kept for the royal standard, which not being hoisted on board the *Victoria and Albert*, indicated her Majesty's wish to avoid public ceremony—probably owing to the death of the ex-King of the French.

Upon taking leave, the captain and officers expressed the pleasure they had derived from our visit, and paid us an unexpected and graceful compliment, by causing the band to play our National Anthem as we descended the ship's side. A curious incident occurred, which I must record. In pulling off to the frigate, I was telling my companions of my former intimacy with Commodore Bainbridge, a name well known and highly respected in the service of his country. After passing a well-merited eulogium upon the private and public character of that distinguished man, with whom I had the good fortune to travel from

Quebec to the Falls of Niagara, I remarked to Claxton—

"I shall start the subject of the Commodore—I hope you will back me up."

"I think," responded he laughing, "that the Baltimore affair and the *Cockchafer* story will be my theme."

"I advise you not to touch upon those subjects," I rejoined, "or one of the gallant officers will have you out on the sands, rifles at fifty paces."

"I'll be cautious," said the captain, "but it would cause a pretty considerable deal of fun."

No sooner had I got on board than I delivered my credentials to Lieutenant Holl, who received me with marked civility. I then introduced my friends, who were as warmly welcomed, and I took an early opportunity of alluding to the late Commodore Bainbridge, and the happy hours I had passed in his society.

"Well, that is strange, very strange," remarked the lieutenant. "I could'nt have believed it. He was a good man."

The lieutenant paused, and I feared I had touched upon some tender ground, when he continued—

"Only to think that you should have named him to me who married his youngest daughter."

"Let me congratulate you," I continued, "she was a charming person."

From that moment all reserve vanished, and we talked over by-gone days. Deeply interesting as the conversation was to me, it was tinged with no little degree of melancholy when I remembered that out of the merry party which lionised the towns of Quebec, Montreal, and Kingston, visited the Falls of Montmorenci, La Chaudière, and the mighty cataracts, and traversed the lakes and rapids (a party consisting of the gallant Commodore, his friend the Postmaster General of New York, three of the fairest of Columbia's daughters, myself, and a brother officer)—only one remained.

I have alluded to Captain Claxton and his story of the Baltimore affair, in which he took a part, and the *Cockchafer* story, and as I feel, perhaps, my readers will have as great a longing to hear the story as I have had to hear the one of "Old Grouse in the gun-room," with which his Worship Hardcastle was wont to keep his servants in a roar, I will lay it before them. Before I do so, however, I must give you a brief account of the Baltimore affair, and how, when, and where the *Cockchafer* incident happened, and I cannot accomplish this better than by giving the captain's own words, or at least the spirit of them.

The hostilities that were being carried on between France and Great Britain had led to a series of misunderstandings between the United States and our country. Napoleon had (as the American minister declared) revoked his anti-neutral decrees, and our Government was called upon to repeal the offensive ordinances—" the system of blockade, and the seizures of supposed British seamen in American ships." Unfortunately, during the embarrassed and disjointed relations of the two countries in 1812, an untoward event occurred, which tended to increase the rancorous animosity that had previously existed, namely, the hostile collision of an American frigate and a British sloop, off the coast of Virginia. The conferences held between our new envoy and Mr. Monroe did not produce a reconciliation, and the message of the President widened the breach. He compared the seizure of the supposed British seamen in American vessels on the " great highway of nations " to that " substitution of force for a resort to the responsible sovereign, which falls within the definition of the war." He affirmed, that, under this pretext, thousands of American citizens had been torn from their country, and subjected to the most severe oppressions. The commerce of the United States had been wantonly harassed, and the most insulting pretensions had been accompanied with lawless proceedings, even within harbours. Not content with this devastation of neutral trade, the British Cabinet had at length resorted to the "sweeping system of blockades" under the name of "orders in council,"—an innovation pregnant with complicated and transcendent injustice.

After a warm debate, in which Randulph and other independent members spoke against any hostile declaration, the discussion terminated with a declaration of war. The 18th of June, a day since famed in the annals of our country, was the one upon which the act of the American legislature was signed by Maddison.

I pass over the invasion of Canada, the surrender of General Hull, the overtures for a reconciliation between the contending powers, the fierce animosity that existed in Congress, and the violent tone adopted by the majority. Suffice it to say that the minds of the people on both sides of the Atlantic were inflamed, and a war unjust in its origin, unnecessary in its object, was carried on with the utmost hatred and rancour. The reckless barbarity of the savage Indians, serving under the British flag, reflected the utmost disgrace upon our arms, and called forth bitter animadversions, not alone from the American Government, but from all the well-thinking people in England.

The war had been carried on with the greatest ferocity, and had degenerated into one of malice and cruelty. Torpedoes, submarine instruments, destructive machines, had been employed against our vessels; such deeds being legalised by an Act of Congress, and vindicated as a set-off to those cruelties practised by our allies.

In vain did the Emperor of Russia assemble a Peace Congress at St. Petersburg, which was attended by three distinguished citizens of the new, and some plenipotentiaries from the old world. The negotiation unhappily failed, and hostilities were resumed. After the conclusion of peace with France, an attempt was made by the advocates of moderation at home to put an end to the conflict. This praiseworthy feeling was, however, frustrated by the zeal of others who wished to avail themselves of the increased force to inflict signal chastisement on the Americans. The Prince Regent, at the prorogation of Parliament, seemed to adopt the views of the latter; he spoke with asperity of the republican government, and alluded to the means now at his disposal to prosecute the war with increased vigour. In consequence of the above declaration, additional troops were to proceed to America, and part of the fleet in which Claxton served was anchored off the Potomac, which it was soon to ascend, as far as practicable, in order to make an attack upon Baltimore. On the night and morning of the 12th and 13th of September, the army (if such it could be called) under Ross, consisting of about three thousand five hundred men, composed of the 4th, 44th, and 85th regiments, and a battalion of seamen and marines from the men of war, commenced its march early, having about twenty or five-and-twenty miles—if my memory serves me—to reach the town it supposed itself destined to attack. Claxton at the head of his men from the *Ramillies* formed a portion of the above forces.

The movement was commenced under most favourable auspices. No effort had been made to prevent a landing. Flushed with the recent success of a march of treble the distance, and its result, which was the capture of Washington, and destruction of its capitol, arsenal, dock-yards, ships on the stocks, a great quantity of naval stores, two hundred and six pieces of cannon, thirty thousand stand of arms, Houses of Assembly and Senate, that portion of the force which had taken part in the above affair looked forward to another entertaining campaign, while those who had only lately joined were equally primed for fun. Confident in the abilities, judgment, and dash of their experienced and brave leader, failure was deemed impossible ; but, alas ! during the first hour of their march, that gallant head was laid low, and a gloom, which reached every individual of the small host, was thrown over the expedition, as Ross was carried, mortally wounded, from the front to the rear by a gang of seamen.

After having led regiments and brigades in the Peninsular war under Wellington, serving in actions of every description, and earning for himself honours and fame that will never perish, their distinguished chief was picked off by a rifle from a bush—not in a fight—not even in a skirmish. No excitement was there, no issuing of orders, no galloping of aides-de-camp, no forming of lines, no rushing to the front, no enemy to fight, but one sneaking shot from the long rifle of some killer of coons, and our only general had fallen.

The Admiral, Sir George Cockburn, was by his side, talking to him at the time, and, it was said, that looking to the quarter from whence the smoke was seen, he caught the eye of another leveller, and probably saved his own life by shaking his fist, calling him names we dare not repeat, and interlarding his remarks with sundry British oaths—

> "Those syllables intense,
> Nucleus of England's native eloquence."

The army advanced as if nothing had happened, under the command of the next in rank, Colonel Brook, and somewhere about noon found itself opposed to the enemy, strongly posted in a wood,

through which passed the high road to Baltimore.
The 4th, under Colonel Faunce, were detached to
take the wood in flank, and (if the attack of the
line, which was speedily formed in front, succeeded)
to intercept the enemy's retreat. This movement
was well intended, but the foe—to use a common
but very significant phrase, "cut and run" almost
as soon as the line reached the enclosure, which was
surrounded with what in England would be called
park palings, rather difficult to get over.

It was a curious sight for soldiers to see about
four hundred seamen, with hats of all forms and
shapes, white cross-belts, long pigtails, which many
of them still delighted in, formed in line and
marching at a quick step to the charge with fixed
bayonets; their line was not well maintained, and
no wonder; but there was no lack of speed, for
their officers were heard to say, "Run forward, my
lads; don't march!"

During all this time the whole were under a
galling fire from the wood. From the British force
only one volley was fired as they neared the palings,
and the moment they began to get over or through
them (for whole rows were pulled down), the enemy,
all except dead, dying, and wounded, rushed through
the wood as closely followed by the pursuers as the
state of their lungs would permit. But the lungs

of the enemy were in better order; they fairly distanced their pursuers, who had the mortification of seeing the 4th only just in time to give one flanking volley, as the rear-guard, if that phrase be appropriate, cleared the wood.

After sending the killed and wounded to the rear, Brook's force advanced, and shortly before sunset came in sight of Chinkapenny Hill, overhanging Baltimore, which appeared strongly fortified; three rows of guns, or entrenchments of some sort, being full of men. Above them was what seemed to be a down, on which, by the aid of glasses, a great many well-dressed females could be discerned, walking in groups with officers in full uniform.

It was evident to those who had long been tasting war in all its shapes and horrors, that this time the Americans were in full force, and were well prepared for as many thousands as our force mustered hundreds; and that before night, many who then looked upon the scene, would probably see the curtain drop on this life's play for ever.

Such, however, was not their destiny. A council of war was held, and about midnight the fires were ordered to be replenished, the forces to form; but instead of advancing, they commenced a well-ordered retreat, after such a night of rain as is only to be met with in the tropics, or on their borders.

About day-break the force halted for an hour, and then proceeded over the same ground. Before evening they embarked from the same spot at which, the morning before, they had landed, not dispirited otherwise than by the loss of their heroic general, nor shorn of their honours—for they had met the enemy vastly superior in numbers, strongly entrenched in a forest; they had attacked and driven him from his cover; and had only ceased from further hostilities against Baltimore when they found how overpowered they were in numbers and guns, and not before a night attack by the bomb-vessels and boats of the squadron on the water, with which we were to act simultaneously by land, had failed, and the failure had been reported.

The British force suffered, comparatively speaking, but little—a score of men or so from each regiment, and from the seamen's brigade, who were in the thickest of the fight. An officer who formed one of the rear-guard to the small army, was not a little surprised about two hours after the retreat, to observe a naval man coming after him on a blood mare, full gallop, without a saddle, and with nothing for a bridle but a canvas cross-belt, strapped on by means of another belt as a head-stall. The officer helped to check the fiery steed as it passed, and was entreated by the rider, who was my friend Claxton, to halt his men, or, in all probability, the whole of the Captain's naval force, about a hundred in number, would be sacrificed. All that the officer could do was to recommend the blue-jacket to push on to Colonel Brook, and state his case, promising him that he would march at the slowest pace possible, as he felt it was impossible for him to halt without orders.

Onwards Claxton went full gallop on the run-away mare. In less than twenty minutes the halt was sounded. Back again came the excited rider, passed through the rear-guard without exchanging a word, and about an hour afterwards joined it with his motley crew, shoes in hand, slip-slopping and rolling along, all but dead beat. Upon inquiry, it appeared that a mistake had been made. The wounded had been carried by this detachment to a creek of the Potomac, about three miles to the right of the line of retreat, while the others were halting. Long before they could have deposited their burthen in the boats sent for them, the main body had recommenced their march, so that they were two good hours behind.

It was supposed and intended that the whole of the above party should embark with the wounded, but as no such orders had been given to Claxton, who was in command, he had marched again to join

the main force. Great was his surprise to find it
gone when he reached the halting ground. It
happened that a wounded officer had been able to
sit upon the aforesaid mare, and as the boats were
not adapted for taking equine passengers on board,
the animal was fortunately brought back, and served
"Jack" a good turn. Many were the jibes and
jeers as the sailors' *reserved* guard passed from the
rear to the front.

"Holloa, Jack!" exclaimed one, "what, been
acting rear-guard?"

"Light infantry, eh?" shouted another. "What,
left behind in the long boat?"

"Hitch your trousers up, you horse marine,
and don't roll to windward," ejaculated a third.

"Steady, steady!" said a fourth; "why, what
have you done with your shoes?"

Claxton enjoyed the joke very much, it being his
first appearance as a "mounted officer;" his blue
jackets, too, were loudly cheered as they passed to
the front, and had the honour of being the first to
embark. Great was the marvel that the Yankees
did not cut off this handful of men belonging to the
Ramillies, who, for two hours at least, were six miles
in rear of the force. To show the pluck of "Jack,"
it must be added that the small party had constantly
formed square to receive cavalry; for one of our

artillery-men, whose horse had run away with him, suddenly hove in sight, and the blue jackets naturally took him for one of a troop of the enemy's cavalry on the look out.

After the affair at Baltimore, when a considerable number of prisoners were taken and brought on board, Sir George Cockburn was greatly annoyed by the Americans calling him Cockburn, instead of Coburn, as the name is usually pronounced, and, having pointed out the proper articulate sound, he was at a loss to understand why they would not adopt it. The fact is, many did it in ignorance, some found it annoyed him, and some were set on by the midshipmen, but all were savage with the admiral for the marauding expeditions carried on by the men-of-war against little vessels. One morning a whole bevy of Yankees were on board, who, as usual, began with the forbidden appellation, Cockburn, "Make a signal," said the Admiral, in a stentorian voice, to the signal midshipman, "for the officer of the *Co-chafer* [the *Cockchafer* was a small man-of-war schooner] to come on board." Doing this, Cockburn looked daggers at the Yankees, who stood in front of a row of young "reefers," trying hard to suppress their laughter. "*Co-chafer*, sir," replied the first lieutenant, in even a louder tone, for he had at once caught Sir George's motives.

"Let me know when the officer of the *Co-chafer* comes on board." During this conversation the majority of the Americans looked aghast, especially when the proper pronunciation had been corroborated by another officer, and one of the Yankees, on taking leave, said, "Good morning, Admiral Co-burn." He then proceeded, muttering to himself, but loud enough to be heard by all, "Co-sure, Co of the walk, Co-boat, Co-pit; well, they all sound tarnation strange to my ears, and, for my part, I reckon Cock-sure, Cock of the walk, Cock-boat, and Cock-pit are more ship shape."

The coast of America, during that war, was blockaded in a way that the invention of steam and iron-plates will assuredly prevent, if another war should take place in our days. The men-of-war were quartered in the American waters. Broke, in the *Shannon*, guarded Boston; Hardy, in the *Ramillies*, New London and the Long Island Sound; Oliver, in the *Valiant*, blockaded Sandy Hook; Beresford, in the *Poictiers*, did the same at Philadelphia in the Delaware. Others in frigates had charge of different ports to the southward. The *Ramillies* in particular, inside Long Island, blockading Decatur and the *United States* and *Macedonian* frigates, took numberless vessels with its boats. Serious questions then arose as to what was to be done with the

prizes, as they were too many and too small to send
to Halifax; and, consequently, a system was followed
which was not strictly *en règle.* Whenever any ships
were taken, the captains were told to come off with
so many dollars and have their vessels back again.
It constantly happened that they did not succeed in
raising the money, but when they did they were not
shy of saying what tarnation fools the Britishers
were for letting them have vessels for three or four
thousand dollars which were worth eight or ten
thousand.   Occasionally, when the captains did not
come themselves, others from Long Island came off
to purchase, and take away the cargoes.   There
were several vessels in the pay of our ships, who,
as will presently be shown, brought us whatever
we wanted, in the shape of fresh provisions or articles of dress—from fresh beef down to a pickled
herring, or a full-dress coat to a shoe-tie.   Every
sort of "dodge" was practised to take in the un-
wary.   I must here premise that, at New York,
men were appointed to examine the quality of the
flour, and mark each barrel according to its relative
value.   Claxton took a vessel with eight hundred
barrels on board; the crew had run it aground, and
saved themselves by escaping in their boats.   The
barrels were all branded with the lowest mark, and
Claxton was about to order the vessel to be set on

fire, when up jumped a burly man, exclaiming—
"Don't burn her, she'll come off easy, she's not
hard a-ground;" and, true enough, she was hove off
and brought alongside the *Ramillies*. As the owners
refused to ransom her, a merchant from Long Island
bought the cargo, and brought another vessel to
take it in. Claxton ordered the transhipment, and
observed that the 'cute purchaser had caused the
low mark to be planed out, and the highest inserted,
thus raising his profit more than fifty per cent.

"I guess," said the Yankee, "I worn't born
yesterday; I can see as far into a mill-stone as the
man that made the hole in it."

One incident of this not very legitimate trading
caused much amusement to the gallant Hardy and
the officers of the *Ramillies*. One night, about
eleven o'clock, Sir Thomas, who was walking with
Lieutenant Claxton on the quarter-deck, heard a
hail, and was told that it was from an American
vessel that had been sent in search of news. A
boat came alongside, and a man walked up the side
of the ship. Both the captain and his lieutenant
were anxious to hear the report, and were all
attention, when the "stranger" exclaimed in a loud
voice, addressing the monarch of the quarter-deck,
"I say, captain, it was a tarnation shame selling
me that cargo of pork—it's from North Carolina,

and not worth a quid of backy." The captain's
dignity was at an end. He rushed into his cabin
and exploded with laughter, while Claxton was left
to appease the infuriated pork-dealer.

Certain privileges were accorded to the dealers
with the English men-of-war, either as buyers or
sellers, and one of them was humoured so far as to
have a sham fight got up in his honour. I will
leave Claxton to tell the story in his own words:—
"We lay at anchor about 1,800 yards from the
Yankee battery at the entrance of New London
river. They tried their shots, and we tried ours,
at an angle of 45 degrees. Ours did not reach the
shore, and theirs did not reach us. In the present
day, we must have kept off double the distance.
We had some American coasters in our employ. It
answered their purpose to be allowed to pass unmolested at night, when coming from Rhode Island,
Newport, to New York, inside the island, and up
the Sound. We were anchored about half way in
their track, and about a nautical mile from the
coast. They were obliged to call at the ship at
night when going east—*id est*, from New York to
Newport—and then they brought the ship all sorts
of supplies, and were off a couple of hours before
day dawn. Going west, or back again, they were
allowed to go by unmolested if, by chance, they
were in sight after dark. They had a system of

marked mast-head vanes, and we knew when and where not to send the British barges (a favourite name in the Yankee papers)—or, in other words, barge, whale-boat, pinnace, yawl, and two cutters— in chase. One night, in my watch, an American captain—I forget his name—said to me, after taking a glass of grog in the wardroom, and after his cargo was discharged, 'Captain' (they called all us lieutenants captains), 'I want you to help me in a go.' 'Well, what sort of a go?' 'Well, captain, the fact is, I am suspected at New York. You take so many coasters, and I keep making so many voyages: and you know, when first we began, I cleared out with live bullocks for St. Eustace— well, they stopped that; then I brought you whole quarters of beef, and whole dead sheep—and, mind, it was winter time—and they have stopped that; and now, what have I been obliged to do, but bring the beef in eight-pound pieces in barrels as flour? Now, if the wind suits, I'll come by next time at midday, and when you see I have got New London open, if you will send the barges in chase, I'll fire a small pair of swivels I have on board, and you fire your boat-guns at me—but only powder, mind, on both sides. Decatur will come out with all the boats of the *United States* and *Macedonian* frigates, take up the fight, and tow me in if the wind falls light. You must get Captain Hardy to agree.'

Well, on a day in February, he did come from the
eastward, beating New York way against a fine
westerly breeze.   I was called by the quarter-
master, who, with the signalman on the look out,
made out his vane, and went to Sir Thomas Hardy.
' Please, Sir Thomas, here's Captain —— coming.
May I man the boats to chase him?'   ' Yes ; take
the pinnace, the whale-boat, and the two cutters—
but don't bother me any more about it, and don't
keep the men away long.'   Away we went, and
very soon Captain —— began firing his swivels,
after bearing up for New London, and very soon
out came ten boats from the *United States* and
Macedonian, and I saw Decatur himself in one of
them.   Powder-firing came to shot-firing, Captain
—— was towed in with cheers, and the British
barges went back to the ship, no one on either side
the worse, and so ended the affair.   About three
weeks after came the smack *Rapid*, Captain ——,
with his next cargo from New York.   We had the
run of Fishey Island, on which was a fine lake ; and
directly he saw me, he handed me an American
newspaper, saying, ' That, I guess, was a proper
well done go.   They carried me in triumph round
the town, gave me the freedom of the City of New
London, and five hundred dollars, for doing what
was headed—Gallant Defeat of British Barges !' "

CHAPTER XIV.

CHAPTER XIV.

It has been the fashion in England to say that the late Duke of Orleans was hostile to this country; but, as far as my personal experience goes, such was not the case. In the year 1832 I went to Boulogne for a few weeks, owing to the death of my sister. During my *séjour* there, the Duke of Orleans arrived, with one of his brothers, and held a reception, which was attended by many Englishmen. As I was in deep mourning, I did not present myself, but wrote down my name in their Royal Highnesses' book. I took care that my visit should not seem made with a view to my being asked to a large dinner the duke was to give that evening; but within an hour of my having written my name, an aide-de-camp came to the *Hôtel des Bains*, where I was staying, with an invitation, which I considered a command, to dinner. I accordingly went, and was most cordially received by both the princes. When dinner was announced the Duke of Orleans requested the Préfet of the department to lead the way, and intimated that I was to follow, and to occupy one of the posts of honour by the side of the illustrious host. No one could be more affable than the unfortunate son of Louis Philippe: he talked of England, of English sports, racing and shooting, and hinted at his readiness to send a horse to Goodwood races when possessed of a racing stud —an event which both he and I lived to witness.

The success of his horse Beggarman, which won the Goodwood cup in 1840, is still in the remembrance of many a turfite; and had his Royal Highness lived, and the dynasty of Louis Philippe continued, there is every reason to believe that the English race-course would have been patronised by the heir to the French throne. The Duke of Orleans was a most liberal and zealous supporter of the turf and field sports, forming a pleasant contrast to his ancestor Egalité, who figured for a few years at Newmarket and Ascot towards the end of the last century. This prince's rapid fall from the height of earthly grandeur to the lowest abyss of earthly misery, imprisonment, and an ignominious death, might act as a warning to others, but I shall content myself with laying his exploits upon the turf before my readers. In 1789, his Royal Highness made his *début* as a sportsman in England, and in the following year sought the fountain head, Newmarket, where he was generally successful. At the Craven meeting, the duke's Boxer was beaten by Mr. Vernon's Scrub, 30 gs. In April his Lambenos yielded the victory to Mr. Fox's Shovel and Lord Clermont's Tallyho. At the same meeting his Royal Highness was again unfortunate, his horse Hocks having been beaten by Lord Barrymore's Fop and by Lord Falkland's Sir Charles. In the first spring meeting, the duke's Fortitude beat Lord Derby's Director, 100 gs., but his luck did not last, for upon the same day his horse Jericho was defeated in a stake of 200 gs., and had, in addition, to pay 100 gs. forfeit to the Duke of Bedford's Skyscraper. Two days afterwards, at the second spring meeting, Lambenos paid 100 gs. forfeit to Lord Grosvenor's Asparagus, and, within eight-and-forty hours, beat a field of ten for fifty guineas. In the first spring meeting, the duke's Fortitude could not stand up against the Prince of Wales's Serpent, or General Wyndham's Osprey, and, in these two events, his Royal Highness was compelled to resign himself to the loss of 200 gs. Jericho, too, was beaten by the Duke of Bedford's Dragon for 200 gs.

A ray of sunshine now appeared to the royal sportsman, for in the first spring meeting Conqueror beat the Duke of Queensbury's Dash, six miles, 300 gs. Where was the Society for the Prevention of Cruelty to Animals in those days?

In the second spring meeting, the clouds again lowered over the House of Orleans. Conqueror was beaten by Butler for the Jockey Club plate, and again at Epsom by Tickler. Jericho was beaten by Sir Charles Bunbury's Smack, for 200 gs., and the duke's Colonel by Wyndham's Pecker for 100 gs. The last of the duke's horses, whose prowess has to be recorded, was a two-year old, named Good Morning, by Trentham, a name which we presume was significant of the duke's farewell to the turf. This flyer happened to win a trial stakes of 50 gs., beating six others, with the odds of six to one against him, and was immediately named for the Oatlands, forty subscribers, 100 gs. each. But as it was beaten in a match over the old course by Mr. Bullock's Contractor, his Royal Highness withdrew it, and paid forfeit.

The death of Egalité's grandson, the late Duke of Orleans, was a sad blow to the French and English turf. Had he been spared, I have little doubt he would have annually presented a cup to be run for at Goodwood, the scene of his racing triumph. As it is, the Orleans Vase, won by my brother the late Duke of Richmond's Mus in 1841, leaves a lasting memorial of the prince's liberality and love of the turf. Sports and sporting literature have greatly increased in France within the last twenty years;

and a talented author, whose name I cannot at this moment remember, has written well upon the subject. The name *Le Sport* includes all manly exercises, hunting, sporting, racing, steeple chasing, coursing, coaching, bull baiting, cock and dog fighting. Every country has its national amusement. Spain boasts of its bull fights—sanguinary remnant of Moorish barbarism, or, as Byron writes,—

> " Such the ungentle sport that oft invites
>   The Spanish maid, and cheers the Spanish swain ;
> Nurtured in blood betimes, his heart delights
>   In vengeance, gloating on another's pain."

Rome and Florence have their races without riders. The land of the Czar has its sports on the ice, and racing, too, though not upon such courses as we are accustomed to. Instead of the " Ditch In," and " two middle miles," we read of turnpike roads twenty and fifty miles in length ; and it is upon record, that some years ago, with a view of proving the superiority of English thorough-bred horses over any others, Count Matuchewitz started Sharper and Mina against an Arabian and Cossack, for a race of forty-eight English miles on a turnpike road, which was won easily by Sharper. During the winter of 1839, another race was made, to be run at Libidian, a town about 120 miles to the south-east of Moscow, where a good race meeting, and an im-

mense horse fair take place annually.   The event is
thus recorded :—

Mr. Koratchugan's ch. c., by Red Rover out of Proserpine,
    four years old   1
Mr. Petrossky's br. m. by Regent out of Fair Ellen, five years
    old   2
Mr. Workoff's br. h. Concert, by Memnon out of Cassandra,
    five years old   3
Prince Tumen's ch. m., by a Persian stallion out of a Calmuck
    mare   0
Mr. Talhoft's br. m. Mouse, of pure Calmuck breed   0
        (The last two stood still at the eighteenth mile.)
Mr. Varle's br. m. Hope, by an Arabian out of a Cossack mare   0
        (Stood still at the sixteenth mile.)

A pretty race between the three English thoroughbred horses for
some distance, but won easy at last. Run in 58 minutes, 54
seconds. The sire of the winner was bred by General Grosvenor,
by Nicol, a Selim horse, out of a Beningborough mare.

Talking of Russia, leads me to give a slight sketch
of a celebrated character who arrived in England
about eighteen years ago. I speak of a young Tartar,
who had been taken by the Russians, some four
years previous, in a skirmish with the Circassians,
and had been offered the alternative of entering the
Russian service, or being exiled to Siberia.   He
chose the former, and was soon promoted to the
command of a small troop of cavalry. One day,
upon parade, his superior officer gave way to the
violence of his temper, and accused the Tartar of
neglect and disobedience of orders. This the young
warrior bore with patience ; but when, in the heat
of his passion, the Russian officer gave him the lie,

and struck him, his blood was up, and, with his
sabre, he cut the tyrant down. Feeling that his
only chance was in flight, the gallant youth stuck
his spurs into the sides of his steed, and was followed
by six soldiers anxious to avenge their commander's
fall. Although they could not literally "catch a
Tartar," they did so figuratively, for four of the pursuers fell under his unerring aim. The others gave
up the chase, but not before they were severely
wounded. After many "hairbreadth 'scapes," and
"moving accidents by flood and field," the young
Tartar and his faithful steed reached England in
safety, and, in the month of August, 1844, they
were safely in the Regent's Park barracks, where
they found the very best "entertainment for man
and horse." Anxious to put the Tartar's sabre
practice to the test, two non-commissioned officers of
the 1st Life Guards turned out with single sticks, to
give him a taste of their quality; and certainly a
more wonderful performance was never witnessed.
With a single stroke of the sabre he cut one of the
foemen's sticks in twenty pieces; and, although
he got rather severely handled over the arms and
shoulders, he succeeded in slicing the other stick
completely down to the guard; then, being pursued,
he threw his lance (covered over and buttoned as a
foil) a length of twenty yards with such precision

and strength, as almost to take the breath out of the gallant Life Guardsman's body. He then went through sundry evolutions, which would not have disgraced Ducrow's circus in its palmiest days— firing pistols at marks with unerring aim at full gallop; throwing himself on and off; picking up his spear at a gallop; throwing his whole body off his horse, and clinging only by his leg so as to present no mark to his enemies; firing pistols between his horse's fore and hind legs, and in his horse's mouth. In short, he gave the spectators the most varied representation of the predatory warfare of his native country. His trusty steed deserves a few words. It was a grey Arabian, about fourteen hands three inches, active, and full of courage. Upon being asked whether he could part with him, the young Tartar clung to his neck, and, patting him with the greatest kindness, exclaimed in excellent German, "No! he is my life, my eyes, my arm, my body, my all. Never, to the last day of my existence, will I dispose of the partner of my cares, to whom I am indebted for my life!"

After the tournament, the warrior was presented with a purse of fifty sovereigns, which the officers of the 1st Life Guards and their friends had collected for him. Shortly afterwards he left England for Constantinople.

"In Germany," says the author of the foreign

sporting work from which I have quoted, "*battues*
are carried on by the higher classes, when the game,
being driven into a small circle, is butchered by the
gunners." To this I can bear witness; for I have
attended a royal *battue* at Vienna, in which every
species of game, from a hare to a red deer, fell a
victim to the guns or *feet* of the exalted personages;
for, literally speaking, nearly as much game was
trampled upon, or knocked on the head, as shot.
An English farmyard, full of hogs and poultry, with
the contents of a hutch full of white rabbits turned
loose in it, would furnish an equally good *battue*.
"In Holland," continues the writer, "the sport consists of shooting wild geese and ducks in winter,
sledging, skating, bowls, billiards, chess, and tennis;
in the East, the jereed exercise in tiger hunting; in
Africa, lion hunting." Our French author writes
most elaborately upon the national sports of England, and proceeds to classify them according to
Bell's Life. His remarks and ideas are occasionally
quaint, sensible, and just; at other times absurd to
a degree. "The place of honour," he writes,
"belongs to the race-horses, and between them is a
line of demarcation. The horses that are to run
for the Derby, at Epsom, are first named, and after
them follow the champions for the Doncaster St.
Leger." Passing over some remarks upon the

Bourse du Sport (Tattersall's), we come to his graphic account of Epsom. "The Derby is a national *fête* in England. The Derby! Where is the Englishman who will not sacrifice his dearest interests to it, his very duties, nay, the presence of his love? The Derby! A wizard potent enough to wrest for a whole day an Englishman from his lethargic gravity. Thousands of vehicles cover the plain, filled with elegant and lovely women; the Queen, with her dazzling toilet and beauty; the highest nobles of England, treating the trainers and jockeys as their equals; the hawkers, the suttling booths, the gambling booths, the betters; every vehicle converted into a dining-room. Oh, the wonderful sight! wonderful even to eyes not English! The signal for starting is given; the horses rush forward; a solemn silence prevails. The horses fly: they would not be so light if they carried all the gold staked on their speed! They approach the goal; the struggle is desperate. Silence has ceased. Some by voice and gesture excite the horse upon which they have staked their fortune. The cries raised by others, though more disinterested, are not less vehement. Twenty horses have started; only two or three return. What a dearly bought victory! But the conqueror has won £30,000 or £40,000. The race being

over, vehicle races begin on the road; there is an
awful confusion; they are driven against one
another, break down, or overturn. The roads are
strewed with shattered poles and wheels; nothing
stops the drunken drivers. One would fancy it a
breaking up of the ice on the Neva, an avalanche
of Mont Blanc, a tempest on the ocean. After
racing comes steeple-chasing and coursing, and
next stag, hare, and fox hunting, with their
fatigues and perils." Hold hard, brother sportsman! Who ever heard in England of fox-hunting
coming after coursing, "calf-hunting," or "currant
jelly" hounds? Here, in accounting for fox-
hunting occupying the fourth rank, the writer has
evidently "found" what is termed "a mare's nest,"
for he says "that he has discovered the reason of
this unjust classification, which is, that in the chase
there is no betting, and that Englishmen reduce
everything to bets." Then come pigeon-shooting
and dog-fighting. Of the latter the writer says,
"It has already begun to degenerate, and we shall
see it presently fall lower still." We sincerely
trust that his prediction may be realised. By way
of episode, he indulges in a few lively "skits" on
our mania for extraordinary feats and betting.
Thus he says, "A Woolwich lieutenant offers to
play a game of tennis against 'All England' for

£50," and adds, "A singular accomplishment for
an artillery officer." "One individual announces
that for £5 he will throw himself from the top of
Waterloo Bridge; while another engages not to
touch any food for ten days." He might have
added, " or to make himself a brute by eating sundry
loaves, sundry pounds of pork chops, sundry dozens
of oysters, and drinking sundry gallons of beer."
After horses, greyhounds, stags, hares, foxes,
pigeons, bull-dogs, bipeds, and gluttons, boxing is
discussed; and here we give our continental friend's
views upon that subject:—" In these combats,
everything is opprobrious and repulsive; ay, everything, from the toothless mouth and the savage
looks of those degraded beings, to the preparations
and precautions destined to prolong the combat.
Each second brings his champion a pail of water
and a sponge, and a bottle of brandy or wine.
The heroes are stripped to their waists, and at
first *totter as much from fear as drunkenness !*"
Fear and drunkenness! Shades of Gregson,
Mendoza, Pearce, Jackson, Cribb, Spring, and
Langan arise, and annihilate the French author
with a look. Surely Shaw, the Life-Guardsman,
whose prowess on the battle-field is well known,
was neither a coward nor a drunkard. Censure the
sport, but libel not its professors. To proceed.

"The murmurs of the spectators soon warn the combatants that they have not come to witness childish play. Vanity prevails over fear, and the combat becomes serious. At every tooth that drops, at every rib that breaks, at every eye that falls out, there are voices that shout 'Bravo!' and hands that applaud. The struggle has already lasted an hour; the boxers are exhausted; they can scarcely stand; their faces are bruised and covered with blood; their bodies present but a huge sore. But they have not fought more than fifty rounds, and a good fight [so we translate *beau combat*] must be renewed at least sixty or seventy. Their seconds apply the sponge to the flowing blood, wash their eyes, noses, and ears, pour wine or brandy down their throats, and the blows resound again, until one of them, exhausted, panting, almost dead, falls down, never to rise again. And yet the crowd is often dissatisfied, and often cries out that there has been cowardice or treachery. Instead of one corpse it would have two. This is the dark side of sport in England; for it is not only the lower classes that are addicted to these loathsome spectacles, the most distinguished men blush not to witness them, and to speculate upon the fists of a boxer with as much *sang froid* as they would upon the legs of a racer."

The above is rather an exaggerated description,
and yet, unhappily, there is too much truth in it.
Prize-fighting has of late years been open to
roguery and rascality; still the good old English
system of settling a difference with the fists is pre-
ferable to the knife. In one instance they fight
and shake hands; in the other, the survivor, if he
escapes the hand of justice, wanders about like a
second Cain, loathed and despised by his fellow-
creatures. In the following remarks we entirely
concur with our French author :—

"In this department of sport (boxing) we shall
never be on a level with the English, and we can
but congratulate ourselves upon it. Let us learn
from them to breed and train our horses; let us
borrow their racing regulations; let us turn to
account their experience and knowledge; let us
even be English in the denominations of our races;
but when their manners stray into cruelty, let us
stick to our own country. Let us leave them in
possession of their bull-dog fights, but let the taste
for hunting be encouraged amongst us, and that
taste will yield us horses and riders. We are still
far from having their numerous hunting equipages,
but already our riders are numerous and bold.
The Prince de Wagram, M. Henri Greffulle, the
Duc d'Aremberg, the Marquis de Vogne, and the

Prince de Challais are inferior to none in science
and spirit. The bright deeds of the Marquis de
Macmahon, the boldest rider in France, have,
perhaps, no rival even in England. As for racing,
Chantilly is our Epsom, and our Derby the prize
given by the Jockey Club, which amounts to
25,000 francs, and can often boast of a field of
more than six-and-twenty horses. The *Société
d'encouragement* bestows its largess and awards
its prizes in the months of May and June, at the
Champ de Mars, Versailles, &c., &c.; whilst in
September the government patronises racing, by
giving plates to be run for."

Since the above was written, a large list of
gentlemen riders might be added, both in racing
and steeple-chasing, many of whom would rank
foremost in any country. Before taking leave of
this work, I must refer to that portion which calls
upon the provincial owners of race-horses " to come
to Paris, and engage in a contest which may some
day be rewarded with triumphant success." This
suggestion has been carried out; the French authorities have established a grand race open to all
nations, and we thank them for it. I am delighted
to find that our continental neighbours have entered
the arena with us at Epsom, Ascot, Goodwood,
Newmarket, and Doncaster; and I beg to endorse

the sentiment of the talented writer, that "exaggerated modesty, or consciousness of inferiority, stifles the very principle of emulation, without which everything declines and goes to ruin."

As an instance of this emulation in a branch which is not generally cultivated on the turf, let me mention a classical discussion which took place, during the first October meeting at Newmarket in 1841 between Lord Palmerston (not in *propriâ personâ*) and the Earl of Winchilsea, then Lord Maidstone, as to the proper pronunciation of the name Iliona. The question was, whether the letter *i* in Il*i*ona was long or short; and the animal, which was Lord Palmerston's property, was at that time second favourite for the Cesarewitch Stakes, which she won by a length. The subject was warmly taken up by the London newspapers, who discussed it day after day. Among the best *Jeux d'Esprit* was the following, entitled, "Puzzler for the Greeks, or the Turfites at fault":—

> "*Air and chorus, 'Bow, wow, wow.'*
>
> "Attend, ye tulips of the turf, renowned upon the field, sir,
> For *jockeyship* to *scholarship* at Tattersall's must yield, sir;
> No longer on a favourite nag embark in speculation,
> But bet your money freely on a *right* pronunciation.
> Bow, wow, wow;
> What a march of intellect! bow, wow, wow.
>
> "Now the schoolmaster is abroad, of proselytes in search, sir,
> And 'mid the knowing racing ranks is flourishing his birch, sir;

And Tattersall may shortly cut his horses and his hammer,
While whips, and boots, and spurs give way to arguments in
    grammar.
               Bow, wow, wow;
        Honour to Lord Palmerston; bow, wow, wow.

" 'Tis said when doctors disagree, with bluster and with bounce,
    sir,
Which doctor's right, and which is wrong, no mortal can
    pronounce, sir;
And long and vainly may we search for Cantab or Oxonian
Rightly to judge 'twixt Maidstonite and learned Palmerstonian.
               Bow, wow, wow;
        Race between the long and short; bow, wow, wow.

" ' By Jove,' cried Bentinck, ' in a trice authority I'll bring, sir,
And in opinion I'm confirmed by sporting brother Byng, sir,
That in no university there ever yet was known a
Grecian to designate the mare as aught but Ilïŏna.'
               Bow, wow, wow;
        ' Clear as mud,' cried bold John Day; bow, wow, wow.

" ' Not quite so fast,' cries Maidstone's lord, well skilled in classic
    lore, sir,
' Ilïŏna she should be call'd, I'll bet you six to four, sir;
And tho' among the fielders here you come it very strong, sir,
I cheerfully will back the *short* if you will back the *long*, sir.
               Bow, wow, wow;
        Certain I shall distance you; bow, wow, wow.'

" ' Had we pronounced it long at school,' cries Gregory and
    Crommelin,
' Upon our shoulders, with a cane, we should have had a
    pommelling;
And now of study in our youth the happy fruit we reap, sir,
And still while conning o'er our *books* we never are asleep, sir.
               Bow, wow, wow;
        Judges good, and no mistake; bow, wow, wow.'

" The *Racing Calendar* lay by, and sport your precious metal,
Let a Greek lexicon be brought the knotty point to settle;
Or send to Viscount Palmerston, and say, we have occasion
Of his mare's name to learn from him the right pronunciation.
               Bow, wow, wow;
        Sure his lordship ought to know; bow, wow, wow.

" ' Then be it so,' cried Mr. Byng, 'and I will bet a quart, sir,
   His lordship says the name is *long* whoe'er may sound it *short*,
     sir ;
   So freely sport your cash, my friends ; I reckon, without banter,
   That *long* throughout will keep the lead and win it in a canter.'
            Bow, wow, wow ;
       Some may then be short of tin ; bow, wow, wow.

" Thus did Lord Palmerston decide, with wonted animation—
   ' The point at issue, you're aware, requires consideration ;
   But as its vast importance to the sporting world I feel, sir,
   I won't observe the strict reserve maintained by Robert Peel, sir.
            Bow, wow, wow ;
       Would we were in place again ; bow, wow, wow.

" ' In my mare's name the ' o ' is *short*, in truth I do not jest, sir,
   In the first Æneid Virgil has the question set at rest, sir ;
   " *Preterea sceptrum, Iħŏne quod gesserat ;* "
   Now, how he would have called my mare each jock can be a
     guesser at.
            Bow, wow, wow ;
       Frank and candid you'll admit ; bow, wow, wow.

" ' And as about the animal so fairly I have dealt, sir,
   I dub her *Hilli-ona*, just as if that way 'twas spelt, sir ;
   And as of sport upon the turf I always was a lover,
   A *mare's* nest in this note of mine perhaps you may discover.'
            Bow, wow, wow ;
       Who'll dispute my scholarship ; bow, wow, wow."

Much has been said and written of late about
the present degraded state of the Turf, but it is
highly illiberal to pass a sweeping denunciation
on the many for the faults of a few. At all times
and in all ages many black (*legged*) sheep have
been found among the racing and betting fraternity.
I well remember acting as one of the stewards at
the Chatham and Rochester races some five-and-
thirty years ago, when a gross piece of rascality

was attempted, which happily I was the means of
frustrating. A friend of mine, a gallant baronet,
who had served in the Guards, had a horse to run
at the above races. Before the start, the trainer,
who went by the name of Lying and Dirty Dick
(the latter as applicable to his person as the first
was to his character), came to me and said he had
received his master's orders to sell the animal;
that he had done his best, but could not find a
customer, and that he should therefore run the
horse in Sir George's colours. By what the modern
fast young men call a "fluke," the animal won the
first heat, greatly to the surprise of every one; and
as the comic Latin grammar says,—

" *Partim astutorum mordebantur,*"
" Part of the knowing ones were bit."

While the jockeys were weighing, "Dick" approached me, and said, "I did all I could, my
Lord, to get to you before the race, but the con-
stables would not let me cross the course. A
gentleman bought the little 'orse just after the bell
rang." "Really," I responded; "pray, what is
the gentleman's name?" "He gave me his card,
it's in my upper coat pocket. He is to pay the
money and have the 'orse delivered up after the
race." Knowing how anxious Sir George was to
get rid of his horse, thinking it possible he might

not pull through another heat, and being convinced
that if I interfered some foul trick would be played,
and that probably the horse would not be allowed
to win, I merely said that his declaration to me as
one of the stewards was a sufficient guarantee to
hand over the plate to the new purchaser should
the race come off in his favour. In the second
heat Sir George's jockey did his best, but was
beaten, and the odds in due course of time were two
to one against him. Congratulating myself that
my friend had got rid of an unsatisfactory horse,
I was about to sit down to write a letter to Sir
George, when " Dirty Dick," with a rueful countenance, informed me that "he had looked everywhere for the gentleman, but could not find him,
and that he began to think he had been 'oaxed
by some unprincipled 'feller.' " " If he has given
no reference," I replied, " and is not to be found,
I shall appeal to my brother stewards as to whether
the bargain should hold good." " There's no
necessity for that," responded the trainer, " as
he h'ant here, I should have said it were h'off."
"Then we understand one another," I responded,
"the horse runs as Sir George's." "Exactly so,"
replied Dick ; and I mentioned the occurrence to
the stewards. The deciding heat came off, five to
two on the winner of the second, and my friend's

horse was looked upon as a dead one; when, to the surprise of all, he won!

Again Dick appeared on the course with a very strange companion, who, rushing forward, led the winner back opposite the Stand. The jockey entered the enclosure, followed by the pair above mentioned; and the stranger, pulling out some notes, handed them over to the trainer. "I looked for you everywhere," said the former; "I was obliged to go to Day's bank to get my cheque cashed." "It's werry unlucky," interrupted Dick, "I wore bound in conscience to tell one of the stewards that I could not find you. I don't know what's to be done. Unquestionably you did say the 'orse was yours; what is to be done?"

During this conversation, which was evidently meant to be heard by me, a gentleman connected with the bank entered the stand, and at once declared that no strange cheque had been presented, much less cashed, within the last two hours.

"The bargain was declared off," I said, addressing the trainer, "and Sir George wins the fifty pound plate."

"I'll not give up the horse," muttered the stranger.

"Settle that among yourselves as best you can," I remarked, "the money for the plate will be sent to the real owner, and if you complete a sale now it will be exclusive of that sum."

Loud words followed, mingled with threats of legal proceedings, but all ended in smoke, and ere the day closed I ascertained that the purchaser was a London horse chaunter, a confederate of Dirty Dick's.

I now come to a most striking event, the celebrated steeple-chase for £1,000, play or pay, between Mr. Osbaldeston's br. g. Clasher and Captain Ross's Clinker. It took place on the 1st of December, 1829, in the neighbourhood of Melton Mowbray, and I was one of the spectators. The weights were 12 stone each; Clasher to be ridden by his sporting owner, and Clinker by Dick Christian. In order to prevent any private trial, the starting and coming in posts were only declared a few hours before the appointed time for starting. The excitement created by this match baffles all description. It was looked upon as a struggle between two first-rate hunting counties—Leicestershire and North-amptonshire—of which the two horses were the respective champions. Clasher was well-known in the Pytchley Hunt, and had come out of the crowd by winning the Welter Stakes at the previous hunt meeting. Clinker, formerly the property of the present Sir Francis Goodricke, was purchased by

Captain Ross for 500 guineas, to run the great
steeple-chase against the late Lord Kennedy for
2,000 guineas, in which he proved successful. His
prowess upon that, as on many other occasions in
Leicestershire, and almost every sporting county in
England, had gained him a great name, and the
Melton men were very "sweet" upon him. At
the hour fixed for the start the principal parties,
accompanied by their friends, and troops of sporting
acquaintances, went away at a killing pace, without
any unnecessary delay. They kept abreast from
the starting post over Burrow Lordship, Twyfleet,
Marfleet Lordship, taking their leaps, many of
which were awful raspers, with the greatest coolness and judgment; and up to the last fence which
separated them from the winning field, it was as
even a race as possible. Here, unfortunately, the
Captain's horse fell, and of course put Dick Christian
hors de combat, while Clasher, taking the leap as
fresh as a four-year old, landed the Squire safely in
the Tilton field. Neither Clinker nor his gallant
rider were hurt by the fall, and so ended one of the
finest races of the sort that ever took place in this
paragon of a hunting country. The distance run
was five miles, which was done in sixteen minutes.

The Captain, resolved not to give in, made
another match with his successful antagonist,

which came off in Northamptonshire on the 5th of
December.   The terms were, Mr. Osbaldeston's
Pilot, 12 st., against Captain Ross's Polecat, 13 st.
7 lbs., owners on, four miles ; the Squire taking
500 sovereigns to 200 sovereigns.   The two horses
had met the previous year in Leicestershire, in a
steeple-chase, even weights, and Pilot had won in a
common canter.   This time half-past ten was named
as the hour for starting, and, punctual to the minute,
a large party of sportsmen were assembled near the
covert.   When the signal was given, away went
the flying coursers at a slapping pace across Harrington Field, by Louthland Wood, to the Army-
tage, on the borders of Leicestershire.   Pilot took
the lead and kept it, and it was soon apparent to
the Melton men that the Captain would be done to
a tinder.   Such was, indeed, the case.   At the
brook near Harrington, Polecat went through instead of over, and from this point the race, which
lasted fourteen minutes, was finally decided.   Nothing could exceed the Squire's riding, which was
steady throughout, never throwing away a chance
by getting elated at his easy victory.   No one knew
better than this lover of field sports that "there's
many a slip 'twixt the cup and the lip," and a slight
mistake, a flounder in a brook, or a " cropper" at
an ox fence, might have changed the places of the
respective horses.

Within the last few years steeple-chasing seems
to have greatly extended its influence, and almost
every county can boast of an annual meeting. I
well remember the time when it was so uncommon,
that the announcement of such an event attracted
the notice of the sporting million. Take, for instance, the celebrated Hertfordshire chases in 1830,
when Lord Ranelagh's Wonder, ridden by Captain
(now Colonel) M'Douall, fully came up to his name,
beating upon one occasion a large field of horses,
and upon another two celebrated horses of that day,
jockeyed by Mr. Codrington and the Honourable
Augustus Berkeley. Of the latter's riding it is
unnecessary to speak, as he was unquestionably one
of the best horsemen of the age—possessing judgment, quickness, and nerves of adamant. What
could exceed the excitement produced by these
steeple-chases, especially the second grand Hertfordshire affair, in which Wonder, jockeyed by
Captain Blane, was placed third, Mr. Caldecott's
ch. m. and ch. h., the former ridden by Mr. Fiske,
and the latter by Captain Becher, taking the first
and second posts of honour. The distance, about
five miles, was done in twenty minutes, sharpish
work, considering the heaviness of the ground and
stiffness of the fences.

From steeple-chasing I turn to boating, a delight-

ful pastime before the introduction of river steamers
played such havoc with it in the more frequented
parts of the river.

> " Some o'er the Thamis row the ribbon'd fair,"

writes Byron in "Childe Harold;" and unquestionably, however agreeable it might have been in
the days of the noble poet to have found oneself
like Dibdin's "Jolly Young Waterman, never in
want of a *fair*," we should scarcely like in these
days to trust any lovely daughter of Eve in a frail
wherry subject to the tender mercies of the steam-
boat captains.   The Thames, like the roads of
England, have been completely sacrificed to steam;
and a morning sail or an evening pull on the water
is now only to be ranked among the pleasures of
memory.   Some seventeen years ago boating was a
great amusement, both to the higher and the
humbler classes; and in those days there were some
splendid six, eight, and ten-oared boats, manned by
the flower of the English nobility.   Now the steam-
boats have entirely monopolised Father Thames;
and since the time these fire-flies have taken possession of the no longer "silent highway," oars
and sculls are at a sad discount.   Who now would
venture his life in a wherry, when, owing to the
modern invention of "steam for the million," boats
are whizzing up and down the river from sunrise

to sunset, dodging in and out, dashing and slashing
very much after the principle of the cutting-in,
panel-breaking coachman of the fourth George's
time ? What would the water poet, that renowned
king of scullers of 1630, John Taylor, have said,
had he lived during the present period; he that was
wont to boast that he often ferried the immortal
Shakespeare from Whitehall to Paris Garden, or his
contemporary Ben Jonson from the Bankside to the
Rose and Hope playhouses ? With his tirade
against coaches, then but lately introduced, what
would he have said to the modern importation of
cabs, 'busses, and other vehicles, from the well-
appointed four-in-hand "team," to a Whitechapel
cart ? The poor water poet must have drowned
himself in his own element, for mark what a picture
he drew even then of the fearful calamity that
assailed his vocation :—"I do not inveigh," says
honest John, "against any conveyances that belong
to persons of worth or quality, but only against the
caterpillar swarm of hirelings. *They have undone
my poor trade* whereof I am a member ; and though
I look for no reformation, yet I expect the benefit
of an old proverb, 'Give the losers leave to speak.'
This infernal swarm of trade-spillers [coaches] have
so overrun the land, that we can get no living upon
the water; for I dare truly affirm that every day in

any term, especially if the Court be at Whitehall, they do rob us of our living, and carry five hundred and sixty fares daily from us. I pray you look into the streets, and the chambers or lodgings in Fleet Street or the Strand, how they are pestered with them, especially after a masque or play at the court, when even the very earth quakes and trembles, the casements chatter, patter, and clatter, and such a confused noise is made, so that a man can neither sleep, speak, hear, write, nor eat his dinner or supper quiet for them."

But the river annoyances do not deter the Oxford and Cambridge University Clubs, the Westminster, Eton, and Harrovians, from continuing to contend for the aquatic championship, and there are a variety of cups and prizes still given, not forgetting Doggett's coat and badge for the Thames watermen. Perhaps one of the most notable events that ever took place was the grand four-oared match for 1,000 sovereigns, between the Harrow and the Guards' clubs, July, 1829. The gentlemen selected for the former club were—Mr. Slater (stroke oar); Mr. Cannon; Mr. Bayford; Mr. Osbaldeston; Mitchell, of Strand Lane, coxswain. For what the watermen called the " Sodger Officer " Club—Captain Bentinck (stroke oar); Viscount Chetwynd; Lord Douglas; Colonel Hobhouse ; Brummell, of Vauxhall, coxswain.

After a most determined struggle, in which both of the crews evinced the greatest pluck and judgment, the Harrow men won by about fifty seconds.

Another aquatic achievement was the grand rowing match from Oxford to London in sixteen consecutive hours, which came off May 12, 1824. It is only fair to the gentlemen by whose skill, exertion, and manly perseverance the arduous task was accomplished, to say that it was a feat never equalled in the annals of the sport. The wager was made between Sir John Burgoyne, Bart., and the late Colonel Standen, and the terms of the match were as follows :—" That six officers of the Third Guards (now the Scotch Fusilier Guards) should row in a six-oared wherry from Oxford to London in sixteen consecutive hours." The crew consisted of Captain Short, Hon. J. Westenra, Douglas, Blane, and Hudson, who with Colonel Standen made up the number. The rowers were to choose their own coxswain, and time was to be kept by watches previously wound in Oxford and London. The boat in which the wager was to be contended for was built for the purpose by Mr. Sullivan, of Millbank, after the plan of the Marquis of Worcester's *Fancy*, a boat remarkable for its speed. The wager arose from a bet made by Lord Newry, about seventeen months before, that he would row the

same distance in eighteen hours with five of his
servants trained for that purpose. Some dispute
arose as to his winning his match; but on a
chronometer being sent down to Oxford, he was
declared to have won by one minute, having had
wind, tide, and everything in his favour. Not
only Sir John Burgoyne, but most of the knowing
ones, as well as the amateurs, and the members
of the majority of the river clubs, were ready to
offer three and four to one against the accomplishment of the wager. It was settled that the
12th of May should be the day for deciding the
match, and application was made by Colonel
Standen and his friends to the commissioners of the
locks between Oxford and London for their assistance in clearing the beds and pans, and supplying
plenty of water as they passed through. This was
readily granted, and through the arrangements
made by the commissioners nearly half an hour was
gained by the rowers.

On Tuesday morning the gallant crew arrived at
Oxford, retired early to bed, and gave orders to be
called at two, intending to start punctually at three.
By a quarter before three they were attired in their
aquatic costume—blue-striped shirts, crimson neck-
cloths, and white hats. They took in a little brandy
and some sandwiches, and at one minute past three

o'clock, their coxswain, Isaac King, gave the word
" All's ready." The rowers let fall their oars
amidst the cheers of a great number of persons,
and the wherry cleft the stream, starting at the rate
of about eight miles the hour. On arriving at
Bolter's Lock, Maidenhead (half-way), it was half-
past eleven o'clock; half an hour had been lost by
the wind freshing to the east, and the squally
weather. Here, James Cannon, the second coxswain, was taken aboard, and by many " a long
pull, a strong pull, and a pull altogether," the
wherry reached Windsor Bridge by one o'clock.
No time was lost; although every man on board
was fatigued, they pushed on with most determined
resolution, and notwithstanding great difficulties,
owing to the unfavourable state of the weather,
they arrived at Teddington Lock before half-past
five o'clock. In Teddington Lock they took refresh-
ments, and their spirits were raised by the arrival of
a number of their London friends in wherries and
skiffs, who cheered them loudly upon their having
gone thus far so successfully. Thomas Hill, the
third coxswain, was here taken on board ; and considering the wind was in their teeth, and the weather
foul and contrary, they did wonders. It was half-
past five when they left Teddington Lock, and upon
their arrival at Putney Bridge it was exactly six

o'clock. The river was covered with boats from all
the aquatic clubs, but from Teddington to Westminster Bridge, two eight-oared guard-boats cleared
the way for the wherry. The cheering of the spectators excited the liveliest emulation among the
rowers, and kept them from sinking, as it was feared
they would have sunk, under the excessive exertion,
and losing their wager almost in sight of port.
The umpire, Colonel Meyrick, took his station on
Westminster Bridge at six o'clock. The craft on
the river, the bridges, stairs, and wharfs, from which
there was a view of Whitehall Stairs, the appointed
landing place, were crowded with spectators. Several
of the Bow Street patrol were placed at Whitehall
Stairs to keep the peace, and to assist in the debark-
ation. At half-past six o'clock the wherry arrived
at Battersea Bridge, the rowers completely knocked
up, some of them almost bent double, and all of
them much distressed. The tide was now in their
favour, and having taken a little brandy, they bent
once more to their oars, and at a quarter before
seven o'clock arrived at Westminster Bridge. Mr.
Sullivan, the boat builder, towed them to Whitehall
Stairs, where they declared they would have arrived
one hour sooner had the wind been in their favour.
The distance from Oxford to Westminster Bridge is
one hundred and eighteen miles, and it was ac-

complished in fifteen hours and three quarters. The original wager was £200, but no less a sum than £15,000 changed owners upon this occasion.

I had every reason to remember this event, as it cost me a new hat, and a doctor's bill to get rid of a cold which I caught. In the year 1815, while on the personal staff of General Maitland, I had become intimately acquainted with all the officers of the division, and from that period I had never ceased to take an interest in the corps. No wonder, then, that my feelings were raised to the highest pitch of excitement when I saw the match won in such gallant style, and rising to cheer the crew, I lost my balance and fell into the water. My new white beaver hat floated calmly away with the stream until it was captured by a collier in a barge, who, amidst the shouts of the spectators, clapped it knowingly on his sooty head, leaving me to walk home under " bare poles."

In the same year there was a match in which I took the deepest interest, between the Eton and Westminster scholars, for 100 sovereigns, and upon which considerable sums of money changed hands. The Marquis of Waterford pulled stroke in the Eton boat, and won by many boat's lengths. Here I cannot do better than give my personal remembrances of this nobleman. It

was during a visit to Melton when Sir William
Massey Stanley, and his brother Rowland Errington,
hunted the Quorn, that I first became acquainted
with the Marquis. The hounds met at Kirby Gate,
and while riding to cover, Waterford, to whom I
had just been introduced, completely ingratiated
himself with me. His groom was riding a young,
unbroken horse, and upon nearing a stiffish flight of
rails, he said, "That's the very place to try him at.
There, let him go; give him his head." The groom
obeyed, but the animal he rode swerved and refused
several times to face it. "A little more powder,
and he'll do it," exclaimed the owner. Again the
attempt was made, and without success. "He'll
break his neck," said Errington; "the brute won't
rise at it." "Won't he?" rejoined the head of the
Beresford family; "I'll have a try. I never yet
asked a man to do what I would not attempt myself.
Jump off; never mind the stirrups." In a second
the man had alighted, his master had taken his place,
and without putting his feet in the irons, which
were much too short for him, he patted the refrac-
tory animal on the neck, then cramming his spurs
into his sides, and lowering his hands, he seemed
actually to raise the "young one" over the rail.
"Come," he said; "if you can get over one way,
you can equally get back," so turning the astonished

animal short round, he pressed him with his knees, just to remind him that he had some steel "persuaders" on, and away flew the horse, clearing the rail in a most sportsmanlike style. A few days afterwards I breakfasted at Lowesby Hall, then rented by Lord Waterford, and there I was surprised to find in a long conversation I had with him *tête-à-tête*, how much his mind was stored with the writings of the best prose and poetical authors, ancient and modern. What a contrast did this intellect form to a variety of acts of folly which the noble lord perpetrated, some of which would have been heartless, had not Waterford's generosity always compensated those who suffered from his "larks!"

To return to the river. This same year another sporting event came off, namely a grand rowing match for 200 sovereigns, between the Squire (Osbaldeston), with Mitchell, of Strand Lane, and Captain Bentinck, of the Guards, with Cobb, of Whitehall; the terms being to row a pair of oars from Vauxhall to Kew Bridge. At the word "off," Mr. Osbaldeston's boat shot half a length ahead; and the boats remained in this position until within a few yards of Battersea Bridge, when the Captain laid out, and the boats were about even. Soon after the church had been passed the opponents changed places, and from this point the gallant

Guardsman continued to gain, winning the match
at length by four minutes and a half. A wonderful
feat took place in September of the same year, when
Messrs. Bishop and Horneman accomplished the
task of rowing with a pair of oars from London
Bridge to Gravesend, up to Richmond Bridge, and
back to Westminster (a distance of nearly a hundred
miles) in the short space of thirteen hours and
thirty-five minutes — an hour and twenty-five
minutes within the time of the wager. What
made this exploit so wonderful was, that from
Gravesend to Erith Reach, they had a heavy sea
and a dead "noser," as I can vouch for, for it nearly
water-logged their boat, and capsized mine.

In 1830 I was present at a most extraordinary
match against time, made by a distinguished amateur, F. Cresswell, Esq., for fifty sovereigns, that
he and William Lewis, a waterman of Old Swan
Stairs, would row in a Thames wherry from Bil-
lingsgate down to Gravesend, up through Richmond
Bridge, and back to the Old Swan, in thirteen
hours and a half. At starting the odds were two
to one in favour of time. The day was calm,
although it rained heavily for some time, and the
tide in their favour almost the whole of the way to
Gravesend. They turned without landing, so as to
avail themselves of the flowing tide, and on their

return the tide about Sion House was again favourable, the ebb having commenced. Such was the pluck of the gallant men, that they arrived at the Old Swan Stairs at twenty minutes past five, winning their match by an hour and forty minutes.

An aquatic deed of my own caused me no little pride, though it is scarcely fair to mention it after such achievements. I was staying with Ball Hughes at a villa he had for the summer, on the banks of the gentle Mole, near Esher. We had all been at Epsom Races, and were dusty and hot. While lounging on the lawn before dressing, I remarked what a luxury it would be to have a swim. "Can you swim?" asked my host. "Pretty well," I replied. "I'll bet you fifty pounds," continued he, "that you do not jump in head foremost as you are, swim to that tree and back in five minutes." "I suppose if I say done," I replied, "I may take off my hat, and leave my watch in your possession." "I agree to the latter, not to the former. Is it a bet?" "It is." "George," said the Golden Ball, addressing the late Sir George Wombwell, "you must be timekeeper. When William Lennox is ready, you must give the word. He must take a header, swim for that willow tree, touch its branches, and return in five minutes." The word was given, I plunged in head foremost, and found myself regularly "bonneted" under the water, as my hat had slipped down over my face. In a second or two I raised it, swam out, reached the goal, touched the willow, and was back at the starting-place with a minute to spare. In less time than I can take to record it, I ran up to my bed-room, took off my drenched garments, got between two blankets, and was down at dinner wonderfully refreshed in body, and still more in mind by the "refresher" of fifty pounds, which I found under my napkin. Since that period I have never caught a glimpse of the sluggish Mole without being reminded of my aquatic feat.

I was equally successful in winning another wager from "The Golden Ball." The late Earl Fitzhardinge had made me a present of a splendid old hunter, called Goliah, whose wind was too much touched for a gallop, but who was perfect at a walk or a gentle trot, and as a fencer. One day I was driving him in a tilbury in Hyde Park, where, from his beauty and symmetry, he was the admiration of all. Ball Hughes noticed him. "What a hunter he would make!" said he. "He was one of the best in the world," I responded; "and even now he would leap almost any fence in the country: wonderful too at timber; he would fly over those railings." This was an allusion to some high wooden railings that then enclosed the park. "I'll bet you five pounds," said the exquisite, "that he does not." "Done," said I, "I will do it to-morrow." "Oh, no, it must be done at once. The bet I propose is, that you have him taken out of the tilbury, and without saddle clear the highest rail in the park, in a sporting manner. "Done," said I, "with this stipulation, that as the rails are equally high near Kensington Gardens, you select one there, so as to be out of the way of the horse-men and carriages." "Agreed," he said, "and Fred Fitz Clarence shall be the umpire." Fitz Clarence, Ball Hughes, his friend Lloyd, and myself, proceeded to the spot, where I took Goliah out of the tilbury, fastened his traces over his loins, undid the bearing rein, got a "lift" on, and charged the rail, retaking the leap back again into the road. "Fairly won," declared the umpire; "that animal would be worth four hundred pounds if his wind was sound."

The ancient, royal, and noble diversion of hawking has sunk into great neglect among the civilised nations of Europe, yet it is the sport best calculated for the enjoyment of the fair sex. It displays their skill and grace on horseback to the greatest advantage, and it is divested of that danger of broken limbs to which ladies are so liable in following the hounds. With these advantages, it is

strange that this amusement, the delight of the
ancient kings of England, should have sunk into obli-
vion.   It is true that the late Duke of Rutland had
formed the intention of reviving the sport in its ancient
splendour, but his project was never carried out; that
the late Duke and Duchess of St. Alban's introduced
falconry at their *fêtes* at Holly Lodge, Highgate,
some thirty years ago; and that the Maharajah
Dhuleep Singh still carries on the sport in Norfolk.
But these form the solitary exceptions to the rule.
Britain and Thrace are the only countries where we
have any evidence that this diversion was practised
in by-gone ages; and of the latter, Pliny obscurely
alludes to it as being confined to one particular
district. Gibbon observes that hawking was scarcely
known to the Romans in the time of Vespasian,
yet it was introduced soon afterwards, most probably
through their intercourse with the Britons. From
a curious but well-authenticated tract of English
history, it appears that the invasion of this country
by the Danes was occasioned by the assassina-
tion of Lodbrog, the father of Hinguar and Hubba.
He embarked with his hawks and hounds, and
being driven on the coast of Norfolk, grew so
much in favour with the King of the East Angles
for his skill in hawking, that Benre, the king's
falconer, murdered him through jealousy; and the

first motive of the landing of the Danes was to revenge his death.

That ladies were early enamoured of this amusement may be gathered from an ancient sculpture in the church of Milton Abbas, in Dorsetshire, where the consort of King Athelstan appears with a falcon in her hand tearing a bird. Harold, afterwards King of England, is painted going on a most important embassy with a hawk on his hand and a dog under his arm. King John received of Jeffrey Fitzpierre two good Norway hawks, for leave to export 1 cwt. of cheese; and Nicholas the Dane was to give one of these birds every time he entered the kingdom to traffic, the Norwegian breed being held in the highest repute. According to Froissart, King Edward III. had with him in his army "thirty mounted followers carrying birds, besides sixty couple of strong dogs, and as many greyhounds, with which he hunted every day on land or water, as he best liked." During his reign it was made felony to steal a hawk; and to take its eggs, even in a person's own ground, was punishable with imprisonment for a year and a day, and a fine at the king's pleasure. In the reign of Queen Elizabeth the imprisonment was reduced to three months, but the offender had to find security for his good behaviour for seven years, or lie in prison till

he did. Such was the enviable state of the good
old times of England, when people were subject to
capital punishments, fines, and incarceration, by the
most unjust and arbitrary laws, for destroying the
most noxious of the feathered tribe. Henry IV.
granted Sir John Stanley the Isle of Man, to be
held by homage and service of two falcons, payable
on each coronation day; and Philip de Hastang
held the manor of Comberton, in Cambridgeshire,
by the service of keeping the king's falcons.
Henry VI. is represented at his nuptials attended
by a nobleman with his falcon. It will thus be
seen that a person of rank seldom went abroad
without a hawk on his hand, which in old paintings
is made the criterion of nobility. Chaucer describes
Sir Thopis as following this knightly sport :—

> " He could hunt at the wild dere,
> And ride on hawking for the revere,
> With grey goshawk on hande."

And Spenser, in the days of the Virgin Queen,
makes it a prominent feature in the education of
Sir Tristram :—

> " Ne is there hauke that mantleth on her pearch,
> Whether high tow'ring, or accoasting low,
> But I the measure of her flight doe search,
> And all her prey, and all her dyet know."

In the reign of James I. Sir Thomas Monson is

said to have given £1,000 for a cast of hawks. So
lately as 1670, Walton, in his "Compleat Angler,"
speaks of hawking as entering into competition with
hunting or fishing, and gives a list of the various
birds used in the sport, as if it were then much in
vogue. The falcons that were formerly used still
breed in Wales, North Britain, and its isles. The
peregrine falcon inhabits the rocks of Carnarvon-
shire; the same species, with the gyr falcon, the
gentil, the goshawk, and also the lanner, are found
in Scotland. Many difficulties stand in the way of
reviving this diversion, the principal one being the
expense, labour, and perseverance necessary for
training the birds. It also requires an open
country, for trees and hedges, to which everything
flies when pursued by a hawk, spoil the sport.
Hounslow Heath, Salisbury Plain, the site of the
Chobham Camp, and Newmarket Heath, are admirably adapted for hawking, and ere long we trust
that the hereditary Grand Falconer of England,
the Duke of St. Alban's, may be tempted to revive
this ancient pastime of "Merrie England."

The only time that I ever was present at a hawking
party, was at Holly Lodge, Highgate, about the year
1832. The duke (father of the present duke) and
the duchess (formerly Miss Mellon, afterwards Mrs.
Coutts), who resided there for a few weeks during

the summer months, did all in their power to entertain their friends, and, among other amusements,
falconry was suggested. The Grand Falconer appeared in a picturesque costume, attended by a numerous retinue, and followed by the guests, with the
duchess at their head, proceeded to a field where the
game was to be flown at. At a given signal the duke
advanced to the front, glove-guarded, with jesses in
hand. The bird of prey, being hooded, was then
fisted. The quarry, a white pigeon, was quickly let
loose from a trap, and, in a second, the hawk flying
out of the hood, at one fell swoop seized the quarry,
which was soon brought to the ground. The falconer then approached the hawk, encouraged her
with kind tones of voice, drew the body of the prey
away, merely allowing the head to be retained, and,
luring her by a small piece of meat, again fisted,
hooded, and fed her. So much commiseration was
naturally felt for the poor innocent pigeon, more
especially by the gentler sex, that the pursuit was
discontinued, and the party adjourned to another
part of the grounds, where some half-dozen milk-
maids, dressed in Swiss costume, were milking their
cows preparatory to immense bowls of syllabub being
made. The cows, however, decked out in ribbons
and wreaths of flowers, did not behave very well
upon this occasion, and seemed to have no respect

for their aristocratic lookers on. *Dr. Ollapod*, in Colman's clever play of the " Poor Gentleman," tells the old lady *Lucretia Mac Tab* to step out of the path, as " the cows have been there." In the instance I refer to, they gamboled about, and, in many cases, damaged the ladies' dresses not a little.

CHAPTER XV.

CHAPTER XV.

In the course of my literary life, I came in contact with many people of distinction, and saw much of the ways of men of letters. Some of these have been introduced in earlier parts of these volumes, as well as in the former work, to which I have more than once alluded. As an editor, of course I had dealings with contributors, just as, in my capacity of author, I had dealings with publishers. But I decline to expose the weaknesses of either class, the more as I consider their weaknesses, or what pass as such, to be the almost necessary consequences of their position. The irritability, the jealousies, and rivalries of authors, have been often dwelt on, and not always in the best spirit. After reading the valuable works of the elder Disraeli, and seeing the faults of the greatest literary names, it is hardly worth one's while to show that minor authors were more faithful to the bad than to the good example of their leaders.

But the quarrels of authors among themselves

sink into the shade when compared with their attacks
on publishers. We all remember Campbell's toast
to Napoleon at a dinner where many leading publishers were present, and his reason for giving it,
that Napoleon had shot a bookseller. But surely
this feeling is much to be regretted. It is easy for
authors to vent their spleen against publishers, just
as ladies and gentlemen complain of servants as the
"greatest plague in life." But the rejoinder is the
same in both cases—What would you do without
them? My own experience has certainly not confirmed the charges made against publishers.

I have had transactions with Bentley, Tuxford,
Hurst and Blackett, Chapman and Hall, Newby,
and the late Messrs. Colburn and Shoberl, and have
ever been honourably treated. Publishers, like
authors, try to make the best bargain they can; and
when we consider how many books prove a failure,
we cannot be surprised if literary speculators are
wary. It will occasionally happen that a good
manuscript may be rejected, for the judgment of the
reader attached to all publishers' offices is not infal-
lible, and it more often happens that works of inferior
merit find their way to the public. This occurs
when author or authoress publish on their own
account, or guarantee the publisher against loss.
Hence a great mass of mawkish fiction has issued

from respectable firms, and a certain amount of blame has attached to them.

During the course of a long literary experience, I have had many manuscripts forwarded to me, with the modest request that I would read, recommend, and dispose of them; and only in one instance have I been able to carry out the writer's wishes. This was in the case of a very clever book, called "Woman's Temptation," written by a most amiable and talented young lady, the Hon. Miss Mary Dutton. Poor girl! she did not live to reap the benefit of her success. When the manuscript was first sent to me, I received an apologetic letter from the authoress for the manner in which it had been copied, and I found that she had copied it out "fairly" three times. I assured her in reply, that if the composition was as good as the handwriting, nothing more could be desired. Hurst and Blackett at once purchased the copyright, and brought it out, edited by the young lady's stepmother, the Hon. Mrs. Dutton, now Lady Sherborne. In the preface we find the following touching notice:—

"The following pages were scarcely in the hands of the publishers, when the writer of them was taken from among us by a death most sudden and unexpected.

"This is not the place to dwell upon her loss, though what that loss is, none can appreciate but those few who were intimately acquainted with her pure spirit and bright intelligence; and they indeed feel that her place among us can never be filled up.

" Had her life been prolonged, we cannot doubt but that the present work would have been but the earnest of others. But the active brain and the ready hand are now still, beneath the snow-covered grave; she is cut off, even before she had put the finishing stroke to her first work;—and, as the writer's life had been one of almost constant retirement and self-culture, we hope that these pages will be found to be as interesting as they are well-intentioned, and that the remarkable knowledge and insight into character shown throughout, may be looked upon as indications of mental powers of no common order.

"*Feb.* 14*th*, 1860.   " F. D."

In other cases, when publishers have declined the manuscripts, even with the tempting offer of £50 to cover part of the expenses, I have been placed in the most painful position, as it is difficult to satisfy the writers that fair play has been shown them. They quote books which they consider " trashy," " unmitigated rubbish," " wretched stuff," and which have not been so severely dealt with. Under these harassing circumstances I have usually addressed a letter of regret, pointing out the cart-loads of books that are annually published, the effect that cheap literature has produced, as few will purchase a three-volume octavo novel for 31s., when many of our most valuable standard works may be had for a sixth of that price; and the enormous expense of printing and advertising. Usually I have attempted to cheer the disappointed author who has toiled over the midnight lamp, with the following remarks: — "Remember," I have said, "that the author of 'Roderick Random,' 'Peregrine Pickle,' 'Count Fathom,' 'Launcelot Greaves,' Smollet, whose rich genius composed the most original pictures of human life, perished in a foreign land, neglected by an admiring public. His life was a succession of vexations, struggles, and disappointments. 'Burn's Justice' was sold for a trifle; Goldsmith's 'Vicar of Wakefield' was disposed of in the hour of distress; 'Evelina' produced £5 5s.; 'Paradise Lost' sold for £5. Milton's children and the family of Burns received alms from the public. The 'Rejected Addresses' were rejected by all the London booksellers and publishers, and, at last, only realised a small sum." How truly, yet bitterly, has the satirical Nash written, "How many base men that wanted those

parts I had, enjoyed content at will, and had wealth
at command, yet I am a beggar! Men of talent
are preyed on by cormorant publishers, kept under
by dunces, or robbed by sharkish booksellers."
Carey, too, writes—

> " The sellers must be abject slaves,
>   The buyers vile designing knaves."

It is the same in all branches of business, especially in those where speculation enters as largely
as in the publishing trade. Look at the immense
sums paid to known authors for books which have
not been seen by the publisher, and which sometimes do not even pay their printing expenses. If
the publisher is to repay himself for these losses by
a lucky hit, he must have his hands free to make
this lucky hit at the right moment. The publisher does not profess to judge the merit of a work,
but its adaptability to the public.

> " Clever work, sir, 'twould get up prodigiously well,
>   Its only defect is, it never would sell;
>   And though statesmen may glory in being unbought,
>   In an author it's rather considered a fault,"

say Messrs. Lackington, in Moore's "Twopenny
Post Bag." There is, probably, no author, of what
eminence soever, who has not found the truth of
this unpalatable maxim.

But even when the publisher is found, and a

satisfactory sum secured for the copyright, the author's difficulties are not at an end. The printers have next to be dealt with; and as few authors copy their MS. three times over, like the lady I have mentioned, it is easy to imagine that the misprints made are sometimes awful.

Sometimes the mis-spelling of a word renders the expression offensive, or ridiculous. I remember quoting a letter from Wellington to the Duke of Beaufort, telling him that Lord Fitzroy Somerset had been wounded at Waterloo, in which the following line occurred, "Fitzroy is free from fever." Great was my horror to find in the proof, "Fitzroy is free from fear." I altered the word, called the printer's attention to it, yet in the revise the same mistake occurred. Not wishing to do such an act of injustice to the gallant Plantaganet as to let it be thought he was likely to be influenced by fear, and despairing of getting the error corrected, I went off to the printers, and never left the room in which the ponderous printing-machine was at work, until I saw "fear" changed into "fever."

A few months ago I was correcting a paper for a religious magazine, when I found, instead of "entrancing thought," "entertaining thought." Upon other occasions I have met with errors of a most ludicrous nature. In dedicating a work to the late Prince Consort, I found, "with the most gracious submission of his Royal Highness," instead of "permission." In quoting the lines on a picture of Lely, who—

> " On animated canvas stole
> The sleepy eye that spoke the melting soul,"

I found "soul" spelt "sole," a "melting sole;" rather too suggestive of melted butter. In alluding to Wellington's death, instead of "an empire mourns his loss," the printer inserted "an emperor mourns his loss." And again, in the same work, "to dwell on the warlike deeds of Wellington would be supercilious," instead of "superfluous;" and "*Cæsar invictire dicer*," instead of "*Cæsaris invicti res dicere.*" Some excuse is to be made for the printers when the writing is what Tony Lumpkin calls "a damned cramp piece of penmanship, with such handles, and shanks, and dashes, that one could scarce tell the head from the tail; an up and down hand, as if it was disguised in liquor." D'Orsay told me a story of a clerk in the French Foreign Office, who, copying a despatch mechanically from an original not very legible, wrote, "*Demande de coups de pied au Ministre de la Marine*," instead of "*Demande de copie de pièces au Ministre de la Marine.*"

In 1858 much excitement was caused in Cheltenham by a report that the Emperor of the

French had been assassinated. It appeared that a telegram had been received, giving an account of the University boat-race, and the words occurred in it, "The *Emperor* shot a-head." By a slight slip the phrase was turned into "The Emperor shot dead," and of course, circulated throughout the town. I heard of a similar mistake occurring in a French telegram, announcing the arrival of the King of Prussia at Compiègne : "*Le Roi est arrivé ; aujourd'hui théâtre, demain chassé.*"

I sincerely trust that my printers will not make the same mistakes in the letter I am about to quote. But I must preface it by a short statement of the circumstances which called it into existence. In the year 1859 I was editor of the *Review* news-paper, and as at that time attacks on Napoleon III. were very numerous, and, in my judgment, equally unjust, I made that journal an organ for supporting and defending his Majesty against them.

Being anxious that the Emperor should be aware that there were many in England, however humble their pretensions, ready to do justice to him and his views, I forwarded to Monsieur Mocquard, his *Chef du Cabinet*, copies of the papers that were thus friendly to his interests. By return of post I received a letter from his secretary, couched in such courteous and flattering language that I cannot deprive myself of the pleasure of laying it before my readers. It is not my wish to introduce my political views into a work of this nature; but I hope I may be allowed to say that not one of the fears that were entertained by the anti-Napoleon party in this country have been, or seem likely to be, realised. For years the cry of "French invasion" was echoed throughout our land, and the day was all but fixed when our polite neighbours were to pay us an *un*-friendly visit. It was seriously discussed whether the Emperor would take up his quarters at Buckingham Palace or Windsor Castle, should he succeed in his attempt, and whether the Crystal Palace would not form an excellent barrack for the Imperial Guards, Zouaves, and *Chasseurs de Vincennes*. Nay, the spot was named where, according to some supposed fatalist notion of the Emperor, his Majesty was to be shot in Regent Street. All, however, has ended in smoke, not cannon smoke, and England and France are still allies.

Here is the letter:—

"Cabinet de l'Empereur, Palais des Tuileries, le 12 Avril, 1859.

"MILORD,

"Je me suis empressé de communiquer à l'Empereur l'article que vous lui avez consacré. Il a fait éprouver, vous ne pouviez en avoir le moindre doute, une vive satisfaction à S. M. et sans de trop nombreuses occupations, elle vous aurait exprimé elle même combien elle était touchée de cette preuve de sympathie de l'un de ses anciens et honorables amis d'Angleterre. Elle se trouve heureuse dans les jours difficiles de recontrer des hommes comme vous pour la défendre contre d'injustes attaques, avec l'accent de la conviction. S. M. me charge donc et je me félicite, milord, d'être auprez de vous l'interprete de ses sentiments de gratitude.

"Veuillez agréer, milord, l'assurance de ma considération la plus distinguée,

"Le Secrétaire de l'Empereur,

"Chef du Cabinet,

"Mocquard.

"*A Lord William Lennox.*"

Among men of literary eminence I have known I must mention Robert Montgomery, commonly called "Satan Montgomery," not from his having any dealing with that "father of lies," but from the poem he wrote upon that subject. I had been summoned to attend at the Old Bailey, as a witness to the character of an officer who had unfortunately shot his adversary in a duel, and, being acquainted with some of the Aldermen, I was invited to dinner to meet the Judge. Upon taking my seat on the right hand of the learned Judge, I recognised in my next neighbour a reverend gentleman whom I had heard preach a charity sermon at St. Paul's, Covent Garden, some years before, for the benefit of the Westminster Hospital. "I understand," said he, of course after alluding to the state of the weather, "that some 'nobs' dine here to-day, some noble lords."

Thinking it possible that he might indulge in some tirade against my order, I replied, "I only know of one, and that is myself, for the rest of the party are aldermen, and men learned in the law."

"I beg your pardon," said he, rather confusedly, "but—"

I saved him from further explanation by thus interrupting him—"I think I had the pleasure of hearing you preach at St. Paul's for the benefit of the Westminster Hospital, and so impressive were you that you extracted a five-pound note from me."

"I remember the occasion," he replied.

"And moreover," I rejoined, "I recollect the text: it was from the sixteenth chapter of St. Luke, 'To beg I am ashamed.'"

"Your Lordship has a good memory," he answered.

"And so pleased was I with your discourse," I continued, "that I attended your chapel in Charlotte Street, Bedford Square."

" Indeed !"

" And your text was the briefest one I ever heard —' My God.'"

Both the above sermons were truly impressive, but, perhaps, what would now be called a little too " sensational." Montgomery was very theatrical in his action, throwing himself forward as if, not to speak irreverently, he was going to take a header (*à la Colleen Bawn*) from the pulpit. He seemed as proud of his hands as Byron was, and always displayed them prominently. With all this his sermons did not possess those singularly attractive powers, those sterling qualities, that full exhibition of Divine truth, that vital piety, that apostolic labour, that deep searching of the conscience, that rich but simple eloquence, that brilliant but chastened imagination, that affecting earnestness, which characterised a Blount, a Bickersteth, a Chalmers, or, in our days, a Molyneux. His poems, "The Omnipresence of the Deity" and "Satan," were severely criticised by Macaulay, and in some degree deservedly, though I think the "tomahawk" and " scalping" system was carried too far, as the critic descended to personalities. Thus he writes—" We have no enmity to Mr. Robert Montgomery—we know nothing whatever about him except what we have learned from his books, and from the portrait

prefixed to one of them, in which he appears to be
doing his very best to look like a man of genius
and sensibility, though with less success than his
strenuous exertions deserve. We select him because
his works have received more enthusiastic praise,
and have deserved more unmixed contempt, than
any which, as far as our knowledge extends, have
appeared within the last three or four years." The
great historian thus annihilates the clerical author
with a back-hand hit at Martin the painter. Talking
of "Satan," he says, "Of the two poems we rather
prefer that on the 'Omnipresence of the Deity,' for
the same reason which induced Sir Thomas More
to rank one bad book above another, 'Marry, this is
somewhat. This is rhyme. But the other is neither
rhyme nor reason.' Satan is a long soliloquy, which
the devil pronounces in five or six thousand lines
of bad blank verse, concerning geography, politics,
newspapers, fashionable society, theatrical amusements, Sir Walter Scott's novels, Lord Byron's
poetry, and Mr. Martin's pictures. The new designs
for Milton have, as was natural, particularly attracted
the attention of a personage who occupies so conspicuous a place in them. Mr. Martin must be
pleased to learn that, whatever may be thought of
those performances on earth, they give full satisfaction in Pandæmonium, and that he is there thought

to have hit off the likenesses of the various Thrones and Dominations very happily."

The critic, in his "slashing article," alludes to "irreverent familiarity," "grotesque indecency:" would not the last paragraph we have quoted come under those denominations?

I pass to another man of less pretension in the world of letters, but of more true literary celebrity, the late James Smith, one of the authors of the "Rejected Addresses." I have already stated that, in consoling unsuccessful writers, this book was one to which I appealed, and there are few more remarkable circumstances than the history of those amusing parodies. Written for an immediate purpose, and apparently destined to a sudden and brief popularity, they were passed over by all the leading publishers, and finally became a classic in the world of comic writing. Murray, who rejected them when new, and when the smallest sum would have been thankfully received for them, was glad to purchase the copyright at an auction many years later.

Many of James Smith's witticisms had a good circulation in society, though not as large as that of the book by which he is remembered. And like many wits he found himself subject to be robbed of his children, to see his own coin circulating under the name and stamp of another.

I remember his telling me that there ought to be a book kept at some public library, in which a man might register his own joke, and thus prevent the annoyance which he often felt when, at a dinner party, some one laid a claim to one of his witticisms. I think that if jokes are to be made copyright, a book ought equally to be opened for suggestions for the public good. How often does it happen that the merit of a suggestion does not go to the originator, but to some after-discoverer! Having, as I flatter myself, originated an idea which will be adopted by the Government in due course of time, I take this opportunity of making it public. It is now some twenty years ago that I sent a letter to the morning papers, which appeared in one of them at least, suggesting a penny tax upon every railway ticket, with the exception of the parliamentary trains. I pointed out that the tax would be easily collected, and at a very small cost. In a correspondence I had with some of the leading editors subsequently, when I revived the question, an objection was raised that it would be a hardship for a person travelling from London to Richmond to pay as heavy a tax as if he were journeying to Edinburgh. I replied that the case was equally hard with respect to the post, as a letter from Grosvenor Square to Bond Street was charged as much as one from London to Dublin.

At that time the inland revenue stamp had not been introduced, or I might have added that it seemed a hardship for a man who drew five pounds from his bankers to pay as much as a millionaire did when signing his name to a cheque for a hundred thousand. When my old and highly valued friend Disraeli was Chancellor of the Exchequer for the second time, I reminded him of a letter I had addressed to the public papers upon the subject of the railway tax during his first occupancy of that post, but the Right Honourable gentleman, while thanking me, did not avail himself of the suggestion.

I knew Thomas Haynes Bayly intimately, and a kinder-hearted creature never existed; his wife, too, was pretty, clever, charming, and lady-like. As a song writer few excelled him, and many of his ballads attained a world-wide reputation; for years "Isabel," "We met," and "My Pretty Blue Belle," were regularly *organ*-ised by every Italian grinder in London and the provinces; a few of his farces were highly popular, and "Perfection" is still to be found among the stock pieces of the theatre. Bayly's whole heart was set upon his lyrical and dramatic works, as I can prove to my cost. In the year 1832 I went over to Boulogne for a few weeks, and hearing that the Baylys were in the town, I went to their house on the evening of my arrival,

after dining at the *table d'hôte* of the *Hotel des Bains.*
As they were at home, I was ushered into the
drawing-room, where I found Mrs. Bayly seated at
the pianoforte, and her husband with a manuscript
in his hand, spouting the words of a musical farce
he had just written.

"I am so glad to see you!" said he, in his
blandest tone; "and now you are here you must
act as audience, and take the critic's seat in the first
row of the pit."

After listening for more than an hour to the
reading of the new farce, and to the entire music,
vocal as well as instrumental, from the overture to
the finale, praising or offering suggestions as to
what I considered might be an improvement, I rose
to wish them good night. I pleaded as my excuse
for leaving them the drenching I had got in my
three hours' passage across from Dover, with the
wind blowing half a gale from the southward.

"Oh! you must remain a few minutes longer,
just to hear my last new ballad, and the first scene
of an opera I have nearly finished."

"I will come in some other evening," I responded,
"I feel quite chilly and uncomfortable."

"Only ten minutes," he replied, "and this glass
of absinthe will warm you thoroughly."

Fortifying myself with a tolerably large glass of

this delightful but pernicious liqueur, I again seated myself, and soon found that my host's minutes were hours, for the deep tones of a neighbouring church clock sounded midnight before the opening chorus had been gone through. " I shall be locked out of my hotel," I exclaimed, seizing my hat and hurriedly wishing the fanatico and his wife good-night. In my haste to get away I stumbled against something under the gateway, which, from the kick I unintentionally gave it, very soon showed signs of animation. My first impression was that it was a thief lurking about either to attack a stray individual, like myself, or to break into the house; and under this view of the case, I pictured to myself a fellow with the ominous letters T. F. (*travaux forcés*), which in English appear T(hie)F. branded on his arm, seizing me by the collar and strangling me outright, after the improved fashion of the modern garotter. To rush back to the bell, to pull it violently, to call "help!" to find Haynes Bayly standing aghast, lamp in hand, inside the door which he had opened, was the work of a moment.

"What has happened?" he exclaimed, "you have frightened my wife out of her senses;" here the lady herself appeared to corroborate, by her scared look, her husband's statement.

"Get my court-dress sword," said the poetaster, "it is in the drawing-room."

"And a lanthorn and the poker," I added, for the figures of a man erect and another kneeling or crouching, apparently enveloped in a cloak, were still visible under the dark *porte cochère*. In a few seconds Mrs. Bayly re-appeared with the light and weapons, and as we were about to proceed cautiously, to ascertain who the intruders were, leaving the lady and her French maid in a state of extreme alarm, great was our surprise and, I may add, greater was our delight, when suddenly, by a sort of pantomimic transformation, the erect figure appeared as an Italian organ player, and the couchant one as his anti-Bass instrument. To add to our astonishment, the Murillo-looking boy commenced an air which was quite unknown to me.

"My 'Isabel,' I declare," said my companion, in an ecstacy of delight.

"Who would have thought it your 'Isabel?'" I repeated.

"Yes, and my 'We Met,'" as the wandering musician changed from the former to the latter air. "I never expected to be so honoured out of England," continued Haynes Bayly, placing a five-franc piece into the hands of the astonished boy.

" *Tante grazie, Signori miei,*" said the dark-eyed son of Italy, who little thought when he took up his "lodgings" for the night "on the cold ground," that

he would have been awakened from a dream of his
sunny land by a stranger administering so liberally
to his relief. His astonishment would have been
considerably increased had he known that the donor
was the composer of the two airs he had played
on his organ. With a hope of further reward, he
continued to grind away these tunes during the
whole six weeks I remained at Boulogne, much to
the satisfaction of Haynes Bayly, who heard his
"Isabel" in every part of the town.

Bayly was the author of a novel entitled "The
Aylmers," which was so caustically written that it
gave dire offence to a female relative of his, who
fancied herself the object of his vengeance. Certainly
the character drawn was the vilest that ever could
be imagined, but as Haynes Bayly was one of the
kindest-hearted creatures in the world, it is difficult
to believe that he would appear in the odious part
of a slanderer against one of the gentler sex, especially when the object of the malicious attack was
a relative. Many of the residents and visitors at
Bath, where the scene of the novel was laid, warmly
espoused the cause of injured innocence, and the
author was denounced as a libeller by a clique
which probably feared its turn would come next.

Glad, indeed, should I be if I could include the
next name on my list among authors proper. But

though Prince Talleyrand left his Memoirs written, and the reading world has been looking forward curiously to the date he assigned for their publication, there seems reason to fear that the death of the appointed editor will prove a further obstacle. Such a caustic talker may well be supposed to have left still more caustic writings.

Although I had often met Talleyrand at Paris when I was on the staff of the Duke of Wellington, I never had the pleasure of forming one of a party *en petite comité* with him at dinner, until the year 1834, when he accepted an invitation to dine with Henry and Mrs. Webster. The party consisted of eight, that most sociable number; and as the host was known to be an excellent judge of cookery, we all anticipated a gastronomic and intellectual treat. It was well known to us all that the Prince was a *gourmet* of the first water, that his culinary department at Paris consisted of four *chefs*—the *rôtisseur*, the *saucier*, the *pâtissier*, and the *officier*, the latter superintending the dessert. In all, ten men were employed to minister to his tastes. But besides this we had all read of Talleyrand's witty sayings, and were now anxious to hear some new ones from his own lips. In ninety-nine cases out of a hundred where men are expected to make themselves funny, they fail to provoke a laugh; but such was not the case on the occasion I refer to, for Webster with much tact devoted his conversation to the luxuries of the table at home and abroad, and reminded his guests of the gastronomic saying, that a good dinner ought to be eaten in solemn silence. After the cloth had been removed (for *diners à la Russe* had not yet been introduced), instead of a table cloth stained with the juice of the grape, a bright polished mahogany, in which you could see your opposite neighbour's face, shone in all its splendour. In lieu of fruit which had become stale and vapid from the fumes of the dishes and the heat of the room, fresh products of the garden and hothouse were placed with the wine on the board, and an air of comfort prevailed which soon brought out the humanities, and put every one in a good humour.

There is nothing more extraordinary than the change of manners, customs, and dress, that has taken place within the last fifty years; it is as wonderful as the introduction of gas, railways, telegraphs, and chloroform. Up to the middle of the first half of the present century drunkenness was unblushingly carried on by the upper ten thousand, and noblemen and gentlemen reeled, in an awful state of intoxication, into the drawing-rooms, where the ladies were assembled. Now, within twenty minutes of the departure of the gentler sex, "John

informs the company that he's taken up the tea,"
and a drunken man is a *rara avis* among the higher
classes. But our grandfathers would have denounced any one as a wine-bibber who touched a
glass of the juice of the grape during the day, and
a man would have been scouted from society who
smoked a cigar or clay pipe in broad daylight. I
well recollect when the late Duke of Devonshire was
suffering from some affection of the throat, and a
mild Havannah was recommended him by the faculty
as an antidote against the biting cold easterly winds,
that he was universally censured by those who did
not know the reason of his walking along Piccadilly
with a cigar in his mouth. Then the dress—but I
have alluded to that already. So great was the art
of neckcloth tying, that a book with illustrations
of the various ways of accomplishing this necessary
appendage to costume, was published under the
title of "Neckclothiana." Few people who now
enjoy the luxury of a Byron tie and collar, would
fancy the misery of having the neck encased in
more than a yard of stiff-starched cambric, three or
four inches in depth, of the solidity of a soldier's
leather stock of the old school, and furnishing
a sort of first lesson in garotting. Nor would
the exquisite who now attends the best balls in
London in his polished bottines, loose pantaloons,

and Gibus hat, be reconciled to tight light coloured net " oh,-no,-we-never-mention-thems," the white silk stockings, a speck on which when descending from the carriage was fatal to the evening's amusement, the white waistcoat, frilled shirt, and cocked hat of other days. I well remember during the riots in London, caused by the appearance of Queen Caroline, being quartered at the "Adam and Eve," Kensington, and the effect produced on the minds of the drivers of the market-carts, the fruit women, labourers, and mechanics as I walked home from Almack's or some other ball, in this conspicuous attire, about four or five o'clock on a fine morning in June or July. Once when I was just passing the door of a private lunatic asylum then and still in existence on the London side of Kensington, I was taken for one of its inmates who had made his escape, and but for the interference of a guardian of the night who happened to recognise me, I should probably have been politely requested to enter.

But to return to Webster's dinner. No sooner had the faultless claret gone its round, than our host led up to topics which he thought would interest his distinguished guest, and repeated some of the clever sayings attributed to him. The Prince appeared to be delighted at the homage paid to his talent, and kept up a brilliant conversation, full of sparkling gems, which, however, would be deprived of half their splendour without the "setting." One original witticism I remember which caused a hearty laugh. The subject turned upon the large families English ladies have, and I mentioned that I was one of fourteen; another of the party said that, much to the horror of his father, he was the thirteenth born. "Horror!" responded Talleyrand, "had the father complained to me I should have said, '*Ah! je reponds qu'a présent vous devez être à votre aise (à vos treize).*'" From all I saw of Talleyrand, I should say his witticisms were of a much higher order than those of ordinary punsters. Puns or not, there was always some meaning in them, while many of the best jokes we hear from other men are a mere verbal jingle.

What can be more pungent than Talleyrand's answer to an indiscreet querist, who asked him, "*Eh, bien! M. le Prince, que s'est-il passé aujour-d'hui au conseil?*" "*Il s'est passé quatre heures, monsieur.*"

Another time when some one remarked to the Prince the audacity of a thief who, after robbing a haberdasher's shop, wore a splendid neckcloth which formed part of the spoil; "*Parbleu,*" replied Talley-rand, "*ne voyez-vous pas que c'était pour mieux cacher son coup.*"

Again, how perfect is his answer to Madame de Staël, who asked if she and her rival Madame de Fl—— fell into the river, which he would first attempt to save. "*Ma foi, Madame*," he replied, "*vous m'avez l'air de savoir mieux nager*." He was equally ready at repartee in his boyish days. Two young friends walking arm-and-arm with him were attempting to chaff him, and after enduring their attempt a little time, he said, "*Je vois bien que vous voulez vous moquer de moi, et je vais vous donner une idée juste de mon caractère. Je ne suis pas précisement un sot, ni absolument un fat; je suis entre les deux.*"

One of the severest characters given of Talleyrand was from the pen of George Sand, in the *Revue des Deux Mondes*. It is given in the form of a dialogue between two friends, supposed to be walking near the Château de Valençay, and the person of the Prince is described in the following savage terms :—

"Cette lèvre convexe et serrée, comme celle d'un chat, unie à une lèvre large et tombante, comme celle d'un satyre—mélange de dissimulation et de lasciveté; ces linéamens mous et arrondis, indices de la souplesse du caractère; ce pli dédaigneux sur un front prononcé; ce nez arrogant, avec ce regard de reptile; tant de contrastes sur une physionomie

humaine révélant un homme né pour les grands
vices et les petites actions."

The writer then proceeds to picture a day at the
Château :—

"Demande par quel dévouement, par quelles
bonnes actions sa journée est occupée ; ses gens te
diront qu'il se lève à onze heures, et qu'il passe
quatre heures à sa toilette, temps perdu à essayer
sans doute de rendre quelque apparence de vie à
cette face de marbre, que la dissimulation et
l'absence d'âme ont pétrifiée bien plus encore que
la vieillesse.

"A trois heures, te dira-t-on, le Prince monte en
voiture, seul, avec son médecin, et va se promener
dans les allées solitaires de sa garenne immense.

"A cinq heures, on lui sert le plus succulent et
le plus savant dîner qui se fasse en France.

"Après ce festin, dont chaque service est solem-
nellement annoncé par les fanfares de ses chasseurs,
le Prince accorde quelques petits instans à sa famille,
à sa petite cour.

"A l'entrée de la nuit, le Prince remonte en
voiture avec son médecin, et fait une seconde
promenade.

"Le voici qui rentre, et sa fenêtre s'illumine
là-bas, dans cet appartement reculé, gardé par ses
laquais en son absence avec une affectation de

ymstère si solemnelle et si ridicule. Maintenant il va travailler jusqu'à cinq heures du matin. Travailler! . . .

"Nature entière fais toi muette et immobile comme la pierre du sépulcre! le génie de l'homme s'éveille, le plus habile et le plus important des Princes de la terre va se courber sur une table, à la lueur d'une lampe, et du fond de son cabinet il va remuer le monde avec le froncement de son sourcil."

As a contrast to the fearful severity with which the French writer denounces the "voluptuous hypocrite," we will quote an English character of the Prince which appeared in the columns of the *Morning Post.*

"Talleyrand," says the writer, "was born lame, and his limbs are fastened to his trunk by an iron apparatus, on which he strikes ever and anon his gigantic cane, to the great dismay of those who see him for the first time—an awe not diminished by the look of his piercing grey eyes, peering through his shaggy eyebrows, his unearthly face marked with deep stains, covered partly by his shock of extraordinary hair, partly by his enormous muslin cravat, which supports a large protruding lip drawn over his upper lip, with a cynical expression no painting could render; add to this apparatus of terror, his dead silence, broken occasionally by the most sepulchral guttural monosyllables. Talleyrand's pulse, which rolls a stream of enormous volume, intermits and pauses at every sixth beat. This he constantly points out triumphantly as a rest of nature, giving him at once a superiority over other men. Thus, he says, all the missing pulsations are added to the sum total of those of his whole life, and his longevity and strength appear to support this extraordinary theory. He likewise asserts that it is this which enables him to do without sleep. 'Nature,' says he, 'sleeps and recruits herself at every intermission of my pulse;' and, indeed, you see him time after time rise at three o'clock in the morning from the whist table, then return home and often wake up one of his secretaries to keep him company, or to talk of business.

"At four he will go to bed, sitting nearly bolt upright in his bed, with innumerable night-caps on his head to keep it warm, as he said, and feed his intellect with blood; but, in fact, to prevent his injuring the seat of knowledge if he tumbles on the ground; and he sits upright from his tendency to apoplexy, which would no doubt seize him if perfectly recumbent.

"We may remember the newspapers stating he was found a few years ago, his head having dropped from his pillow, so drowned in blood that no feature was to be seen. Although he goes to bed so late, at six or seven at latest he wakes and sends for his attendants. He constantly refers to the period when he was Minister of Foreign Affairs, and when this power to live without sleep enabled him to go out and seek information, as well as pleasure, in society, till twelve or one o'clock. At that hour he returned to his office, read over all the letters that had arrived in the day, put marginal indications of the answers to be given, and then on waking again at six, read over all the letters written in consequence of his orders. . . . . . All we shall add further is that Talleyrand is not a man of imagination nor of invention. He never could make an extempore speech in his life. His forte is his impassibility and his cool and perfect judgment. He is very silent, and is always stimulating those who approach him to talk on the important subjects of the day. He will listen for hours to the opinions of men of mediocrity; and out of all he hears makes up those webs in which other politicians get involved like giddy flies. To this power of judgment Talleyrand adds that without which neither statesmen nor generals can ever succeed, namely, exceedingly good luck."

Talleyrand died in Paris on the 17th day of May, 1838, at the age of 84, and was buried at the

Church of the Assumption, where his body was to
remain until the vault at Valençay was finished to
receive it. The asperities that had been levelled
against him when alive, were continued after his
death, and many of the French newspapers in
describing his funeral, launched forth into the most
bitter invectives against a man who was declared to
have "served, mocked, deceived, and betrayed all
governments." Strange that such a man should
have been decorated with the highest worldly
honours; but, as a French writer remarks, "In
France success absolves from every crime, from
every infamy, and confers every virtue, and every
species of distinction."

The Prince was invested with the following
orders :—Knight of the Holy Ghost, Grand Cross
of the Legion of Honour, Knight of the Golden
Fleece, Grand Cross of St. Stephen of Hungary,
the Elephant of Denmark, Charles III. of Spain, the
Soter of Greece, the Sun of Persia, the Conception
of Portugal, the Black Eagle of Prussia, St. Andrew
of Russia, the Crown of Saxony, and St. Joseph of
Tuscany.

I will conclude this chapter with an anecdote
of a noble author whose political life has been more
fruitful than his literary life, and who, though a
staunch and true reformer, was not a first-rate

shot. One day, when enjoying a day's sport with a friend in the country, and when pheasants and hares were numerous, the noble lord made no addition to the bag. On taking leave and feeing the gamekeeper, he remarked, "I suppose I'm about the worst shot you ever saw." "Not at all, my Lord," responded the man, "I've seen many a worse; you misses them all so cleanly, my Lord."

CHAPTER XVI.

CHAPTER XVI.

AMONG those who have honoured me with their friendship, I know no one for whom I entertained a more profound respect and deep regard than the late James Goding. He was a man of excellent sound sense, was devoted to the arts and sciences, and was a perfect judge of music and painting. His hospitality was proverbial; and many a delightful dinner have I enjoyed with Lady Jane and himself in Belgrave Square. The house was full of the finest specimens of Harlow, Watteau, Schneider, Hondekooter, and other masters; and his collection of old plate, glass, and china was second to none. Goding had the organ of "decoration" strongly developed, and could select Venetian frames, carved work, quaint devices, ancient church fittings, old marqueterie, and other valuable articles, from some obscure shop, and with his wand of Aladdin convert them into the most beautiful objects of

decorative furniture. His great passion was for
violins and violoncellos, and he spared no expense
in purchasing the finest instruments that could be
procured. With pride would he show the far-
famed Cremona upon which Paganini had won his
English laurels; from that he would turn to the
splendid base which had often been heard at
the popular concerts of ancient music, held in the
Hanover Square Rooms. Goding was devoted to
music; and as among his wife's relatives many
were first-rate amateur vocal and instrumental
performers, no evening passed at his house without
a concert, in which he himself, as a violinist, took
part. Nor were his *réunions* confined to amateurs;
for he would ever assist rising talent, and many
friendless artists had cause to trace their after success to the patronage Mr. Goding extended to them
when unknown to fame, and struggling to obtain
a hearing. Few men worked harder to gain an
honourable independence than did Mr. Goding.
Every morning he was to be found at his desk at
the Lion brewery in Lambeth, attending to the
business of that important and lucrative concern.
If a friend dropped in (and during the year legions
of friends did drop in), he was invited to a frugal
but excellent lunch, consisting of the best bread,
the finest cheese, the nicest butter, and a perfect

glass of unadulterated ale or porter. After the
duties of the day were over, Goding would visit
all the brokers' shops in the New Cut, in the hopes
of finding some old furniture, then proceed to St.
Martin's Lane, to look out for a violin; and from
. thence to Wardour Street, for objects of *vertu*.
Had Mr. Goding been brought forward as a candidate for parliamentary honours, and been successful, he would have proved himself a most
valuable member of the House of Commons. Indeed, so extensive was his knowledge upon many
political subjects, especially upon the malt tax, that
he received the thanks of the late Sir Robert Peel
for some able letters he addressed him upon that
vexed question. Goding was extremely proud of
the eulogium bestowed upon him by the premier,
and was justified in quoting, with a slight altera-
tion, "Approbation from Sir Hubert Stanley is
praise indeed." There was another event which
gratified Goding not a little, and that was, the
employment of his splendid team of dray horses
to convey the equestrian statue of the " Iron
Duke" from the factory at Paddington to Piccadilly. Goding's death was a severe blow to his
relatives, friends, and acquaintances, and the poor
at large, as in him they had ever found a kind

husband, a hospitable friend, and a most liberal benefactor.

Few men have earned themselves a greater reputation for their labours in the cause of the poor than a well-known peer, of whom the following story is told.

On the occasion referred to, his lordship was visiting a ragged school, near which was a room devoted to the instruction of young girls. After inspecting the boys' department, he went to the other, and at the request of the matron commenced asking a variety of questions of a scriptural nature, to which he received very satisfactory answers. Just as the noble lord was about to take his leave, he addressed a girl somewhat older than the rest, and among other things inquired, "Who made your vile body?" "Please, my Lord," responded the unsophisticated girl, "Betsy Jones made my body, but I made the skirt myself."

A similar reply is recorded of another charity scholar, who was under examination in the Psalms, "What is the pestilence that walketh by darkness?" "Please, sir, bugs."

Perhaps the most efficacious remedy against this plague, failing ordinary soap and water, which is generally inimical to beasts of that species, would be the water of Winifred's well, which is said to

possess such miraculous properties. It was on a
tour in Wales, that I paid a visit to this singular
spring. Leaving Chester early, I breakfasted at
Holywell, called by the Welsh "Treffynnon," or
the "Town of the Well." The spring issues from
a rock, and has been celebrated for many ages for
the miraculous efficacy traditionally related to have
been imparted to its waters by St. Winifred, to
whose memory the fountain is dedicated. The well
is covered by a small Gothic building erected by
Henry VII.'s mother. Eighty-four hogsheads of
water are thrown up every minute, so that a tee-
totaller might revel there. The legendary story of
its origin is curious. Winifred, who is said to have
lived in the early part of the seventh century, was
a beautiful and devout virgin, the daughter of
Thewith, a nobleman of these parts, and niece to
St. Benno, who having obtained leave from her
father to found a church upon his possessions here,
took her under his care, in order to assist her in
her religious exercises. Cradorus, the son of King
Alen, admired the beauty of her person, and resolved an attempt upon her virtue. It is said that
he made known to her his passion on a Sunday
morning, after her parents were gone to church.
She made an excuse to escape from the room, and
immediately ran towards the church. He overtook

her, says the tradition, on the descent of the hill, and enraged at his disappointment drew his sword, and struck off her head. The head rolled down the hill to the altar, at which the congregation were kneeling, and stopping there, a clear and rapid fountain immediately gushed up. St. Benno snatched up the head, and joined it to the body, when, to the surprise of all present, they immediately re-united, leaving only the mark of a white line encircling the neck. Cradorus dropped down upon the spot, where he had committed this atrocious act, and the earth swallowed him. Winifred is reported to have survived her decapitation fifteen years, and to have died Abbess of Gwytherin in Denbighshire.

After leaving Holywell I reached Mostyn Hall, which was erected in the time of Henry VI. The old mansion has a venerable appearance; the park is beautifully broken, and slopes finely to the sea, facing the north-east, where the trees grow close to the water-edge. During the time that Henry, Earl of Richmond, was secretly planning the overthrow of the House of York, he passed concealed from place to place, in order to form an interest among the Welsh, who favoured the cause on account of their respect for his grandfather, Owen Tudor, their countryman. While he was at Mostyn

Hall, a party attached to Richard III. arrived there
to apprehend him. He was then about to dine,
but had just time to leap out of a back window,
and make his escape through a hole which to this
day is called the "King's Window." Richard ap
Howell, then Lord of Mostyn, joined Henry at the
battle of Bosworth, and after the victory received
from the king, in token of gratitude for his preservation, the belt and sword he wore on that day.
Shortly after my visit to Mostyn Hall, I saw an
advertisement in the *Times*, announcing that a
piece of plate was about to be presented to the
popular owner of it, and calling upon artists to
furnish an appropriate subject for it. It occurred
to me that the scene at Bosworth Field, at the
moment when the gallant Henry VII. was presenting the trusty weapon that had been by his side
during the battle to Richard ap Howell, would be
very suitable. I at once sketched out a plan,
pointing out the figures of the different personages
I wished to be introduced: 1. The Lord of Mostyn
on his knees; 2. The king presenting the sword;
3. Broken lances and swords, tattered banners;
4. Wounded horse, and dead trooper.

With this plan, I wrote a few anonymous lines
to the committee, suggesting the idea, and great
was my delight when I found my suggestion

adopted.   A letter informed me of it, and requested
me to give the names of any silversmiths I might
wish to recommend for executing the testimonial.
My reply was " Garrard, or Storr and Mortimer.   I
give their names as they come in the alphabet, for
both are equally good."   The lot fell to the latter,
who, thanks to the talent of the artist they employed,
fully, nay more than fully, carried out my idea,
and my friend Lloyd Mostyn received a testimonial
worthy of his public services and private worth.

One of my most agreeable reminiscences of a
country house was a visit I paid to the late Sir
William Massey Stanley at Hooton Hall, Cheshire,
now the property of Richard Naylor, Esq.   Few
that knew Sir William as "a man about town,"
would have believed what a metamorphosis came
over him, not out of the sound of Bow bells, but
out of the range of White's bow window.   From
a good-humoured, indolent man of fashion, thinking of nothing but the *haute volée*, or *volaille*, as
I once heard it pronounced, he became a practical
country gentleman, entirely conversant with the
management of his estate, park, garden, farm,
stables, and mansion.   The result was, that Hooton
was second to no other ancestral home of England.
The establishment, both in house and stables, was
excellent, the living faultless.   There was no want

of amusement for the guests; horses and carriages were at their service, and they were allowed that delightful boon of doing what they liked best. Dinner was punctually at seven o'clock; and, to keep up a time-honoured custom, supper was served at eleven o'clock, the interim being devoted to cards or billiards. We seldom sat down to dinner under fourteen, as three or four neighbours were generally invited.

Sir William Massey Stanley was a most gentlemanlike, liberal, and warm-hearted friend, and no man was more liked and respected both in Cheshire and Leicestershire. For some years he and his brother, Rowland Errington, kept the Quorn hounds, and I had the good fortune to pay them a week's visit at Melton. They lived in a remarkably good and tolerably large house, but not spacious enough to accommodate all their guests; so they rented another, which furnished sleeping apartments, with a sitting-room common to all, for their friends. At the time I refer to, Francatelli was the *chef de cuisine*, and a better one, if perhaps we may except the inimitable Ude, never existed. It was here that I first saw a plan, which has since been very commonly adopted (would it were universally!)—a bill of fare at breakfast. Instead of having the tea, coffee, and all the *gourmet* accessories introduced at once, and thereby depriving them of that heat which is so essentially necessary, a list was made out of certain matutinal delicacies which were ready in the kitchen to be sent up at a few moments' notice. Small tables were arranged, coffee-room fashion, so as to enable any one who came early or late, to sit down at once and enjoy a good hot breakfast in comfort. The same plan was carried on at Woburn Abbey under the late Duke and Duchess of Bedford; and there, in a room called the Canaletti room, from its walls being decorated with the choicest pictures of this master, groups of two, four, or more, might be seen forming a snug coterie.

To return to Melton: the dinners and wines were first rate, not alone at the Stanley's, but at the Old Club, and Lord Wilton's, though, as "comparisons are odious," I will refrain from awarding the palm to either. Suffice it that the three establishments were perfect.

Although there was no gambling at Melton during the time I refer to, the stakes at whist were high; but there is a great distinction between gambling at games of chance, such as hazard, *rouge et noir*, and *roulette*, and playing at the scientific game of whist. In the former, thousands may be lost at one sitting; in the latter, when equal players contend against one another for any length of time, the result is not very ruinous to either party. One evening, after an excellent run, in which I was admirably mounted by Errington, and one of Francatelli's most successful dinners, whist was proposed ; and, unfortunately, Lord Waterford, who was to have made one, had not arrived. We were seven at dinner, and as dummy was not patronised, it was impossible to make up two rubbers without my joining. When urged to do so, I pleaded my inability to compete with such first-rate players, adding, that the stakes, five-pound points, and twenty-five on the rubber, were far beyond my means. " If you only promise to return suit and not revoke," said Sir William, " I'll stand the whole or any part of the stakes you like." " Let's cut for partners," exclaimed Rowland Errington, " we'll all stand an equal risk." This was agreed to, and with a tremulous feeling I drew a card, hoping that I should fall to the lot of one of the " Stanley brothers ;" but such was not the case. My partner was Sir Francis Goodricke, than whom a better sportsman never existed. He has now for many years given up the sports of the field, and in a more useful career has attended to the " one thing needful," proving, by his example and influence, a great blessing to those around him,

more especially the humbler classes. The deal fell
to my lot, and again I felt nervous. "Let me
make one stipulation," said I to my partner,
"which is, that whatever errors I commit, you will
not notice them; it will only flurry me, and do no
good." "Agreed," responded Sir Francis. Happily for me I had such a splendid hand that nothing
but a revoke could have made me lose. We scored
a treble. Then began the betting on the odd trick
and the rubber, and again I quailed; another hand
nearly as good was dealt me, and, to my horror, a
fatal mistake lost me two tricks. Upon expressing
my regret, my partner good-humouredly said,
"Never mind, we score two by honours." More
betting ensued, and the third hand decided the
rubber, and put me out of my misery by our gaining the odd trick. "A treble, a double, the rubber, and bet, seventy pounds!" said Sir Francis,
as he took out his pocket-book and entered the
amount. "Here's your sovereign that you stood
upon the game," he continued, "and now for
another." I looked awe-struck, for I knew full
well how I should fare with a bad or ordinary
hand. At that moment Lord Waterford was announced, and much to my delight, and I have no
doubt to that of Sir Francis Goodricke, his lordship took my place, for another rubber or two

would probably have been attended with what is
called by tradesmen "an alarming sacrifice."

As the earlier part of my life was passed abroad,
and in country quarters in England, where my
finances would not allow me to indulge in a good
stud of hunters, I had little experience in the field,
and all I could expect to do was to follow some
good man at a respectable distance, and look more
to him than to the hounds. Upon one occasion I
had the good fortune to go in the wake of Lord
Wilton, the very Crichton of manly sports, and
getting a good start, I saw for the only time in
Leicestershire, the find and the finish. Even upon
other days, when I was thrown out, and contented
myself with keeping in the line of the second horses,
there was much to delight me, both by the cover
side, and in the town of Melton. It was a glorious
sight to see the well-mounted huntsman, whippers-
in, and the pick of English Nimrods, to look at the
well-trained pack, to listen to the cheery horn, the
melodious tone of "gone away!" while the acme
of gratification was to hear the "who-whoop," or
coronach, over the fallen foe. In the town it was
a most agreeable off-hunting morning's occupation
to walk through the respective stables and reflect
on the intrinsic value of each animal, and the enormous sums expended upon horseflesh.

Although an old friend of mine, Frederic Tolfrey, who took part with me in our private theatricals at Quebec, and another highly-valued acquaintance, Henry Corbet, in his "Tales and Traits of Sporting Life," have paid me most flattering compliments upon my race riding, I never felt myself to be either a first-rate horseman, or a good man across country. The author of "The Sportsman in Canada" called me a second James Robinson; but all I lay claim to is having been patient, and a tolerable judge of pace. As on the plains of Abraham I always rode my father's horses, which were superior to the rest, I naturally got more praise than I deserved; and once having established myself as a popular jockey, I was "put up" upon all the best horses. When upon my return to England, at Goodwood, Stapleton Park, and Lambton, I found myself in company with the late Delmè Radcliffe, Kent, Honourable Augustus Berkeley, John White, and other first-rate performers, I felt my inferiority. I was always fond of hunting, but it was a recreation I could not always afford to indulge in, except when mounted by friends. Through the kindness of Ball Hughes and George Payne I have hunted in Northamptonshire; I have just recorded my experiences with Sir William Massey Stanley and his brother at Melton; the late Sir David Baird

mounted me during one winter in Scotland, and the
present Earl Bathurst did the same upon one occasion in Austria. The late Sir John Gerard mounted
me in Lancashire, Sir Francis Goodricke gave me
the pick of his stable one day in Warwickshire, the
late Lord Fitzhardinge constantly mounted me in
the Cheltenham and Berkeley counties, Sir Philip
Egerton lent me some first-rate " copers " in
Cheshire, a worthy friend and constituent of mine,
when I represented King's Lynn in Norfolk, gave
me a day with the harriers, and at Leamington,
when I hunted two winters *à mes frais*, I got many
an extra day with the Pytchley, through the kindness of that neatest of all riders, Saunderson.

Upon two occasions I proved that what I wanted
in judgment I made up in courage, and upon both I
placed the lives of two very valuable hunters in
jeopardy. The first event came off at Vienna, when
a grand hunt was got up by Sir Charles Stuart, afterwards Marquis of Londonderry, to amuse the crowned
heads and others then assembled at the Congress.
The fox, a bagman, was turned out within a few
miles of the Imperial city, and after a scurry of
some fifteen or twenty minutes, crossed the Danube.
Being a light weight, and admirably mounted, I got
a good start and kept it; one or two of my own
countrymen, among them the present Marquis of

Anglesey, then a dashing cornet in the 7th Hussars, and a few noble Hungarians, were also in the first flight, but they were too discreet ever to allow such an idea to enter their heads as charging the swollen and fast-flowing river. Headstrong, as I then was, and elated with the thought of setting the field, I dashed into it, and providentially landed in safety on the opposite bank, many yards below the spot to which I tried to pilot my horse. Great was my horror to find my good-natured cousin (then Lord Apsley) looking aghast at the risk I had run of depriving him of a valuable animal, and a fool-hardy relative. Of course a few flatterers congratulated me on my prowess, while one whose good opinion I valued more than all others—I allude to the late Duke of Wellington, to whom I was an *attaché*—pointed out the folly I had committed.

Many years afterwards I was staying at Oulton, the hospitable seat of Sir Philip Egerton, who mounted me on a remarkably clever hunter called Swing. Galloping along an open field in company with the Master of the Hounds, Sir Harry Mainwaring, the hounds running at a tremendous pace, I observed many of the field bearing away to the left. "Is there anything impracticable?" I inquired. "Nothing to stop you," responded the baronet; "go straight a-head, the fox is making for that spinny. I must

nurse my horse a little." After this intimation
away I went, heedless of what Sir Harry was doing,
and found myself alone in my glory. For a time
all went smooth, when my attention was attracted
to the mast of a barge, not a hundred yards off.
"A canal," said I inwardly, "and Sir Harry has
done me." There was nothing left me but to give
up the run or charge the water, and there was no
craft for me to jump in and out of, as Tom Smith,
le roi des chasseurs, once did. So clapping spurs into
Swing, I went at the canal, lighting in the
centre. Then came the plunge, the struggle, the
shivering feel that accompanies such ducking,
the swim, and the scramble out. Fortunately I
landed in safety, looking more like a half-drowned
rat than an humble follower of Nimrod. Sir
Philip Egerton and many of his friends were hor-
rified at the state poor Swing was in, and the
matter was not improved by a remark that no one
would have insured my steed and myself for any
consideration, as, except at the place where my
horse had accidentally gained his footing, it would
have been next to impossible to have made a landing. "What became of the fox?" I inquired,
after stammering out a hundred apologies to my
kind host. "Oh, we killed it in that spinny, and
thanks to the bridge not five hundred yards to your

left, were all in at the death." To my great satisfaction Swing was not the worse for his hydropathic
treatment, and I escaped with a trifling cold.

I recollect one other instance in which I ran the
risk of being drowned. Hunting with the old
Warwickshire previously kept by that first-rate
sportsman Thornhill, Augustus Berkeley and myself
found ourselves one day alone with the hounds, the
waters were out, and the huntsman and field wisely
preferred going a little out of the way to secure
terra firma. There was a bridge over the river,
but the gate had been so dammed up that to open
or leap it was impossible. "We must try lower
down," said the captain, "follow me." We got on
the meadows, which were so covered with water
that the course of the river was not visible. Yard
by yard we crept on, cautiously feeling our way, until
all of a sudden we both found ourselves in deep
water, and how we ever got out I know not. No
sooner had we gained the dry land than we found a
lady whom I had mounted on a favourite Arabian
horse of mine, anxiously awaiting to see the result
of our aquatic expedition. "The hounds are
making for yon wood," she said. "Amulet [as
my steed was called] has thrown a shoe, but I
insisted that my husband should not remain with
me." "What's that?" exclaimed Augustus, as his

ready ear caught the well-known sound, "they are running into him, come along." Away we went across a ploughed field, and at a distance of a few yards from the wood we found the fox caught in a steel trap, the leading hounds close upon him. In less time than I can describe it, Augustus Berkeley was off his horse, the animal was extricated from the iron jaws of the trap, and transferred to those of the pack, "who-whoop" was shouted by the captain, the brush presented to the fair huntress, and the steel trap thrown into a ditch. After a time the huntsman and some of the field came up, and as we had agreed to keep our counsel, not a word was said as to the trap; although we afterwards communicated the circumstance to the master of the hounds, with a view of checking a system that might have proved baneful to hound as well as fox. Augustus, myself, and the fair equestrian were complimented upon being the chosen few in at the death. The way the "Flying Squirrel" carried me during the early part of the day, was so satisfactory, that I got a handsome bid for him, and as it was the last day of the season I accepted it.

These records of my own hunting adventures lead me to speak of one who was as distinguished in the field as he was valued in all other walks of life, one to whom I am indebted for much sport and for more kindness.   I allude to the late Mr. Morrell, of Headington Hill.

Mr. Morrell was born in 1810, and like a worthy scion of a most worthy sire, he inherited a strong love for field-sports.   His father hunted the Headington harriers from 1820 to 1832.   This pack originally consisted of fourteen couple of the old Southern breed, but when "Jem Morrell," as he was familiarly called by his intimate friends, became master, he kept it up by drafts from Mr. Drake's, the Heythrop, and the Blackmore Vale, and raised the pack to twenty-five couple, all level to a nicety, twenty-one inches high, and very fast.   So famed were the Headington harriers that Jem Hills, the huntsman, no mean authority, said, if he had them for one week, he would kill any fox in England. When Mr. Morrell became an M. F. (master of fox-hounds) the harriers were sold to Mr. Locke, of Ashton Gifford, in Wiltshire, who kept them for two seasons, and then passed them on to Sir John Cam Hobhouse, afterwards Lord Broughton. To return to the Squire.   He was educated at Eton, and there fostered that love for every manly pursuit, which characterised him to his latest day.   As a practical and theoretical follower of the "noble science," as a good shot, and as a thorough and liberal supporter of the sports of "Merrie England," the late owner of Headington Hill was second to none.

I know not what studies Mr. Morrell took most delight in when an Eton boy, but I should rather fancy from his tastes in maturer life, that he must have selected those passages from the classic authors which treat of the chase; and that among old English writers, all who eulogise that pursuit must have been his favourites. I can readily believe that he preferred Somerville to Livy, Beckford to Euripides; and unquestionably the breeding, feeding, and exercising of his hounds were such as to place them on the same, if not upon a higher footing than those of Sparta. They were quite up to their work, so forcibly described by the Bard of Mantua, and could

> " Urge the bold chase, and joining in full cry,
> O'er hills and dales, thro' thickest woodlands fly."

I am far from meaning to convey that Morrell did not go through the usual routine of a public school education with credit to himself, or that he was at all deficient in his scholastic duties; but all his leisure hours were devoted to sport. He was of a kind and humane disposition; and no one felt more acutely the unfortunate death of a schoolfellow, a younger brother of the present Earl of Shaftesbury, who was accidentally killed in a pugilistic encounter at Eton. Morrell conveyed the unfortunate sufferer from the shooting fields to his dame's.

I pass over a few years, and bring my readers to that period when Mr. Morrell first became a master of foxhounds, which was in 1848, when, by the unanimous voice of a large meeting of influential gentlemen, he was called upon to hunt the old Berkshire country. No sooner had he been installed as master than he addressed a circular letter to the owners of covers, informing them of his having succeeded Mr. Morland, expressing a hope that no objection would be made to their covers being drawn as heretofore, and stating that his desire would be uniformly to cultivate a good understanding with those noblemen and gentlemen whose property was comprised within the limits of the hunt. Before issuing this address, Mr. Morrell had retained the services of John Jones as huntsman; William Boorer as first, and James Stacey as second, whip. Of the antecedents of these respected servants it will suffice to say that Jones came from Lord Southampton to Mr. Morland. He was a light weight, an excellent horseman, always with his hounds, quick at his work, made his casts boldly, and persevered as long as there was the slightest chance of getting up his fox. Added to this, he was a first-rate kennel-man—no small recommenda-

tion in a huntsman. William Boorer came from
Mr. Morland, having previously lived with Mr.
Thwayts, in South Berks. He was a good servant;
and many a fox owes his death to old Will's thrill-
ing tally. James Stacey came from the Vale of
White Horse. He formerly whipped in to the
late Earl Fitzhardinge's hounds. He was, and we
are happy to say is still, an out-and-out horseman,
an excellent whipper-in, in every sense of the
word, and sails over a country like a workman.
Stacey now hunts the Linlithgow and Stirlingshire
hounds.

Mr. Morrell, who was an excellent judge of
horseflesh, next proceeded to purchase horses for
himself and his men, and was eminently successful,
as was proved by the prowess of Little Wonder,
Memnon, Magnum Bonum, England's Glory, Sir
Warwick, Marlborough, Wild Rose, Minerva, Mammon, Milesias, Buckland, Mischief, Marquis, and
others.

The unfriendly disposition which many gentlemen of landed property, in various parts of the
kingdom, have too often shown to the preservation
of foxes, not alone to the great mortification of
sportsmen, but to others whose liberal minds have
a strong conviction of the general benefits which
accrue where foxhounds are established, was un-

known in the old Berkshire country, where every
one seemed to put his shoulder to the wheel, to do
as much as he could to promote "the chase, the
sport of British kings," as Pope describes it. The
good-fellowship and friendly feeling evinced for the
worthy and liberal master of the hounds was proved
by the wonderful show of foxes during the whole
period that Mr. Morrell hunted the O. B. H.;
gentry, landowners, and farmers all uniting to preserve the wily animal, and vying with each other
as to the number of cubs their broad acres could
produce.

I have already alluded to Mr. Morrell as a master
of harriers; and if I wished to prove that I was
not influenced by any private feeling towards the
departed, I could transcribe the highest possible
panegyrics from the best written sporting works of
the day. Such quotations, however, would swell
my work too much, and I will content myself with
saying that the run from Jackson's Oak was never
surpassed—"the hounds running into a splendid
hare after a very fast run of one hour; distance
nearly eleven miles, almost straight." The writer
adds—"No one was better placed than Mr. Morrell
throughout the run." After hunting the country
for ten years, Mr. Morrell retired, and a sale of
hounds and horses took place at Tubney Kennel.

The amount realised for the former was 2,600
guineas, averaging £32 12s. 3d. per couple; the
horses averaged £119 15s. 8d.; those bought in
were afterwards disposed of for 200 guineas more
than the reserve price. The whole sale amounted
to £6,365 2s. Mr. Morrell bought in twenty-five
couple of hounds, which he lent, and afterwards
gave, to the Vale of White Horse. Whether this
act of princely munificence, amounting (according
to the above average) to £819 12s., was duly appreciated, we will not pause to inquire. It assuredly
was not approved of by the members of the O. B. H.

As a master of foxhounds, few could equal Mr.
Morrell; his hounds were beyond the reach of criticism, and the management, both in the field and in
the kennel, was as near perfection as possible. In
addition to this, the worthy master's hospitality was
unbounded; and no sportsman ever came within
reach of the old Berkshire without being made
heartily welcome at Mr. Morrell's board. The
glories of Tubney are over, but they will live in
the remembrance of every true lover of the manly,
invigorating recreations of old England, and be
handed down to posterity as a bright epoch in the
most palmy days of fox-hunting. The testimonial
presented to Mr. Morrell, at Abingdon, by the old
Berkshire men, will prove a lasting memorial of the

respect which they entertained for him; and in
retiring from his mastership, there was but one
feeling that pervaded every class, from the earth-
stopper upwards, and that was regret at losing so
excellent a sportsman and so good a fellow. The
memorial consisted of a massive silver plateau, made
by Garrard, representing the death of a fox, with
an equestrian statue of Mr. Morrell, accompanied
by his huntsman, Clarke, dismounted, and surrounded by hounds. The following is inscribed
upon the plateau :—

"This group, commemorative of days in the old
Berkshire country, is presented to James Morrell,
Esq., by his friends and neighbours, in testimony of
his excellence as a sportsman, and of his great
liberality, urbanity, and kindness as master of the
O. B. H. from 1847 to 1857."

When Mr. Morrell ceased to sport the "pink,"
and to carry the cheering horn on his saddle bow,
he contrived to amuse himself and his friends with
his greyhounds and his gun.

Before concluding this part of the subject, I must
record a feat of the late owner of Headington
Hill which he performed on Little Wonder. This
animal, only fourteen hands high, carried his master
in the capacity of steward over the watercress
ditch at an Oxfordshire steeple-chase, which was

pronounced by Jem Mason to be a yawner, and
which only two contrived to get over.

In February, 1853, Mr. Morrell was appointed
high sheriff of the county; and in 1860 he gave a
grand banquet to Lieutenant-Colonel North, and
the officers and members of the Oxford City Rifle
Corps, which was attended by the Lords-Lieutenant
of Oxfordshire and Berkshire, the Bishop of Oxford,
the Vice-Chancellor, &c. In proposing Mr. Morrell's
health, the Duke of Marlborough said, "No one
thing, however, contributed more to the greatness
and prosperity of this country than its commercial
activity; and it was very gratifying to find men,
by steady, earnest application, amassing for themselves an independent fortune, and at the same time
attaining the highest position and respect. He
thought they would agree with him, that his
respected friend was one in whose person the justice
of these observations was exemplified. His commercial prosperity represented what an Englishman
might attain by uprightness and integrity of conduct; while his acts showed that in amassing wealth
which God had placed in his hands, he desired to
make his neighbours happy, and to promote every
'object of public usefulness, as a magistrate, a neighbour, and a citizen, and in aiding and abetting this
glorious volunteer movement, and bringing all in

one united feeling of good will and fellowship."
Upon the principle of the old English gentleman
immortalised in song, Mr. Morrell proved that in
feasting the rich "he ne'er forgot the poor;" for
having generously determined that the humbler as
well as the higher classes should participate in this
celebration, he had distributed at the Town Hall
3,000 pounds of mutton, 2,000 quartern loaves, and
2,000 quarts of beer, to 1,500 poor families residing
in Oxford, the total number of persons who thus
shared his bounty amounting to 5,556.

To show the disposition of Mr. Morrell to support
ancient feasts and festivals, it must be added that he
ever kept up the good old custom of celebrating harvest home, thus following in the steps of his honoured
sire.   The labourers upon his own estate, and upon
that of his neighbour, Farmer Fry, were all invited to
the annual gathering.   It was indeed a joyous sight
to witness the sons and daughters of labour lay by
their toil for a day, to indulge in harmless recreation.   Let us accompany them to a large tent which
had been erected for the occasion in the farmyard of
Blackbird Lees, where they did justice to the ample
fare provided by their liberal host.   The "luxuries
of the season" consisted of beef, mutton, veal, pork,
rabbit pies, and plum puddings; two excellent
barrels of beer were tapped, and were as much

enjoyed by the humble tillers of the land as claret cup and iced champagne are by the upper ten thousand. After the meal, pipes were lit and dancing commenced, a fiddler having been engaged for the occasion. The peasants, clad in their Sunday attire, led forth their rosy-cheeked partners, who skipped over the green sward, if not with the lightest of step, yet with the lightest of hearts. Listen to the laugh, the jest; watch the mirth and merriment of the younger folks as they trip it on the "light fantastic toe;" and mark the joyous yet more sedate looks of the matrons, and their "gude old men," as they gaze upon a scene where—

> " Each village lass is proud to wear
> Her newest gown and bonnet,
> While dames of threescore whisper near
> And moralise upon it."

How they danced! They never seemed to tire, old and young, light hearts and happy times :—

> " The dancing pair that simply sought renown
> By holding out to tire each other down."

It was a joyous scene, and will long be remembered, not alone by the recipients of Mr. Morrell's kindness, but by all who witnessed it. The stream of public feeling is evidently in favour of occasional freedom from toil. Rest from labour is a privilege that ought to be granted to every animated being;

and in all ages of the world, recreation has been the
resource of all, without reference to rank, sex, or
condition.   I would ask the canting lachrymose
ascetics, who unhappily exist in our day, and who
consider the enjoyment of the humbler classes a
crime, why the mind of the hardy son of the soil is
to know no respite, why the sturdy arm is never to
move except in toil, and why popular diversions
and manly exercises are to be enjoyed exclusively
by the higher orders ?   National advancement will
not be retarded by public sports duly regulated;
and England will rue the hour when harvest homes,
May-day, and Christmas revels are banished from
the land, where once they flourished, and where
legal provision was made for public pastimes.

Headington Hill, as Mr. Morrell's mansion is
called, is a mile and a half from Oxford, commanding a most beautiful view of this seat of learning,
and of the surrounding country.   A more lovely or
salubrious spot cannot well be imagined.   According
to local authority, the colleges in Oxford and other
public buildings have been principally erected with
stone dug in Headington quarry.   A field called
Court Close is said to be the site of one of the
palaces of King Ethelred, of which a gateway and
part of the walls were in existence until within the
last fifty years.   It was during his reign that the

Danes burnt the city, in retaliation for the general massacre of their countrymen, by order of that monarch. Headington Hill is a modern building, containing all that good taste and ample means can produce. The rooms are spacious and lofty, combining comfort with elegance, and so well regulated with regard to heat and cold, that during the most sultry day in July, or the bitterest wintry evening in December, the temperature is exactly what it should be. The hall, drawing-rooms, dining-rooms, and library, are splendidly decorated, and the billiard-room is as snug a room as ever was built; its walls are adorned with portraits of the old Berkshire hounds and celebrated hunters. How often have I listened to the departed host describing the brilliant runs, as he pointed out the horse that carried him through an arduous day, and the hounds that so nobly did their duty! It was a real pleasure to hear Mr. Morrell talk of hunting; his heart and soul were in it, and as he was ever a man of business, the diary, which he kept regularly, was full of practical information. In the dining-room, where hospitality reigned for months throughout the year, there is a fine picture, painted by Grant, of Mr. Morrell mounted on his favourite milk-white hunter, Memnon, with three of his first-rate hounds— Foreman, Rutland, and Musical. This picture is rendered ten times more valuable from the fact of its having been presented to the owner of Headington Hill by some friends in Oxfordshire and elsewhere. The dining-room reminds me of rather an amusing occurrence. During my visit there in 1863, the ladies complained a little of the awful time the gentlemen sat over their wine, and threatened us with the severest penalties if we did not join them earlier. I was appealed to as the person of the highest rank, and as we had some fair syrens staying in the house, who delighted all with their singing, I promised to exert my influence with our host, to devote more time to the muses, and less to Bacchus. In this I was ably seconded by the majority of males, albeit a few preferred "the flow of the regal purple stream" to the charm of melody. "What, limit me [for I had alluded to the advice of his medical adviser] to a glass of wine after dinner!" said Mr. Morrell. "That 'early-closing movement' won't do at Headington Hill; but as I am in the minority, I agree so far, that we will only drink one glass after nine o'clock." Upon the following morning I walked into Oxford with a view of purchasing the largest glass I could find, and at an old curiosity-shop in the High Street saw one of Brobdingnag dimensions, well suited to drink wine out of from the large tun

at Heidelberg. I purchased it, and extraordinary
as it may appear, Mr. Morrell's initial was engraved
upon it. Upon sending it home, I ascertained from
the butler that it held two bottles of champagne ;
I therefore requested him to have it placed upon
the table before his master, with a slip of paper
inscribed "Memorial in behalf of the early-closing
movement." Not a word was said until our host
was about to take his seat, when he espied the glass.
"Ah, that's right," he said; "something like a
glass ; fill it with champagne and hand it round as
the loving cup; we can, if any one wishes it, have
our last glass of claret in it after nine." Poor
Morrell, he enjoyed the joke heartily, and was
highly pleased with the donor.

The grounds, although not very extensive, are
beautifully laid out, with clumps and avenues of
fine forest trees, spreading their luxuriant branches
over the verdant sward. The lodges are elegant
and unobtrusive, with small patches of flower-
gardens, in which the rose, the honeysuckle, the
geranium, the verbena, and the mignonette delight
both eye and nose. The house commands one of
the finest views imaginable. From its windows the
venerable domes and steeples of the far-famed city
are clearly visible. Amongst the most prominent
objects that can be seen by the naked eye, or con-

jured up in that of the mind, may be mentioned
the tower, battlement, and pinnacle of Magdalen
College, and the shady retreat known as Addison's
Walk, in the College gardens; the imposing majesty
of the tower of St. Mary's; the elegant spire of All
Saints, exhibiting in some degree a mixture of the
Gothic and Grecian styles; the spacious and well-
proportioned dome of the Radcliffe Library, rising
to the height of eighty feet from the floor; the
ancient tower of St. Aldate's; the embattled tower
of St. Michael; the ancient Norman style of St.
Peter-le-Baily; the diversified and interesting gra-
dations of architectural science exhibited in the
Cathedral of Christ Church; the tower and ogee
dome containing the huge bell, "Great Tom of
Oxford;" the extensive front of University College,
blending ancient English with the Italian style;
the highly-enriched turret of Balliol; the mixed
architecture of the Tuscan, Doric, Ionic, and Corinthian orders of Merton; the battlements of New
College; the beautifully ornamented tower of All
Souls; the spacious quadrangle of Brazenose;
the picturesque college of Worcester, situated near
the Isis; the Bodleian Library; Clarendon Printing
House; Astronomical Observatory; and the elegant
arched gateway of the Botanic Garden, said to have
been designed by Inigo Jones.

At a distance the hills rise in graceful swellings, while beneath the river Cherwell rolls its ceaseless course. East, west, north, and south the gay landscape, the fruitful fields, the picturesque villas, the rural cottages, the ivy-clad churches, the luxuriant woods present themselves to the view; while far to the north a glimpse may be caught of Vanbrugh's noble edifice, the palace of Blenheim, and that stately column which perpetuates the memory of the signal victory obtained over the French and Bavarians by "the hero not only of this nation, but of this age," John Duke of Marlborough.

Nothing could exceed the liberality both of the late Mr. and Mrs. Morrell, the latter of whom established and supported a most excellent school for the children of the poor; and Mr. Morrell, amid his love of sport, never forgot one of the golden rules of life, that of lending a fostering hand to those in distress; of him, ay, and it equally applies to her, it may be truly said, in the words of one of the brightest luminaries of the Scottish Church:— "When he looks around him on the world, he is soothed with the pleasing remembrance of the good offices which he has done, or at least studied to do, to many who dwell there. How comfortable the reflection, that him no poor man can upbraid for having withheld his due; him no unfortunate man can reproach for having seen and despised his sorrows; but that on his head are descending the prayers of the needy and the aged, and that the hands of those whom his protection has supported, or his bounty has fed, are lifted up in secret to bless him." In less than ten months from the time I visited Headington Hill, poor Morrell and Mrs. Morrell were called to their long account. I attended the funeral of the former, and never was truer grief displayed by all classes than that with which they saw their friend and benefactor consigned to the earth.

CHAPTER XVII.

T 2

CHAPTER XVII.

QUESTIONS have often been asked as to the origin of some of the cant phrases of the day, and I believe no one has discovered the meaning of—"There you go with your eye out"—"What a shocking bad hat"—"Does your mother know you are out?"—"Go home and chain up ugly" — "Go it, my cripples, crutches is cheap"—"Who's your hatter?"—"Mind your pretty feet"—and other senseless exclamations. I can, however, throw a little light upon the subject, and can vouch for the paternity of one—"I'm not aware." One summer, when returning from Hampton Court races, on the box of a four-horse drag, with poor Charley Sheridan, who possessed a large portion of the talents of that truly able family, by my side, we overtook an elderly gentleman on the bridge, whose rotund appearance no amount of Bantingism could have reduced, and who hailed us to pull up. Our well-bred amateur coachman, Fitzroy Stanhope, obeyed the summons, and Sheridan, descending from his seat, asked the stranger his pleasure.

" I see you are full outside and in," was the reply; "you drive a little too fast, coachman, during these crowded days; who is the proprietor of your coach?"

" I am not aware," responded the descendant of the immortal Richard Brinsley.

" Not aware!" echoed the other, the blood mounting in his rubicund face, and giving us the idea that a fit of apoplexy would follow. " When does the next coach go by?" he continued, " I prefer a pair horse to your scampering four."

"I am not aware," again said Charley, with a most bland and winning smile.

"And your name, Sir, for I presume you are guard."

" I am not aware."

"Come along, my boy," said Fitzroy, "we shall be late," as Sheridan proceeded to resume his seat.

"Late!" exclaimed the obese gentleman, "why, what o'clock is it?"

"I am not aware," shouted Charley, as we drove off, at the rate of twelve miles an hour, towards London, leaving our "fat friend" in a great state of excitement. During our dinner, which took place that evening at Crockford's Club, the subject turned upon "cant words," and a small wager was made by Sheridan that he would get "I'm not aware" into as great a popularity as belonged to other sentences. The expiration of the Goodwood race week, which was shortly to follow, was the time allowed for the general introduction of the phrase.

"Of course you'll assist me," said Charley, addressing me.

"You may depend upon my services," I responded, and fully did I act up to my promise. Upon reaching Goodwood House, where fifty questions were put to me, as honorary secretary of the racing club, I replied "I am not aware," until, at last, others caught up the words, and the phrase became general. After dinner, on the second day, I replied to General Peel, who asked me what time the races began, in the cant phrase; but he retorted upon me, for on my asking the name of one of his young horses, he answered, "I am not aware."

"So let it be," said I, "an excellent name," and from that moment the son of Tranby was called "I am not aware."

With such notoriety the phrase soon became universal, and Sheridan won his wager. The loser, reversing the usual custom upon such occasions, gave the Hampton Court "drag" party an "I am not aware" dinner at the Castle Hotel, Richmond, where the utmost fun and merriment prevailed. Fitzroy Stanhope headed the vocal department, and was ably supported by Charles Sheridan, who sung, among other things, some lines he had adapted to the air of "Sweet Jenny Jones," the subject being the universally known and highly respected head waiter at Limmer's. The first verse ran as follows :—

> " My name is John Collin, head waiter at Limmer's,
> At the corner of Conduit Street, Hanover Square,
> Where my chief occupation is filling up brimmers,
> To solace young gentlemen laden with care."

Unfortunately I cannot remember the other verses, which were replete with point, and which were sung by the sweetest of voices.

While upon the subject of cant phrases, I must not forget one which, though not meant by the utterer to be personal, gave offence to three kind-hearted men. Among other celebrities of his day was Edward, commonly called Mike, Fitzgerald, the son of the noble but misguided political partizan, Lord Edward, who was shot in the struggle for his arrest, A.D. 1798.

Mike had served in the 10th Hussars, and formed

one of the "Elegant Extracts" already alluded to.
He had always a quaint expression at hand, and
one day at Paris, when a large party of Englishmen
and foreigners had assembled at the *Cercle aux
Etrangers*, previous to dining, some hesitation took
place as to the "order of going." Instead of saying,
with Macbeth, "You know your own degrees, sit
down;" or with his strong-minded wife, "Stand not
upon the order of your going, but go at once," the
ex-hussar shouted out, "Go it, my cripples, crutches
is cheap!" when, to his deep dismay, he found that,
among the party of his own countrymen, three were
cripples, the late Lord Stair, Henry Drummond,
and another, whose name I forget. To apologise
was to make the affair worse, so Mike rattled on, to
try and divert the attention of all; but although his
voice was merry, his heart was sad, for he knew that
he had unintentionally wounded the feelings of three
as good creatures as ever lived. To show to what
extent the love for slang names was carried, Lord
George Bentinck, than whom a more refined and
noble-minded nobleman never existed, named two
of his horses "All round my hat" and "Here I go
with my eye out;" the pedigree of the former by
Bay Middleton out of Chapeau d'Espagne, may have
warranted the allusion to the hat, although it was
rather far-fetched, and the same remark may apply

to "Here I go with my eye out," who was a sister to Bramble.

At the time of the railway mania I embodied several of the cant phrases of the day in the following song, which I am afraid will be only too generally understood, or rather appreciated :—

STAGGING FOR THE MILLION.

" *Litera* scrip-*ta manet.*"

To the air of " Bow, wow, wow."

Oh, have you heard the news of late, how all the world were
  stagging it;
The money flowed so plenteously that all the folks were bagging it;
Patrician lords of high degree were mixing with the rabble,
For where's the man "wot" can be found that don't in railways
  dabble?   Stag, stag, stag.

Among the herd you'll find divines, knights, lawyers, soldiers,
  sailors,
With outlawed " gents," sweeps, K.C.B.'s, cads, blacklegs, tinkers,
  tailors ;
And Melton men who quit the chase, and take to *stays* for sporting,
And lots of pretty London *dears* who go a *Capel Courting.*
                                                  Stag, &c.

The soldier quits the warlike *line* for civil engineering ;
Across the equinoctial *line* no more the sailor's veering ;
In *Hudson's* Bay he anchors now ; alas, deluded ninny !
He finds his locker full of *scrip*, his purse without a guinea.
                                                  Stag, &c.

Retaining fees to peers are sent, to soften opposition,
And e'en high dames for railway shares will on their knees
  petition ;
And members of the Lower House, who their constituents cozen,
Will feather well their nests, then sit, and hatch schemes by the
  dozen.   Stag, &c.

Provisional committee men, with "Lawyers Quirk and Gammon,"
Have pocketed some paltry pelf by bending thus to mammon.
Stag-nation comes at last, 'tis said; the shareholders look daggers,
John Doe and *Roe** will end the game; the *stags* have got the
    staggers.   Stag, &c.

Perhaps there is no word of a truly slang nature more constantly employed than the verb to
"chouse." In the *Tatler*, number 213, we find—
"However they may pretend to chouse one another,
they make but very awkward rogues; and their
dislike to each other is seldom so well dissembled
but it is suspected." The word is a very expressive
one, and the origin of it deserves a brief notice.
"A chious," writes W. Gifford, "was an envoy
sent from the Porte on special occasions, for the
Turk at that time kept no ambassadors in any part
of Europe; and the term is applied to a cheat or a
swindler in consequence of a circumstance which
took place in 1609. Sir Robert Shirley sent a messenger, or chious (as our old writers call him) to
this country, as his agent, from the Grand Signior
and the Sophy, to transact some preparatory
business. Sir Robert followed him at his leisure as
ambassador from both those princes; but before he
reached England his agent had chioused the Turkish
and Persian merchants here of £4,000, and taken

* John Doe and Richard Roe were well-known characters when
arrest for debt was the law of the land; debtors being sued at the
suit of the above parties.

his flight—unconscious, perhaps, that he had
enriched the language with a word of which the
etymology would mislead Upton and puzzle Dr.
Johnson. Two other chiouses are mentioned by our
annalists, as visiting us in 1618 and 1625. These,
however, were more respectable characters, and are
only noticed for the degree of pomp with which
James and Charles I. respectively received them."
After all, chouse is not so remote from cozen (an
old word from the Danish *kosa*) but that we may
easily believe something very like it had long been
familiar to us. The frequent use of the word, however, at this period, is undoubtedly owing to the
celebrity conferred upon it by the knavery of Sir
Robert's chious. In "The Alchemist," written by
Ben Jonson, and acted in 1610, the following
dialogue between *Dapper*, the lawyer's clerk, and
Face occurs :—

> " What do you think of me,
> That I am a chious?
> *Face.* What's that?
> *Dapper.* The Turk was here.
> As one would say, Do you think I am a Turk?"

Ford introduces the word in his comedy of "The
Lady's Trial"—

> "Gulls or Moguls,
> Tag, rag, or t'other, hoger mogen, varden,
> Skipjacks, or chouses."

Shirley, too, in "Honoria and Mammon," writes—

"We are in a fair way to be ridiculous. What think you, madam, chioused by a scholar?" Butler quaintly says—

> " He stole your cloak, and pick'd your pocket,
> Chous'd and caldes'd ye like a blockhead."

And again—

> " He that with injury is griev'd,
> And goes to law to be relieved,
> Is sillier than a sottish chouse,
> Who when a thief has robb'd his house
> Applies himself to cunning mon,
> To help him to his goods again."

After thus stating the origin of the word, I will illustrate it by a case to which it is thoroughly applicable, and which was never equalled in the Turkish dominions. I will not give the names, as I believe one of the party is still living, albeit since the period I refer to he has become a wiser and a better man. The circumstance took place at a fashionable spa, some twenty or five-and-twenty years ago, and the principal performers were three oldish birds and two fledglings. A dinner was got up at the house of one of the former, and after " potations pottle deep " of champagne and claret, a game of hazard was proposed. At first the stakes were trifling, but they gradually increased, counters representing fives, tens, and twenties, were introduced, and a succession of bowls of hot punch being brought in, the young players began to feel the effects of it. Pen and ink were called for, I O U's given, and it was not until three o'clock in the morning that the party broke up. One of the fledglings was to leave early by the coach, and while dressing he was surprised by a visit from the host.

"I am come," said the latter, "to pay you the hundred pounds I owe you."

"Hundred pounds!" replied the other, who had taken a hasty glance at his account. "You are mistaken. You owe me nothing."

"Nonsense, my fine fellow, here it is," showing a betting book. "The fact is you were so drunk you forgot to enter it."

"That may be the case, for I own during the last hour the punch got the better of me. I fear I was mortal drunk."

"Well, you did not stand alone; young —— was equally so."

"Oh, he was in a very bad way before we sat down. He gave me his account to look over, which I have not yet had time to do."

The host handed over the hundred-pound note, the young man still hesitating whether he ought to receive it. However, after a little persuasion, he placed it in his pocket-book, with a remark that, should the mistake be discovered, he would willingly refund.

"'That paying back is a double duty,' as old Jack

Falstaff says," responded the host. "You'll find it all right."

A knock was heard at the door, and another of the elderly party entered.

"I don't wish to dun you, old fellow," said he, addressing the pigeon; "but when you look over our account, you will find you owe me five hundred."

"Five hundred!" echoed the astonished youth. "I know young —— owes you a balance. You and I are quits."

"Please, sir, the coach is at the door," said the butler. "Shall I put your luggage in?"

"Never mind the coach," said the host. "If there is any mistake, pray have it rectified. Nothing is so bad as mistakes in money matters."

"You are quite right," remarked the victim. "I will go up by the night mail. Give the coachman this half-crown for his trouble in calling. The fare to London is paid."

The party met at breakfast; and the result will be easily anticipated. The young man having received a hundred pounds, and having declared that both he and his brother fledgling were so tipsy that they knew little of what had occurred, could not make a stand against the demands of the old birds, who, playing into one another's hands, choused the two youths of nearly eighteen hundred pounds.

The affair caused a good deal of sensation at the

time; but, as the leading chious was a professed
duellist and an excellent shot, few dared to bring the
affair to light upon the evidence of two self-acknow-
ledged drunken men. I know not whether any of
the party were conscience stricken, and refunded
their ill-gotten gains. We read daily of the Chancellor of the Exchequer receiving large sums from
those who have defrauded the State, why should
not those who have robbed their neighbours be
equally anxious to make what is called "a clear
breast of it," and disgorge their roguish gains?

During a somewhat lengthened period "about
town," as it is termed, I have occasionally met with
men who were wont to introduce subjects with a
view to getting up a bet, which, if taken, they
were certain to win. There are a variety of ways
of "plucking the fledglings." One is by quoting,
or getting a confederate (for these sharp prac-
titioners generally run in couples) to quote, some
popular passage, and then wager as to the author,
or correctness of the lines. The following is a
favourite "trap." "Welcome the coming, speed
the parting guest," says one. "I wonder where
they come from." Walter Scott and others are
named. "I'll take the odds," says the getter up
of the robbery, "I name one against the lot."
"Done!" says a greenhorn. Homer is named;

and after pretending to search the Iliad and Odyssey through, the latter is found to contain them.

> " Hail, great Atrides!
>   True friendship's laws are by this rule expressed,
>   Welcome the coming, speed the parting guest;
>   Alike he thwarts the hospitable end
>   Who drives the free, or stays the parting friend."

This probably gives rise to another; for, as the blood-hound who has once drawn blood is seldom sated, so the *escroc* continues, " 'Parting guest!' I fancy some one calls it the 'going guest.' " A bet ensues, and it is soon discovered that Hobbs wrote as follows :—

> " Love him that stays, help forth the going guest."

From Hobbs to Hudibras is the next move, and the confederate cites the often misquoted lines—

> " He that's convinced against his will,
>   Is of the same opinion still."

Upon wagers being made, it turns out to be, "He that complies against his will." Another productive quotation is—"Though last, not least;" which few are aware is from "Julius Cæsar." Then, again, the lines—

> " For he that fights and runs away
>   May live to fight another day,"

are quoted, and Hudibras named as the author. Bets are made, and Sir J. Mennes proves to have written them; Butler's lines being—

U

" For those that fly may fight again,
　Which he can never do that's slain."

Of course the subject is not always a literary
one, occasionally the size of different squares—
Belgrave, Grosvenor, and Lincoln's Inn Fields—
are brought on the *tapis;* the distances from one
place to another; the question as to whether the lion
crest of the Percy family stands alike at Northum-
berland House as at Sion, are all discussed, ending
with a bet—that is, whenever a greenhorn can be
found.　A good story is told of the late John
Mytton.　He was upon one occasion at the Royal
Hotel, at Chester, during the races; and going
into the room where the ordinary was to be held,
he saw a friend of his industriously counting the
number of legs of the tables and chairs.　The Squire
of Halston retired unperceived, and waited his opportunity.　After a considerable quantity of fiery " military" port had been drunk, the man of figures
began cautiously, by saying, " How hot it is! I
wonder how many candles are a-light in this room."
From candles the subject got to the furniture, when
the sharper continued, " I'll back myself to name
the number of legs of chairs and tables, against
any one naming the number of candles."　No one
was bold enough to make the bet; but when he
proceeded, " And I'll lay a ' pony' that I name the

number of legs nearer than any one else," he was stopped short by Mytton saying, "Done, for a pony or fifty!" "Fifty!" and the wager was booked. "Who'll be umpire?" said the man—the "leg," it would be more appropriate to call him. "The chairman, if he will be so kind," responded Mytton; "and, to prevent mistakes, let each write down his guess, and hand it over to the umpire." This was done; the legs of the chairs and tables were counted, and the Squire won by four. "I'll not take the money," said Mytton; "it shall go to the Infirmary, or some local charity." To account for the above unexpected result, and to add another to the diamond-cut-diamond cases, it must be mentioned that Mytton, suspecting a trick, had sawed off four legs before dinner—a pretty broad hint that the roguery was discovered.

I remember a case in which a trick of the kind was played, thoughtlessly enough, but the remembrance of it haunted the perpetrator for years afterwards. A youth was out fishing with his father, and caught a fine trout, which he declared weighed three pounds. The father, who was some yards off, said it looked little over two pounds to him, and the youth offered a bet of a shilling that the fish turned the scale of three pounds. The father lost, never suspecting that his son had inserted his pen-

knife in the throat of the fish, so as to add the
weight which was wanted.

I have often fallen in with some of those characters known as "cool hands."   Among the number
I may mention the late Colonel Copeland, of the
Bays, a popular man in his regiment, and equally so
among sporting men.   One day during the time I
had a seat in the House of Commons, I was engaged
to dine with John Philip Beavan, in Sackville Street.
Beavan was a solicitor, a parliamentary agent, and
occasionally assisted extravagant young men about
town with temporary loans.   I met him first at the
Inverness Lodge of Masons, and afterwards at a
public dinner at Hertford, where he was retained
for the liberal member, the late Tom Duncombe.
From this an intimacy sprung up, and I was his
guest occasionally at dinner, meeting at his house
many of the most agreeable members of society.   On
this occasion I had been at the " House," and, in the
temporary absence of the Speaker, had occupied his
chair, and upon reaching Beavan's house, the drawing-room was almost dark, so much so, that it was
scarcely possible to recognise the assembled company.
After I had made my bow, and shaken hands with my
host and hostess, Colonel Copeland was announced.
" I should apologise for being late," he said, " did
I not know that I am not the last; I've just come
from the House of Commons, where I left ' Anatomy

Bill'* in the chair, and as Granby Calcraft told me he dined with you, I felt I should be in time." To hear myself thus familiarly called by one I had never been introduced to, much less spoken to, surprised me not a little; but I must do Copeland the justice to say that, when he heard I was present, he offered me the *amende honorable*, and we were friends ever after. Talking of Colonel Copeland reminds me of a novel match which took place in the month of October, 1841, between that gallant officer and Lord Huntingtower, the colonel driving an unicorn against Lord Huntingtower's four-in-hand, twice round Hyde Park, for one hundred guineas: one horse in each team was allowed to break out of a trot, and the race was won easily by the unicorn.

The coolest of all cool hands I ever met with, was a young man whose conduct went so close to the verge of swindling, that one hardly knew which name ought to be applied to him. The event occurred while I was staying at Leamington some thirty years ago. Among those assembled there to enjoy the sports of the field was an old acquaintance of mine, Coesvelt. He was a man of most gentlemanlike manners, agreeable conversation, and exquisite taste. His collection of Italian pictures included some

* This nickname was given me on account of the active part I took when the Bill in question was brought before the House.

splendid specimens of Raphael and Parmigiano, and
if his love for the chase was not so ardent as his
admiration for the arts, if he admired Diana less
than Clio, he was still enough of the sportsman to
enjoy a gallop with the Warwickshire.　Coesvelt
was as simple minded as a child, and he could
not bring himself to believe that trickery was
ever practised, at all events by those who bore the
mark and wore the garb of gentlemen.　A strong
instance of this occurred during the first winter I
passed at Leamington.　One morning, when looking
out of the club window at the Regent, my attention
was attracted by a stranger who was mounted upon
a remarkably clever handsome chesnut horse; his
dress was peculiar, consisting of a military blue
frock coat, elaborately ornamented with black braid,
a foraging cap with gold band, a pair of military
trousers with a broad silver stripe, and boots with
fixed brass spurs.　" Who is the new arrival ? "
asked one.　" An officer from Birmingham," responded the other.　As I had a letter to finish
before going to meet the hounds at Ufton Wood, I
thought no more of the new comer until I reached
the cover side, when I saw him in conversation with
Coesvelt, Henry Williams, and other of my acquaintances.　The former beckoned to me, and was just
beginning to say, " Allow me to introduce ——,"

when a cry of "Gone away" was heard. Perceiving
his intention, I hastily exclaimed, "After the run,"
and in a moment I was going best pace across an
excellent hunting country. Our fox was headed
by some Leamington idlers, and was shortly killed.
When on my way home I overtook the stranger and
Coesvelt, who at once introduced him to me as
Mr. Penson, of the Carabineers. "Are you quartered near here?" I asked. "At Birmingham,"
he responded. My attention was caught by the
silver lace, which I knew was not worn by the
regulars, but I accounted for it by fancying the
wearer had exchanged from the yeomanry into the
cavalry. Nothing more occurred, except that I
overheard the young officer accept Coesvelt's invitation to dine with him at the club, and accompany
him to the ball which was to take place that evening
at the public rooms. "I shall be happy to avail
myself of your kindness," he responded, "as far as
dinner is concerned, but, unfortunately, I have
brought no evening clothes with me." "Oh, I can
manage that," replied the unsuspecting friend, " I
have no doubt I can fit you out; and what with
my wardrobe, and a visit to the tailor's, a haberdasher, and a shoemaker, you may depend upon a
proper suit." This was agreed to, and I thought
little more of the matter until the ball commenced,

when I saw the stranger engrossing the general
attention, for it had been bruited about that he
was a young man of family, fortune, and position,
who had only recently joined that gallant corps, since
commanded by an excellent officer, and downright
good fellow, Colonel Richmond Jones.   The master
of the ceremonies was introducing Mr. Penson to all
the rank and beauty then assembled at this celebrated Warwickshire Spa.

It happened that among my partners were two
young ladies who had a brother in the Carabineers,
and who remarked to me, that they thought the
new cornet was not very well up with respect to
the names of his brother officers.   The same idea
had flashed across my mind, for a remark that had
fallen from him showed me that his intercourse
with his regiment must have been extremely
slight, if even it existed at all.   Upon the following
morning the "illustrious unknown" was introduced into the club as an honorary member, and as
my suspicions were still excited, I took the trouble
to send for a monthly army list; and while the
porter was gone for that, to look over the last fortnight's *Gazette* to ascertain whether the name of
Penson appeared in either.   While thus employed,
the hero of my search approached me, and made
the usual common-place remark concerning the

weather. After a few moments, I summoned up courage to ask him point blank how long he had joined his regiment. "Within the last fortnight," he responded; "I am stationed at Birmingham at present with a recruiting party." I thought this strange, but said nothing, determined to wait until an army list was procured, which I found would be not until the afternoon, as it had been necessary to send to Coventry for it.

During the day I happened to stroll into one or two shops, the owners of which casually informed me, that through my recommendation Captain Penson—he had received brevet rank—had given them handsome orders. This information placed me in an awful fix. On the one hand, I did not wish to damage the stranger's character, on the other, I felt some compunction lest the tradesmen should suffer by my not declaring that I knew little or nothing of him or his antecedents. Determined to have the mystery cleared up, I sought Coesvelt, and unburthened my mind to him, and he at once entered fully into my feelings. "I think," said he, "in justice to Mr. Penson, ourselves, the Leamington visitors, and tradesmen, that the affair should be thoroughly investigated; at the same time, I believe the young man will really prove to be what he states himself." "I hope he may,"

I responded, "but I have my doubts. What say you," I continued, "to calling at once at the Clarendon Hotel, and openly telling Mr. Penson that his conduct has created some little suspicion, and that for his own sake we wish it cleared up?" "We cannot do better," replied my friend, "and you shall be spokesman. I will leave all to you." It was now near six o'clock, so we at once proceeded to the hotel, where we were told that Mr. Penson was dressing for dinner, as he was engaged to partake of the hospitality of a baronet, at that time very popular at the Spa, though long since dead. After waiting a few minutes in Mr. Penson's sitting-room, that gentleman made his appearance, splendidly equipped in a new coat, embroidered waist-coat and trousers. Coesvelt's bow was a little formal, and mine was not as friendly as usual, for I felt "ryled" at my name having been made use of without my sanction.

"May I ask," said I, "the name of the colonel of your regiment?"

"Oh! certainly," he replied, mentioning that of the full colonel, not the commanding officer.

"I am aware of that," I said, "but I refer to the lieutenant-colonel."

"Really," he answered, "I have joined so lately that I am not aware of it."

"And yet," I proceeded, "as you say you are on a recruiting party, you must first have been at head-quarters?"

"Oh yes, I was there for a month."

"And the adjutant's name?"

"Let me see, I forget that; but I know General the Hon. Robert Taylor is the colonel."

"I don't mean," I interrupted, "the full colonel, but the lieutenant-colonel."

"General Taylor," he responded.

At this my companion rushed forward, seized hold of the speaker's hand, shook it warmly, and said, "I am delighted that you have gone through the painful ordeal, and come out of it so honourably."

"One word, Coesvelt," said I, dragging him by the hand from the room into another that was open. "That young man is a barefaced impostor; Edward Wildman commands the regiment; he does not even know his name, or that of the adjutant; and he would not have been appointed to the recruiting service without having been at least two months at head-quarters."

"I will go back," replied Coesvelt, "and denounce him to his face."

"Let us consider calmly what is best to be done," I responded; "we must warn the landlord of this

hotel, and the tradesmen, as to the character of
Mr. Penson; but first we will 'beard the lion in
his den,' and tell him of the step we consider it our
duty to take."

But the *soi-disant* "plunger" was not to be
caught; no sooner had we left the room, than he
made a hasty retreat through the window, got into
a fly, drove to Warwick, and by the middle of the
following day was safe home at his father's house
at ———. For four-and-twenty hours afterwards,
nothing was talked of in Leamington except the
" fashionable military swindler;" and loud and deep
were the denunciations of those he had victimised.
Upon the second morning after his departure, a
letter came from the youth's father, who was a
most respectable solicitor, to Coesvelt, expressing
his deep regret at his son's conduct (which he attributed more to a love of fun and excitement than
to downright dishonesty), and stating that he would
be answerable for all the debts he had contracted.
The letter concluded by saying, " When my son
first appeared at Leamington, he had no idea whatever of assuming a character to which he was not
entitled, that of holding a commission in the Carabineers; but upon being told that he was looked
upon in that light, his vanity got the better of him,
and he accepted the peacock's feathers which had been

thrust upon him. Accept, then, his and my apologies for the annoyance he has caused you and your friends, and make some allowance for his youth."

In reply, Coesvelt promised to explain the affair to all interested in it, sent in the bills, which were immediately paid, and in ten days the wonder had ceased to form the topic of conversation, and Penson (such was his *nom de guerre*, not his real name) was entirely forgotten. Some of the young ladies felt rather disgusted at having sacrificed so much of their time to the stranger, whom they all denounced as the worst dancer with whom they ever had the bad fortune to figure. The real "Simon Pure" of the gallant Carabineers declared that it was fortunate he was away, or a breach of the peace might have ensued. The adventure was not without its moral; it pointed out the mischief of forming too sudden acquaintances without proper introductions; it gave a practical hint to tradesmen not to trust every one that gave an order; and it gave poor Coesvelt a lesson that he remembered to the last hour of his existence. If he had a weakness, it was a pardonable one, namely, that of thinking the world better than it is, and never suspecting that any one could act dishonourably.

Another instance of a "cool hand" occurred whilst I was residing at Gee's Farm. A friend of mine, who is now no more, proposed to pay me a visit for a day or two, and as I had known him for some years I readily assented to his proposition. Thinking it probable that he would wish to extend his stay, I said in reply, that I hoped the day or two meant from Monday till Saturday, on which latter day I was engaged from home. I would suggest that the same plan should be followed in all country visits, and that the host or hostess should name the extent of the visit. The vague term, "a few days," is difficult to understand. There is another plan equally good, which was successfully adopted by the late Duke and Duchess of Gordon, at Gordon Castle, and which was peculiarly necessary in Scotland, where friends and neighbours propose themselves to pay flying visits, extending to weeks, not days. The method was to place a large printed board in the hall or passages, with the names and numbers of the bed-rooms, opposite to which was written the date of arrival of one guest, and underneath the date of the expected arrival of another to the same apartment. So that unless the visitors wished to follow the example of "Box and Cox," and have one bed between them, the first occupant departed on the morning the second was expected. Nor was there any breach of hospitality or any indelicacy in the proceeding, for

all were treated alike, and in the event of the host
and hostess wishing any particular friends to remain
over the given time, it was very easy to transfer
the new comers to other apartments. In my case
my cool friend arrived, made a thorough hotel of
my house, borrowed my horse to ride, my phaeton
to drive, breakfasted early or late as the fancy took
him, dined at home when it suited him, went off,
before the cloth was removed, to the theatre, and
expected supper upon his return. In common
courtesy I was bound to submit to this, and my
consolation was that in a week I should be rid of
him. Friday approached, my friend was more con-
siderate and attentive, and proposed dining quietly
and passing the evening with me. I asked a few
acquaintances to meet him, and the evening went off
pleasantly. On wishing him "good-night" (and
as Barham, Hook, Beazley, Walpole, and some
other choice spirits had dined with me, it was late
before we thought of retiring) my off-hand visitor
said, " Really, you have made my time pass so
agreeably, that I hope you will not think me cool
if I ask you to allow me to stay a few days longer."
I looked aghast, and was about to stammer out some
excuse, when my friend interrupted me, " This is
rather dry work; I think I will have a glass of
brandy and soda" (here he rang the bell and gave

his order); "and, by the way, I know what you are
going to say; you are on guard to-morrow,
dine with your mother on Sunday, and are
engaged to Cupid (this was Walpole's nick-name)
on Monday. I have arranged for that. I am
acquainted with lots of guardsmen, and if I commence my foraging excursion at guard-mounting to-
morrow, I have no doubt I shall be asked to St.
James's, especially as I am staying with you. You
will give me lunch at the Horse Guards. On
Sunday I can do a little family duty at Richmond.
No dinner here—only a snack from the servants'
dinner before I go; and Walpole kindly asked me
to be of the party on Monday. So you see I shall
not mar any of your enjoyments. By the way,
perhaps you will lend me your phaeton to-morrow;
I could set you down at the Regent's Park Barracks,
and then drive down to St. James's Street, and on
Sunday it would do you all the good in the world
to ride down to Richmond, and 'Drummer' too,
as he is getting too fat." Under the circumstances, it was impossible for me to refuse, and my
friend was booked for another week.

During this period the talent of my cool friend
again came into operation. I was engaged on the
Wednesday to dine with my old amateur friend
John Dawkins. We were to dine early, as the late

Earl Fitzhardinge, then Colonel Berkeley, his brother
Augustus, and Dawkins, were to act at the Tottenham Court Theatre that evening. Punctuality was
of course the order of the day, and just as we had
all assembled in the drawing-room, with only five
minutes to spare, who should drive up to the door
but my cool friend. Dawkins hearing a loud rap,
left the room, to tell his butler, who was busily pre-
paring the wine, not to admit any one; but he was
a moment too late, for my friend had already gained
the hall. All that my host heard was, "I wish to
say one word to Lord William Lennox;" and being
a well-bred man, he went forward, said that I was
up stairs, and that he would call me down into his
morning room. "All I required," proceeded my
persevering friend, whose olfactory senses had
already "nosed" the dinner, "was to ascertain
whether Billy Lennox had kept a place for me. I
am on my way to Long's, to have an early chop,
for I would not be a moment late for the world."
"Why not stay and dine here?" said Dawkins,
"and we can all go together." "Oh, I could not
think of such a thing; your table is probably full;
no—excuse me; I'll just say one word to Lennox,
and meet you there." "My friends are actually
descending the staircase," continued my host. "You
must join us—I will take no denial. I have a place

vacant, for Richard Jones sent an excuse; he is in
the first piece at the 'Garden' this evening."
"Since you are so pressing," responded the hungry
visitor, "I must yield."

In less than two minutes we were all seated
round Dawkins's hospitable board.   The week
passed away, and happily my friend had "sponged"
himself into another friend's house in the Regent's
Park, so on the Saturday he took his leave,
having as a matter of course borrowed my
phaeton to take him there, and my landlord's cart
for his luggage. "By the way," said he, "your
servants have been most attentive, I think I ought
to 'tip' the boy, the groom, the cook, and the
housemaid."   "Such 'buckshees,'" I responded,
"are totally opposed to my notions; I pay my
servants liberally, and if I did not entertain friends
I should diminish the establishment."   "Well, old
fellow," he replied, "one must do in Rome as the
Romans do, so a sovereign among them won't hurt.
Let me see, I'm rather short of cash, could you
lend me a sovereign?"   "Not for that purpose,"
I answered.   "Never mind for what purpose;
just hand over twenty 'bob' in silver if you have
it." For a moment I reflected; the old story flashed
across my mind, that the only way of getting rid
of a troublesome visitor was to advance him money,

so I gave him the sovereign, which he divided equally between the "boy" and housemaid; and although he called occasionally upon me, his memory was treacherous, for he gave me the pleasing satisfaction of remembering that my servants were not only paid against my principle and wishes, but that the gratuity came out of my pocket, and never returned to it.

I could name another instance of a cool hand which nearly led to a serious quarrel. Happily for me, I was not the hero of the story, though I happened to be present when it occurred. A small party of friends were dining at the house of a most hospitable officer, who had served in the army; the dinner was excellent, the wine faultless, when just before the ladies (there were only two present) left the room, the Amphitryon, who was a perfect specimen of "London Assurance," asked one of his guests, "whether he would rather look a greater fool than he was, or be a greater fool than he looked?" After a slight pause, the object of the jest replied, "Of the two I would rather look a greater fool than I am." "Oh, that's impossible," responded the other. A slight laugh followed, which was succeeded by a dead silence, for all present saw that anger and resentment were strongly depicted upon the victim's countenance.

"I suppose you are in a hurry, gentlemen, for the ladies to take their departure," said the hostess with considerable tact, fearing angry words might arise; "but you must postpone your hunting and shooting anecdotes for the present, for we both wish to hear about the military fancy ball, which is shortly to come off." This gave a slight turn to the conversation, but the struggle was going on in the mind of the offended guest, as to the line he should adopt. A meeting at Norway with pistols at twelve paces crossed his mind, an open demand of whether insult was meant next entered his brain, to be followed up (in case of the affirmative) by hurling a missile in the shape of a bottle of wine at the host's head, of course after the ladies had retired.

The lady of the house saw that mischief was brewing, and with a most winning smile she turned to the irate man, and said, "You of course are invited to the ball, and if not engaged, I must try to get you into my season's quadrille." All except the host, who was either unaware, or pretended to be so, of the offence he had given (for I omitted to say it was the first time his "butt" had dined at his table), were on the tenter hooks of suspense and anxiety as to the result, when with a most praiseworthy magnanimity, the offended guest

responded, " I scarcely feel competent to join that
set, except perhaps as ' All fools' day,' a character
which, it seems, your husband thinks I am most
qualified to take." " Fool," said the host, "no
one will take you for that; but help yourself, here's
your good health, and pass the bottle." This
restored good fellowship, and the rest of the evening
passed off very pleasantly. Somewhat later I
hinted to the jester that he had run a great risk of
getting himself into a scrape, and that some years
ago he would have probably been paraded at Chalk
Farm at eight o'clock in the morning with a hair-
triggered pistol opposed to him. " 'Pon my life, old
fellow," he replied in a sort of Dundreary style, " I
meant no offence; some one sold me, and I thought
I'd take a rise out of another in revenge."

I remember a practical jest being played off
after a dinner at a gallant admiral's which nearly
led to an awful disturbance. The individual
selected for the butt was a good-humoured young
Life Guardsman, who was elegantly got up for
dinner and a ball. The trick was to get two
saucers, one of which had been blackened with
burnt cork, and for the jester to lure on his victim
to follow his movements. He began first by extending arms, and going through sundry mild
gymnastic feats, in which he was of course followed.

He then took the two saucers, giving the blackened one to his friend, and holding it so high that the dark colour of its inside was not seen; he then dipped his finger into his own clean saucer, and made sundry hieroglyphic marks on his forehead and cheeks, which being imitated by the unhappy wight, rendered his face of an Ethiopian hue. "Is that all?" asked the victim, perfectly unconscious of his Othello look. "No," responded the other, "you must bow to the looking-glass." The young soldier did so, and the angry expression of his countenance showed that he was boiling over with rage. Happily the good-humoured master of the house appeased him, and took him off to his dressing room, where the blackamoor was soon turned white. The joke, however, was one of extreme bad taste, and a fatal rencontre might have been the result some years ago.

After these instances of coolness and practical jokes, carried out to the full extent, it may seem almost an act of vanity on my part to mention a harmless trick I played on a worthy second-hand dealer. It was during the time I was quartered in the Regent's Park and Knightsbridge Barracks with the Blues, that I became acquainted with a most estimable member of the Hebrew persuasion, who was ever ready to exchange a "Bersian"

(meaning Persian) carpet for old epaulettes, aigui-
lettes, gold embroidery, or lace. He was a German,
Zimmerman by name, but whether connected with
the family of that eminent medical and philo-
sophical writer, to whom we owe the elaborate
dissertation on "Solitude," and the excellent
"Treatise on Experience," I know not. Certainly experience and the profitable results of
it had not been lost upon him, and he was the
ready purchaser of every article, from a diamond
brooch down to an old pair of jack boots. In after
life Zimmerman rose to a higher position, published
his life, and dealt in articles of *vertù* and *bijouterie*.
Upon one occasion, in an exchange of a sword knot
for a small piece of china, I found the latter slightly
damaged, and upon remonstrating with the Israelite
he naturally replied that the gold of the sword knot
had somewhat lost its former lustre, and that "hish
vay of doing bisnish" was never to return goods
once bought, or to take them back if sold. "All
right," I replied, "in future we will deal upon
those terms." Nothing occurred for some time
worth recording, until one day, after I had left the
regiment, I was sitting alone in my chambers in
Regent Street, when Zimmerman was announced.

"Have you anything to dispose of, my Lord?"
he asked, laying down on the floor a large empty

bag, which he was in great hopes would be filled before his departure.

"I have nothing at present," I responded; "besides which, you never bid for any rubbish I wish to part with, nothing under plate or jewels suits you now."

"I beg pardon, my Lord, I am always happy to purchase anything, from a door mat to a pearl necklace."

"I'll put that to the test," I replied; "what will you give me for that warming-pan?—a most useful article during this cold frost?"

A bright copper warming-pan was in the corner of the room, placed there to be called for by the man of whom I bought it.

"I only bought it yesterday morning," said I. "Remember, in future I warrant nothing sound."

Thinking that if he took the warming-pan it might lead to another deal, he offered me about a third of its original cost, and I accepted his offer. He then gave me a set of studs in exchange for some old uniforms, and, having completed the morning's business, he requested me to send for a cab for him. Upon its being announced, and his having carefully packed his bag, he proceeded to take possession of the copper article, which shone as bright as the sun at mid-day.

"Why, what is this?" he exclaimed, as, turning the warming-pan round, he called my attention to a large hole in it.

"Oh, that is easily repaired," I said; "you know the terms upon which we deal."

For a moment Zimmerman looked put out, but soon recovered himself, and muttered, "I've made a bad morning's work."

Finding he took it in such good part, and never intending to let him stand by his bargain, I returned him the money, advising him in future never to "buy a *pig* in a poke,"—rather an unfortunate simile to make to a Hebrew.

"I do not mind taking the warming-pan," said he, "at a fair price, now I have a cab at the door."

"Have it by all means," I replied, "and I'll throw it in for nothing."

Another adventure with Zimmerman occurred some twenty years afterwards, when I was residing in that very diminutive house at the corner of Hay Hill in Berkeley Square, which D'Orsay always likened to a grand pianoforte. A friend of mine who had just sold out of the army was anxious to dispose of his old military equipments, and asked me to see Zimmerman upon the subject. In consequence of this the latter called, and having inspected the articles, made an offer for the whole lot. While considering what was best to be done, to accept or not to accept the sum proposed, I heard a loud knocking at the door, and upon its being answered, recognised the voice of an old and kind friend, the Honourable Edmund Byng, who said, loud enough for me to hear, that he must see me if but for a moment.

"My Lord is very busily engaged with a foreign gentleman," said my lad from the country, who now would be dubbed "page."

"Only one word," responded the visitor, opening at the same time the door of the tiny dining-room in which I was transacting my business. I made a sign to Zimmerman to be silent, and welcomed the new comer.

"I have a few friends coming to dine with me to-day," said Edmund, "and perhaps you will make one—quite an impromptu affair; Charles Kemble and Frederick Yates will be of the party." To this proposition I gladly assented, and was then in hopes that my visitor would take his departure; but, with an anxiety to show attention (as it afterwards proved to be the case) to a distinguished foreigner, he remained, asking me, *sotto voce*, to introduce him to my friend.

Not liking to expose our vocations in the "old

clo'" line, I approached Zimmerman, and told him
not to say a word, or the bargain should be off;
then turning to Byng, I said, "This gentleman is a
German; he has a taste for the stage, and I am
anxious to bring him out on the boards as *Shylock*."

"I never saw a finer expression," responded this
true and liberal patron of the drama: "a splendid
eye, not a bad stage figure. Would he give me a
taste of his quality?"

"Impossible just now," I replied; "perhaps upon
some future occasion."

Knowing that there was one subject which would
excite the ire of the Jew, and bring forth a burst
of anger, I approached him, and said in an under-
tone, "You had better come back later; I expect
Craven Berkeley here immediately." This allusion
to one at daggers drawn with the Jew produced
the desired effect; for Zimmerman contracted his
eyebrows, muttered curses deep, not loud, and
hurried out of the room.

"Bravo, bravo!" said Edmund Byng; "a fine
deep-toned voice; I should like to introduce him
to Charles Kemble. May I run and ask him to
dinner?"

"Not to-day," I answered; "his engagements
will not permit it."

"Well, don't forget that if at any time I can be

of service to your friend, I shall be delighted."
With this he took his leave, but reverted at dinner
to the subject of a real German-Jewish *Shylock*.

"I almost fear," said Kemble, "that, however
talented a foreigner might be—and there have been
some artists of resplendent genius, male and female,
both on the French and German boards—that the
accent would not suit the lines of Shakespeare.
Still, I shall be happy to hear the gentleman go
through a scene from the 'Merchant of Venice.'"

What strange revolutions have been brought
about! I have lived to see Fechter and Colas
produce the greatest effects in the most sublime
plays of the immortal bard, and draw down plaudits from every part of the house; nay, more, to
have read their histrionic triumphs recorded by the
pens of the ablest critics of the day.

There never was a kinder or more hospitable
creature than Edmund Byng, who, despite his eccentricities, could boast of a legion of friends. His
dress was always most peculiar; trousers, high-
lows, and an oddly cut coat not being quite the
costume for dinner parties, and yet he perseveringly
appeared in it. His dinners, too, were eccentric.
If he had a party of twelve, he would have one sole,
his favourite fish, for each; instead of entrées, he
had joints; and often have I seen an aitch bone of

beef, a leg of pork, a fillet of veal, and a ham, smoking on his board. His standing joke was to tell his company that woodcocks, snipes, wild ducks, pheasant, partridge, golden plover, or whatever game was in season, would be introduced in the second course, and now and then a greenhorn, acting upon this information, would wait for the promised luxuries. Great, then, was his disappointment at finding, when the covers were removed, that a plum or college pudding did duty for the woodcock and snipe. How heartily did the host chuckle when he called out, "Help Mr. —— first; he has waited for that bird; or would he like some of this?" Poor Byng! his loss was deeply deplored by a large circle of friends, and by no one more than by the chronicler of his kind, though eccentric, actions.

CHAPTER XVIII.

CHAPTER XVIII.

IT is now about thirty years ago that I passed two winters at that queen of spas, Leamington; and a more delightful place it was never my good fortune to visit. The Warwickshire hounds, under that first-rate sportsman, Thornhill, hunted four times a week within easy distance of the town. The Pytchley occasionally enabled us to join them; and by sending a horse over night to the Broadway country, a run with the late Lord Fitzhardinge's hounds could be ensured. Dinner parties, balls, concerts, and private theatricals were the order of the evening, while an excellent club held at the Regent Hotel was an agreeable lounge throughout the day. Jepthson was at that time in the zenith of his professional glory, and was always ready to promote every sort of gaiety. Sir Thomas Mostyn kept open house, so did the Dormers, the Dillons, the Tichbornes, the Somervilles, the Eastnors, and others, all vying with one another to render the spa agreeable.

Among the visitors there was Sir Charles Chad, whom I had known some years before at Brussels, and whose son had a great taste for theatricals. Young Chad consulted me upon the propriety of getting up a few performances for charitable purposes, and I promised him every assistance in my power; but the task was greater than I had anticipated. In the first place, there was no theatre at that time in Leamington, no actresses whose services we could retain within an easy distance of it, and last, not least, there was a strong prejudice against theatrical amusements, which was shared by many of the leading residents and visitors. When I canvassed my friends and acquaintances to join the *corps dramatique*, I was met with every sort of objection. The married ladies did not wish their husbands to mix themselves up with professional actresses; the single ladies thought a ball or even a carpet dance so much better than any private play; the old ladies quoted the opinions of the Reverend Mr. Close, at Cheltenham, and denounced the undertaking as one that ought not to be patronised. The lords of the creation were equally difficult to manage. One objected to the expense, another to the plays I suggested, a third to the part I proposed; and I

became nearly disheartened, when a fortuitous circumstance occurred.

This was the arrival of a strolling company of
players, who advertised a performance in the assembly-rooms. Chad and myself attended it ; and, after
the play was over, we had an interview with the
manager, and found him most willing to enter into
our views. My propositions were that he should
act as stage manager and prompter, and that the
ladies of his company should give us their assistance.
To these he gratefully acceded ; and our next step
was to see Elliston, the proprietor of the rooms. I
had known his father, the great William Robert,
intimately, and the son at once promised me his aid.

A meeting of the amateurs was then called, and
only five attended, including Chad, Glanville (of the
21st Fusiliers), Dr. Jones, Donnithorne Taylor, and
another, whose name has escaped my memory. Chad,
the promoter of the undertaking, had set his heart
upon acting *Dr. Ollapod*, in the "Poor Gentleman;"
and from a specimen I had seen of his histrionic
powers, I reckoned greatly upon him; but, although
a host in himself, it was impossible with so small a
force to fill up the characters. So I suggested other
pieces with fewer personages—" Charles II.," " Ma-
trimony," " How to Die for Love," &c. The first was
objected to as having been so recently played by the

strollers, and the others were not considered of sufficient importance to set before a paying audience.

After other propositions, which were opposed, we were just about to abandon the scheme, when I made a suggestion which was carried unanimously. It was to advertise a series of dramatic performances in the Leamington papers, and trust to volunteers joining our ranks when they found we were in earnest. Past experience had proved to me that such would be the case; and in this instance my anticipations were realised, for in eight-and-forty hours after the announcement that in the course of three weeks the "Poor Gentleman" and the " Review " would be acted at a new theatre about to be erected in the assembly-rooms, I had more applications from aspirants to theatric fame than I could attend to. Another meeting was called, the parts cast, and a rehearsal named. In the meantime Elliston and myself were busily employed in hiring scenery from the Warwick theatre, raising a stage, and dividing the room into pit and boxes.

The morning of the rehearsal arrived; my stage manager and prompter, accompanied by his wife and two young ladies, were present, and as all the amateurs were nearly perfect, I began to congratulate myself upon the success of the undertaking, more especially as many tickets had been sold, and places secured. A second rehearsal was called, when to my great dismay I found that the duties of my managership were almost too much for me. One amateur had thrown up his part in disgust, and another wished to have a more prominent one in the farce if he consented to act the walking gentleman in the comedy. Having arranged the above little matters, I fondly flattered myself all difficulties were got over, when the manager's wife came forward and said, in rather a pompous tone, that the character I had assigned her was not at all suited to her abilities. Before I could recover from my astonishment, the *prima donna* put in a claim to have a song introduced both in play and farce.

It required no ghost to tell me that there was a regular mutiny in the camp, and that unless I took some very decisive step to quell it, we should soon be left without actresses. Requesting the company to be seated, I called for pen, ink, and paper, and sent to the Regent Hotel, where I kept my horses, for my groom to come round immediately, mounted and ready to convey a letter for me. After penning my despatch, which I showed to my colleagues, I addressed the mutineers in nearly the following words :—" Ladies, the characters assigned to you are those you have been in the habit of performing, as I see by the playbills. If, however, you object

to them, I have only to remark that your engagement is at an end.   This letter which I have
addressed to Mr. Penley, whose company is now
acting at Coventry, will, I have no doubt, remove
all difficulties, for I took the precaution of ascertain-
ing what his views were when a hint was given
me of what has since occurred.   On behalf of my
friends and myself, I beg to assure you that it is
our wish to make your engagement as agreeable and
remunerative to you as possible; but we prefer at
once to cancel it, sooner than run the risk of having
difficulties thrown in our way."   A penitential
apology was the result of this address, and from
that moment nothing could be more loyal than the
conduct of the ladies.   Our first play went off
admirably.   The room was crowded to excess, and
the plaudits were loud and enthusiastic.   Another
performance was arranged—"Charles II." and
"Bombastes Furioso"—which was equally successful.   In the first piece, Chad, Donnithorne Taylor,
and Glanville—the latter as *Captain Copp*, and the
two former as the *Merry Monarch* and *Rochester*—
covered themselves with dramatic fame.   There
was one incident which ought to be recorded.
Chad required a dress, and I recommended him to
apply to Nathan, the celebrated costumier.   His
letter was characteristic:—

" SIR,—I wish a dress sent here next Monday for "Charles II." I am five foot ten, and perfect symmetry.

" Your obedient,

" C. CHAD."

The order was attended to, and the dress fitted admirably.

During the whole of the performances, Elliston had been indefatigable in his exertions; and feeling that they ought to be rewarded, I proposed, during supper, after the second performance, that we should repeat "Charles II." and "Bombastes Furioso," for his benefit, allowing him to act *Megrim* in the interlude of "Blue Devils"—a favourite character of his father, and one which he was well up in. To my great annoyance, I found one dissentient, who objected to perform if a professional took any part. In vain I tried to combat his arguments, he was obdurate. "Then," said the others, "the play must be abandoned." "Not at all," I replied, "I will pledge myself to get a substitute, much as I regret being compelled to look out for one." We parted, and I lost no time in applying to my friend Augustus Berkeley, who was then at Cheltenham, asking him to join our company. In the meantime, I had told the manager to study the part in case his services were required. The posters were out, announcing a performance for the benefit of Mr. Elliston, giving the characters; but, instead of filling the vacated one with a name, I inserted "by an amateur of distinction." It soon oozed out that I had written to Cheltenham; and a rumour was spread over the town that some of the amateurs who had made a sensation at Cheltenham, Gloucester, Tewkesbury, Birmingham, and Worthing, under the late Earl Fitzhardinge, were to join my corps. Such, however, was not the case, as Augustus Berkeley's engagements did not permit him to come to my rescue, willing as he was to serve me. In the meantime the seceder thought better of it, expressed his regret in the handsomest manner, and was soon reinstated in his former place.

As the *prima donna* had behaved extremely well, and I was anxious to give as good a performance as possible upon Elliston's night, I felt most anxious to afford her an opportunity of showing forth her vocal powers, which were really of no very mean order. This young lady's ambition had been to sing Bellini's *chef-d'œuvre*, "*Ah, non giunge;*" but how could it be introduced into "Charles II." or "Bombastes Furioso," more especially as the part of *Distaffina* was in the hands of another? "May I not sing it between the acts?" asked the syren in a most beseeching tone, one that would have nearly melted the heart of a rhinoceros. "Impossible," I responded. "I have had at least a dozen applications from some of the amateurs to sing songs, and I have been compelled to refuse one and all." "But in the case of a professional lady," continued the other, "you might, perhaps, make an exception to the rule?" "I regret to be obliged to say no; but I will throw out a suggestion that may meet the difficulty." The syren was all attention. "You are aware," I proceeded, "that although in 'Bombastes Furioso' there is only one female character, a second is referred to, namely—

> " Scrubinda the fair,
> Who lives by the scouring of pots
> In Dyott Street, Bloomsbury Square."

"I remember," replied the young lady, "the *General* raves about her." "It has occurred to me," I continued, "that I could introduce an interview between this fair beauty and *Bombastes;* write some dozen lines for them to recite, previous to her singing a translation of '*Ah, non giunge;*' and thus afford you, by an additional scene, the opportunity you covet." "Oh, pray do!" she said. "It will be the making of me." "In the course of the day you shall hear from me," I replied; and I immediately set to work to fulfil my promise.

The scene was arranged—a room in Dyott Street, with the fair *Scrubinda* carrying on her vocation. After a few doggrel rhymes, in which she mourned the absence of her conquering hero, she commenced her *bravura :*—

> " Ah, non giunge !
> I no fun see,
> Now my hero is gone to the wars.
> Dear Bombastes,
> My heart aghast is,
> At the thought of wounds, gashes, and scars.
> Loved Furioso,
> My future sposo,
> Such sad thoughts quite madden my brain ;
> And poor Scrubinda
> From the window
> Will dash herself thus to cease all her pain."

Just as the lady was about to realise her threat, the *General* made his appearance, declaring that absence had increased, rather than diminished, the ardour of his love. Throwing himself upon his knees, he exclaimed, in words taken from an old burlesque of mine on "Kenilworth"—

> " I for your beauty, dearest maid, am dying,
> And at your feet I lie."

When she replied, naïvely—

> " I see you're *lying*."

A quarrel then ensued, and the hero so lately dubbed Duke of Strombello, narrowly escaped a severe con-

tusion from a pewter pot, which was aimed at his
head. At rehearsal, I had some little trouble with
the representative of *Distaffina*, who threatened to
throw up her part if another Statira appeared on the
boards; but this difficulty was got over, and the
farce was advertised, with an additional character
and scene, in the course of which Bellini's celebrated song was to be introduced. The whole went
off very well. "*Ah, non giunge*" met with an
enthusiastic encore, and the syren was prouder than
any peahen that ever strutted in a farm-yard. For
some months I heard no more of private or public
theatricals, till one day, when travelling to Cheltenham with my friend Donnithorne Taylor, to hunt
with the Berkeley hounds at Dumbleton. Passing
through Stratford-on-Avon, I perceived my name in
large letters at the top of a playbill. Stopping the
post-boy, my companion and myself descended, and
were not a little amused at reading the following
notice :—

" For this night only : 'Bombastes Furioso,' with
a new scene and song, written expressly for Miss
Selina Craven, to Bellini's celebrated air of ' *Ah
non giunge*,' by the Right Honourable Lord William
Lennox." Lower down appeared the cast, "*Scrubinda
the Fair*, by Miss Selina Craven, in which character
she will introduce a song written for and sung by

her, with unbounded applause, at the Amateur
Theatricals at Leamington." A third notice stated
that "the new scene, which produced such a risible
effect upon a large and fashionable house, and the
song that had been enthusiastically encored, on the
occasion of the benefit of Mr. Elliston, son of
William Robert Elliston, were from the versatile
pen of Lord William Lennox."

Any passer by, who did not take the trouble to
read through the poster, would have been attracted
by the following names in huge type: "Miss Selina
Craven, Lord William Lennox, William Robert
Elliston, and Bellini," headed by "Concentration
of vocal, literary, and dramatic talent."

While I am on the subject of private theatricals,
and my efforts as a dramatic author, I must allude
to a far more recent occurrence. When the Town
Hall at Hounslow was opened, in 1859, I was
called upon to deliver the inaugural address, and to
write a prologue for the amateur theatricals which
were got up for the occasion. I quote the newspaper
account of the opening :—

" The Hounslow Town Hall was opened for public
use on Wednesday, June 22nd, 1859, when, at eleven
o'clock A.M., a party of nearly five hundred persons of
the town and neighbourhood assembled in the large
room, to listen to the addresses of the chairman of

the directors, R. A. Frogley, Esq., H. Bullock, Esq., and other gentlemen connected with the institution. Mr. Frogley commenced the proceedings in a very able and appropriate speech. He referred to the building, pointing out the moral benefit that was likely to accrue to the public from such an undertaking, and concluded a most admirable address, by saying that, in the absence of Baron Pollock, Lords Carlisle and Ripon, he had prevailed upon Lord William Lennox to deliver the inaugural address. After a most animated and interesting detail as to the origin and erection of the hall, the state of the finances, and the objects of the committee, by Mr. Bullock, Lord William Lennox advanced to the front of the platform, and, amidst the most flattering cheers, spoke as follows :—'Ladies and Gentlemen, when I first entered this hall I was not aware that I should be called upon to take any part in the proceedings of the day; it is true that, last week, I received an application to address you on this occasion, but I respectfully declined the proffered honour, because I felt how totally incompetent I was to the task, and that there were many gentlemen connected with this town and its vicinity who could be found to do greater justice to the cause which has brought us together. You have heard the appeal made to me by your respected townsman,

my valued friend, Mr. Frogley, and that appeal,
backed by your kind expression, has left me no
alternative but to obey the call you have made.
Indeed, I do not look upon myself as a volunteer,
who is proverbially considered better than two
pressed men, but as one of the latter class, forced
into the service.   Mr. Frogley's request reminds me
of the usual remark of a police constable, who, in
conveying a culprit to the station-house, seizes him
by the collar, exclaiming, in the most polite manner,
" I wish to use no compulsion, but you must come
along with me."

" ' Perhaps a happier illustration might be found by
referring to the days when the heath at the out-
skirts of the town enjoyed a very unenviable
notoriety.   Many an unsuspecting traveller or
simple-minded Londoner, who wished to escape
from the heat and turmoil of the metropolis to
enjoy the balmy breeze that swept over the then
open barren heath, found himself suddenly stopped,
and in courteous phraseology told to " stand and
deliver," with the agreeable assurance that in the
event of a refusal, his brains would be scattered to
the winds.   Now, without meaning to compare my
friend, Mr. Frogley, to one of the heroes of the
road, I cannot help feeling myself in the position of
the unsuspecting traveller—the victimised cockney

—who, having quitted London for a quiet day in the country, finds himself arrested in his progress, and called upon to "stand and deliver"—a speech. The very demand has so scattered my brains, that I fear I shall not be able to collect them sufficiently to address you upon the more serious and sober reflections that naturally arise in the breast of every one who witnesses the completion of an undertaking fraught with benefit of the greatest magnitude to the inhabitants of this town and neighbourhood. Among the gigantic strides that have been made within the last few years in the march of improvement, there are few things more striking than the rapid advance which has taken place with respect to the education of the million, and the facilities of affording them useful information and entertainment. Schools for all classes, for all denominations, for all ages, have been opened—where the adults may make up for former neglect, and where children clothed as Lazarus was, can find ready admittance; but the work would only be half finished, if, after teaching people to write, read, and reflect, you did not furnish them with books and institutions similar to the one that has this morning been inaugurated with a view of affording them intellectual recreation. Indeed, it would be worse than mockery, if, after enlightening the mind and

giving the recipients a craving for improvement,
you did not open channels through which useful
instruction might flow.   To accomplish so desirable
an end, this hall has been erected, and there is every
reason to believe that the result will prove most
beneficial to the inhabitants at large.   If my
memory does not fail me, I think it is Addison that
says, " I consider a human soul without education
like marble in a quarry, which shows none of its
inherent beauties until the skill of the polisher
fetches out the colours, makes the surface shine, and
discovers every ornamental cloud, spot, and vein
that runs through the body of it.   Education, after
the same manner, when it works upon a noble mind,
draws out to view every talent, virtue, and perfection which, without such helps, are never able to
make their appearance."   But we must ever bear in
mind that, although

> " 'Tis education forms the common mind,
>   Just as the twig is bent the tree's inclined,"

it occasionally may be turned from a truthful, right,
and proper course.   It is, then, the bounden duty
of all to exert every human method to direct education in the proper channel, and the most effectual
way of promoting so desirable an object, is to
provide standard works that will raise the moral
feelings and elevate the soul, instead of encouraging

the perusal of volumes calculated to inflame the mind of the reader with disaffection, immorality, and irreligion. To carry out this view, I trust that the time is not far distant when a library of useful knowledge will be added to the institution. There is another method of improving the mind, and it is one which is now carried on with the greatest advantage to the masses; I allude to lectures on Bible knowledge, geography, astronomy, geology, history, philosophy, biography, architecture, literature, temperance, provident habits, engineering, mechanism, and other popular subjects. I hope sincerely, then, that when the days set in, the directors of this institution will have it in their power to welcome their friends and neighbours to an intellectual feast. Among the unspeakable blessings of being born in a land where wisdom and knowledge flourish, may be mentioned the deep interest with which many of our greatest men—I speak of intellect, not wealth—have stepped forth boldly as the champions of popular education, and by their works and labours, have contributed largely to the public good. Among these, the name of Brougham first occurs, as the father of cheap literature, and the founder, in conjunction with Dr. Birkbeck, of mechanics' institutions. Nor must we forget the highly-cultivated intellect of a Stanhope; the keen judgment, the laborious re-

search of a Macaulay; the picturesque vigour of a
Carlyle; the grace of the gifted poet, essayist,
novelist, and senator, Bulwer; the glowing language, forcible in its application, vivid in its description, touching in its appeal, the acute insight
into men and things, of a Dickens; the versatility
and vigour, the profound thought, of a Thackeray,
whether in laying bare the follies of "Vanity Fair,"
or the vices of the unworthies who figured during
the reigns of the four Georges; the careful re-
search in sifting the mass of facts and fiction
of bygone history of a Harrison Ainsworth; or
the instructive and amusing lectures of an Albert
Smith.   Let us then hope that some of the
above gifted men, and others, whose names do not
occur to me at this moment, may be found to
come forward in the cause of the educated com-
munity—a far different body from the educated
class—to delight and instruct them by their
writings.

"'Had I not already occupied so large a portion of
your time, I might refer to Hounslow as it was, and
Hounslow as it is.   I might enter into an erudite
dissertation as to the derivation of its ancient name,
Hundislawe, of its historical associations, when many
a conference took place between four peers and
twenty knights of Louis the Dauphin of France, and

the same number of nobles and knights on the part
of Henry III. of England, or dwell upon its ancient
priory, which was founded in the thirteenth century.
I could turn to the heath—to its Roman road and
camp, to the tournaments, which were so dangerous
to the public peace in times of baronial discontent,
held there in the reign of King John, to the forces
that have been assembled upon it in the days of
Charles II., and James II., and to the encampment
of the army of the Duke of Marlborough, in 1740;
I could dilate upon the deeds of the highwaymen,
who for so many years carried on their depredations
in this then wild district.   I could draw a romantic
sketch of the days when the noise of clanking chains
was heard at the junction of cross-roads, and other
spots, and when a whitened skeleton told that a
criminal had expiated his crimes upon the gallows.
But I pass from such subjects to one more congenial
to your tastes, and one which I trust will " point a
moral" if it does not "adorn my tale;" I allude to
the rapid march of improvement that has shown
itself in the cultivation of the land.   The waste
land has been tilled and enclosed, and, as if by the
wand of Aladdin, neat villas, picturesque cottages,
and substantial homesteads, have sprung up in the
place of dreary hovels, tenantless buildings, and dila-
pidated sheds, giving an air of comfort and civili-

sation to this once barren spot. And does not this suggest another vast improvement? Why should the earth alone be drained, ploughed, and prepared for crops? Does not the human mind require equal care? Are there not weeds to be plucked up? Are there not flowers to be planted? Are there not seeds to be sown? Ought not the light of the days we live in to be carried into the former dark abodes? If you assent to this proposition, as I feel assured you do, then have you done your best to complete this good work by the ready support you have given to this truly national undertaking; and in conclusion may I offer up a fervent prayer that the work nurtured by your fostering care, and shone upon by the sunny smiles of the fairer portion of the creation, whose exertions have been so conspicuous, will by God's blessing ensure a plentiful harvest.' George M. Dowdeswell, Esq., then proposed a vote of thanks to his Lordship, which was enthusiastically agreed to, and after Lord William Lennox had briefly acknowledged the compliment, the meeting broke up."

The inauguration was soon followed by some theatrical performances, in which many of the gentry round Hounslow took a part. The prologue which I was requested to write, as already stated, ran as follows :—

Gent. Like a young lover, in whose anxious face
His modest yet ambitious hopes you trace,
To plead the cause of our untutored band,
And claim indulgence from their friends, I stand:
Yet let us hope no critics fill our pit,
Severe and conscious of o'erwhelming wit,
For to amusement we a nobler aim
Would add, and the Town Hall your mite shall claim.
Should we then fail, we trust at least the cause
Of our endeavours merits some applause.
Should we succeed, no plaudits loud,
No acclamation from the crowd
We seek :—be this our highest prize,
A smile from beauty's cheek—a tear from beauty's eyes.
                              [*Enter a lady.*

Lady. Cease your " soft sawder," here's a pretty mess !
'Twas I that should have spoken the address.
The men have no *address.*

Gent.   That fact confessing,
Yet ladies oftentimes give men *a dressing*
In curtain Caudle lectures.

Lady.   Stop, 'tis certain,
We *prize* no *Prys* who peep behind the curtain.

Gent. Excuse me, madam.

Lady.   Silence, not a word !
I claim a woman's rights, and will be *heard.*
The common *herd* 'gainst female sceptre rave.
(Britannia never yet has been a slave.)
Dare to invade our isle; on such occasion
We'll not be *napping* during *Nap's* invasion.
Decked out in steel, we'll form that " small red line,"
That is, I mean to say, red crinoline.
Maids, wives, and widows—dashing volunteers ;
Our *grand dams*, too, will furnish *granny dears*,
To rally round the throne, and take our stand ;
Our watchword " Liberty, our Queen, our Native Land.'
Then let the *Zouaves* approach, they'll quickly see
" *Zouav*iter in modo, fortiter in re."
And *Buono*-Johnnie—John Bull, hale and hearty,
Won't dub Napoleon a *Buono-parte.*

Gent. But I've *appealed* to friends.

Lady.   What's the male creature after ?
Why, such *appeals* will bring down *peals* of laughter.
"Cause and applause" "be to our foibles blind,
And to our merits very, very kind."
Why sue for favour ? as the turfites say,
Hold out your simple motto—" Play and pay."
Your stale, unprofitable, *flat* remarks have scattered
My poor ideas.

Gent.   Madam, the *flat* is *flattered.*

Lady. I must *collect* them.

Gent.   They're worth *recollecting* ;
Like Town Hall dividends, are they worth *collecting ?*
That is, at present.   Nay, don't look askance,
The market's buoyant ; shares will soon advance.

Lady. Let's leave the "keen encounter of our wit,"
While I address the stalls—you called it pit.

Gent. 'Tis true, pit *rhymed* to wit, and in this frosty season
We look much more for *rime*, you know, than reason.

Lady. Give me the word [*aside to prompter*] ; I've quite forgot
      my part.

Gent. As amateur, pray don't take that to heart.

Lady. Oh, I remember [*reads part*]. "Downfall of the stage,"
" The winter theatres."   " Bad degenerate age."
The Bard of Avon patronised at Court.

Gent. Excuse me, madam, prithee cut it short.

Lady. Muse o'er the glories of the bygone scene,
Where stately Siddons—soul-inspiring Kean—
Majestic Kemble— held their potent spell—
"Thou last of all the Romans, fare thee well "—
Plaintive O'Neil—Jordan, pure Nature's child,
In long link'd sweetness—

Gent.   Madam, draw it mild.

Lady. Yet there are those in this degenerate age
Whose sunny smiles revive the drooping stage ;
Who offer homage to dramatic fame,
And nobly foster Shakespeare's honoured name.
Hail to Victoria—daughter of the isles—
The love of millions, who state care beguiles
With scenes from Avon's bard.   Long may she sway
O'er loyal hearts.

Gent.   Long, long may we obey.

A very ludicrous mistake which might have been attended with unsatisfactory results occurred at Hounslow on the occasion of an amateur play. The piece selected was Bulwer's "Lady of Lyons," in which a very learned doctor who practises in the Divorce Court, and a most talented lady, Miss Katherine Hickson, were to take the parts of *Claude Melnotte* and *Pauline*. The other characters were to be filled by professional ladies and gentlemen from London. A lady, well known in Hounslow for her hospitality, and her anxiety to promote the interest of the town, had taken upon herself the *rôle* of manageress, perhaps the only one she was unable to fill successfully. She had previously asked me to take a part, but I excused myself, saying I had not been on the boards since my return from Canada. This led to an inquiry as to the characters I had studied, and among others I mentioned a favourite one, *Major Sturgeon* in the "Mayor of Garratt." "I won't forget," she said significantly; "and if we ever claimed your services, how long would it take to get ready in the part?" "A few hours," I replied; "for I played it once or twice at Brussels, and three times at least at Quebec." Nothing more was said, and the eventful morning arrived, when the last rehearsal was to take place. Mrs. F. had sent a telegraphic message to me, urging my

attendance at the rehearsal, and as I had offered
upon all occasions to make myself generally useful,
I fancied I might be called upon to prompt the
play, or superintend the stage department. Upon
reaching the Town Hall, I found many of the performers anxiously awaiting my arrival, and heard
the prompter say, "Now his lordship is here, we
can go over his scenes." Before I had time to
inquire the meaning of a remark that fell from
Miss Hickson, "How fortunate it is you are up in
the part!" Mrs. F. had joined me. "How kind of
you!" she said. "I've got your dress ready—a
military frock coat, with this silk sash, sword, and
forage cap, which I have borrowed from the officers:
all you require is a pair of Napoleon boots, and I
have sent to Simmons for them. He furnishes all
the dresses." "What can you mean?" I asked.
"Why the *Major*, you told me, you had acted it
very often," responded the lady. "Last night, the
gentleman who had undertaken the character was
so imperfect, that we gladly dispensed with his
services, and I have just sent to the printer to strike
off some new playbills announcing the fact of your
having consented to act the *Major* at a short
notice." "*Colonel Damas* wanted," cried the call-
boy, in a squeaking voice. "*Colonel Damas!*" I
exclaimed. "Yes," said the lady innocently.

" *Colonel* or *Major Damas*, was not that the character you told me you had so often performed in
Canada?" "Why," I responded, "the play has
only been written a few years; Bulwer's dramatic
fame was not even in prospective existence when I
was at Quebec. It was *Major Sturgeon*, not *Colonel
Damas*, that I prided myself in playing." "What
an awful mistake I must have made!" rejoined
Mrs. F.; "I knew it was a *Major* or a *Colonel;* but
what's to be done?" after a pause she continued,
"It's now only one o'clock, could you not study it
by seven o'clock?" "Impossible," I replied,
"but there's no time to be lost, I will start at once
for London, and procure a substitute." So suiting
the action to the word, I made the best of my way
to the station, proceeded to London by rail, sought
a theatrical stage manager, with whom I was on
terms of intimacy, and returned at six o'clock, with
a gentleman fully competent to take the part. The
play went off well, Dr. S. and Miss Hickson acted
admirably, and in the after-piece of "Boots at the
Swan" Captain Boucher of the 5th Royal Irish
Lancers acted *Jacob Earwig* in a manner fully equal
to Robson.

Upon a previous occasion Mrs. F. had nearly got
me into a scrape similar to the one above recorded.
On the opening of the new theatre at the Town

Hall the play of "The Honeymoon" was selected.
In casting the parts, Mrs. F. said, "You must
reserve a good low comedy part for a young friend
of mine. He acted admirably last Christmas in a
burlesque." "He can have *Jacques*," I replied,
"the mock duke, *Lopez*, the country clod, or *Lampedo*, the half-starved apothecary. *Lampedo* will
just suit him; he is tall and thin." Having
agreed to the above proposition, I thought no more
of the business until the morning of the first
rehearsal, when all the *corps dramatique* were
assembled. As a professional gentleman attended
as prompter, I took up my station in a front seat,
that I might note down any shortcomings, and
make any suggestions that might occur to me. All
went well until the scene where *Lampedo* was to
appear, when, to my great surprise, a lad entered
with a school-boy look, hands in pockets, and perfectly unfitted, from his age and size, for the grown-
up apothecary. I listened with amazement. Young
Fitzhardinge Lye, for such was his name, recited
the part admirably, was letter perfect, and most
anxious to do justice to the character he had undertaken; still, when he had to talk of his wife and
children, the effect was so ludicrous, that I feared
if I allowed the play to go on with such a cast,
Tobin's clever comedy would be converted into a

screaming farce. Some of the performers flocked round me, urging me to make a change; but, anxious as I was to effect it, many difficulties arose. In the first place, I was desirous not to hurt the feelings of the boy, his mother, or Mrs. F.; secondly, I knew no one who would take the part; and, lastly, if I found one, few amateurs, when thus called upon, would have time to study it. "We will go on with the rehearsal," I said, "and come to me after it, Lye. You conceive the character very well." While the rehearsal was in progress, I went over to Mrs. F.'s house, read the character of *Lampedo*, and altered it to that of the apothecary's boy, making him say, "What will my master and his wife and children say?" In short, I adopted the plan of the country manager who, finding that the youth who was to represent young *Norval* was too nervous to utter a line, rushed on the stage in a Highland garb, and said, "This young gentleman's name is Norval: on the Grampian hills this young gentleman's father feeds his flocks, a frugal swain; whose constant care was to increase his store, and keep his only son, this young gentleman, at home." Upon returning to the Town Hall, I told the company that I had taken a very great liberty with the author, and, with the wand of a harlequin, had changed the "full-aged" apothecary to a druggist's "hobble-de-hoy." The result was satisfactory, and few amateurs ever received more genuine applause than did Fitzhardinge Lye on the above occasion. But the word "satisfactory," and the near shave I had in making the performance so, reminds me of a story attributed to Douglas Jerrold. Some one took him a play called "The Factory Boy." "I don't quite like the name," said the author, with mock humility. "Then call it the Unsatis-factory Boy," the wit replied.

CHAPTER XIX.

I HAVE alluded more than once in the course of these volumes to the time when I sat for King's Lynn; and my bloodless election for that borough has been recorded in a former work. The mode of choosing a candidate at King's Lynn certainly forms a striking contrast to that adopted by some of the larger towns, as I shall now proceed to show. A story is told of Mr. Coke, of Norfolk (afterwards Lord Leicester), which, though it had a great effect on the career of Lord George Bentinck, does not appear in Mr. Disraeli's life of that nobleman. When Mr. Coke was residing at Holkham, a deputation from King's Lynn (which was then a close borough) came to ask him to recommend a candidate for a vacancy caused by the death of one of the members. Mr. Coke was out shooting, and while waiting for him two of the aldermen saw a fine stalwart man, who seemed by his costume to

be a gamekeeper. "Would you like, gentlemen, to
look round the garden?" said he. "We shall be
delighted, my good man," responded one of the
deputation. Shortly afterwards the owner of Holkham made his appearance, and one of the aldermen
was about to fee the gamekeeper guide, when he
was interrupted by Mr. Coke expressing his regret
that he should have been out of the way, and
adding that he was glad Titchfield had done the
honours of the garden. Again the alderman put his
hand to his pocket, and was about to say, "Titchfield, here's half-a-crown for you," when, to his
surprise, Mr. Coke said, "By the way, gentlemen,
let me introduce you to my friend, the Marquis of
Titchfield." The worthy aldermen looked at one
another, evidently fearful that their manner had
not been such as they would have wished it to have
been towards the eldest son of the Duke of Port-
land. "But your business, gentlemen?" inquired
Mr. Coke. It was easily told. "I do not think
you can do better, gentlemen, than take a Bentinck
for your member." Happy at the opportunity
afforded them of making some little reparation for
the act of *betism*, they readily assented; and from
that day until the death of the late lamented Lord
George Bentinck, a member of that family represented King's Lynn in Parliament.

Among the curiosities of this town, there was a very ancient register-book belonging to the corporation, and known as the "Red Book," from the original binding having been of that colour. It is thought to be the oldest English paper book in existence, and the leaves have become reduced by age to a loose cottony substance, so much so that they threaten to fall to pieces when touched. The book numbers a hundred and fifty leaves. The first entry is a transcript of the will of Peter de Thornden, burgess of Lynn, dated 1309; the latest entry is on page 100, with the date of 15 Richard 29. Since I saw the above old relic, I am happy to hear that the authorities have had each leaf carefully resized, and the book will now last for many years to come.

I will now cross to the other side of England, and show the promised contrast by reference to the Liverpool election of 1830, when the town was contested by William Ewart and J. E. Denison, Esqs. The contest lasted from Tuesday, the 23rd, to Tuesday, the 30th of November: 4,335 freemen voted, and Ewart was returned; but the election was vitiated in consequence of gross bribery and corruption among the voters. Denison's colours were red and dark blue; Ewart's, pink and sky blue.

Before giving my impressions of the contest, I must dwell for a moment on the immense growth of Liverpool and Birkenhead since the beginning of the century. In 1801, the population of Liverpool was 82,295; in 1811, it had risen to 104,104; in 1821, to 138,154; in 1831, to 201,751; in 1841, to 286,487; in 1851, to 375,955; and in 1861, to 443,874. The Aladdin-like transformation of Birkenhead has been described in terms of equal rapture by a provincial journalist and a noble diplomatist. The former writes—"A new Carthage has arisen on the left bank of the Mersey; and here, if you ascend as far as Oxton, the lines of Virgil will not be inappropriate :—

> ' They climb the next ascent, and looking down,
> Now at a nearer distance view the town ;
> The prince with wonder sees the stately towers
> (Which late were huts, and shepherds' lowly bowers),
> The gates, and streets ; and hears from every part
> The noise and busy concourse of the mart.'

All is bustle, life, and activity. New streets, spacious squares, market-places, churches, chapels, crescents, paragons, and parades, have risen up, while picturesque villas dot the environs. The new Birkenhead improvements will consist of a new dock, two basins, a canal, an extended quay, and a railway to transport raw materials, and bring back manufactured goods. The site of the new city affords many advantages—pure air, good water, and proximity to one of the finest garden parks in England." The noble lord thus writes:—" I have made a very agreeable trip to Birkenhead, which is a place rising, as if by enchantment, out of the desert, and bidding fair to rival, if not eclipse, the glories of Liverpool. Seven years ago there were not three houses that side of the Mersey; there are now about 20,000 inhabitants; and on the spot where within that time Sir William Stanley's hounds killed a fox in the open field, now stands a square larger than Belgrave Square, every house of which is occupied. It would have been worth the trouble of the journey to make acquaintance with the projector and soul of this gigantic enterprise, Mr. Jackson. With his desire to create a great commercial emporium, proceeds, *pari passu*, that of improving and elevating the condition of the labouring classes there; and before his docks are even excavated, he is building houses for 300 families of workpeople, each house to have three rooms, to be free of all taxes, and plentifully supplied with water and gas, for half-a-crown a week each family. These houses adjoin the warehouses and docks where the people are to be employed; and there is to run a railroad to the river,

where every man liking to bathe will be conveyed for one penny. There are to be washhouses,
where a woman will be able to wash the linen of
her family for two-pence; and 180 acres have been
devoted to a park, which Paxton has laid out, and
nothing at Chatsworth can be more beautiful. At
least 20,000 persons were congregated there last
Sunday, all decently dressed, orderly, and enjoying
themselves. Chapels, and churches, and schools,
for every sect and denomination, abound. Mr.
Jackson says he shall create as vigorous a public
opinion against public-houses as is to be found in
the highest classes. There are now 3,000 workmen on the docks and buildings, and he is about
to take on 2,000 more. Turn which way you will,
you see only the most judicious application of
capital, skill, and experience — everything good
adopted, everything bad eschewed, from all other
places; and, as there is no other country in the
world, I am sure, that could exhibit such a sight
as this nascent establishment, where the best interests of commerce and philanthropy are so felici-
tously interwoven, I really felt an additional pride
at being an Englishman."

From this description of the scene of battle I will
return to the contest itself.

I happened to be on my way to Scotland, and had

agreed to pass a day with a friend, now no more, but then residing at Liverpool. During dinner, the conversation turned upon the all-engrossing subject, the pending election. "It will be one of the hardest contests ever fought," said one; "thousands will be spent upon it, and as for fun and excitement, there will be no end to them. Almost all the public-houses are thrown open by one party or the other, and all who wish to see the humours of an election had much better take up their quarters in the town for the next fortnight." Pressed by my friend to stay at least for the first few days, I readily assented; and I am happy that I did so, for the remembrance of the scene will never be effaced from my memory. Upon the following morning the polling-booths were opened, and through the assistance of a staunch partisan of Denison's, I got an excellent seat close to a central booth, near the Mansion House. The streets were filled with pedestrians, all wearing the badges of their favourite candidates; processions of men with banners and bands of music paraded the town; carriages filled with electors were to be seen everywhere; and their windows were crowded with well-dressed ladies, waving their handkerchiefs and ribbons to the assembled multitude. The first real insight I got into the proceedings, was when a man with a huge red and dark blue cockade upon his breast and his hat, made his way up to the booth. "Whom do you vote for, Mr. ——?" "I vote for corporation candidate." "That won't do, sir." Some one in the crowd seeing the colour of his ribbons, said, "Denison's your man." "All right. I vote a plumper for Denison;" then turning to a gentleman who had placed himself near the polling-clerk, "but I look to you, Mr. ——, for the money."

At night the scene was more wonderful than even during the day, for so anxious were the committees of both candidates that none of their partisans should be tampered with, that they had them assembled at different taverns, where they were kept till taken up to vote; not that they were kept there *vi et armis*, for the liquor they received was in a great measure an inducement.

Among other houses, my companions and myself visited a celebrated tavern of that day, called the "George the Fourth," and there we saw a sight to which Hogarth's pencil or Charles Dickens's pen could alone do justice. An immense room was crowded with persons of both sexes, singing, drinking, smoking, dancing, shouting, and hurraing. The smell of tobacco, mixed with that of every spirituous liquor that is known in England, was not very agreeable to the olfactory senses, while the noise was deafening. "Let me out," cried one; "When does the polling commence?" asked another; "More brandy," shouted a third; "Pipes and a bowl of punch," bellowed a fourth; "Hurrah for Ewart, and the pink and sky-blue colours." Some, *Bacchi pleni*, or overcome by Morpheus, were lying extended on tables and chairs, a few were quarrelling, others came to blows; in short, it seemed as if the humours of Donnybrook Fair, the orgies of a flash ken in St. Giles's, and the tumult of a prize fight had joined on this occasion to support the liberty of election. All were utterly regardless of the cry they set up of "No bribery," and far more faithful to the great constitutional maxim inscribed on so many publichouses, "To be drunk on the premises." So great was the sensation created by this celebrated election, that the scene I have attempted to describe was introduced into a French piece called "Richard Darlington," where the author not only made it appear that the free-born electors of England were confined like prisoners until their votes were recorded, but that many had been placed on board ship, and sent on a fortnight's cruise until the poll had closed. At this distance of time I should not like to name the almost fabulous sums that were expended on this contest. The bribery was so gross, that after the passing of the Reform Bill a motion was brought forward in the House of Commons to disfranchise the freemen who had taken part in the contest, but this was not carried. I myself felt some difficulty upon the subject of my vote, being fully aware of the practices that had been adopted; still I felt that under the new Reform Bill a recurrence of such evils would be avoided, and that by-gones ought to be by-gones. This view of the question did not satisfy O'Connell, who, in replying to some remarks I had made, regretted that I, "so liberal a reformer, should throw my shield over bribery."

The number of men who were once wealthy and have ruined or embarrassed themselves by a contested election, is far from being small. In olden times it was an established principle that every vote had to be paid for; and when we add the expenses of bringing up voters to the poll at a time when locomotion was costly, the expense of treating when liquor was heavily excised, we need not wonder at the way in which estates have changed hands, and rich families descended from their former position. A modern novelist speaks of a contest at which one of his characters " distinguished himself immensely, and ruined the family." I could point to places near London which were once proud estates, but are now let on building leases, and break out in crops of brick villas and houses under all conceivable names, and in every conceivable style of architecture. Well if their former owners did not take a further downward step, and land in some debtors' prison.

I am reminded of this end of so many good fortunes and careless lives by a visit I once paid to the Queen's Bench Prison, where I found at least fifty of my acquaintances whom I had lost sight of. I have often called on George Colman, Sir Lumley ' Skeffington, and others, in Melina Place or other precincts of the prison known as "within the rules"; and I found them living as luxuriously as if they had been at their own homes. I had also occasion to visit the Fleet Prison, the first beginnings of which are very curious.

The Fleet Prison was of great antiquity, and is mentioned in the first of Richard I. (1189), who confirmed to Osbert, brother to William Longshanks, Chancellor of England, and his heirs for ever, the custody of his house or palace at Westminster, with the keeping of his gaol of the Fleet at London. In the early times it was tenanted by offenders of rank; in the reign of Henry VI., 1453, Thomas Thorpe, Speaker of the House of Commons, was committed to it. A MS. in the British Museum gives "the names of all Bishops, Doctors, &c., that were prisoners in the Flytte for Religion synce the fyrste year of the Reygne of Queen Elizabeth, A.D. 1558," and, continuing about nine years, mentions eight priests, six doctors, and three bishops confined there for hearing and performing Mass. It was also a prison much used for offenders committed by the Star Chamber. From the reign of Charles I. until that of Victoria, it became appropriated to debtors, and those guilty of contempt against the Court of Chancery. In 1667, Sir Jeremy Whichcot, to whom and his heirs the office of Warden had been granted, rebuilt the prison.

Before the passing of the Marriage Act, during the reign of George II., the Fleet Prison was a notorious resort for the celebration of clandestine marriages, a sort of metropolitan Gretna Green. Persons of broken character, or no character at all, termed "Plyers," who walked in the street before the prison, were employed as touters to solicit custom; and signs were displayed over the apartments used as chapels. One of these signs represented a male and female hand in conjunction, with the words "Marriages performed within" underneath. The abuse arose from an oversight in the existing law, which punished clergymen solemnising such marriages by nothing more than a fine; to a person already incarcerated for debt, a fine was a nullity, and, having nothing to lose, he was able to set ecclesiastical suspension at defiance. The "noose" business became so thriving that some unconscientious ministers voluntarily resided within the precincts of the prison for the purpose of officiating, and in the chapel of one Keith six thousand persons are said to have been married within a year. Registers were kept, and for a length of time were admitted as evidence of marriage in the Courts of Law; but as in many instances false entries were made, they lost their authority.

Few persons living in the present day can be aware of the severity of the laws of arrest for debt some few years ago. It was in the power of a tradesman to incarcerate any debtor for an account not even delivered, and the expenses attending such an arrest often exceeded the amount claimed. I well remember being called upon one morning to visit a very old friend of mine, Granby Calcraft, who had been pounced upon by the Sheriff's officer, and lodged safely in a sponging-house, in Carey Street, Lincoln's Inn, for a debt for which he was legally, though not morally, responsible. At that period arrests were of daily occurrence, and it appears by Parliamentary returns that, in the eighteen months subsequent to

the panic of December, 1825, as many as 101,000
writs for debts were issued.   In the year ending
5th January, 1830, 7,114 persons were sent to
the several prisons of London, and on that day
1,547 of the number were yet confined.   On the
1st of January, 1840, the number of prisoners for
debt in England and Wales was 1,732.   In Ireland the number was under 1,000, and in Scotland
under 100.

Upon reaching the sponging-house, I found that,
without feeing the Cerberus, I should find some
delay in seeing my friend.   Having done what was
handsome, I was ushered into the front drawing-
room, which was neatly kept and gaudily furnished,
an organ, as it appeared to me, being the principal
object.

"Quite in your line, Granby," I said, after
having fully discussed the question of the arrest,
"an organ."

"Like the poet's chest of drawers," he replied,
"it has 'a double debt to pay;' it assumes the form
of an instrument by day, at night, by a pantomimic
process of touching a spring, it is converted into a
bed."

It would be tedious to enter into the cause of
Granby's incarceration.   Suffice it to say that he
could have lived at the Clarendon, under Jaquiere

the best hotel in London, for the sum he was charged
at his new temporary abode. A messenger cost five
shillings, stationery was equally extravagant, and
this, with apartments, attendance, hire of linen,
plate, washing, eating, drinking, and lights, amounted
to an awful sum. By the advice of his lawyer,
much against his own inclination, Calcraft agreed to
go to the Fleet, and take the benefit of what was
called the white-washing Act. I strongly backed
the solicitor's opinion, as the debt was for a thousand pounds, and the responsibility of it had fallen
on my friend by a suicidal act of one who had gone
joint security with him for a loan, of which Calcraft
had not touched a penny. After satisfying the legal
sharps, Granby was transferred to the Fleet prison,
where I lost no time in calling upon him. On my
approaching the door, the sound of a bell called my
attention to a small box, on which was painted
" Remember the debtors," and in which many a
shilling and copper had been dropped. As I entered
the racket court, where my friend was, I was quite
surprised at the number of faces that I recognised, and
the number of persons who addressed me. Of course
a loan was the object of their communication.
Calcraft took me to his room, a small apartment, as
scantily furnished as a barrack room is by the
authorities; however, it was a paradise compared

to the den in Carey Street, for the windows were not barred, and there was free access to the courts below. There was a market held within the walls of the prison, so that, with a tolerably stocked purse, a debtor was not very badly off. Friends were allowed to visit during the day, but after a certain hour were locked in for the night. Having paid my footing, by treating the poorer debtors to a more substantial meal than they were accustomed to enjoy, I was allowed to walk about without being molested, and, with one exception, was never again importuned for money. That exception was by an officer of one of the smartest hussar regiments in the service, whom I had known by sight, and had once met at dinner. He was at his window, enveloped in a splendid brocaded silk dressing-gown, with a velvet smoking cap on, puffing his cares away under the soothing influence of a handsome hookah. As I passed he dropped me a three-cornered note, written on scented pink paper, and containing the following lines :—

"Dear Ld. W.,

"Your old friend Frederick T——, whom you knew in Canada, dines with me next Monday week. As, of course, you will be at Goodwood races, if you could get me half a buck of the Halnaker venison, or even one of Southdown mutton, four-year old, I should be extremely obliged.

"Yours truly,

"————.

"P.S.—Be careful to pay the carriage, or the authorities may 'tap it on the shoulder.'"

As I was not disposed to comply with this cool request, I took no notice, further than to write a civil answer. After a few weeks Calcraft was emancipated, and the pain of leaving was great, for he felt nervous in again seeing his friends. They, however, rallied round him, no one more so than the Marquis of Clanricarde, who got Granby a post in New York, where he died. He was a clever, kind-hearted creature—no one's enemy but his own. His unfortunate marriage with Miss Love was a thorn in his side; for why she waited until *after* her marriage to elope with a nobleman who had offered her his protection *before* marriage, is a mystery I cannot divine.

CHAPTER XX.

CHAPTER XX.

IN the first chapter of the present work I have recorded my early impressions of Goodwood, and if I return to the subject now it is in order to pay my tribute to the memory of my eldest brother, the late Duke of Richmond. Charles Gordon Lennox, fifth Duke of Richmond, succeeded to the title and estates on the lamented death of his father, the fourth duke, in 1819. He was born in 1791, and educated at Westminster. In 1810 he was gazetted to the 13th Light Dragoons, and served on the staff of the Duke of Wellington during the rest of the Peninsular War. At Orthez he received a dangerous wound; a musket ball lodged in his chest, and was never extracted.

On succeeding to the title, my brother kept Goodwood closed for a time as a mark of respect to his father's memory. During this period he cleared off all encumbrances on the estate, and ever afterwards studied in all ways to improve it. Fond as he was of hunting and shooting, he took the deepest interest in agriculture, and parted with his deer to secure increased accommodation for his South Downs. It is in connection with sport at Goodwood that an anecdote occurs to me showing the extreme good humour and kindly feeling my brother displayed towards his family.

Although he was methodical in his affairs, and strictly attentive to public and private duties, no one enjoyed harmless sport and innocent mirth more than he did. Occasionally his younger brothers, myself among them, would take advantage of his kindness, and get up a joke against him. I recollect upon one occasion, during the shooting season, that he remarked the heads of game which were not accounted for, and, turning round to me, said, "I think, William, you must send away many a hare and pheasant to your friends." "I wish I had a chance," I replied. "By the way, can you let me have a brace of pheasants some day next week?" "Out of the question," responded "my Grace," as the Sussex labourers called him, thinking if "my Lord" was right, "my Grace" must be equally so: "I have so much to give away." "Oh! I understand," I continued, "the free and independent electors require some." "Not alone as electors," he replied, "for I give to my tenants, whatever their politics are." A little of what modern young men call "chaff" followed, and the subject dropped. We shot through the Halnaker farms, and, as it got dusk, the Duke said, "We must give up for to-day; bring me all the game that has been killed." Intent on mischief, I hastily withdrew, when the well-known voice of my brother hailed me. "I hope you are not helping yourself." "Oh, no," I replied, "I'm looking for a brace of pheasants I shot in the turnips." After a pause, I joined the party, which consisted of the late Lord Raglan, and Sir Charles Rowan, attended by Palmer the keeper, half a dozen beaters, and the man with the game cart. "Why, what on earth have you got in your side pockets?" asked Richmond, as he perceived something bulky in each, with a pheasant's feather protruding. "Nothing," I answered, "that you would care to have. I must walk home quickly, as I have a letter to finish." "Leave the pheasants behind you," added my brother. "What pheasants?" "Those you picked up in the turnip field." "Oh, you are welcome to all I got in the turnip field; here, Palmer, help me out with them.". That trusty keeper approached on one side, while I addressed a "clod" on the other, and said, "Take it out of my pocket." They dived simultaneously into the extensive pockets of my velveteen shooting jacket, and produced, not two specimens of those beautiful birds which originally were confined to the banks of the Phasis in Colchis, and were afterwards abducted from the borders of that river to the classical land of Greece, but—my reader will start when he reads it—two immense turnips. The gamekeeper looked abashed, Raglan and Rowan tried to suppress a laugh, as did the beaters, when the Duke said, most good-naturedly, "There, you may have the turnips, but I suppose the next thing you will ask for is a leg of Southdown mutton." Anxious to get the pheasants I had jocosely been accused of abstracting, I bided my time; and one morning, coming down at rather an early hour, I found my brother with a trusty friend arranging who were to receive the game killed during the week. I listened to the names as they were read out, with the claims attached to each. At last one was mentioned and approved of as having, although a Whig in politics, lent his valuable aid at an anti-free-trade-in-corn meeting recently held at Chichester. "By-the-way," I said, "a gentleman attended that meeting whose speech has given so much offence to the free-trade party that three of their leading organs of the press have devoted columns to attacking him in no measured terms. Here is one of their attacks." Without mentioning the name of the individual, I read a few lines to corroborate my statement. "If," said my brother, "I have been in the habit of sending him game, I have no objection to continue to do so, but not as a reward for supporting a just cause." "I can vouch for his having had game," I responded; "and moreover that he will take it as a compliment, and not as a reward for his exertions last Monday." "What is his name and address?" continued the Duke. "Lord William Lennox, No. 1, Berkeley Square, London," I responded. "Well, you deserve it," he replied; "not for your speech, which went a little too far, but for your sharpness in bringing about your wish." Of course, having gained my point, I told my brother that I would wait until a later period in the season; but as the return of "killed" had been great, the game was sent to my London address, to be forwarded to a friend for whom I had applied for it.

One of my brother's schoolfellows at Westminster was the late Sir James Graham, and the friendship formed there lasted through life. On one of Sir James's visits to Goodwood, an amusing circumstance occurred. Among the guests was the "Admiral," as he is called, *par excellence*, from the fact that his services in the navy are as conspicuous as those on the turf, and that it may be said of him that he was as much at home *in* the Downs as *on* the Downs. Henry Rous was sitting next to the Netherby baronet, at that time First Lord of the Admiralty, and during dinner was devoting his conversation entirely to him. After the ladies had left, the gallant sailor still engrossed Sir James; and some wags, of whom I am in candour bound to say I formed one, wrote on a scrap of paper, "Work the first lord for a ship, you can't *pique* him too much." This latter phrase applied to the frigate of that name, which Rous brought safe across the Atlantic from the St. Lawrence to Plymouth without a rudder. The servant to whom we entrusted this precious scrap, instead of giving· it to the gentleman next to Sir James Graham, gave it to Sir James himself, who read it, smiled, and passed it to his neighbour. Rous blushed, a regular honest blush, and began to stammer out some explanation; but this was needless, for no one enjoyed a joke more than the worthy baronet.

It is not often that one high official conveys a censure of the conduct of another, and Sir James Graham was not First Lord of the Admiralty at the time when the censure, to which I am about to refer, was conveyed. But the case was none the less curious. It was told me by my brother-in-law, Lord Fitzhardinge.

Fred Berkeley, as he was called before he was raised to the peerage, was travelling from Newmarket to London with my elder brother, the late Duke of Richmond, and they stopped upon their way to dine. The Duke of York met my brother at the door, and insisted upon his dining with him. "I cannot, your Royal Highness," he responded, "unless you will permit me to bring Captain Berkeley with me." "Bring him by all means," said the then Commander-in-chief. Upon entering the room where the Duke of York was, Fred was received in a most friendly way. His Royal Highness said afterwards, "I believe, Captain Berkeley, you were tried by a naval court-martial?" "I beg your Royal Highness's pardon," said the gallant officer, a little nettled; "it was my brother Augustus, who afterwards served in the 10th Royal Hussars. I have had the honour of holding a commission for many years, and far from being tried by a court-martial, I am not aware of ever having been reprimanded." "I quite understand your annoyance at the mistake," proceeded the Duke, extending his hand; "all I wish to say is, that in asking the question, I intended to have added, that had I been First Lord of the Admiralty instead of Commander-in-chief, I should have promoted your brother. If I recollect right, he was the last to leave the ship, and when he did, he swam on shore with the order book fastened to his head." Frederick Berkeley then recounted the whole circumstance, which completely exonerated his brother; indeed, the strongest proof of that was, that Admiral Keats, who presided over the court-martial, after the verdict was given, wrote on a slip of paper, "I shall be happy to take you on board my ship as a lieutenant." So disgusted, however, was Augustus Berkeley with the whole proceeding that he declined the offer, quitted the navy, and entered the sister profession, where he acquitted himself as a gallant soldier throughout the Peninsular Campaign. Had he remained in the navy he would, judging from his antecedents, have proved himself one of the best officers in the service. The circumstance narrated by Captain Berkeley was as follows.

Augustus Berkeley was the officer of the watch on board the *Lively* frigate, when she struck on a rock and went to pieces. Going on duty at twelve o'clock at night, he was told by the officer whom he relieved, that the ship was under the master's orders, and he acted accordingly. Berkeley, who knew the coast well, informed the master that he was out of his reckoning, but he was not attended to. All of a sudden, the cry of "breakers a-head" was heard. In this critical position, the

lieutenant of the watch, who was an excellent seaman,
piped all hands on deck, told the men to be silent,
and obey his orders, and was about to execute some
manœuvre. Unfortunately, the captain, who had
been roused from his slumber, rushed on deck, and
through some mistake, gave an order which at once
brought about the catastrophe. The *Lively* struck,
her foremast went over the side, and actually formed
a means of escape from the vessel. When all hands
had left the ship, with the exception of the captain
and lieutenant of the watch, the latter said, "Perhaps, sir, you will land, so as to let me be the last
on board." "No," replied the other, "I will not
leave the deck so long as there is any one on
board." Upon this, Augustus Berkeley rushed to
the drawer of the binnacle, took the book out of it
in which the order to attend to the master was
entered, and fastening it to his head, jumped over-
board and swam ashore. A court-martial was
ordered, and Berkeley was slightly reprimanded,
instead of being promoted. While he was under
arrest at Malta, a strange circumstance occurred.
The young officer was confined to his cabin, under
the guard of a sentry at the door. One night he
had a dream, in which he fancied he saw his father
by the side of his berth, who said, in a kind voice,
"Never mind, my boy, you will be acquitted."

Upon waking, so strong was the impression on his mind that he had seen his father, that he said to the marine on duty, "You've been playing me a trick by allowing some one to enter my cabin." "Not a soul has passed me, sir," responded the astonished sentry. "Nonsense," continued the other, "I have seen my father, who talked to me." The marine looked more astounded than ever, but nothing further occurred until some time after, when Augustus Berkeley heard from England of his father's death; and, strange to say, the earl died almost at the same hour and the same day when his son dreamt he conversed with him. What made this more wonderful was, that the Earl of Berkeley was in excellent health when his son last heard from him. The Duke of York entirely removed every unpleasant feeling from Frederick Berkeley's mind by remarking, "I now remember that Augustus Berkeley served well in the Peninsula, and but for that unfortunate Quentin affair would have probably been still in the army."

Few of the country seats of England are more delightfully situated than Badminton, the seat of the Duke of Beaufort; and I never recollect passing a more agreeable day than I did there in the summer of 1863, upon the occasion of an agricultural *fête*, a cattle and flower show. The house is handsome and spacious, the rooms lofty, the gardens well stocked, and the park picturesque and extensive. The drive from Worcester Lodge to the house, through a splendid avenue of fine old forest trees, placed in clumps, and not in the usual formal line, reminding the spectator of a body of soldiers at "open order," is magnificent. Upon the walls of the principal rooms may be seen some choice pictures, representing many distinguished members of the Somerset family (and what family has been more distinguished?) intermixed with landscapes and sea views by the best masters, ancient and modern. In the drawing-room is a very faithful likeness of the late Duke, than whom a more popular nobleman never existed. But it would exceed my limits to give a *catalogue raisonné* of all the works of art. There is one thing that strikes the visitor upon entering the house, which is, that it is evidently the mansion of a British sportsman. Although the furniture of the drawing-rooms and library shows that female taste has been called into play, there is a look throughout that stamps it as being connected with the chase. The sporting pictures in the one billiard room; the stuffed wolf, that succumbed to the Duke's pack during the winter of 1862, in France; the riding-whips in the hall; the deer's horns;—all furnish unmistakable

proofs that the Beauforts have been staunch sup-
porters of the "noble science." When I add to the
above, that dogs are such especial favourites with
the family, that they are freely permitted to roam
throughout the house, little more need be said. Let
me for a moment "hark back" to by-gone days and
by-gone heroes.

Badminton, in the hundred of Grumbalds Ash,
lies six miles south of Tetbury, four miles north-
east of Sodbury, and twenty miles south of Gloucester. The manor continued four hundred years
in the family of the Botelers, and was sold by
Nicholas Boteler to Thomas Somerset, third son of
Edward, Earl of Worcester, afterwards created
Viscount Somerset, of Capel, in Ireland. This
nobleman left an only daughter, Elizabeth Somerset,
who, dying unmarried, gave the estate to Henry
Somerset, Lord Herbert, afterwards Duke of Beaufort. The family is descended from John of Gaunt,
fourth son of King Edward III. John, surnamed
of Gaunt, from his birth in that city, was progenitor
of the Duke of Beaufort. He married, first,
Blanche, the youngest daughter and co-heiress of ·
Henry, Duke of Lancaster; secondly, Constance,
eldest daughter and co-heiress of Peter, King of
Castile and Leon; and thirdly, Katherine, the
widow of Sir Ottes Swinford. His issue by his

third wife were John Beaufort, created Earl of
Somerset, Henry Beaufort, who was Bishop of
Winchester and Cardinal of St. Eusebius, known by
the name of the "Rich Prelate," and a daughter,
Joan Beaufort, married first to Lord Ferrers, and
secondly to the Earl of Westmoreland. The issue
of John of Gaunt, King of Castile and Leon, Duke
of Aquitain and Lancaster, Earl of Richmond,
Derby, Lincoln, and Leicester, and Steward of
England, by his last wife, were called Beauforts,
from a castle of Anjou in France, where they were
born. From the time of Richard II. to the days of
Victoria, the Somersets have been united by marriage to the most distinguished families in the
realm.

"This family, since the destruction of Ragland
Castle in the Great Rebellion, have here fixed their
residence, which in respect of stately buildings,
beautiful gardens, large parks, and whatever can
make a place delightful, is esteemed one of the
noblest seats in England." So wrote a chronicler
of olden times; and if that eulogium were then
just, how much more would it be at the present
day, when modern refinement and comfort have lent
their aid to beautify the mansion! The first creation was Baron de Bottefort, by writ, 1308.

The Duke's fox-hounds and kennels are second to

none in the United Kingdom. All the best blood may
be found in the Badminton hounds, as the sires and
dams have been carefully selected from the choicest
packs in England. When I last passed an hour
with the Duke "on the flags," there were sixty-five
couples of old and sixteen and a half couples of
young hounds. The kennels are spacious and airy,
and every attention is paid to the hounds by that
first-rate huntsman Clarke, who excels as much in
the field as he does in the kennel. The Duke is
always admirably mounted; and, as he is usually in
the first flight, it requires a good horse to carry
him. The huntsman and whippers-in are equally
well provided for. There are few men more
deservedly popular than the present Duke, and his
amiable Duchess is equally so. They both feel the
truth of the Scotch poet's lines,—

> " The rank is but the guinea's stamp,
> The man's the gowd for a' that ; "

and by relieving the distresses of their poorer
brethren, by encouraging the manly sports of England, by mixing in friendly intercourse with their
neighbours, they have earned something brighter
than the most sparkling gems that glitter in their
ducal coronets—the affection of all around them.

Much as we English boast of our old nobility,
we are no less proud when we find the lustre of

ancient descent combined with truly noble qualities
in some of our great commoners. And it would be
hard to point to any one of whom this is truer
than Frederick Peter Delmé Radcliffe. This distinguished gentleman claims direct descent from the
Earls of Derwentwater, being descended in unbroken
line from Radcliffe of the Tower, in Lancashire, and
Earl of Sussex. His residence is Hitchin Priory,
where his family have lived ever since Henry VIII.,
expelling a brotherhood of White Carmelites, bestowed the edifice and domain upon Sir Ralph
Radcliffe. He is also " doubly blended with the
line " of those who boast "the blood of all the
Howards," his grandmother, Lady Betty Delmé,
and her sister, Lady Frances Radcliffe, being sisters
of Frederick, Earl of Carlisle. Educated at Eton,
he joined the Grenadier Guards at the age of
eighteen; but as that distinguished corps was then
in the dawn of the "piping time of peace," he could
only shine foremost as a sportsman. He gained his
full share of credit and success as a gentleman
jockey, making his public *début* at Hampton, and
winning the gold cup on Ball Hughes's Elephanta,
not named in the betting, against Lord Wilton, the
Berkeleys, and the best amateurs of the day. In
the Red House pigeon-shooting club, of which he
was an original member, he was the best of the

young ones; and on the grand trial for what was called the "All England Stakes," a sweepstakes amounting to 400 sovereigns, shot for by Lords Kennedy, Pollington, Anson, Hon. George Anson, Captain Ross, and "the Squire" (Osbaldeston), with other crack shots, he was on the fifth day left alone as outsider, to shoot off the ties with Captain Ross, the first favourite. After each killing nine birds, the Captain missed, and the outsider had only to kill one to carry off the "blue ribbon" of the trigger. By a fatality the deciding bird flew directly towards the young Guardsman, who, waiting for its rise, killed it in the air, and it fell behind him, which in those days reckoned as a miss. Subsequently, during one spring meeting at Newmarket, the late Mr. Peareth, who had practised daily until he had brought down his twenty-nine out of thirty, and often all thirty to a certainty, sent a challenge to the whole of the members of the Red House Club, then at Newmarket. All the members declined, for different reasons, but Captain Radcliffe accepted. The match at twenty-five picked birds, for £50, came off at Bottisham, four miles on the Cambridge road, on the Saturday of the race week, amidst a great concourse of people. Mr. Peareth killed twenty-three, and Captain Radcliffe twenty-four, out of the twenty-five blue rocks. He also shot an amicable match at partridges, late in October, with the present Lord Verulam, winning by one bird and a shot, killing twenty-one in twenty-five; Lord Verulam, then Lord Grimston, twenty in twenty-six. But it was not until he left the Guards, after succeeding to his property, and appearing on the hustings as proposer of Lord Grimston for the county, and by his speeches at various public meetings, that he became celebrated for fluency and eloquence attained by few who have not gone through the mill at St. Stephen's. He could not only harangue a mob, but reply off-hand to an opponent with astonishing facility. He twice refused the offer of being returned for the county, the deputation on the first occasion, long before railways were introduced, undertaking to pay the very turnpikes to Westminster. A love of country life and rural sports prevailed over all ambition.

The "Country Squire" was contented, as far as letters are concerned, with the fame attached to several choice little poems, innumerable hunting songs, and *jeux d'esprit*. The lines on Hunting and Yachting are stereotyped as a gem of the first water, and he is responsible for many of those epigrams and conundrums which are household words with the many, though few, very few, are

aware of their paternity. It is not with what he
has been, might have been, or is, in the literary
world that we have to deal. We represent him as
a sportsman, and we shall best convey an idea of
his general qualifications in the words of two *literati*
of the first class. Sir Edward Bulwer Lytton, at a
large agricultural meeting, at which his friend and
neighbour had spoken with wonted brilliancy, in
rising to propose his health, said—" He was proud
to exhibit to Mr. Dallas, the American Minister, so
rare a specimen of unrivalled combination of talent
as that of a country gentleman able to hold his own
in every field sport with all his fellows, and no less
qualified to take his seat in the cabinet of the states-
man, or the closet of the scholar and philosopher."
The late Right Honourable John Wilson Croker, at
a great dinner of the Literary Fund, in London, said
—" The whole *Punch* party have been fairly beaten
at their own weapons by the 'Country Squire' (the
nom de plume under which the choicest productions
have appeared), associated with them in theatricals
at Knebworth ; and were I called upon to bestow
the prize for the greatest amount of wit and pun-
gency, I should not hesitate to award it to the
Knebworth epilogue." This epilogue for Ben
Jonson's play of " Every Man in his Humour,"
was composed and recited by the author at the

express request of Sir E. B. Lytton. After the
eulogy of such a critic as Mr. Croker, it will be
interesting to lay the work in question before my
readers :—

KNEBWORTH PRIVATE THEATRICALS, 1850. EPILOGUE TO "EVERY
    MAN IN HIS HUMOUR." WRITTEN FOR THE OCCASION BY
    F. P. DELMÉ RADCLIFFE, ESQ.

Enter OLD KNOWELL (F. P. Delmé Radcliffe, Esq.) *and* WELLBRED
                (Henry Hale, Esq.).

> *Knowell.* At last the play is over.
> *Wellbred.*   Yes, and all,
> Thank Heaven, has ended with the curtain's fall.
> *Knowell.* Be thankful 'tis well over; think how kind
> All those in front have been to those behind.
> *Wellbred.* Kind, truly in applause. What will they say
> When they get home? that is the question.
> *Knowell.*   Nay,
> That is a question we cannot decide;
> All I can say is—I believe all tried
> To do their best.
> *Wellbred.*   Well, e'en Don Ferdinando,
> You know, can do no more than a man can do.
> *Knowell.* We were of course prepared for admiration
> Of those bright London stars, that constellation,
> The light of any sphere.
> *Wellbred.*   'Twere thought, I ween,
> A dainty dish to set before the queen.
> I'm not surprised that they have raised a fuss,
> But that they condescend to play with us—
> With rustics like myself, and one or two more.
> *Knowell.* Why, because "Every man is in his Humour."
> In truth, they all have proved themselves right hearty
> In their alliance with the "Country Party."
> Kitely was great—as he had been before.
> *Wellbred.* You must admit Old Knowell was a bore.
> *Knowell.* An' if he were, Wellbred might let that pass.
> *Wellbred.* Softly; hem! Shakespeare; "Write me down an
>   ass."
> *Knowell.* As touching Shakespeare—*you* know, I suppose
> That Knowell was the part great Shakespeare chose

To act himself.   Would that his soul divine
Could shed a fostering influence on mine.
 Wellbred. A FORSTERING influence, I think you said?
That brings me back to Kitely.   On that head,
Kitely *was* great, beyond my powers of speech.
 Knowell. And Matthew stuck to Bobadil like a LEECH.
 Wellbred. By Pharaoh's foot, that oath with the humour
  chimes.
Perhaps they will be buttered in the *Times.*
 Knowell. Talk not to me about the *Times* or *Herald,*
Give me three pennyworth of DOUGLAS JERROLD.
Amongst that party there are pretty pickings;
But say, can newspaper describe CHARLES DICKENS?
Author and actor; manager; the soul
Of all who read or hear him! on the whole,
A very "Household Word."
 Wellbred.   That's true.   But still,
With stores of sweets and worlds of wit at will,
They can't do without LEMON.
 Knowell.   Devil doubt it:
How do ye think they'd make their *Punch* without it!
All act together! none for self alone.
Did you mark *Downright?*
 Wellbred.   Plainly cut in STONE.
 Knowell. A precious stone.   But last, not least, I beg,
Regard the touches of AUGUSTUS EGG.
 Wellbred. Now, how about the ladies?
 Knowell.   For my part
I have got *their* perfections all by heart.
 Wellbred. Hush! what will DICKENS say to such sweet word?
 Knowell. Why, that his lady emulates her lord.
A word on her sad accident; but quite
Impromptu, not intended for to-night.
Oh, may she soon recover from her sprain,
To tread with us, her friends, these boards again.
 Wellbred. That fall sank all our spirits: but in need
'Tis said a friend is found a friend indeed.
Successful friendship has our cares allayed—
 Knowell. Ay; and the case relieved by LEMON aid.
For Bridget, say, could HOGARTH's self compare
In portraiture with this our Thespian fair?
 Wellbred. Go back from Hogarth, if you please, to Homer—
You'll find Thalia has become a ROMER.

Knowell. Indeed ! since she thought proper here to roam,
It seems to me she finds herself at home !
The three together carry all before 'em ;
Their sex applaud them, and the men adore 'em.
   Wellbred. Bravo ! I go with you and with your whim ;
We have all done bravely.
   Knowell.   " How we apples swim ! "
But let us now no longer jest or jeer ;
I have a word in earnest for your ear.
Say that to-night we have not played in vain—
Would'st thou, another evening, try again ?
   Wellbred. Why, that depends on circumstance ; in fact,
Upon the play they might propose to act.
Would that I had to choose !
   Knowell.   What hast thou hit on ?
   Wellbred. Why, on your choice—we swear by Bulwer Lytton !
On this occasion he has cast aside
Productions worthy of parental pride ;
Discarded all the offspring of his pen,
And shelves himself to make way for old Ben.
   Knowell. Come, don't get prosy when you should be funny ;
Of course we all should like to get up *Money.*
But let us think no more of that we have not ;
We may be satisfied with what we have got.
Congratulate our Host on his success :
Try what he will, he can have nothing less.
He has gained the object of his aim and ends—
Well pleased his guests, and entertained his friends."

The two songs, headed respectively " Hunting *v.*
Yachting," and " Yachting *v.* Hunting," shall also
follow :—

             " HUNTING *v.* YACHTING.

  " Some love to ride o'er the ocean's tide—
     There are charms in the dark blue sea ;
  But nerve at need, a gallant steed,
     And the life of a hunter for me.
  We plough the deep, or climb the steep,
     With heart and hand as brave
  As those who steer their bold career
     Far o'er the foaming wave.

" There is that in the sound of horn and hound,
    Which leaves all care behind ;
And the huntsman's cheer delights the ear,
    Borne merrily on the wind.
Oh ! give me a place in the stirring chase,
    A dull sky and a southern breeze,
You may rove in vain o'er the mighty main,
    Ere you find any joys like these.

" *March*, 1835. "

" YACHTING *v.* HUNTING.

" There is much of alloy in the hunter's joy—
    Hounds, horses, and elements failing—
But little I know that affects my prow,
    Give me the wild rapture of sailing.
One moment we rise, as a bird to the skies,
    On the foam of the billow's crest ;
The next in the green of the deep, between
    The big waves we appear to rest.

" There are few that have seen, and not any I ween
    Among landsmen can form any notion
Of wonders divine, known to me and to mine,
    Known only to sons of the ocean.
To the hunter I yield all the game of the field,
    But I fear neither battle nor wreck ;
When my sails are unfurled I have wings for a world,
    And I move like a king on my deck.

" *November*, 1836."

Perhaps, however, the part the Squire likes best, is that of the author of " The Noble Science," a work which is admitted to be without equal for instinctive information and for classical style. Of no one was it ever so truly written as of this Squire " *Gaudet equis canibusque ;* " and we are sure that he is far more jealous of the honours belonging to feats by which he has fairly earned his spurs

than of any credit he may have gained by his pen
or tongue.   Touching the latter, we must not omit
that he is possessed of the rare gift which was
nearly monopolised by the late Theodore Hook,
and has constantly electrified the whole assembly
at the largest parties at Woburn Abbey, and other
country seats, with no other possible preparation
than a review of the guests congregated for the
first time at dinner.   He can enact the improvisa-
tore, extemporise to any given air a song replete
with point, and bringing into rhyme the names of
all present, coupled with the events of the day,
alike past, present, and prospective.   For three
years he hunted, chiefly on his own extensive
estate round Hitchin, a pack of dwarf fox-hound
harriers, which he disposed of to Sir J. Flower,
on taking the fox-hounds, and hunting that part of
Hertfordshire and Bedfordshire previously under
the mastership of Mr. (now Sir Thomas) Sebright.
Here, for five seasons, with a good stock of old
foxes, and incessant labour in collecting an effective
pack (drafting at once all but fifteen couples of that
to which he succeeded), and in the second season
having sixty-five couples, which reached perfection
by the third, he showed an amount of sport quite
incredible, and laid the foundation of a system since
ably followed up by Lord Dacre, to whom Mr.

Delmé Radcliffe resigned the hounds in 1839, in consequence of a serious failure in health. He dabbled a little on the turf, owning nothing better than platers, such as Norman William, Cottager, Wilna, and others, calculated for his own riding. But in 1834, when contending for a hunters' stakes, seeing T. Wisby on a mare called Vesper leaving him hopelessly behind, he quitted the course, and steering so as to cut off a mile, and see her win, at once purchased the mare for three hundred and fifty guineas, altering her name to Lady Emily, after the present Lady Craven. With this superior animal, in the course of the next three seasons, he won twenty-two out of twenty-nine races, twenty of which were ridden by himself. In those days he seldom missed Newmarket, and betted heavily; many a book-maker could testify to his laying and standing a thousand between first and second for the Derby; but of late years his visits to the Corner have been rare, and his speculations limited. He has been an expert angler ever since he caught the leviathan trout, of Eton days, off the Cobler, and, like many of our leading fox-hunters, has been devoted to yachting, being an *élève* of the late Lord Yarborough, and an old member of the Royal Yacht Squadron, and having made more than one trip to the Mediterranean.

That "like begets like" is a proverb amply sustained in the Delmé family. The grandsire (husband of Lady Betty, the toast of the town, and the reigning beauty of the Court of Queen Charlotte) was never surpassed as a sportsman, perhaps as a fast man. Being the owner of Erle Stoke, in Wiltshire, another seat in Berkshire, and Cam's Hall in Hampshire, he had stag-hounds, harriers, and fox-hounds at those respective places. He had teams of greys, black and cream colours; at his town mansion, in Grosvenor Square, dinner was served daily, during the season, at five o'clock P.M., for any eight friends who chose to put down their names, the host himself rarely appearing, unless, as was often the case, any member of the royal family had signified his intention of dining. He was the leading whip, unrivalled in putting horses together, driving, in the same team, one horse in a plain snaffle and another in a Chifney. He taught the Prince of Wales, afterwards George IV., to handle the ribbons, and every year drove a tandem, with relays of horses, from Grosvenor Square to Castle Howard. At his death, no less than ninety-five of his horses and ponies were put up to auction at Tattersall's. His son, the father of our Squire, entered the 10th Hussars, then commanded by the Prince of Wales, whose friendship

he enjoyed through life, riding all his races at
Bibury, and managing his stud, in which capacity
he continued as Gentleman of the Horse both to
George IV. and William IV., when the colours of
the monarch adorned the turf. As an amateur
jockey he had no equal, as may be gathered from
the fact that, for a great sweepstakes of one thousand
guineas each, between Lord Foley, Lord Egremont,
and Sir John Shelley, Chifney and Buckle being
engaged for the two former, Sir John sent to Hitchin
for Delmé, who won a severe race by a head between
the two, the third beaten by a neck. He could ride
jockey weight, and was put up more than once by
his confederate, the Duke of Rutland, for the Derby
and Oaks.　Mr. Delmé, of Cam's Hall, and Captain
Delmé, R.N., both breed and run a few race horses.
The latter bred the best horse of his year, Alarm.
The fourth generation have been too much distinguished both in the army and navy, in the
Crimea and India, to have appeared as sportsmen,
but they are doubtless "chips of the old block."
I will not enter into domestic matters affecting the
subject of this brief memoir, further than to say
that, amidst a large share of the sweets, he has
endured many of the afflictions of this life; but I
am happy to find that he is in good preservation, as
appears from his prowess with the hounds.　He

lost his left eye by an accident out shooting, but I heard a first-rate gun-maker, who had seen him shoot, say that he would not advise any one to offer him many dead birds in a pigeon match. His seat on a horse has ever been acknowledged a pattern, and without being a bruiser, like his friend Robert Grimston, he could always bring his theory into practice, and ride as well as write on the method of putting horses at their fences.

I have been informed by one of the best men with Lord Dacre, that Squire Delmé, as they call him, still continues to go as well as any one, when any one has to go, and that in the best runs of the season he is always in the first flight. Frederick Delmé Radcliffe affords a living illustration of the country gentleman described by a popular writer :—
" A country gentleman naturally stands in a great station ; he is one of the strongest links in society between Government and the lower orders of mankind ; and he is a real blessing to the district where he lives, when he unites the four great characteristics of a country gentleman, a good neighbour, an excellent magistrate, and a first-rate sportsman."

The Honourable John Coventry, brother to Lord Coventry, was one of the best horsemen of his day, and his seat and hand on horseback were perfect.

He reminded one of the epigram addressed by
Ben Jonson to William, Earl of Newcastle :—

" When first, my lord, I saw you back your horse,
  Provoke his mettle and command his force
  To all the uses of the field and race,
  Methought I read the ancient art of Thrace,
  And saw a Centaur past those tales of Greece,
  So seem'd your horse and you both of a piece.
  You showed like Perseus upon Pegasus,
  Or Castor mounted on his Cyllarus,
  Or what we hear our home-born legend tell
  Of bold Sir Bevis and his Arundel."

John was for some time in the 10th Hussars, and
was an especial favourite with the illustrious colonel,
the Prince Regent. He was also a sportsman of
the highest order, a good rider to hounds, and an
unerring shot. One evening after the Worcester
race ordinary, the conversation turned upon equestrian feats, and a wager was proposed that no one
at the table could ride to London and back in six-
and-twenty hours, the event to come off that night
without any preparation, or any one in advance to
order horses. John accepted the bet, which was for
a hundred pounds, and named himself to perform
the undertaking. His horse was ordered round, and
having changed his dress, he started late at night
on his solitary ride. The weather was bad, the
night dark, and the roads heavy, the respective
ostlers not a little out of temper at being
awoke—not for a pair, or four, but for a single

poster. But his pluck kept him up, and upon his return to the turnpike near Worcester, he had an hour and a half in hand. A large assemblage of friends were upon the look-out for him at the Star Hotel, and greeted him with cheers. But when an inquiry was made for the maker of the bet, he was not to be found. It afterwards transpired that the unprincipled better had planted himself close to the turnpike gate with a watch in his hand, and finding that, bar accident, the upshot must be against him, had cantered off, and was not heard of for many a long day. We need scarcely add that when he was heard of, the hundred pounds were not forthcoming; so poor John had the fatigue and expense of a journey on horseback of two hundred and thirty miles, with no result, save giving further proof of his indomitable courage.

CHAPTER XXI.

CHAPTER XXI.

I now come to a subject which demands the utmost
ease and grace, a lightness of pen to carry us
smoothly over the floor, a care in steerage to keep
us from shocks and collisions. Muse of the many
twinkling feet, inspire me! I sing of dancing—or,
rather, I don't sing of it, for it has been sung before.
Byron, whose infirmities opposed his own dancing,
was unnecessarily severe on that of his neighbours.
And yet it is plain that he envied them the enjoyment in which he could not partake. We may
remember that when there was a dispute in the
green-room at Drury Lane about some dance, the
noble lord was appealed to as umpire, and that he
said sadly to some friend who came in the next
moment, "Had you been here a few seconds ago,
you would have heard me appealed to as arbiter in
a question of dancing; me, whom fate has forbidden
ever to dance a step!" Other poets have not been
so opposed to the dance. Moore has celebrated it

in the "Twopenny Post Bag," by an allusion to
the figures of chalk which the feet of the dancers
gradually obliterated.   And even if no poets were
found to sing of dancing, it would not lose its hold
upon society.   In the crowded ball-rooms of London, where movement of any other kind is impossible, and in the more airy halls of country mansions,
the same giddy maze whirls on without interruption.

One of the pleasantest of these scenes was that
which took place at Boyle Farm, on the 30th of
June, 1837.   This was the day fixed for the grand
fête given by Lords Chesterfield, Castlereagh,
Alvanley, De Ros, and Robert Grosvenor.   A
more magnificent entertainment never took place
in this or any other country, for there was everything that money could produce, or good taste
suggest.   The day was threatening, but towards
the afternoon it became bright, and the entire road
swarmed with carriages filled with all the *élite*
of fashion.   Towards five o'clock the principal
guests had assembled, and, at half-past, about four
hundred and fifty sat down to dinner, under a large
tent on the lawn, and fifty to the royal table in the
conservatory.   During the repast the Tyrolese
minstrels sung their choicest airs, and after it was
concluded, Mesdames Caradori, De Begnis, Fanny
Ayton, Vestris, with Veluti and other popular

operatic artists of the day, rowed about in gondolas
on the river, some in masks, warbling forth barcaroles
and gondolier songs.   The evening was perfect, and
as soon as it grew dark, the walks, shrubs, trees,
and grottoes, were all brilliantly illuminated with
coloured lamps, the light reflecting on the "silver
Thamis."   At about nine o'clock the dancing commenced, and we must again resort to Moore for the
description of it :—

> " Next turn we to the gay saloon,
>   Resplendent as a summer noon,
>   Where 'neath a pendent wreath of lights,
>   A zodiac of flowers and tapers—
>   (Such as in Russian ball-rooms sheds
>   Its glory o'er young dancers' heads)—
>   Quadrille performs her mazy rites,
>   And reigns supreme o'er slides and capers,
>   As with a foot that ne'er reposes
>   She jigs . . . .
>   Wearing out tunes as fast as shoes,
>   'Till fagged Rossini scarce respires ;
>   'Till Meyerbeer for mercy sues,
>   And Weber at her feet expires."

Our London young ladies are too much accustomed
to three balls a-night during the season to remember
that there are others to whom a ball is a rarity and
an event.   Think of their excitement when a ball
is announced; the preparations, the dresses, the
wonder who will be there, and who will be their
partners, the talk expended on the ball before it
takes place, while it is going on, and after it is

over. Then the trouble of getting to it in country places. All these things have to be taken into account among the concomitants of a ball, and they would surprise us if we could have a full list of them.

An ingenious statistician has published an elaborate article in one of the papers on the balls and *soirées dansantes* that have taken place at Paris during the carnival of 1864, that is to say, from the 6th of January (Twelfth-night), to the 9th of February (Shrovetide), both inclusive. His researches and calculations, it should be premised, are confined to private and official balls, and the public balls at the opera, casinos, &c., are excluded. Our statistician tells us that within the above period not less than 130 balls, on an average, were given in Paris. For each of these about 250 invitations were issued, giving an aggregate of 32,500 persons, of whom one-third at least may be set down as "active performers" in the waltz, polka, and quadrille. Thus, for every evening for five weeks, between 8 and 10 p.m., Asmodeus might have beheld the strange sight of from 15,000 to 16,000 ladies having their hair dressed, donning their ball-room attire, scolding their maids, and admiring themselves in the glass. Simultaneously, an equal number of the *sexe laid* were forcing their feet into

tight patent leather boots, putting on white chokers, and investing themselves in that lugubrious costume known as evening dress. Then followed another important operation—65,000 hands putting on white kid gloves. To convey our 32,500 ball-goers to their destination, from 12,000 to 15,000 cabs at least were necessary. Having laid down these figures to his satisfaction, our statistician proceeds to calculate what all this "dressing," "gloving," "cabbing," and dancing represents:—
"This year the season was a short one, having lasted only thirty-six days, which, at 130 balls per night, gives us a total of 4,680 balls for the whole season. Now, the least that a person giving a ball can expect to spend is 900 francs (£36). The givers of these entertainments will, therefore, have put into circulation a sum of 4,212,000 francs. But what the entertainers have to spend is a joke when compared to what comes out of the pockets of those who are 'happy to accept their kind invitations.' Taking the number of guests at 32,500, they would require from 12,000 to 15,000 cabs, to be conveyed to the ball and back. Let us strike an average of 25,000 drivers at 3 francs each; this gives us 75,000 francs (£3,000) a-night, or 2,700,000 francs for the season. Then we find 32,500 pairs of gloves—or 130,000 francs per

night, or 4,680,000 francs for the season. Then comes a grave question which specially interests the ladies. I assume," proceeds our statistician, " and I trust I am not guilty of exaggeration, that every lady wears the same dress four times, and I am so reasonable as to suppose that each dress costs no more than 200 francs. Well, considering that, on an average, 16,250 ladies honoured balls with their presence every night this season, this gives us about 146,250 ball dresses, or 29,250,000 francs. In addition there is the hair-dressing—an item which represents about 50,000 francs per night, or 1,800,000 francs; then we have 8,000 pair of satin shoes, which represents 64,000 francs per night, or 2,304,000 francs per season. Let us add for flowers, bouquets, a variety of unmentionable trifles, perfumes, &c., at 30 francs per head and per night, which gives 17,550,000 for the season; and the following will present an accurate *résumé* of what Paris has spent for dancing from January the 6th to February the 9th :—

	Francs.
Coach hire	2,700,000
Gloves	4,680,000
Dresses	29,250,000
Hair dressing	1,800,000
Satin shoes	2,304,000
Bouquets	1,800,000
Knicknacks, jewellery, &c. . .	17,500,000
Giving a total of . . .	60,034,000

" If to the total we add the 4,212,000 francs expended by the people who *give* balls, the expenditure
of men's evening dress, chokers, patent leather boots,
and so forth, (which, estimated at 5,000,000 francs,
200,000 francs more, is below the mark), we arrive
at the total, 69,246,000 francs for thirty-six ball
nights."

Of all these balls, those which occupy the highest
place are, of course, the state balls given at Buckingham Palace. We know from Pepys what they
were in the time of Charles II.; it will heighten
the contrast between those times and our own if
we quote the passage from his diary.

" December 30, 1662. Mr. Povy and I to
White Hall, he taking me thither on purpose to
carry me into the ball this night before the king.
He brought me first to the duke's chamber, where
I saw him and the duchess at supper; and thence
into the room where the ball was to be, crammed
with fine ladies, the greatest of the court. By-
and-by comes the king and queen, the duke and
duchess, and all the great ones; and after seating
themselves, the king takes out the Duchess of
York, and the duke the Duchess of Buckingham,
the Duke of Monmouth my Lady Castlemaine, and
so other lords their ladies, and they danced the
Brante, which, according to the *Dictionnaire de*

L'Académie, is an '*Espèce de danse de plusieurs personnes qui se tiennent par la main, et qui se menent tour à tour.*' After that the king led a lady a single Coranto ; and then the rest of the lords, one after another, other ladies ; very noble it was, and great pleasure to see. Then to country dances, the king leading the first, which he called for, which was, says he, 'Cuckolds all awry,' the old dance of England."

At present, as has also been the case during the last few reigns, a state ball is a very different affair.

The height of ambition among the upper ten thousand is to receive an invitation to the Queen's Ball ; and many are the schemes laid to conciliate the Lord Chamberlain, in the hopes of attaining that distinguished honour. In the days of George III. and Queen Charlotte few under a certain rank were invited to state parties, which might therefore be strictly called aristocratic assemblies ; and the fourth George, in a great measure, kept up that exclusiveness which he had been accustomed to in his father's court. William IV., the warm-hearted sailor king, reigned in the troublesome time of Reform agitation, and being free from that failing, too often attributed, with justice, to royalty, namely, the abandonment of old friends, caused the door to be opened wider. In this he was encouraged by what are termed the "whippers in" of the Houses of Lords and Commons, who thought to secure sundry votes in the House by extending the "Court suffrage." From. that moment the barrier was thrown down; "every one," as the saying is, attended levées and drawing-rooms; and the list of the aspirants to ball and concert honours amounted to near 4,000. The difficulty of selection was now increased a hundred fold, and occasionally names were omitted that would have been present under the old *régime*, and *vice versá*. Under our present gracious sovereign every attention has been paid to merit, whether ecclesiastic, clerical, military, naval, political, scientific, diplomatic, or literary; and her Majesty and the late Prince Consort showed marked attention to all who had served their country in either capacity. An anecdote is told, and I believe it to be true, that a certain member of the legal profession who was a strong supporter of the then existing administration, called upon that important member of the Government who looked after the patronage of his party, and said, "I have no ambition to gratify, I have always voted in the House of Commons in favour of your party. My wife has called my attention to the names of many who are honoured by invi-

tations to the state balls whose claims she, perhaps,
erroneously imagines are not greater than her own."
The legal M.P. was interrupted in the blandest
manner. "If I had the selection, depend upon it
your lady's wish would be gratified." "Excuse
me," continued the other, "I believe certain invitations are sent to the wives of those who support
the Government; and not to occupy your time further, if my support is to be looked for, my wife
must not be excluded." I heard this story before
the ball in question, and whether or no the hint produced an effect with the ministerialist, and he mentioned it to the Lord Chamberlain (for, of course, her
Majesty was never made aware of the circumstance),
the result was, that the lady and her husband were
present for the first time.

I well remember attending a state ball at Carlton
House during the time of the Regent, which was
a splendid affair. There was no crowd, ample room
for dancing, and a supper, at which the ladies at
least could sit down. The balls at St. James's
Palace, under William IV. and Queen Adelaide,
were equally good, although the numbers occasionally marred part of the enjoyment. It was a
very nervous and formal affair to be called upon by
the Lord Chamberlain to dance in the quadrille
before the King and Queen, in which her present

Majesty Queen (then Princess) Victoria took part ;
but it once fell to my lot to be so called, the
Princess dancing with the Prince of Orange, the
Duke of Cambridge, then Prince George, being her
Royal Highness's *vis-à-vis*. Nothing could be more
graceful than the Princess's movements.

Since the building of the new ball-room at Buckingham Palace, nothing can exceed the brilliancy
of the balls; the rooms, except that in which the
royal party assemble, being free from crowd. Those
guests who do not wish the formality of passing the,
throne, and making their bow or curtsey to the
Queen, attend before her Majesty makes her appearance, and as the sovereign passes through the
apartments she graciously notices all those who
form the line. One of the most brilliant balls was
given in 1842 ; it was, I believe, the first *bal cos-
tumé* ever given at Court during the reign of the
Guelphs. Honoured with an invitation, I was
looking forward with delight to witness so splendid
an entertainment, in which every one could select
the most becoming costume, when the death· of my
mother prevented my attendance. At the second
costume state ball the dresses were confined to the
reign of George II. and III., the ladies and gentlemen to appear in powder. However becoming such
a dress was to many who possessed fine features, it

marred the look of others, and unquestionably the impression was that the first ball was the greater success.

The subject of State entertainments leads me to mention a dinner at Windsor Castle on the Ascot Cup day of 1840 or 1841, for which I received a royal command.

Ascot Races have undergone wondrous changes since I first remember attending them, in the year 1814, just before I went to Paris with the late Duke of Wellington. My uncle, the late Duke of Gordon, then Marquis of Huntley, called for me at Donnington, where I was finishing an education scarcely (if the truth is to be spoken) begun, at a private tutor's. The night before the races we slept at Botham's, Salt Hill, and at an early hour found ourselves upon the race-course. The meeting consisted of the Prince Regent and his suite, a few of the neighbouring noblemen and gentry, some officers from Windsor and Hounslow Cavalry barracks, and a fair sprinkling of London fashionables, added to a tolerably large number of tradesmen from Windsor, Staines, and Egham, and some dozen or two yeomen and farmers. It was upon this occasion that I had the honour of being introduced to the heir to the throne. Nothing could be more courteous than the manner of his Royal Highness, and I was included in the invitations to lunch in the royal stand. The same honour was conferred upon me some twenty-seven years after, during the reign of our gracious Queen Victoria, when a splendid repast was prepared in Tippoo Saib's tent, and when the entertainment exceeded in luxury that of her Majesty's royal uncle, the modern Sardanapalus. The same may be said of the state dinner at which I was present. Unforeseen business having brought me up to London on the previous evening, I found the greatest difficulty in procuring any sort of conveyance to the castle, almost every horse and vehicle being engaged for the Ascot Cup day. While wondering what I should do (I need not say the Windsor railway was not opened, the Great Western having only commenced its operation the last day of June, 1841), I met the late Earl Fitz-hardinge, who had been invited to dine at the Castle, and who kindly offered me a seat in his carriage. He, too, had fortunately engaged a dressing-room at the White Hart, as the evening dress, *culottes de rigeur*, was not quite the costume to wear in London, and during the drive to Windsor. One thing which struck me particularly was the punctuality of her Majesty and the Prince Consort. Although fatigued with the bustle, excitement, and dust of the day, they entered the drawing-room a few minutes before the dinner was announced, and after graciously noticing the guests, proceeded at once to dinner. There was another peculiarity, which was, that after the Queen and the ladies retired, the Prince only remained twenty minutes, an example which I should be glad to see followed everywhere.

At the hour named on the card I found myself in the Castle; and before the Queen and her beloved consort entered the drawing-room, nearly a hundred guests had assembled. After a most dignified yet affable recognition to the party, her Majesty was led to the dining-room, which on that occasion was in St. George's Hall. It is a splendid gallery, upwards of two hundred feet in length and thirty-five in width. The ceiling is divided throughout its whole length into compartments, on which are emblazoned the armorial bearings of all the Knights of the Garter from the institution of the order. The knights on the corbels, in complete suits of mail, are Edward III. and his son the Black Prince; and there are kingly portraits from the first James to the last George. Along the sides of the hall are shields emblazoned with the arms of the various knights; and in other spaces are large shields, bearing the cross of St. George, and encircled by the garter and its well-known motto, " *Honi soit qui*

mal y pense." There is no spot more likely to
revive associations of by-gone days, and bring to
the mind's eye a review of the stirring times and
warlike deeds of our country. But to the apartment now arranged as a banqueting hall. At each
end were buffets, seventeen feet in height and forty
in breadth, covered with crimson cloth, and encom-
passed with carved Gothic framework, upon which
the massive gold plate was tastefully displayed.
Immediately opposite the seat appropriated to her
Majesty, and within a recess, was a pyramid of
plate, comprising the tiger's head captured at
Seringapatam; over it the Iluma, formed of precious
stones, presented by the late Marquis of Wellesley
to George III. Above the Iluma was a cup,
formed of a shell, embellished with gold and silver,
surmounted by the figure of Jupiter, resting on an
eagle, the base supported by Hippocampi, several
vases rich in precious stones and ivory; and the
national cup, with figures of St. George, St. Andrew,
and St. Patrick, the emblems being formed of rare
jewels. The table extended the whole length of
the hall, and covers were laid for 100. Gold
épergnes, vases, cups, and candelabra were ranged
down the centre of the table. The celebrated St.
George candelabrum was placed opposite the
Queen's seat. It is perhaps the most beautiful

specimen of plate in the world. The upper division contains the combat of England's patron saint with the dragon ; the lower has four figures in full relief, supporting shields bearing the arms of England, Scotland, Ireland, and the plume of the Prince of Wales. I must not omit to mention the shield of Achilles, and the massive gold salt-cellar made to represent the white tower of the Castle. The wine coolers are copies of the Warwick and other well-known classical vases. The hall was splendidly illuminated, and the bands of the two regiments quartered at Windsor, in the cavalry and infantry barracks, were stationed in one of the galleries. On duty at the entrance were the yeomen of the guard, anciently called " *bouffetiers,*" now universally changed to " beefeaters."

During dinner the bands played some popular marches, overtures, waltzes, and quadrilles, from the works of Mendelssohn, Beethoven, Labitzky, Mozart, Ries, and Musard. The repast was splendid, and served on an entire service of gold plate. The attendance was complete, and there was less bustle and confusion in this party of nearly a hundred than I have often seen in a small circle of ten or twelve. The wine of every description, from " humble port to imperial Tokay," was handed round during dinner ; while Francatelli, who then presided over the culinary department, walked round the table to see that the respective *plats* were properly served. At a quarter before nine grace was said, and after the dessert and wine were put upon the table, the Lord Steward gave "The Queen." All stood up except her Majesty, who graciously bowed her acknowledgments. "God save the Queen" was then played. After a brief pause, the health of the Prince Consort, then Prince Albert, was given, and drunk standing, the band playing the "Coburg March." The effect was most imposing; the martial strains of the music, a hall replete with every attribute of regal munificence; a well-dressed company, the female portion of which sparkled with diamonds and other precious stones, produced an effect more like a fairy scene than a substantial pageant. At half-past nine the Queen rose from table, the ladies following her Majesty and the Duchess of Kent to the drawing-room. The Prince Consort then again took his seat, and in about twenty minutes his Royal Highness and the guests joined her Majesty. The Waterloo Chamber was thrown open, and its pictorial treasures, so historically connected with the deeds of our countrymen during the present century, could not fail to create the deepest impression. It was truly interesting to walk through the corridor and guard chamber, and see the fine collection of arms, consisting of oriental matchlocks, helmets, shields, spears, and swords. Among the latter were those worn by the Chevalier St. George in 1715, and by the Pretender in the fatal 1746. It was interesting to gaze upon the coats of mail worn by Charles, Prince of Wales, in 1620, Lord Howard in 1588, Duke of Brunswick in 1530, Lord Essex in 1596, and Prince Rupert in 1635, and to trace out the workmanship of that exquisite silver shield inlaid with gold, executed by Cellini, and presented by Francis I. to Henry VIII. on the far-famed Field of the Cloth of Gold. The great treat of the evening was the appearance of Madame Rachel, who, aided by two or three French actors, gave scenes from some of her most popular plays. Nothing could be more successful than her performance, unaided as it was by dress, scenery, or decorations. A little before twelve o'clock, her Majesty, after addressing in flattering terms the talented *artiste*, and bending graciously to the assembled guests, retired, leaning on the arm of Albert the Good, and, after some slight refreshment, the company departed.

During a long and rambling life, it has fallen to my lot to attend many banquets at home and abroad. I have had the honour of dining with Louis XVIII. at the Tuileries, Versailles, and St. Cloud; with Louis Philippe at the Palais Royal; with Charles X.,

the Dukes of Angoulême and Berri, at their respective châteaux; with the Emperor Alexander,
at one of his grand reviews; with the Emperor of
Austria at Vienna; with the King of Holland at
the Hague; with William IV. and Queen Adelaide
at the Pavilion, Brighton; but among them all,
I never witnessed any entertainment which came up
to the one I have been describing, with Victoria I.,
at Windsor Castle.

The art of cooking has greatly improved within
the last forty years in England, and this is chiefly
to be attributed to our intercourse with the Con-
tinent. Formerly, French cooks and men cooks
were seldom heard of; and the *entrées*, *assiettes
volantes*, and *entremets* which now grace the majority of London and provincial tables were unknown.
Who in the days of George III. would have dreamt
of a cutlet "*à la Victime?*" Indeed, many may
not be aware from whence the name of a victimised cutlet could arise. The story goes, that
Louis XVIII., or some other Heliogabalian monarch,
was in a weak state of health, and required great
nourishment. His *chef de cuisine* was consulted,
and he promised to introduce something that would
prove palatable, as well as strengthening. The dish
was served by the *artiste*, who on taking off the
cover, displayed a cutlet looking as if it had been
up the chimney, black, burnt, and dry.

"Why, what is this?" inquired the royal *gourmet*.

"Wait, your Majesty," responded the *Cordon Bleu*. "Do not judge by appearances." Then with great adroitness he removed the top and bottom burnt cutlets, showing one done to a nicety, and imbibing all the juice of the other two. "See, your Majesty, I have victimised two cutlets in the attempt, but one remains worthy of your royal favour."

But it is not the excellence of the royal fare, nor the honour of being admitted to the royal table, that has impressed this dinner on my memory. The thought which first recurs to my mind in connection with it is the thought of the Prince Consort, and the sad loss England sustained in his untimely death. I am aware that during his life the Prince never possessed that popularity which he so fully deserved, and which would have cheered him so much in all his efforts. But those efforts were never once relaxed because they were not rewarded. The Prince was content to persevere in what seemed to him the right path, even if his wishes for the welfare of England were misrepresented, and his labours received unthankfully. Perhaps few are aware of the secret influence he exercised for good when he was accused of exercising an open influence for harm. One of the most striking instances of the good he did for England was made public the other day by the Secretary for Foreign Affairs, and, I need not say, was learnt with surprise, even by those who might have been prepared for it. Speaking of the demands made by the English Government on America in the affair of the *Trent*, Lord Russell said, in the House of Lords, on Thursday, March 23rd, 1865, " I am bound to say, in mentioning these facts, that there is one circumstance connected with them which does the highest credit to the memory, good taste, and discretion of the late Prince Consort. At the last moment, after her Majesty had approved the despatch, we received a letter from the Prince Consort, in which he said that some of the expressions used in the despatch might be considered too abrupt, and suggested other phrases which he thought might make it more easy for the Government of the United States to accept the request which it conveyed. These phrases were adopted by the Government, and embodied in the despatch, and doubtless tended in some degree to render the document more acceptable to the United States Government."

Such was the action of the Prince Consort in the sphere of public life. No one would know that the suggestion of a few conciliatory phrases proceeded

from him, and perhaps altered the whole tone of
affairs.   Yet at such a moment it is impossible to
exaggerate the weight and value of a few conciliatory phrases.   The two nations were trembling on
the verge of war.   On the one side there was duty,
on the other honour.   What the duty of England
demanded, that her flag should be free from insult,
might seem to the honour of America more than
could be granted.   One harsh word might have set
the world in a blaze.   And this one harsh word is
prevented by a man who found that the slightest
interference on his part was apt to be resented and
suspected; a man who was constantly being told
that his relation to English affairs was purely personal; a man whom nothing but the highest sense
of the welfare of his Queenly consort and his adopted
country could have led to take such a step in the
face of public suspicion and private hostility.

So much has been written of the Prince's affability in private life that I will confine myself to
one anecdote which bears upon it.

In the month of June, 1844, the Emperor of
Russia was in England, and a review of the troops
that could easily be got together in Windsor Park,
took place.   Her Majesty, albeit in general good
health, was about to increase her family, and her
strict injunctions to the late Duke of Wellington,

then Commander-in-chief, were, that the royal
salute should be dispensed with. Orders were accordingly given to the officer commanding the
artillery, and the Queen, at the appointed hour
proceeded to the ground. While going along the
Long Walk, and when within some few yards of
the spot where the troops were collected, her
Majesty again referred to the subject, expressing
a hope to the "Warrior Duke" that no mistake
would occur.

"None can occur, your Majesty," responded her
faithful and loyal subject—"I've issued strict
orders upon the subject."

Scarcely had the latter word been uttered than
the noise of roaring artillery was heard, and the
royal salute, which had been so much dreaded, was
fired.

"Order them to cease firing," cried the Duke, to
one of his aides-de-camp, who galloped off at a
tremendous pace to carry out his chief's instruc-
tions; but it was too late to countermand the order.
Acting upon the impulse of the moment, the "hero
of a hundred fights" sent another aide-de-camp to
the officer commanding the artillery, saying that
they were to retire to the rear, and take no part in
the review, as the disobedience of his orders so
specially given would be a subject for inquiry.

The review proceeded, and during the day it oozed out that the error had occurred through the mistaken but well-intentioned zeal of an officer of the militia, acting for the day on the staff of the Commander-in-chief, who, perceiving the royal and imperial *cortège* arrive, had himself galloped forward to give the order for a royal salute. Concluding that some change had taken place in the arrangements, and strengthened in such a supposition by the hasty approach of a staff officer from the saluting point, the officer gave the fatal order which deprived him and his gallant corps of the honour of taking part in the evolutions of the day. It happened that the artillery officer, than whom a braver and more distinguished officer never existed, had been honoured by a command to dine at Windsor Castle, and with fear and trembling for the first and only time in his life, he made his appearance. His first step on arriving was to consult one of the lords in waiting to the Prince Consort, who had served throughout the Peninsular war, and at the battle of Waterloo on Wellington's personal staff. The noble lord, who was aware of the whole circumstance, took an opportunity of speaking to the Prince, pointing out the delicate position in which the commanding officer of the artillery stood in having, by royal command, to attend a dinner given in honour of a review in which he had been unable to take a part. The Prince, with that kindliness of disposition, and consideration for the feelings of others, for which he was so peculiarly conspicuous, at once crossed the room, and spoke a few words in season, which gladdened the heart of the brave soldier. · At dinner his Royal Highness again addressed a few words to him across the table, thereby showing all the distinguished party that the Queen entirely exonerated the supposed offender from the slightest particle of blame. It was by such acts as these that "Albert the Good" endeared himself to all Englishmen.

The *Northern Whig* has given so interesting an account of the last hours of Prince Albert, from a letter which was written by a member of the Queen's household, shortly after his lamented decease, that I cannot refrain from inserting it. The extremely confidential position which the writer held at the time not only gives the assurance of perfect reliability, but invests the following lines with a very special interest. After describing the grief and fears of the whole household for the Queen, the writer speaks of the personal loss sustained in the death of Prince Albert :—"How I shall miss his conversation about the children! He used often to

come into the school-room to speak about the
education of the children, and he never left me
without my feeling that he had strengthened my
hands, and raised the standard I was aiming at.
Nothing mean or frivolous could exist in the atmo-
sphere that surrounded him; the conversation could
not be trifling if he was in the room. I dread the
return of spring for my dear lady. It was his
favourite time of the year; the opening leaves, the
early flowers, and fresh green, were such a delight
to him; and he so loved to point out their beauties
to his children, that it will be terrible to see them
without him. The children kept his table supplied
with primroses, which he especially loved. The
last Sunday he passed on earth was a very blessed
one for the Princess Alice to look back upon. He
was very ill and very weak, and she spent the afternoon alone with him, while the others were in
church. He begged to have his sofa drawn to the
window, that he might see the sky and the clouds
sailing past. He then asked her to play to him,
and she went through several of his favourite
hymns and chorales. After she had played some
time she looked round and saw him lying back, his
hands folded as if in prayer, and his eyes shut. He
lay so long without moving that she thought he had
fallen asleep. Presently he looked up and smiled.

She said, 'Were you asleep, dear papa?' 'Oh, no,' he answered; 'only I have such sweet thoughts.' During his illness his hands were often folded in prayer; and when he did not speak, his serene face showed that the 'happy thoughts' were with him to the end. The Princess Alice's fortitude has amazed us all. She saw from the first that both her father's and her mother's firmness depended on her firmness, and she set herself on the duty. He loved to speak openly of his condition, and had many wishes to express. He loved to hear hymns and prayers. He could not speak to the Queen of himself, for she could not bear to listen, and shut her eyes to the danger. His daughter saw that she must act differently, and she never let her voice falter or shed a single tear in his presence. She sat by him, listened to all he said, repeated hymns, and then, when she could bear it no longer, would walk calmly to the door, and then rush away to her room, returning soon with the same calm look and pale face, without any appearance of the agitation she had gone through. I have had several interviews with the poor Queen since. The first time she said, 'You can feel for me, for you have gone through this trial.' Another time she said how strange it seemed, when she looked back, to see how much for the last six

months the Prince's mind had dwelt upon death
and the future state; their conversation had so
often turned upon these subjects, and they had read
together a book called 'Heaven our Home,' which
had interested him very much. He once said to
her, 'We don't know in what state we shall meet
again; but that we shall recognise each other, and
be together in eternity, I am perfectly certain.' It
seemed as if it had been intended to prepare her
mind and comfort her—though of course it did not
strike her then. She said she was a wonder to
herself, and she was sure it was an answer to the
prayers of her people that she was so sustained.
She feared it would not last, and that times of
agony were before her. She said, 'There's not the
bitterness in this trial that I felt when I lost my
mother; I was so rebellious then; but now I can
see the mercy and love that are mixed in my trial.'
Her whole thought now is to walk worthy of him,
and her greatest comfort to think that his spirit is
always near her, and knows all that she is doing."

"The news of the premature death of Prince
Albert," wrote a Berlin paper, "has produced a feeling of the deepest grief at Berlin. The whole country deplores his loss as a great family disaster. The
same feeling will evince itself throughout the whole
of Germany, which never ceased to love the Prince

as one of her own sons, and to venerate him as one of the most honest political men of this century. The Prince, on his part, despite his sincere attachment to his adopted country, had not forgotten his native land, and on more than one occasion had shown his serious solicitude for its interests. When, after a temporary misunderstanding between the two countries, so detrimental to both, a better feeling sprang up between Prussia and England, Prince Albert certainly contributed greatly thereto by his influence. His loss is a great one, not only for Great Britain, but also for us. Of the heart-rending grief of the Crown Princess I shall not speak; it will be fully understood by every delicate mind. The despatches received the day before yesterday fully prepared us for the sad catastrophe. The news of his death was received in the middle of the night. A supplement to the *National Gazette* announced it this morning to the public. It caused quite a consternation in every class of the population of Berlin. I scarcely feel able to write to-day. Under the impression of so sad an event all other matters give place to it."

With this last and noblest character I close my portfolio of sketches. It may seem but a sad ending, yet the word "farewell" is of itself a sad one. An author always longs to make his readers linger

on the last pages; and how can I tempt my readers ·
more than by appealing to the memory of the great
loss all England has suffered, and the great and
good Prince, the "silent father of our kings to
be"?—

> " We have lost him: he is gone:
> We know him now: all narrow jealousies
> Are silent; and we see him as he moved,
> How modest, kindly, all accomplished, wise,
> With what sublime repression of himself,
> And in what limits, and how tenderly;
> Not swaying to this faction or to that;
> Not making his high place the lawless perch
> Of winged ambitions, nor a vantage ground
> For pleasure; but through all this tract of years
> Wearing the white flower of a blameless life,
> Before a thousand peering littlenesses,
> In that fierce light which beats upon a throne."

THE END.

PRINTED BY VIRTUE AND CO., CITY ROAD, LONDON.

www.ingramcontent.com/pod-product-compliance
Lightning Source LLC
Chambersburg PA
CBHW030946110726
47900CB00004B/1153